CREATOR OF *WAGONS WEST*,
ONE OF THE MOST ENDURING AND
EXCITING SAGAS IN FRONTIER
FICTION, DANA FULLER ROSS
INTRODUCED AMERICA TO THE
LEGENDARY HOLT DYNASTY.
NOW THE PROUD AND PASSIONATE
FOREBEARS OF WAGONMASTER
WHIP HOLT FORGE THEIR WAY
WESTWARD TO CREATE A TRADING
EMPIRE, FACING THE INTRIGUE OF
DEADLY ENEMIES FROM OTHER
LANDS . . . AS WELL AS RUTHLESS
TRAITORS FROM THEIR OWN.

**AN ALL NEW EPIC ADVENTURE OF
UNFORGETTABLE MEN AND WOMEN—
SEIZING THEIR DESTINY, FORGING A
TRAIL TOWARD THE FUTURE, AND
FULFILLING THE HEROIC PROMISE
OF AN UNTAMED LAND . . .**

JEFF HOLT Though he prefers peacemaking to trouble, he is as fierce in a fight as any man. Now he must battle for his company's future—and his life—in an isolated, frozen land.

MELISSA MERRIVALE HOLT A captivating southern beauty with a sharp business sense, she has at last found happiness with her husband, Jeff Holt. Now she must choose between her love for Jeff and the challenge of the raw frontier.

CLAY HOLT Jeff's older brother, this consummate man of the frontier has an explosive temper and is deadly with knife, fists, and gun. Now he must play a waiting game, controlling his fury as he seeks to unmask his nation's most treacherous enemy.

SHINING MOON Clay's proud Sioux wife, like Clay she feels happiest in the wild places of the West. She alone can tame his heart, but can she tame her longing for the home she left behind?

MATTHEW GARWOOD A young boy filled with anger, he has begun to frighten his foster mother, Shining Moon. But she doesn't know how dangerous he really is, and by the time she does, it may be too late.

INDIA ST. CLAIR As skilled and dangerous as any man, she is an expert sailor and a passionate lover. But her beauty conceals a lifetime of secrets—even from the man she loves.

NED HOLT Cousin to Clay and Jeff, he is a big brawny man in his twenties. He has traveled the world, but he has never met anyone like the beautiful India St. Clair.

PROUD WOLF Shining Moon's younger brother, he has come east to learn the white man's civilized ways. But his love for a white woman will arouse the savagery and hatred those civilized ways conceal.

AUDREY STODDARD The daughter of the headmaster at an all-male academy, she flirts with her father's students, but gives her heart only to Proud Wolf—whom society forbids her to love.

Bantam Books by Dana Fuller Ross
Ask your bookseller for the books you have missed.

*Wagons West * The Empire Trilogy*
HONOR!
VENGEANCE!

Wagons West
INDEPENDENCE!—Volume I
NEBRASKA!—Volume II
WYOMING!—Volume III
OREGON!—Volume IV
TEXAS!—Volume V
CALIFORNIA!—Volume VI
COLORADO!—Volume VII
NEVADA!—Volume VIII
WASHINGTON!—Volume IX
MONTANA!—Volume X
DAKOTA!—Volume XI
UTAH!—Volume XII
IDAHO!—Volume XIII
MISSOURI!—Volume XIV
MISSISSIPPI!—Volume XV
LOUISIANA!—Volume XVI
TENNESSEE!—Volume XVII
ILLINOIS!—Volume XVIII
WISCONSIN!—Volume XIX
KENTUCKY!—Volume XX
ARIZONA!—Volume XXI
NEW MEXICO!—Volume XXII
OKLAHOMA!—Volume XXIII
CELEBRATION!—Volume XXIV

The Holts: An American Destiny
YUKON JUSTICE—Volume Seven
PACIFIC DESTINY—Volume Eight
HOMECOMING—Volume Nine
AWAKENING—Volume Ten

*Wagons West * The Frontier Trilogy*
WESTWARD!—Volume One
EXPEDITION!—Volume Two
OUTPOST!—Volume Three

THE EMPIRE TRILOGY
BOOK 2

VENGEANCE!

Dana Fuller Ross

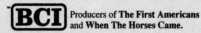

BCI Producers of **The First Americans** and **When The Horses Came.**

Book Creations Inc., Canaan, NY • George S. Engel, Executive Producer

BANTAM BOOKS

NEW YORK • TORONTO • LONDON • SYDNEY • AUCKLAND

VENGEANCE!

A Bantam Book/published by arrangement with Book Creations, Inc.

Bantam edition/February 1999

Produced by Book Creations, Inc.
Lyle Kenyon Engel, Founder

ISBN 0-553-57765-4

Published simultaneously in the United States and Canada

PRINTED IN THE UNITED STATES OF AMERICA

OPM   10 9 8 7 6 5 4 3 2

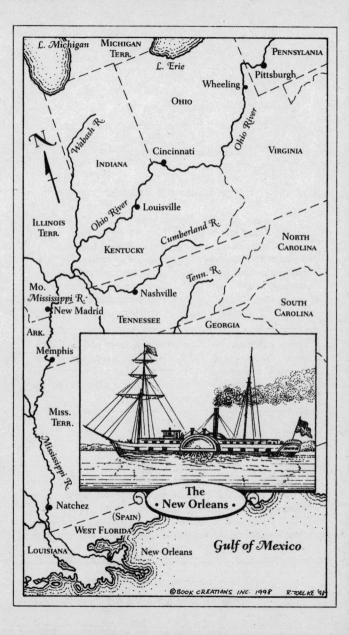

The
• New Orleans •

©BOOK CREATIONS INC. 1998   R·TOELKE '98

CHAPTER
ONE

*A**laska!* The very name stirred a man's soul. Jefferson Holt leaned back in his chair and gave his full attention to Lemuel March, his cousin-by-marriage.

"I wouldn't say that the place is a paradise, mind you. Too blasted cold for that, though I'm told the summer months are tolerable. But from all reports, the Russians are doing a booming business there in furs."

"Beaver?" asked Jeff.

March shook his head. "Seal and otter, for the most part. And then there's the timber, and the fishing."

Jeff snorted. "That's a long way to go for trees and fish. There's plenty of both to be had a lot closer to home."

"True, true." March sat forward in his chair, hands clasped together and anticipation shining on his lean, weathered face. "But that may not always be the case, and if we're well established in Alaska when the time comes that her natural resources are even more valuable, we'll be in a position to make a fortune."

Jeff could not argue with that reasoning. Although he himself had been an entrepreneur for only few years, he had already learned that success often depended on being in the right place at the right time.

"And Alaska is a frontier," March added, "most of it wild and untamed. I thought that might appeal to you as well, Jeff."

Frontier. Lemuel knew him well, Jeff had to admit. The frontier held magic for him, had always called to the blood that flowed in his veins—Holt blood.

He and March were sitting in the parlor of the stately house in Wilmington, North Carolina, where Jeff had made his home for the past two years. The house had belonged to his late father-in-law, Charles Merrivale, who had founded the mercantile business that had grown into the Holt-Merrivale Trading Company. Jeff had returned to Wilmington less than twenty-four hours earlier from Washington City, where he had spent several weeks assisting his older brother, Clay, in a secret investigation on behalf of former president Thomas Jefferson. The Holt brothers had found themselves in deadly danger on several occasions during the affair, but that was behind them now. Jeff had come home anticipating peace and quiet for a change.

He should have known better.

Instead he had found his wife and his business associate about to embark on a venture that was risky at the very least, perhaps outright dangerous. Lemuel March, who owned a fleet of sailing ships, had in Jeff's absence persuaded Melissa, Jeff's wife, to join him in an undertaking to open up the Pacific Ocean for trade. The bounty of the Hawaiian Islands beckoned in the middle of the vast sea; China and its market in tea and spices and other exotic goods lay at its distant western shores. And farther up the coast of North America was the far-flung wilderness of the Alaskan territory, controlled by Russia. Who knew what riches awaited the bold adventurer?

Lemuel March was eager to find out, and so was Melissa Holt. In fact, Melissa had planned to be on the first March ship to make the voyage to Alaska, a ship scheduled to sail from Wilmington in a matter of days.

Somehow, knowing his wife as he did, Jeff had not been surprised by Melissa's plans. She had always had an adventurous streak—she would never have married a Holt otherwise—but the demands of motherhood and running the Holt-Merrivale business kept it safely suppressed most of the time.

"It's certainly an intriguing idea, Lemuel," Jeff said now as he crossed one long leg over the other. "But it's going to be dangerous, too."

March shrugged. "Stepping into the street is dangerous. A man can be run down by a wagon full of whiskey barrels. All life is a risk, Jeff."

Jeff was all too aware of that. His own life had hung in the balance many times during the past handful of years.

The door into the parlor opened, and Melissa came into the room. As always when he saw his wife, Jeff felt his heart give a little leap. She was beautiful—thick brown hair, delicate features, a slender but sensuous body. Jeff's first impulse was to go to her, draw her into his arms, and give her a long, lingering kiss. But the anxious frown that furrowed her brow warned him that such a gesture would not be particularly welcome at this moment.

"Well?" she demanded bluntly. "Are we going ahead with the plan or not?"

A grin spread across Jeff's ruggedly handsome face as he got to his feet. He had let Melissa and Lemuel worry too much about what he was going to decide, he realized a little sheepishly. Almost from the first moment Melissa had told him about the Alaska plan, Jeff had supported it but had not said so.

"As far as I can tell," he said, "the potential gains far outweigh the risks. We'd be foolish not to grab this opportunity."

A bright smile lit up Melissa's face as she hurried

forward and embraced her husband. "I knew you'd feel that way, Jeff. That's why I agreed when Lemuel first suggested it."

Jeff put a finger under Melissa's chin, tipped her head back, and lightly brushed his lips across hers. "And if I hadn't gotten back from Washington City when I did, you would have sailed right off to Alaska."

"Well," murmured Melissa, not bothering to deny it, "someone had to go along to keep an eye on our investment."

Lemuel March cleared his throat. "Am I to assume now that both of you will be making the journey?"

Jeff looked over his shoulder and replied, "No, just me. Now that I'm here, there's no need for Melissa to go."

But when he turned back to face his wife again, he saw an angry light shining in her eyes. He knew he was in for a fight.

"Fight! Fight!"

The shout carried over the docks along Wilmington's waterfront, bringing workers and sailors at a run to witness the bare-knuckles battle. Two men stood toe to toe at the foot of the gangplank leading to the deck of the *Lydia Marie*, a March ship. They were slugging it out, trading powerful punches without even attempting to block each other's blows. It was a bloody, brutal way to fight, and since neither man was willing to give ground, the one who could absorb the most punishment and remain on his feet was the one who was going to win.

A punch rocked Ned Holt's head back, and he blinked rapidly to clear away the blood dripping into his eyes from a cut on his forehead. Vision still blurry, he slammed his fist in the direction of his opponent, feeling the impact shiver all the way up his muscular arm as the blow connected with Donnelly's nose.

Both men were big, with corded muscles in their arms and brawny shoulders that strained against the fabric of their shirts. Ned was a few inches taller, rangy and rawboned compared to the stockier Donnelly. Ned was younger, too, and had a longer reach, but that did not necessarily give him the edge in this fight. Donnelly had sailed the seven seas, worked on docks all over the world, and traded blows in dozens, perhaps even hundreds, of similar fights. Punching him was like punching a block of wood.

Donnelly's right fist crashed into Ned's breastbone. Ned staggered back a step, the first time either man had budged since the fight began. Donnelly was quick to press his advantage. His left fist shot out and caught Ned on the jaw. Lights exploded behind Ned's eyes, and a red-tinged blackness began to close in on the edges of his vision. He threw a right at Donnelly's head, but the punch only skimmed the side of the man's closely shaved skull. The near-miss threw Ned off balance, and he stumbled forward.

Donnelly kept pounding him, hooking blows viciously into his belly. Through the roar of blood in his head Ned could barely hear the yelling of the crowd. He hunched his shoulders and bent over, trying to protect himself from Donnelly's punches. That was the worst thing he could have done, he realized an instant later, because Donnelly's right came looping around to his jaw with all the power of the man's stocky body behind it.

The rough wooden planks of the dock scraped Ned's face as he landed. The black tide closed in, and it would have been so easy to let it sweep him away to some place where he could stop hurting.

But through the haze in his eyes he saw a slender figure standing at the front of the crowd, saw the fear in the deep brown eyes. With a roar of rage he pulled himself free from the sucking grasp of the black tide and reached out to grab one of Donnelly's ankles. He yanked as hard as he could, and Donnelly went down like a felled tree.

Drawing on reserves of strength he hadn't know were there, Ned scrambled to his knees and met Donnelly with a punch as the man tried to get up. Both of

them sprawled down again. Wood splinters gouged
Ned's fingers and palms as he pulled himself along
and threw himself on top of Donnelly. His weight
knocked the breath out of the man's lungs. Ned got his
fingers around Donnelly's throat, lifted, smashed his
head back down against the planks. Again and again,
as if Donnelly were a rag doll, he slammed his head
downward.

Then strong hands grabbed Ned's arms, hauled
him up, and pushed him back. Ned tried to pull away,
but his strength suddenly deserted him. Weak as a
baby, he would have fallen had the men not been holding him up and slapping him on the back in congratulations. He gasped, wishing they would stop; each
hearty blow made his head ring like an anvil.

Somehow he wound up sitting on a piling by the
edge of the dock, his chest heaving as he tried to draw
air back into his burning lungs. He lifted a trembling
hand and wiped some of the blood from his eyes.

"Let me," a voice said softly from beside him.

A wet cloth touched his face. It felt like heaven.
Ned groaned as the cloth swabbed away the blood. He
saw some of Donnelly's friends dragging the man
away. "I . . . I didn't kill him . . . did I?" he rasped.
His voice was harsh, ugly, and sounded as if it belonged to someone else.

India St. Clair chuckled. "It would take more than
bouncing off that dock a few times to dent Donnelly's
head," she said. "He was already starting to come
around. They'll dash a bucket of water in his face and
pour a bottle of rum down his throat, and he'll be fine."

Ned managed a tired grin. "I could do with some
of that myself," he said. "The rum, I mean."

"Then come along," India said. "I'll buy you a
drink."

Ned shakily got to his feet, and India held his arm
as they started toward the waterfront tavern known as
Red Mike's. Her grip was surprisingly strong, considering that she was a woman and little more than half
Ned's size.

Not that India's gender was readily apparent. She was clad in the loose-fitting tunic and trousers many sailors wore, and a sailor's cap was perched on her close-cut dark hair. When she had first gone to sea several years earlier, she'd had no trouble passing as a young man and had worked as a cabin boy. Now she was a full-fledged member of the crew currently signed on to the *Lydia Marie*, but only Ned and the ship's owner, Lemuel March, knew she was a woman.

And Ned knew that better than anyone, for he and India had been lovers for more than a year.

When they were seated at a table in Red Mike's, Ned looked down disgustedly at his torn, bloodstained shirt. "Another one ruined," he muttered.

India pushed one of the buckets of beer she had carried from the bar over to him. "Whatever possessed you to goad a man like Donnelly into a fight?" she asked. "He's won brawls in every port from here to Madagascar."

"This is beer," Ned said, frowning at the bucket. "I thought you were getting rum."

"Your mouth's a red ruin, my lad. Rum would burn it. That beer's going to be bad enough."

Ned lifted the bucket and downed a healthy swallow. He winced and cursed as it burned his cut and swollen lips, as India had warned it would. "I got tired of his swaggering around," he said, answering India's question. "He thinks he knows everything there is to know about sailing."

"He probably does," India pointed out. "More than you, at least. It was only a few years ago that you were sitting in Pittsburgh, a bloody landlubber through and through."

Ned winced again, this time at India's candor. But she was right. Until he came to New York with his cousin Jeff Holt, Ned had never entertained any notion of going to sea. In New York he had met India, as well as Lemuel March, and from there he had sailed to North Carolina with Jeff. Before he knew it, the sea was in his blood. It was as if he had been born to have a deck under his feet.

But Ned still had things to learn about the life of a sailor. He probably should have steered clear of Donnelly, he thought ruefully. The man was a braggart and a bully, just the sort that had always rubbed him the wrong way—probably because in his earlier years Ned had been much the same way. But that was before he had met his cousin from the wild frontier.

India sipped her beer, then said, "I wish Donnelly was sailing on the *Beaumont* instead of the *Lydia Marie.* I don't like to think about the two of you being on the same ship all the way to China."

Ned shook his head and instantly regretted the gesture as pain shot through his skull. "Don't worry," he told India, gingerly rubbing his forehead. "I'll keep my distance. Donnelly will have no reason to cause trouble."

"You beat him," India said. "That's all the reason a man like him needs. It'll stick in his craw."

"Then he'll just have to cough it up," Ned said lightly.

He was afraid India was right, though. In a few days the two March ships would sail from Wilmington, the *Beaumont* bound for Alaska, the *Lydia Marie* for China by way of the Hawaiian Islands. A long voyage, mused Ned.

And he would probably have to watch his back every league of the way.

Clay Holt drew back on the reins, bringing his horse to a stop on a hilltop overlooking the triangular point of land where the Allegheny and Monongahela Rivers came together to form the Ohio. Sprawled across the point was the city of Pittsburgh, a growing, bustling settlement that was the hub of traffic on the river. Clay had been here before, on this very hilltop, in fact. He and his brother Jeff had been on their way to Washington from the Holt family homestead near Marietta, Ohio, summoned by a message from beyond the grave. Clay and Jeff had not stopped in Pittsburgh, not even to visit their aunt and uncle. They had been in too great a hurry to reach Washington.

This time Pittsburgh was Clay's destination, and the destination of the young man beside him as well.

Lieutenant John Markham let out a groan as he stood in the saddle and eased muscles made sore by long days of hard riding. "Thank God we're here at last," he said. "We can look forward to making the rest of the trip in the elegant comfort of a riverboat."

"This isn't a pleasure trip," Clay reminded him. "We're hunting a murderer."

The two men made a sharp contrast. Clay looked every bit the rugged frontiersman in tall black boots, rough homespun trousers, a linsey-woolsey shirt, and a broad-brimmed hat of black felt. A North & Cheney flintlock pistol was tucked behind his belt on the left side; on the right hung a heavy-bladed hunting knife in a sheath decorated with a rawhide fringe. Clay carried a long-barreled flintlock rifle across the saddle in front of him. His face above the short black beard was tanned to the color of old leather, and his deep-set blue eyes were keen and piercing.

The lieutenant, on the other hand, had the air of the city about him, despite the road dust that coated his brown suit, white shirt, silk cravat, and beaver hat. Normally he would have been wearing a natty blue and white army uniform with a high-peaked hat, but he was here with Clay unofficially, acting as a special investigator on behalf of Thomas Jefferson and other men high in the government. His youth, along with his fair hair and open, guileless face, made him seem mild-mannered, even ineffectual. But the former president would not have sent Markham on this mission had he not demonstrated his abilities as a covert agent in the past.

"I haven't forgotten why we're here," Markham said, "nor am I likely to. The man who was working with Gideon Maxwell in Washington, whoever he is, is threatening the security of the entire country. And he may well be the man responsible for the death of your friend Captain Lewis."

Clay's jaw tightened at the memory of Meriwether Lewis. As a member of the Corps of Discovery half a dozen years earlier, Clay had followed the captain all the way to the Pacific and back. Lewis had deserved a better death than a pistol ball in the head at a lonely Tennessee roadhouse. And he deserved to be remembered as something better than a lost, pathetic suicide.

But that was what history might well record, Clay reflected. He suspected that Lewis's death had something to do with an immense and terrible plot that was threatening the young country. But few people were aware of it, and that was the way Jefferson and the other government men wanted to keep it. No use in panicking the citizens with the news that half the country was on the verge of being lost in a gigantic land grab.

Jefferson had given Clay Holt and John Markham the enormous task of finding the conspirators before they succeeded. The first step was uncovering the identity of the politician who had sold out his country and hatched the traitorous scheme in concert with Gideon Maxwell, a powerful figure in Washington City's criminal underbelly.

Maxwell was dead now, but his death had come too late. A huge chunk of the Louisiana Territory was already at risk.

Clay, Jeff, and John Markham had established that Maxwell's partner was one of three men, all members of the United States Senate: Charles Emory, Morgan Ralston, and Louis Haines. The senators were in Pittsburgh, preparing to board the steamboat *New Orleans* for its unprecedented voyage down the Ohio and Mississippi Rivers to its namesake: the Crescent City, New Orleans.

Clay and Markham would be on that boat as well.

Heeling his horse into motion, Clay started down the hill toward the city. Markham sighed and fell in alongside him. They had traveled light from Washington City, bringing only what they could carry in their saddlebags, and they had made good time. There was no real hurry; the *New Orleans* was not scheduled to leave Pittsburgh for several days yet. But Clay hoped they might solve the mystery that had brought them here even before the boat set off on its journey.

After all, he had a wife waiting for him in Ohio, waiting to return with him to their true home in the Rocky Mountains.

She had grown to womanhood in a land where death was ever present, a land where bloody-handed raiders could come screaming out of the night with little warning to cleave heads and carry away women and children, a land where nature itself was harsh and unforgiving. She knew the value of keen ears, open eyes, and a healthy mistrust of the unknown.

That was why her gaze never left the boy as he carried the basket of eggs into the cabin and set it on the table. She knew that Matthew Garwood was dangerous.

And yet, for the past several weeks, he had done nothing to make Shining Moon suspicious. He had been helpful, friendly, even cheerful as he worked around the Holt family farm in Ohio, not far from the great river and the settlement of Marietta. He was like a different boy, and Shining Moon sometimes had to remind herself that this was the same child who had mutilated small animals with a knife, who had laughed and failed to help her when she had fallen into the old well in the woods behind the barn. She was more than halfway convinced he had deliberately lured her into the well, and worse, that he had played a part in the death of her friend, Cassie Doolittle. The old woman had died when her two-wheeled cart overturned on top of her, dragged to the bottom of a hill by a runaway mule. Shining Moon was not certain how Matthew could have caused that tragedy, and yet . . . and yet . . .

"Thank you for gathering the eggs, Matthew," she said, summoning up a smile.

"Is there anything else I can do for you, Shining Moon?" he asked.

She shook her head, remembering how difficult it had always been to get Matthew to to help with anything until recently. Perhaps he really had changed. "Castor and Pollux may have something for you to do in the barn. Why don't you ask them?" she suggested.

"All right." Matthew left the cabin, and Shining Moon heard his footsteps as he trotted toward the barn. Castor and Pollux Gilworth, the burly twin brothers who took care of the Holt farm, were out there with a cow that was struggling to give birth. Shining Moon hoped that Matthew would not be in their way.

She reflected on the boy's brief history, on the long-standing feud between the Holts and the Garwoods, begun when both families had settled in the area a score of years earlier. She knew about feuds. Her own people, the Teton Sioux, had battled with the Crow, the Arikara, the Blackfoot, and the other tribes of the plains and mountains. The tribes raided back and forth, shifting the balance of power constantly over the years. Warriors were killed, women and children were taken as slaves, whole bands were forced from land that had always been their home.

According to Clay and Jeff, the Holts had never really wanted trouble, but the Garwoods, for some distorted reason, had decided they were mortal enemies. The Holts had had no choice but to defend themselves. The rumor that Clay Holt had fathered a child—Matthew—with Josie Garwood and then abandoned her had only exacerbated the tension between the families.

Clay was not Matthew's father; Shining Moon knew that now. But when Josie had died, killed by a madman in the tiny settlement of New Hope far to the west, Shining Moon had offered to take her son and raise him as her own. Clay had warned darkly that there might be trouble, but Shining Moon had been determined.

Now she understood what Clay had meant. Matthew's uncle, Josie's own brother, Zach, had fathered the boy. Bad blood added to bad blood. Even now, Shining Moon shuddered when she thought of it.

Clay had brought her to Ohio for a reunion of his family, and he had left her on the farm after receiving the summons to Washington. The Marietta postmaster had brought a letter from Meriwether Lewis—who had died two years earlier—informing Clay of a land grant he was due that had mistakenly never been awarded. Clay had gone to Washington to claim the land, and now, long months later, he had not yet returned. Shining Moon had recently received a letter in which he promised to come as soon as possible. He had been asked to undertake a special mission for his country, he wrote, although he was vague about who had asked him and what the mission was.

One of the Gilworth brothers clumped into the cabin, his hands stained with blood. He wore a broad grin on his bearded face, however, so Shining Moon guessed that the birthing had been successful.

"Got us a pretty little calf out there, Miz Holt," he said. "Took a little doin', but we managed. Ol' Bessie did most of the work, anyway." He jerked a blunt thumb toward the door. "Want to go take a look?"

Shining Moon smiled and shook her head. "I must begin preparing our evening meal. Matthew brought in the eggs for me again."

"That boy's gettin' to be a regular little beaver when it comes to chores. Why, he even helped when Pollux an' me was tryin' to get that calf turned round the right way. He was right there with a bucket of water or anything else we asked him to fetch."

Shining Moon hesitated, then said, "I have thought that perhaps . . . perhaps the evil spirits inside Matthew have gone away." She did not know how else to say it.

Castor frowned. With his bushy beard and thick, dark eyebrows, the big man looked quite fierce. "I wouldn't count on that," he said. "I'm glad the boy's behavin' himself these days, but it might not last. Course, he had a long talk with your brother when he was here, and I don't know what they said to each other. Maybe Proud Wolf finally got through to Matthew where none o' the rest of us ever could."

"I hope that is true, but until I know for certain . . . I will be careful."

Castor nodded solemnly. "I reckon that's best. It may not be fair to the boy, if he really has turned over a new leaf, but I'd rather be a mite unfair than catch a knife in the gizzard when I wasn't lookin'."

He was right, Shining Moon knew. Not for the first time, she wished that Clay would return. She wished that her brother had been able to stay longer during his visit to the homestead on his way east.

But by now Proud Wolf was hundreds of miles away, she knew, in the city the white men called Cambridge, Massachusetts, and no doubt he was faced with problems of his own.

The fist seemed to explode in Proud Wolf's face, knocking him backward. He felt himself falling and could do nothing to stop it.

He sprawled on the ground, blinking up at the spreading branches of the big tree behind the academy's kitchen. The leaves blotted out the early evening stars, but the moon rising in the east cast a silvery glow over the broad lawn that surrounded the Stoddard Academy for Young Men.

"Had enough, redskin?" hissed the figure looming over Proud Wolf. The young man raised his clenched fists. "Or do you want some more?"

Proud Wolf rolled over and came up on his hands and knees, pausing for a moment to clear his head. Breathing deeply, he waited until the world had stopped spinning. He heard laughter from the other students gathered around him and Frank Kirkland.

Frank was laughing, too, a nasty, mocking laugh. Almost from the first day Proud Wolf had arrived at the Stoddard Academy, Frank had treated him with open contempt. He had not been surprised when the young man from Connecticut goaded him into this evening's rendezvous.

Earlier in the day, Frank had deliberately bumped into the desk in the library at which Proud Wolf was working. The inkwell on the table had tipped over, spilling a pool of ink on the composition the Sioux youth had been laboriously writing. Proud Wolf's response had been instantaneous—and angry. He had come to his feet and his hand had moved toward his belt, where he would normally have carried a tomahawk and a hunting knife had he been in his homeland.

But he was no longer in the high valley nestled in the beautiful Shining Mountains, the peaks the white men called the Grand Tetons. And instead of his buckskins, he wore white man's clothes. His thick dark hair was pulled back and bound tightly. His only weapon was the quill pen still clutched in his hand. He had dropped the pen on the table, glared at Frank Kirkland, and said in a low voice, "You meant to do that."

"Prove it, redskin," Frank had sneered. "You can't. But if you want to do something about it anyway, I'll see you under the tree behind the kitchen an hour after sundown tonight."

Proud Wolf had nodded curtly, accepting the challenge.

When he arrived behind the kitchen at the appointed hour, he had found not only Frank but nearly a dozen other students waiting, watching him with undisguised hostility. Proud Wolf had surveyed them and asked scornfully, "Am I to fight all of you?"

"I fight my own battles," Frank had snapped. "The boys just want to see me teach you a lesson, you heathen."

"I am not a heathen," Proud Wolf could not resist saying. "The Black Robes—you call them priests— taught me about God."

Frank had waved off Proud Wolf's protest. "All you Indians are heathens and savages. Everybody knows that." He stepped closer, taking off his jacket and handing it to one of the other young men. As he balled his fists, he went on, "I'm going to teach you that we don't want savages around here mixing with civilized folk."

His fist flashed toward Proud Wolf's belly.

Proud Wolf stepped aside easily, only to discover that he had underestimated his opponent. Frank's move had been a feint, and his other hand caught Proud Wolf flush on the jaw. As the blow rocked Proud Wolf back, Frank bored in relentlessly, pounding a couple of punches to Proud Wolf's midsection, then one into his face. That was the blow that had knocked Proud Wolf on his back.

Now, as he listened to the hooting and laughter of Frank and the other young men, a red rage burned through him like a prairie fire. With a sharp cry he surged up off the ground and threw himself at Frank, tackling him around the waist and bringing him down heavily. They rolled from side to side on the grass as they grappled. Frank flailed at Proud Wolf with his right fist while he tried to get his left hand around the young Sioux's throat.

Proud Wolf blocked the blows, caught hold of Frank's left wrist, and twisted. Frank howled in pain. Proud Wolf levered Frank's arm behind his back and slowly forced him facedown against the grass. With a little more pressure, Proud Wolf could easily have popped Frank's arm out of its socket.

As he dug his knee into Frank's back, Proud Wolf reached around with his other hand and wedged it under Frank's chin. He jerked back, lifting Frank's head at an unnatural angle. The skin of Frank's neck was stretched tight, ready for the knife slash that would grate on bone and sever arteries so that blood would fountain out and take Frank's life with it. . . .

Only there was no knife in Proud Wolf's hand, and the man trapped helplessly beneath him was not a true warrior, only an arrogant white fool. Had Frank Kirkland been a Blackfoot, Proud Wolf would not have hesitated to kill him. Between gritted teeth he said, "With one heave of my shoulders I could snap your neck like a rotten twig, white man. Remember that next time you decide to teach me a lesson."

"Let him go." The voice was cold and hard, and it was accompanied by a metallic clicking. "Let him go or I'll put a ball in your head, Indian."

Proud Wolf glanced up without releasing Frank. He was not surprised to see William Brackett stepping forward from the cluster of students. Will was the one who usually took the lead, the one whose approval Frank Kirkland would do almost anything to gain. Nor was Proud Wolf surprised to see a pocket pistol in Will's hand, glinting in the moonlight. The little flintlock's hammer was drawn back, and at this range, even in this uncertain light, Will could hardly miss.

"You must be disappointed, Will," said Proud Wolf, his lips drawing back from his teeth in a sneer. "You thought your pet here would give me . . . what do you white men call it? A sound thrashing?"

"Let him go," Will Brackett repeated.

Before Proud Wolf could decide whether or not to comply, light suddenly spilled around the corner of the kitchen. Several of the young men scattered, running from the light, while Will stepped back quickly and shoved the pistol under his jacket. Proud Wolf let go of Frank and scrambled to his feet.

A tall man with a severe face and a shock of white hair appeared at the corner of the small building, holding a lantern aloft. He glared at the young men revealed by the circle of light, then looked down at Frank Kirkland, who still lay on the ground gasping for breath.

"What the devil is going on here?" demanded the newcomer. His gaze fell on Proud Wolf. "I should have known you'd be involved in this."

"I have caused no trouble since I have been here, Mr. Stoddard," Proud Wolf said.

Jeremiah Stoddard, the headmaster of the acad-

emy, snorted in contempt and indicated Frank Kirkland with his free hand. "What do you call this?"

A cur, thought Proud Wolf, but he said, "Frank and
I were . . . wrestling."

He had been among white men for too long, Proud
Wolf thought ruefully. Lying came too easily to him
now.

"Wrestling?" Stoddard repeated skeptically.

Will Brackett stepped forward. "That's right, sir,"
he said. "The boys and I had heard that Proud Wolf's
people are noted for their wrestling ability, so we asked
him to demonstrate a few holds for us."

"In the dark, behind the kitchen?"

"We didn't think it would be appropriate in our
residence, sir," Will replied. He bent to grasp Frank's
arm and help the gasping youth to his feet. "I'm afraid
things got a bit carried away. You know, the enthusiasm of competition. Isn't that right, lads?"

The other students chimed in their agreement.
Even Frank nodded shakily.

Will could have told Stoddard that the moon was
nothing but an inflated buffalo stomach with a candle
inside it and the headmaster would have believed him,
Proud Wolf thought with disgust. Of all the students at
the academy, Will Brackett was Stoddard's favorite.
And Will knew it.

Stoddard grunted and lowered the lantern a little.
"All right. But this is still a disgusting display and not
at all the sort of thing young gentlemen should be en-
gaged in. I want all of you back in your quarters immediately."

"Yes, sir," Will said briskly. "Let's go, boys." He
held out a hand, beckoning to Proud Wolf.

Will wanted him to join them, Proud Wolf realized,
to fall in step with them and go back to the massive
pile of ivy-covered mortar and stone that served as
their home at the academy. Proud Wolf wanted no part
of such a show of false friendliness.

"Go ahead," he told Will and the others. "I will be
along shortly."

Will hesitated, then shrugged. He could not challenge Proud Wolf's decision without making Stoddard suspicious. He slapped a still-shaky Frank Kirkland on the back and led his group of followers around the kitchen.

Stoddard waited until they were gone, glowering at Proud Wolf. "You don't fool me, you know," he said after a moment. "You don't fool me at all."

"Such is not my intention, Mr. Stoddard."

"Bringing you here was Professor Hilliard's idea," snapped Stoddard. "It was a damn foolish notion, if you ask me. You can't take an Indian out of his natural surroundings and expect him to act like a white man."

There were many things Proud Wolf could have said to that. For one, he was not sure he *wanted* to be like a white man. From what he had seen of them, they were, with a few exceptions, a cruel, venal race. But he did want the same education that the academy offered to Will Brackett and other young white men. The fire to learn burned brightly within him. That was the reason he had agreed to the proposal offered by Professor Abner Hilliard, who had journeyed thousands of miles to the west to find the young man mentioned in the journals of his late friend and colleague, Professor Donald Franklin. It was Hilliard's idea that a young man of Proud Wolf's natural intelligence could succeed at the academy and, ultimately, at Harvard, where Hilliard taught, despite Proud Wolf's lack of formal schooling.

So far, though the work had been difficult, Proud Wolf felt sure that he was proving Professor Hilliard correct. And more importantly, the challenge of learning new things filled him with excitement.

The only drawback had been the reaction of the other students, led by Will Brackett and Frank Kirkland. Outside the classrooms they had made life as miserable as possible for Proud Wolf.

"I don't want any more . . . wrestling," Stoddard went on when Proud Wolf said nothing. "Do you understand?"

"Yes, sir."

"Frank Kirkland's father is a wealthy, powerful man. If he knew you'd hurt his son . . ." With another snort of disgust, Stoddard turned away. "Get on inside," he said over his shoulder. "Unless you'd rather sleep under the stars like a savage."

That was exactly what he would have preferred, Proud Wolf thought with amusement, but he would not give Stoddard the satisfaction of seeing him behave "like a savage." He set off toward the residence building instead.

He had gone only a few feet when someone called his name softly from the shadows. He stopped. The person at the real core of Will Brackett's hostility stepped from the darkness and glided toward him.

Audrey . . .

CHAPTER
TWO

T he look on Melissa's face reminded Jeff of a
storm sweeping over the high country, full of
thunder and lightning and the possibility of utter
devastation.

"You cannot be serious," she said angrily.

At least she'd had the grace to wait until they were
behind the closed doors of their bedroom to challenge
him, Jeff told himself, instead of lighting into him in the
parlor in front of Lemuel March. He felt a prickly irritation anyway, and he snapped, "I'm dead serious. The
trip to Alaska is going to be much too dangerous for
you and Michael."

"We were already planning on going," Melissa
shot back. "Or have you forgotten that you weren't
even here when the plans for the trip were made?"

Jeff took a deep breath and tried to calm himself. "I
haven't forgotten. And good plans they are. You've always had an excellent head for business, Melissa. If I
had come back here from Ohio with you and found the

business in such bad shape, I don't know that I could have set things aright any better than you have. Probably not as well."

"Well, it's certainly gracious of you to admit that I've done a good job," Melissa said with a sniff.

"It's the truth," Jeff said simply.

And it was. Cutthroat competition from an unscrupulous rival merchant had almost put the Holt-Merrivale Company out of business. Melissa suspected that the man had been responsible for the piracy, arson, and outright murder that had plagued the company for several months. She had explained all that to Jeff, including the hair-raising tale of how she had almost been killed herself in the fire that had come close to destroying their warehouse. The story had made Jeff more determined than ever to see that Melissa was never placed in harm's way again.

Then there was the question of Michael, their young son. Although he was an inquisitive, adventurous, sturdy child, Jeff could not allow him to go along on such a hazardous journey.

Melissa turned away from him, holding her body stiffly. "You are the stubbornest man I've ever met," she said.

"Since that includes your father, that certainly puts me in select company."

As soon as he spoke, Jeff knew he should have kept the thought to himself.

Melissa did not rise to the bait, however. Instead she asked, "What would you have done if you had come home a few days later and found us already gone?"

"Why, I'd have come after you, of course," Jeff said without hesitation. "I'd have found the fastest sailing ship I could and caught up with the *Beaumont* before it reached South America. Then I'd have sent you home."

"And if I'd refused to go?" She turned and faced him. "What would you have done then? Tied me up and flung me in the hold of the other ship like so much cargo?"

"Don't be ridiculous."

Melissa's expression softened slightly. "Jeff, I understand you want what's best for Michael and me. You want to protect us and keep us from harm."

"Well, I'm glad you understand that much."

"And you may be right about the trip being dangerous." She stepped closer and put a hand on his arm. "But don't you see, Jeff? Every time we're separated, something happens to prolong the separation. We were apart for years when I was . . . when Michael was . . ."

He knew what she was trying to say. Through the manipulations of her father, who had opposed their marriage, Jeff and Melissa had not seen each other for some two years, had not even known where the other was. Melissa had been pregnant when they parted, although Jeff had not known that, and Michael had been born while they were separated. Jeff had been unaware that he had a son until the couple was reunited, when he met the toddler for the first time. Michael was now a bright, curious four-year-old.

Being apart for so long had devastated both Jeff and Melissa. Then had come the "simple" trip to Washington City, in the course of which Clay and Jeff were persuaded to take on a long, dangerous, secret assignment for Thomas Jefferson. Jeff realized what Melissa was afraid of: The voyage to Alaska and back would take months at the very least, months during which they would be separated yet again.

Suddenly Jeff was no longer so certain he was right. Any sea voyage had its perils, of course, especially one as long and arduous as the trip around South America and up through the Pacific to Alaska. And there was no way to predict what dangers might be awaiting them in Alaska itself, a land few people knew anything about. But they would have one of the best crews on the seven seas—Lemuel March would see to that—and more importantly, Jeff himself would be there to protect Melissa and Michael. It was presumptuous, Jeff realized, to think he could handle *any* danger, but the Holts had never lacked for confidence in their own abilities.

Then, too, he reminded himself, Melissa had been in deadly danger at home in Wilmington while he was off in Washington with Clay. She could have died in that warehouse fire just as easily as she might from any threat Alaska could hold.

"Why don't you say something?" Melissa suddenly burst out. "You're just standing there frowning at me!"

"I'm thinking," Jeff said solemnly, "thinking that perhaps you may be right about this matter."

Her eyes, her beautiful brown eyes, widened in surprise. "Do you mean it?" she asked in a half-whisper.

Jeff nodded. "Of course I do. I wouldn't tease you about something like this, Melissa. I'm still worried about what might happen, but at least we would be together."

"Then . . . Michael and I can go?"

Jeff hesitated. A part of his brain clamored that the decision he was on the verge of making was an unwise one. But he ignored the warning and smiled at his wife. "Hell, what good is a man's better judgment if he can't go against it once in a while?"

Melissa stepped closer, coming into his arms as he lifted them instinctively to embrace her. She put her arms around his waist and hugged him tightly, resting her head against his chest. "Thank you," she said softly. "I wasn't sure I could bear to be apart from you for so long again."

Jeff stroked her hair for a moment, then put his hand under her chin and tipped her head back so that he could kiss her. Melissa's lips were warm and sweet, and he felt the same passionate longing for her that he always did when he kissed her. He slid his fingertips down the graceful curve of her neck and then onto her bosom, until the soft mound of her breast filled his palm. He cupped it, squeezing gently. Melissa moaned deep in her throat and opened her lips to him. Jeff pulled her more tightly against him.

He was a lucky man, he thought, to have a wife with such an adventurous spirit that she could face a long, dangerous journey with excitement and determination.

He only hoped he never had reason to regret the decision he had made this day.

"Audrey." Proud Wolf said her name aloud. Then his breath seemed to freeze in his throat. He stood gazing at her in the moonlight, awestruck once again by her beauty.

Audrey Stoddard was the youngest child of the headmaster and his wife and the only one who still lived here at the academy. She was seventeen, several years younger than Proud Wolf but already a woman full-grown. There was no doubt of that.

Thick hair that shone bright auburn in the sunlight now fell in dark waves around her head, reflecting silvery glints of moonlight. She wore a gown that was much too thin for the cool, late-summer evening. The neckline was cut low enough to reveal the upper slopes of her full breasts, and to his shame Proud Wolf found his eyes being drawn to them. He looked away, hoping Audrey had not noticed.

She held out a hand toward him, and he took it without thinking. Her slender fingers were cool and smooth and soft as they folded around his palm.

"What happened?" she asked breathlessly. "Father heard that there was going to be some sort of trouble between you and one of the other boys."

Proud Wolf was not surprised. Jeremiah Stoddard had his spies among the students, young men eager to please their headmaster by carrying tales to him. Will Brackett was one of them, though Proud Wolf doubted that even Will was devious enough to have slipped word to Stoddard of a fight that he himself had probably instigated.

"It was nothing," he said in reply to Audrey's question.

"Is that . . . a bruise I see on your face?" Audrey sounded more impressed than concerned.

Proud Wolf lifted a hand and touched his cheek where Frank had punched him. He managed not to wince at the pain. "As I said, nothing."

"It was that horrible Frank Kirkland who fought with you, I'll wager," Audrey went on. "This isn't the first fight he's been in. I think Father should expel him from the academy. He probably would if Frank's father didn't have so much money."

At least Audrey was perceptive enough to see what was important to her father, thought Proud Wolf.

"And I don't know why Will is such good friends with him," Audrey added. "They're nothing alike."

Ah, that was where she was wrong. Will and Frank had much in common, including a dislike of those they considered outsiders, interlopers—such as Proud Wolf. And there was another basis for their friendship: Frank was a toady who would do anything Will hinted he wanted done. As such he was quite valuable to Will, who wanted to keep his own hands clean.

Audrey could not see that, however, Proud Wolf knew. She might be insightful where her father was concerned, but she turned a blind eye to Will's faults. Proud Wolf had learned that much from observing the two together. He had seen the way Audrey looked at Will; he had heard her laughter when Will spoke. She was charmed by him.

Like a prairie dog frozen in place by the glittering eyes of the snake slithering toward it . . .

Proud Wolf kept these thoughts to himself. Aloud he said, "You should not be out here after dark. Your father would not like it. And are you not cold? You should wear a shawl."

Audrey sniffed. "You sound like my mother." She tossed her head, and her hair moved like dark wings in the moonlight. "As for my father, his bluster no longer frightens me. I've heard it my entire life."

"Perhaps you should go inside anyway," suggested Proud Wolf. "The air is growing chill—"

She stepped closer to him. "I know the best way to get warm."

Before he could comprehend what was happening, she was in his arms. He embraced her as she lifted her head and found his lips with hers. Her warm, soft breasts pressed into his chest. The kiss made Proud Wolf's blood race and the pulse pound in his head. The heat of Audrey's body seared him even through two layers of clothing, and he felt a surge of desire so intense it was almost painful.

And yet, in the back of his mind he was aware that they were standing out in the open, in the moonlight, where anyone who cared to look could see them. If Jeremiah Stoddard happened to come outside again, he would fly into a rage and perhaps even attack the young man he regarded as a godless savage.

With regret, Proud Wolf broke the kiss and stepped back. Audrey made a little sound of disappointment. He rested his hands on her shoulders and said firmly, "This is not right."

"What's wrong with it?" she demanded breathlessly.

"Your father or someone else will see—"

"Let them! I don't care. I've been wanting to kiss you ever since the first day you got here. I know you must think me a hussy, but I can't help it."

Proud Wolf thought back to the day of his arrival at the Stoddard Academy. Audrey had looked at him with interest when Professor Hilliard introduced the two of them, but he hardly would have guessed that she wanted to kiss him.

"It is not good for us to be doing this," he insisted.

"On the contrary, I think it is very good indeed. Didn't you like it, Proud Wolf? Don't you like kissing me?"

How could he answer that? Truthfully, he had enjoyed kissing her very much. But if he told her that, it would only encourage her. She might even start to think that she was . . . in love with him!

He recalled the Sioux maiden known as Raven Arrow. She had been in love with him, and that love had led indirectly to her death. Proud Wolf had been profoundly affected by what had happened to Raven Arrow, and only after visions of a spirit cat had appeared to him—visions he was sure had been sent by her—had he been able to move on and accept the challenge of coming east with Professor Hilliard.

Loving a Sioux Indian could only lead to problems for Audrey Stoddard. He could not allow that to happen. With that in mind he looked at her, so beautiful in the moonlight, and said, "You are not of my people. I have no interest in kissing a white girl."

Even in the dim light he saw her eyes widen with surprise, then narrow to angry slits. Her hand flashed up, and she would have slapped him across the face had he not reached up and easily caught her wrist.

"Oh!" she exclaimed.

"I am sorry," he said.

"I . . . I don't want your apologies, you . . . you redskin! Let go of me!"

Proud Wolf released her wrist and stepped back. She glared at him for a moment, then turned and walked off stiffly, the long gown swirling around her legs. She vanished into the shadows beneath the trees.

Proud Wolf gave a long sigh, then shook his head. He had hurt her with his words, he knew, and he hated it, especially because they had been a lie. Her kiss had been so exciting and tempting that it had taken all his self-control not to pull her into his arms once more.

He looked around, searching with his eyes for any movement in the night, listening with his ears for the slightest sound that did not belong. When he was certain that no one was lurking nearby, he walked toward the large brick building in which the academy's students were housed.

Ill-advised though Audrey's actions had been, no lasting harm would come of them, he told himself.

Other than the fact that the memory of the kiss and the way she had felt in his arms was now burned permanently into his brain.

"Clay! Come in, come in. It's good to see you again, son!"

Clay grasped the hand his uncle Henry extended and shook it vigorously. Henry slapped him on the back with his other hand and went on, "We got your letter saying that you were coming, but it only arrived yesterday. You almost beat it here, Clay."

"We made good time on the trail," Clay said. He turned to indicate the young man who had come into the house with him. "This is my friend, John Markham." The two men had decided to keep the fact that Markham was a lieutenant in the army a secret from those who had no need to know it.

Henry shook hands with Markham. "Any friend of Clay Holt's is more than welcome in this house, Mr. Markham. I'm glad to meet you."

"Thank you, sir," replied Markham. "We appreciate your hospitality."

"It's not hospitality. Clay's family."

Clay turned at the sound of a door opening and saw his aunt Dorothy coming into the room. "Clay!" she said as she threw her arms around him. "I'm so happy to see you." She stepped back with her hands on his arms and looked him up and down. "You've gotten thin. You need some good home cooking."

Clay smiled. "Yes, ma'am, I reckon I do. I've been eating my own cooking for a spell."

Dorothy turned to Markham. "And this must be the young friend you mentioned in your letter."

"John Markham, ma'am," the lieutenant said, "your humble and obedient servant." He took her hand and lifted it to his lips.

Dorothy laughed and blushed, and Henry said in a mock growl, "You have a rather European way with the ladies, don't you, young man?"

A clatter on the steps leading to the second floor

announced the arrival of three more family members. They fairly flew down the stairs, and in the blink of an eye Clay found himself surrounded. His brother Edward was pumping his hand, his sister Susan was hugging him around the neck, and his youngest brother Jonathan was squeezing his other arm. All three were whooping and chattering and asking one question after another.

Clay had not seen his brothers and sister since the Holt family reunion at the homestead in Ohio several months earlier. Edward was a strapping young man in his late teens, Susan was a blond beauty several years younger, and Jonathan stood poised on the brink of adolescence. They looked happy and healthy, and it did Clay's heart good to see the faces he loved so well.

"I just knew you'd come by here on your way back from Washington," Edward was saying. "Did you get your land grant?"

The grant, owed by the government to Clay as a member of the Corps of Discovery, was what had taken him to Washington in the first place, although he had not expected the trip to become so complicated and dangerous. He said to Edward, "Yes, I've got it. As pretty a piece of ground as you'd ever want to see, in the shadow of the Grand Tetons along the valley of the Snake River."

Edward's eyes grew large. "I want to go there with you!"

"So do I!" Susan added.

"Me, too!" Jonathan piped in.

Clay grinned. "Not this trip, I'm afraid." As their faces fell, he added, "But sometime in the future, when things have settled down some, there'll be a place there for you if you want it. That's a promise."

He did not mention that Bear Tooth's band of Sioux also made their home in the valley of the Snake, or that south of the Sioux village lay the tiny settlement of New Hope. There was plenty of room there for everyone. That was one of the things Clay loved most about the West.

As he spoke, though, he wondered if he could ever fulfill his promise. Would things ever settle down for the Holts? If the past few years were any indication, it was unlikely. But he could hope. It would be pleasant someday to be an old man with all his family gathered around him, his adventuring days over. He smiled to himself. It was a dream to cling to, anyway.

In the meantime, he had come to Pittsburgh for more than a visit with the family. He introduced Markham to his siblings, then left them all talking in the hallway as he steered Uncle Henry into the parlor. In a quiet voice he asked, "Have you heard of a steamboat called the *New Orleans?*"

Henry nodded. "Of course I have. I suppose every businessman in Pittsburgh knows about the *New Orleans*. If Captain Roosevelt can really take her all the way down the Mississippi, it's going to make a big difference in our trade up here. Hell, it'll make a difference for the whole country."

"I reckon you're right," Clay said. "And that's why Markham and I are here, to board the *New Orleans* for its trip downriver."

Henry raised his eyebrows, then looked at him shrewdly. "You're up to something, Clay," he said. "Something you don't want to tell me about."

"Something I *can't* tell you about," Clay corrected. "I've been sworn to secrecy, but I can tell you that I'm acting in the best interests of the country."

Henry snorted as he walked to an armchair and sat down. "You didn't have to tell me that. Your pa and I fought in the war to make this nation free. No Holt would ever turn against it, and that's the gospel." He pursed his lips and frowned. "Not unless it was Ned. That boy was always a pure vexation to his mother and me."

"Ned has changed a lot since he took up with Jeff a couple of years ago," Clay assured him. "He's grown up, and he's turned into quite a sailor, too, or so I'm told."

"That's what he says in his letters, whenever he can be bothered to write to his old ma and pa." Henry shook his head. "Well, he's a grown man, and I suppose it's time I stopped worrying about him. That's easier said than done, though." He took a deep breath. "You were asking about the *New Orleans*."

"Do you know where she's docked?"

"I surely do."

"Could you take Markham and me down there tomorrow?"

"Of course," Henry said. "I'm not sure you and your young friend will be able to book passage, though. I've heard tell that the boat's already full up with important folks who want to be part of the first trip."

"Some space on the deck to roll our blankets at night will be all we need, if it comes to that. But I reckon once I've talked to Captain Roosevelt, he'll find room for us."

Henry held up his hands. "Keep your secrets, son. I'll not pry into your affairs. Anyway, some of the folks who have already booked passage may back out and come home once they realize how rough the trip is liable to be."

"Is Roosevelt expecting trouble?" asked Clay.

"From what I've heard, Roosevelt and his partners, Fulton and Livingston, are just about the only ones who have any confidence that the *New Orleans* can make it all the way downriver. The keelboatmen and flatboatmen who have been hauling goods up and down the river for years all swear that a steam-powered boat can't handle the snags and the shifting currents. Of course, it will be better for them if Roosevelt fails. If those big steamboats start going up and down the river, it'll hurt business for everyone else on the Mississippi."

Clay had never particularly trusted the twin ideals of change and progress, but he was practical enough to know that his uncle was right. If Captain Nicholas Roosevelt succeeded in his gamble, life all along the Mississippi would change.

But that was not Clay's concern right now. His job was to find a traitor.

Markham came into the parlor, trailed by Dorothy and the children. The lieutenant wore a slightly harried look on his face. Grinning, Clay asked, "Are those young uns about to talk your ears off, John?"

"Oh, no," Markham replied quickly. "I'm enjoying our conversation. They've, ah, asked me a great many questions about Washington City."

"And you never did tell us exactly what it is you do there, Mr. Markham," Edward reminded him.

"I'm a writer," Markham replied. That was the story he and Clay and Thomas Jefferson had agreed upon to explain his trip down the Mississippi. "I'm going to write about my travels."

"You mean write them in a book?" asked Susan.

"Yes, that's the idea."

"Can I read it?" Susan's eyes were shining, and she had put one hand on Markham's arm. Clay suppressed a chuckle. It was clear that his sister was smitten with the handsome young lieutenant.

"I'll see that you get a copy when it's published," Markham promised.

"Oh, thank you! I'll be looking forward to it so much," Susan said, never taking her eyes off his face.

"You can have an old book if that's what you want," Jonathan said. He turned to Clay. "Will you send me a cap like the one you used to wear? The one made out of a racoon's skin?"

"I'll see what I can do when I get back to the mountains," Clay said. He did not add that it might be a long time before he returned to the land he had come to regard as his true home.

"Well," Henry said, "at least you can stay and visit with us for a few days. The *New Orleans* doesn't leave until Sunday." He clapped a hand on Clay's shoulder. "It's good to have you with us."

"It's good to be here with some of the family again," Clay said sincerely.

But even as he spoke, he knew that the most important member of his family was not here, and until he could be with Shining Moon again, he would not be truly complete.

CHAPTER
THREE

It was a gorgeous early autumn day, and the Holt farm was bustling with activity. Castor and Pollux Gilworth had already harvested the corn and wheat crops, but there was still plenty to do. Apples hung heavy on the trees in the small orchard, and hogs had to be slaughtered. Shining Moon had decided that she and Matthew would be responsible for picking the apples and leave the grisly task of hog butchering to the Gilworth brothers. Since Matthew seemed to have turned from his old ways, she thought it best to avoid the barn and what Castor and Pollux would be doing.

No need to remind the boy of the things he had done in the past with animals and sharp knives. . . .

The orchard, several neat rows of trees, was not far from the cabin. "Fella name of Chapman came through here not long after Castor and me went to work for Clay and Jeff," Pollux had explained to Shining Moon. "He had a bunch of seeds in his pack, and he gave some of them to us to plant. This is the first year the trees have borne much fruit." He smacked his lips. "That means plenty of deep-dish apple pie." He added with a sigh, "Ol' Miz Doolittle sure made a good one."

The mention of Cassie had revived sad memories for Shining Moon, and Pollux had immediately apologized when he saw the look on her face. She had smiled and assured him it was all right.

Now, as she stood at the edge of the orchard and looked at the trees, their branches festooned with ripe, rosy apples, she thought of Cassie again and wished the old woman could be here to see them. She could almost hear Cassie's ribald, cackling laugh.

Matthew hefted a straw basket as he stood beside Shining Moon. "Are we going to pick those apples or not?" he asked, a hint of the old surliness in his voice.

"Yes. We are going to pick the apples." Shining Moon picked up her own basket and the short ladder she had brought from the cabin.

"I get to climb the ladder," Matthew said excitedly.

"All right," Shining Moon said with a smile. She carried basket and ladder over to the nearest tree. "We will start here."

She propped the ladder against a low-hanging branch and steadied it with her hands as Matthew scrambled up the rungs and into the middle of the tree. He plucked the apples and dropped them down to Shining Moon, who caught them and placed them carefully in the baskets so they would not bruise. The work went quickly, and by midmorning it seemed to Shining Moon that she and Matthew had made good progress.

"We should stop and rest for a while," she called to Matthew as he finished picking a tree clean of fruit.

"It's all right with me if we go on," he said. "I'm not tired."

"The apples will still be there in a little while. Come down and sit with me. We will rest."

Matthew shrugged, clambered down the ladder, and sank cross-legged onto the ground. Shining Moon sat a few feet away, carefully arranging her skirts around her. She had become accustomed to wearing the clothing of white women, so unlike the soft, sturdy buckskins of her people, but she still found dresses overly fussy and inhibiting.

The air was crisp and cool, and the warmth of the sun felt good. Matthew reached over to one of the baskets and picked out an apple. "I'm going to eat one," he announced.

"That is a good idea." Shining Moon chose one for herself and bit into it, relishing the sweet, juicy tang.

"I wish we had apples in the mountains," Matthew said around a mouthful of fruit.

Shining Moon nodded. "When we return, we will take seeds with us and plant them. Soon the valley of my people will be covered with apple trees."

Actually, the cold season in her homeland was probably too long for apple trees to thrive. But perhaps, with plenty of care and attention, she could coax a few seedlings to life, and eventually the trees might bear fruit.

But will I? she suddenly wondered. She had been with child once, before a brutal attack had ended the budding new life. Since then, though she and Clay had shared the pleasures of the flesh as often as they could, none of the seeds he had planted within her had taken root. Because of what had happened to her, she might never be able to bear a child.

Perhaps that was why she had been so eager to take Matthew in and raise him, she thought. She had never been one to ponder the ways of her god, of Wakan Tanka, nor did she normally waste time brooding about the whys and wherefores of her own actions. She lived in the here and now, not the past or the future. But there were moments when questions like this one nibbled at the edges of her mind.

"Why are you staring at me?" snapped Matthew. "What did I do?"

Quickly, Shining Moon shook her head. "Nothing," she said. "I was thinking of my homeland. Your homeland, now."

Matthew looked off into the distance. "I don't have a home. Not anymore."

"That is not true." Shining Moon gave in to impulse and reached out to rest her hand on Matthew's shoulder. "Your home is wherever your family may be." *And Clay Holt and I are your family now,* she added to herself.

Matthew pulled away. "My family's all dead, 'cept for Uncle Aaron, and he might as well be since he decided he wanted to get along with the Holts. The Holts killed all the rest of my family."

With a pang Shining Moon wished she could have avoided this conversation. All it was doing was bringing up bad memories for Matthew. She tossed aside the apple core and stood up, brushing off her dress. "We must return to our apple picking," she said briskly.

Matthew sprang to his feet. "I don't want to pick any more damned apples!"

"Matthew—" Shining Moon began warningly.

"I won't do it!" He spun around and dashed away, running along the rows of trees until he reached the edge of the orchard.

Shining Moon watched him run toward the barn. Her mouth was a taut, angry line, but the anger was directed as much at herself as at the boy. She should not have brought up the subject of family. But it was difficult not to dream, to dream that one day Matthew would feel the same way about her and Clay as they did about him—or rather, the way she had felt about him before Cassie's death and her own mishap in the old well. Whether she wanted to admit it or not, those events had strained whatever tenuous bond had existed between her and Matthew.

And Clay had never liked the boy or known how to go about the job of raising him. Clay was a good man, but Matthew was a Garwood, and as such he would have to prove himself to Clay, would have to earn Clay's affection and trust. Matthew had refused to do anything toward that end. Indeed, he had gone out of his way to prove that Clay's opinion of him was well placed.

With a sigh, she turned toward the apple baskets. She would have to continue the gathering by herself. She had just picked up a basket when she heard an angry shout from the barn.

The voice belonged to one of the Gilworth brothers. And from the sound of it, something was seriously wrong. Shining Moon threw the basket back on the ground, hitched up her skirts, and ran toward the barn, her sleek brown legs flashing under the white woman's dress.

She hurried through the open double doors, saw nothing amiss, and plunged down the center aisle between the stalls and through the doors at the other end. Outside was the pen in which Castor and Pollux were slaughtering hogs, and as Shining Moon came out of the barn, she paused and instinctively averted her eyes from the blood and entrails scattered on the ground. She saw the Gilworths standing nearby. One of them was holding Matthew, who was struggling futilely, his feet dangling off the ground. The other brother was clutching his upper right arm, and crimson welled between his tightly clenched fingers.

"What happened?" Shining Moon asked, breathless from running—and from fear.

"Stabbed me, he did!" the wounded Gilworth brother exclaimed. "Came running out of the barn and stuck me in the arm with a knife! He might've put it in my back next if Castor hadn't grabbed him."

Shining Moon saw the knife lying on the ground where Castor had apparently knocked it from Matthew's hand. Castor's huge arms were wrapped around Matthew now, immobilizing him. Shining Moon willed herself to remain calm as she said to Pollux, "Let me look at the wound."

The sleeve of Pollux's shirt was already torn and bloodstained, so he ripped it off from the shoulder, exposing an ugly gash in his arm. Shining Moon did not wince at the sight. She was Sioux; she had seen many knife wounds before, most of them worse than this one.

"We will clean it," she said. "Can you move your arm?"

Pollux nodded, grimacing as he demonstrated. "Hurts like the devil, but everything seems to be working."

"Good. When the wound is clean, we will pack it with moss and bind it. The moss will suck out any poison."

"I reckon you know what you're doing," Pollux said. "I'll put myself in your hands, ma'am." He glanced at Matthew, who had finally stopped fighting. "What set him off like that?"

"I spoke of things I should not have," Shining Moon said bluntly. "Your injury is my fault."

"Not hardly, ma'am," said Castor. "You weren't the one who put that pig-sticker in Pollux's arm. 'Twas the boy."

Matthew twisted and writhed again as profanity streamed from his mouth. He cursed Castor, Pollux—and Shining Moon most of all. "You damn redskin whore!" he howled.

Shining Moon ignored his words, but she could not ignore the hatred behind them. All the progress she had thought they were making these past few weeks had been an illusion. Matthew was still the same boy he had always been: filled with bitter, violent hate for the Holts and anyone connected to them.

Jeff fought down the apprehension that welled in his chest at the sight of the *Beaumont*, the majestic schooner that would take him, Melissa, and Michael around Cape Horn and up the Pacific coast of North America to Alaska.

Not that he was worried about the seaworthiness of the ship itself or the abilities of its crew. March ships were some of the finest vessels built in New England, and the crews were handpicked by Lemuel and his captains. If any ship could safely make the long voyage to Alaska, it was the *Beaumont*. The ship was sleek and beautiful, from its needlelike prow to its low cabins to its squared-off stern. With over two dozen sails fluttering from the crossbeams of a trio of towering masts, it was the very embodiment of speed worked in canvas and polished wood.

What made Jeff uneasy was his memory of the only other trip he had made on a sailing ship. He had been sick nearly the entire voyage, heaving the contents of his churning stomach over the railing several times a day.

"Maybe this time will be different," he muttered to himself.

"What did you say, dear?" Melissa asked from beside him.

Jeff shook his head. "Nothing important," he replied, hoping that Melissa would not press the issue.

Michael chose that moment to pull loose from Melissa's hand and go dashing up the gangplank to the deck of the ship. "I want to look for our cabin!" he called over his shoulder.

Melissa picked up her skirts and hurried after him. "Michael! Come back here! It's not safe to run around on the ship while it's being loaded!"

That was his son, all right, Jeff thought with a smile as he watched the towheaded boy disappear around a corner of the fo'c'sle. Adventurous to the core, even a little reckless sometimes. Jeff quickly followed Melissa, knowing that she would not be happy if he left her to run down the boy by herself.

Before he could join the pursuit, he was stopped at the top of the gangplank by a stout figure in white trousers, blue coat, and a cap bearing a gold insignia. The man extended his hand. "Mr. Holt? Welcome aboard, sir. I'm Captain Niles Vickery."

Jeff had no choice but to stop and shake hands. "I'm pleased to meet you, Captain," he said, "and I know we have a great deal to discuss, but right now I probably ought to help my wife catch up to our little boy—"

"That would be the lad right there, I take it," said Vickery, pointing with the index finger of a plump hand.

Jeff looked and saw Ned coming toward him with Michael perched on his broad shoulders. Melissa and India were behind them. Ned grinned at Jeff. "Lost something, cousin?"

"Yes, a little hellion who's going to be in trouble if he does anything like that again," Jeff said gruffly, for Michael's benefit.

Ned swung the boy to the deck and set him on his feet. "There you go, Whip," he said.

Jeff saw Melissa roll her eyes at Ned's use of the nickname. Ever since Jeff had taught Michael the rudiments of using a bullwhip, Melissa had fought a losing battle against the name, which looked as if it was going to stick with everyone but her. Out of consideration for her feelings, Jeff tried not to use it when she was around, but sometimes he slipped, too. It suited the boy so well.

Michael looked up at Jeff. "I was just looking for our cabin."

"We'll find it soon enough. I'm sure it's below-decks. In the meantime . . ." Jeff waved a hand at Captain Vickery. "Wouldn't you like to meet the captain of the ship?"

Michael's eyes grew large as he stared up at Vickery. "Are you really the captain?"

"That I am, laddie," replied Vickery.

"You must have been a sailor for a long time."

"Man and boy, nigh onto forty years," Vickery confirmed. He held out a hand. "If you want to come with me, I'll take you up to the bridge and let you get the feel of the ship's wheel."

Michael turned excitedly to Melissa. "Can I?"

She smiled. "Go ahead."

Michael took the captain's hand and skipped happily toward the stern. Jeff watched the two of them go, then said to Melissa, "I'm sorry he ran off like that."

"He wouldn't be a Holt if he didn't run off every

now and then." She turned to Ned. "Thanks for catching him."

"The sprout pretty much ran into me," Ned replied with a grin.

"What are you doing here on the *Beaumont*?" Jeff asked. "I thought you two were shipping out on the *Lydia Marie*."

"We are," India said. "We are just over here saying good-bye to some mates of ours."

"But we'll be dropping anchor in the same ports along the way around the Cape," Ned said. "So it's not as if we won't be seeing any of you again for a while."

The plan called for the two ships to travel together until they had rounded the southernmost tip of South America. Then their routes would diverge, the *Lydia Marie* heading northwest toward the Hawaiian Islands and the *Beaumont* continuing northward to Alaska.

Ned slapped his cousin on the shoulder and went on, "In fact, we'll be seeing a lot of you from the *Lydia Marie*, since you're probably going to be hanging over the rail of this ship, too, as you did when we sailed down here from New York."

"Don't even joke about it," Jeff said grimly. "This time it's going to be different."

"Think you've got your sea legs, eh? Well, I hope you're right."

So do I, Jeff thought. Otherwise, a long voyage was going to seem much, much longer.

"A hundred and forty-eight feet from stem to stern," Captain Nicholas Roosevelt said proudly as he gestured toward the blue-painted vessel behind him. He had reason to be proud, Clay thought. The *New Orleans* was the most impressive steamboat he had ever seen. At forty feet wide, it was also the largest. A massive paddlewheel was set amidships on each side, just ahead of the tall smokestack that jutted from the center of the boat. Fore and aft of the paddlewheels rose a pair of masts with sails attached so that the *New Orleans* could take advantage of the wind if necessary. A row of low-ceilinged cabins ran down the center of the boat at deck level. The bridge was located in a small wheelhouse just ahead of the paddles. The hull was gracefully rounded, and the boat sat fairly low in the water, unlike the flatboats and keelboats that regularly plied the waters of the Ohio and Mississippi Rivers.

"Please don't take offense, gentlemen," Captain Roosevelt went on, "but I'm a busy man, as you might expect. What can I do for you?"

Clay and Markham had caught Roosevelt just outside his waterfront office. He was a solidly built man with a shock of dark hair and bushy side-whiskers. His dark eyes shone with a light that Clay recognized: Roosevelt was a dreamer, an explorer, an adventurer—the sort of man who did not like to be told that something could not be done. Clay felt an immediate kinship.

Markham said, "My associate and I need to speak with you on a matter of utmost urgency, Captain."

Roosevelt snorted. "Everyone thinks that what they're doing is a matter of utmost urgency, son. So if you can't spit it out—"

"Thomas Jefferson sent us," Clay said simply, keeping his voice low so that he would not be overheard in the hustle and bustle around them.

Roosevelt looked at him sharply and took a deep breath. "Well, now, that's a different story." He jerked his head toward the small building that served as his office. "Come inside."

Once they were in the office and the door was closed behind them, Roosevelt regarded Clay and Markham through narrowed eyes and asked, "What do the two of you have to do with President Jefferson?"

"We're working on his behalf," said Markham as he reached inside his coat and brought out a folded piece of paper. "On behalf of the United States government, actually, but at Mr. Jefferson's request. I believe this letter will make everything clear." He handed the paper to Roosevelt.

The captain took it, unfolded it, and quickly read the words written there in Jefferson's bold script. He grunted. "If Thomas Jefferson really wrote this—" he began.

"He did," Clay said.

"Then it seems I have no choice but to give you all the help I can." Roosevelt passed the document back to Markham, who put it away. "What do you require, gentlemen?"

"Passage on the *New Orleans*," Markham said.

Roosevelt frowned. "Every cabin is booked. I've had to extend invitations to several politicians from Washington City who seem to think it will do them good to make the voyage with me. Since my partners in this venture, Mr. Fulton and Mr. Livingston, are hoping to be granted a monopoly on steamboat trade on the Mississippi, they feel it's essential to maintain good relations with the government."

Clay nodded. "One of your passengers is the reason we're here, Captain. I'm afraid I can't tell you any more than that, though."

"A secret, eh?" Roosevelt shrugged. "Well, since it's at the behest of Mr. Jefferson, it seems I have no choice but to find room for you. I must warn you, however, that your accommodations won't be fancy."

"I've spent many a night under the stars on rough trails, Captain," Clay said dryly. "Whatever you have will be fine."

Roosevelt looked shrewdly at Clay. "I'll wager you have seen some rough trails, Mr. Holt. I'll wager you have." He went to the door of the office. "Well, come along, and I'll give you a tour of the boat."

"Are any of the other passengers on board yet?" asked Clay.

"Not that I know of. We won't be leaving for a couple of days."

"All right." Clay was glad the others hadn't boarded. He and Markham would run into Senators Emory, Ralston, and Haines soon enough.

And whichever one of them might be the traitor— whoever had conspired with Gideon Maxwell to steal the western half of the continent and possibly ordered the murder of Meriwether Lewis—that man would know when he saw Clay and Markham that they were still on his trail. There was no other reason for them to be here, especially after everything that had happened in Washington.

Which meant that the trip down the Mississippi, which would be perilous to begin with, would be even more so for Clay and Markham. The man they were after had killed before and would not hesitate to kill again.

As they left Roosevelt's office, a pretty, dark-haired woman was coming down the dock toward the gangplank that led to the deck of the *New Orleans*. Her face lit up at the sight of Roosevelt. "Hello, Nicholas," she said.

"My dear." Roosevelt took her hands and leaned forward to kiss her cheek, then turned to Clay and Markham. "Gentlemen, allow me to present my lovely wife. Lydia, this is Mr. Holt and Mr. Markham. They'll be traveling with us when we leave Pittsburgh."

Clay and Markham took off their hats and nodded respectfully to Mrs. Roosevelt. "Ma'am," Clay said.

Markham asked, "Did I hear the captain correctly, Mrs. Roosevelt? You're traveling on the *New Orleans* as well?"

"Of course," said Lydia Roosevelt. "Why wouldn't I go with Nicholas?"

"Well, ah, I thought perhaps the dangers inherent in such a voyage might dissuade you."

Roosevelt gave a booming laugh. "You've no way of knowing this, Mr. Markham, but two years ago, when my wife here was naught but a blushing bride, she accompanied me down the Ohio and the Mississippi on a flatboat I had specially built, so that I could study the problems of negotiating the rivers with a steamboat. She was a staunch traveler then, and I daresay she still is."

"Nicholas, you will embarrass me." Mrs. Roosevelt regarded Clay and Markham with a keen intelligence.

"I was under the impression, gentlemen, that there were no more berths remaining for this voyage."

"We'll find room for Mr. Holt and Mr. Markham," Roosevelt said hastily. "Don't worry about that, my dear."

"I wasn't worrying, Nicholas. I was just curious."

Clay wondered how much Roosevelt would tell her once they were behind closed doors. Luckily, the captain knew very little about their mission, only that they were acting on behalf of the government. And as he had reflected earlier, their true motive for being here would not be a secret to the man they were seeking, so there was nothing anyone might give away that would endanger their mission.

"I was about to show our new passengers around the boat," Roosevelt said to his wife. "Would you care to join us?"

"Of course. And then I need to discuss a few last-minute details with you."

Roosevelt took her arm. "Very well. Come along, gentlemen."

As they started up the gangplank, Mrs. Roosevelt glanced over her shoulder at Clay and Markham. "What about your wives?" she asked. "Are they traveling with you?"

"I'm not married," said Markham.

"You should be. It's a wonderful institution. What about you, Mr. Holt?"

"My wife isn't with me, I'm afraid. I wish she was."

Even as he spoke, it occurred to Clay that the *New Orleans* would probably be stopping at Marietta on its trip down the Ohio River. He could see Shining Moon at least for a few hours and finally explain to her what was going on and why he had to stay on the steamboat rather than taking her and Matthew back to the mountains.

Maybe, with any luck, he and Markham would have uncovered the traitor by then. It wasn't going to happen before the boat left Pittsburgh, from the looks of things, but there was no reason the job might not be done by the time the *New Orleans* reached Marietta. Clay found himself hoping fervently that it would work out that way.

Because he knew that once he saw Shining Moon, it was going to be pure hell to have to leave her behind once more.

CHAPTER
FOUR

M elissa lowered herself onto the narrow bunk
and sighed. For the next couple of months she
would spend much of her time in this cabin,
and although it was one of the largest on the ship, it
seemed cramped and small. It would seem even
smaller with a rambunctious boy in it. She suspected
that he would be on deck most of the time, however,
but that was a mixed blessing; she would have to
worry about his falling overboard or hurting himself.
Not for the first time, she asked herself if she had made
the right decision by insisting that she and Michael accompany Jeff to Alaska.

If only Philip Rattigan hadn't kissed her . . .

In spite of herself, she found her thoughts wandering back to the night the sea captain had taken her in
his arms. It had been a moment neither she nor he had
expected to happen. At least *she* hadn't. She had always
been faithful to Jeff, had in fact barely looked at another man since her wedding day. But then Rattigan

had come along, tall and dashing and devastatingly handsome, and even the fact that he was allied with Jedediah Corbett, the rival merchant who was trying to run Holt-Merrivale out of business, hadn't kept Melissa from noticing him.

Rattigan had saved her life when hired killers had tried to blow up the warehouse in which Holt-Merrivale merchandise was stored. They had managed to stop the fire before the building burned down, although there was nothing they could do for the guards who had been murdered.

Melissa had no doubt that Corbett, Rattigan's partner, was responsible for the attempted arson, even though Rattigan himself had sworn that he had no knowledge of Corbett's illegal schemes. Rattigan had even indicated that he was going to confront Corbett and end their partnership.

Had it all ended there, she probably would not be on this ship right now, Melissa reflected. But it hadn't ended. When she and Rattigan had staggered coughing out of the smoke-choked warehouse after extinguishing the flames, he had taken her in his arms and done what he claimed he had wanted to do since the moment he had first laid eyes on her.

He had kissed her, long and hard—and God help her, Melissa had kissed him back.

She had not seen him since that night, and she never wanted to see him again. She did not want to be reminded of the hot surge of desire that had shot through her as she found herself in the arms of a man who was not her husband. She did not want to think about the way his mouth had plundered hers so ruthlessly. . . .

Philip Rattigan was still in Wilmington; Melissa had heard rumors about the angry dissolution of his partnership with Corbett. She wished he would go back to England, where he had come from, but there was no indication he was going to oblige her anytime soon. So it fell to her to put some distance between them, as much distance as she possibly could.

She was going to put an entire continent between them. She hoped that would be far enough to help her forget about him.

Him, and that damned kiss . . .

The kiss sent drums of fire pounding along his veins.

"Ah, India," Ned murmured as he drew his lips slightly away from hers, "you drive a man wild!"

"Any man, or just you?" she asked in a whisper.

"It had better be just me!"

She kissed him again, lightly, quickly. "You don't have to worry about that, my lad."

They were huddled in the shadows of an alley next to one of the warehouses that lined the docks. They had stopped at Red Mike's for a drink after leaving the *Beaumont*, and now it was time to get back to the *Lydia Marie*. In less than an hour both vessels would be setting sail from Wilmington, bound for Cape Horn and the broad Pacific Ocean.

But before the voyage began, Ned wanted a few moments alone with India. Once they were at sea, it would be difficult to find any privacy. They had to snatch any opportunity they could to be together, and Ned didn't intend to waste this chance. He brought his mouth down again on India's and tightened his embrace. His right hand slid down her back to the swelling of her hips and brought her more intimately against him.

India's fingers clutched at his shirt, and she let out a low moan. But she whispered, "I don't rut in alleyways, Ned, especially not in broad daylight."

"I know. We'll have to wait for another time. But at least we have this moment, don't we?"

It would all have been much simpler had she not been determined to keep her identity as a woman a secret from the rest of the crew. But Ned understood her reluctance. Many sailors regarded a female on board ship as a bad omen, and the feeling was exacerbated when that woman was a member of the crew.

Some of the men would consider a female sailor fair game for their amorous advances, too.

With a sigh, India leaned her head against his chest and said, "I suppose we'd best be getting back to the ship."

"You're right—" Ned stopped short at the sound of angry voices nearby.

"—ought to crack your skull with a belaying pin, you bastard!"

Ned recognized the voice. It belonged to Donnelly, the sailor with whom he had fought a couple of days earlier. The bruises Donnelly had given him still ached, and now, from the sound of things, Donnelly was about to attack someone else.

"Ned—" India caught hold of his arm as he started back along the alley toward the sounds of fighting.

"I just want to see what's going on," he said, pulling away from her.

"Then I'd better go with you." She hurried to catch up with his long-legged stride.

Ned paused when he reached the mouth of the alley, which opened into a narrow, squalid lane that ran behind the warehouses. He held out an arm to keep India back, but she sidestepped it and stood beside him.

A dozen feet away, with his back toward them, stood Donnelly. The burly sailor's fists were clenched, and he was advancing toward a smaller figure that flinched away from him. "Lemme alone, ya damned bloody ape!" whined the smaller man.

"I'll teach you to mess with me, Yancy," Donnelly growled.

Both Ned and India recognized the little man. Yancy was a sailor on the *Lydia Marie*, a scrawny, balding Englishman who moved around a ship's rigging with such skill and grace it was as if he'd been born there. He had a surly temper, and Ned did not consider him a friend by any means, but Ned was not going to stand by while Donnelly handed him a beating. Not after the run-in Ned himself had had with the bully.

India must have guessed what he was about to do, because she caught at his arm again, but he shook her off and stepped out of the alley. "Donnelly!" he snapped.

Donnelly stopped in his tracks, one fist poised to strike out at Yancy. He looked over his shoulder and said, "Holt."

"If you're determined to fight with someone, shouldn't it be somebody closer to your own size?" Ned asked scornfully.

"Damn it, Holt, stay out of this. It's none of your concern—"

"Anytime you're about to make a brutal ass of yourself, I'm making it my concern."

India said in a low voice, "Ned, we don't know what's going on here."

"That's right, Holt," Donnelly snapped. "You don't have the first damned idea what's going on here."

"Yes, I do." Ned nodded toward Yancy, who was taking advantage of the distraction by edging farther away from Donnelly. "You're about to lambaste poor Yancy here, and he probably doesn't deserve it any more than I did when you decided to attack me."

Yancy, several yards away now, spun around and dashed down the lane. Donnelly jerked his head around in time to see the little sailor duck into the next alley and disappear. Donnelly spat out a furious curse, then swung toward Ned again.

"He's gone, and it's your fault, Holt! You're going to pay for that."

Ned lifted his balled fists. "Come on, if that's what you want."

"Ned," India said warningly.

Whatever else she might have said was drowned out by Donnelly's roar as he charged straight at Ned.

For the second time in three days, Ned found himself fending off an attack by Donnelly. Slugging it out hadn't worked very well the first time; Ned had won the battle, but he was still paying the price in stiff, sore, bruised muscles. This time, as Donnelly came at him,

Ned quickly stepped aside and reached out to grab Donnelly's shirt. He twisted, using Donnelly's own momentum against him, and threw the burly sailor toward the wall of the closest warehouse. There was only one problem with that maneuver, Ned saw to his horror.

India had somehow gotten in the way. Donnelly was about to crash into her.

India darted nimbly out of Donnelly's path and extended a slim leg. Her booted foot tangled with Donnelly's calves, and with a shout he tumbled forward, crashed to the paving stones, and rolled over several times.

Before he could regain his feet, before Ned could reach his side, India was crouched next to him, the point of the thin-bladed dagger in her hand barely pricking the soft skin of his throat. "That's enough," she said, her voice lowered into the husky timbre she adopted in her pose as a young man. "I've no desire to slit your throat, Donnelly, but I will if I have to."

With the knife at his throat, Donnelly could not move. But he did cut loose with a string of sulfurous curses. "You're damned fools, both of you!" he concluded. "You should have left me alone to give that little weasel what he deserves!"

"It's not your job to hand out punishment to the crew," Ned said. "That's the captain's place."

To Ned's surprise, Donnelly laughed. "All right, if that's the way you want it. We'll just leave it to the captain."

"This fight's over," India said, pressing slightly on the knife to emphasize her point. "Remember that."

"Let me up," rasped Donnelly. "I've no more interest in either of you."

India withdrew the blade and stood up. "See that it stays that way," she warned.

Donnelly got to his feet and with a glare wiped away the tiny trickle of blood on his neck. He spat onto the paving stones, then stalked away toward the waterfront.

When Donnelly was gone, Ned turned to India and grabbed her by the shoulders. "What the devil did you think you were doing?"

"Keeping you from being hanged or jailed for killing a man," India shot back. "If Donnelly had hit that wall, it could have dashed his brains out. I just brought him down a little sooner."

Ned shook his head. "That was my fight, India. You had no right to interfere."

"Interfere!" she repeated angrily, jerking free of his hands. "I was just trying to save you from more trouble than you need, bucko. Besides, if you were locked up in a jail cell or swinging from a gallows, I'd have to sail all the way to China without you—"

She stopped short at the faint sound of shoe leather rasping on paving stones. Yancy looked around the corner of the nearest building and asked, "Is he gone?"

"You mean Donnelly?" Ned said. "He's gone, all right. We sent him packing."

Yancy emerged from the shadows of the alley. "I can't thank the two o' you enough. I thought for certain the cobber was going to pound me head to mush."

"I won't stand by and see any man beaten by a larger one," Ned said again.

"Well, I'm much obliged, and I'll tell ye this—old Yance pays his debts, he does. I'll not forget what the two o' you did for me today."

India waved off his thanks. "Just do your job when the ship sails," she said. "That's all the gratitude either of us needs."

"Speak for yourself," Ned said with a grin. "You never know when you might need to call in a favor. What was the trouble about, anyway, Yancy?"

The little Englishman shrugged. "Naught that I could say. Donnelly's just a bully, he is."

"That's the truth," agreed Ned. "Well, we'd best be getting to the ship. Wouldn't want it sailing without us, would we?"

India was still frowning as they made their way to the *Lydia Marie*. Ned couldn't understand what was bothering her, nor why she kept casting suspicious glances in Yancy's direction.

There was nothing wrong with having a new friend, was there?

Jeff stood at the railing of the *Beaumont*, watching with his son as the crew bustled about, preparing the ship for sailing.

"How long will it take us to get to Alaska?" asked Michael. "I want to be there now."

Ah, the impatience of youth, Jeff thought. Of course, he was not that far removed from it himself. He was still a young man, and he understood full well the burning desire to get to wherever it was he was going. Deep down, he agreed with Michael: He, too, wanted to be in Alaska *now*.

Captain Vickery passed them, then stopped and looked back. "I'm on my way to check on the cargo," he said to Michael. "Would you like to come with me?"

Michael glanced up at Jeff. "Can I?"

"I suppose it would be all right," Jeff said. "Just be careful, and do what the captain tells you."

"All right."

"Say 'Aye, Cap'n,'" suggested Vickery.

"Aye, Cap'n!" Michael repeated delightedly.

Jeff watched with a smile as Vickery ushered Michael through one of the hatches that led belowdecks. The boy turned around and climbed down the ladder carefully . . . but not too carefully.

"Where's Michael going?" Melissa asked from beside Jeff.

He turned and looked at her, a little surprised that she had come up without his noticing. He wondered briefly if city living had dulled his senses.

"He and Captain Vickery are going to check on the cargo," he answered. "He'll be safe down below."

"I know. Captain Vickery seems quite competent."

"Lemuel would never have hired him otherwise." Jeff smiled. "What have you been doing?"

"Unpacking our things . . . what few of them I actually could unpack in that tiny cabin."

Jeff nodded. "Space is always at a premium on a sailing ship. We have to leave as much room for cargo as possible in order to make the trips profitable."

"Right now I don't care about profits."

Jeff's smile widened. "I never thought I'd hear that from a hardheaded businesswoman like you."

Melissa did not return the smile. In fact, she looked rather solemn as she said, "All that matters to me is that we're together, Jeff. I hope we're never separated again."

He slipped an arm around her shoulders and drew her against him. "So do I," he said honestly. He had done the right thing to let Melissa and Michael accompany him on this voyage. He was more convinced of that than ever.

Melissa came up on her toes to kiss him, apparently oblivious to the sailors scurrying about their tasks. Her lips pressed hard against his, and when she drew back, Jeff blinked in surprise and asked, "What was that for?"

"You're my husband, aren't you? And a wife can kiss her husband whenever and wherever she wants to, can't she?" There was a fierce intensity to Melissa's voice.

"That's right." Jeff drew her close and stroked her hair as she rested her head against his chest. He had certainly enjoyed the kiss, but what had she meant by those questions?

The proposed trip down the Ohio and the Mississippi by the *New Orleans* had been greeted with skepticism by the people who made their living on those great rivers, but nevertheless, a large crowd had gathered in Pittsburgh to witness the departure of the steamboat. A brass band had marched down to the dock and was playing patriotic songs as passengers arrived and came on board. Senator Charles Emory of Maine, tall and handsome with dark, curly hair, waved to the crowd as he ascended the gangplank. Behind him came Senator Morgan Ralston of Georgia, a white-haired, distinguished son of the South. The last member of the triumvirate, Senator Louis Haines of New York, was smaller and darker than his fellow politicians. Although he lacked their easy charm, he was an effective legislator and had represented his constituents for two terms. The three men were friends and frequent companions at the social gatherings that characterized political life in Washington City.

Clay Holt was quite familiar with the three senators. He has first met them at a party given by Gideon Maxwell in Washington. Later, Clay, Jeff, and Lieutenant Markham had joined them and their families on a hunting expedition to the Virginia woods organized by Maxwell. It was during that outing Clay had discovered that one of the three senators was working with Maxwell on the illicit scheme to gain title to half of the Louisiana Purchase. The problem was that Clay didn't know which of the men was the traitor.

That was what he and Markham had to find out before the *New Orleans* reached the city for which it had been named.

Clay and the lieutenant were already on board. They stood at the aft railing and watched as the other passengers, including the three senators, embarked. Markham said in a low voice, "Are you certain we want to expose our presence so soon?"

"This is a big boat, but not *that* big," Clay replied dryly. "They're going to know sooner or later that we're on board, and the gent we're after is going to know *why* we're here, too. I'd just as soon go ahead and throw a scare into him now, give him more time to worry. For all he knows, we already know which one he is."

Markham looked dubious. "If that was the case, he would have been arrested already. He's probably confident that we *haven't* discovered him."

Clay shrugged. "Then he'll have all the more reason to worry. And a fellow like that makes mistakes."

"My God," Markham exclaimed as he looked at Clay, "you're hoping that he tries to kill us!"

"That might make things a mite simpler." Clay winked at the lieutenant. Leaning against the rail, he watched the passengers for a few moments, then straightened and said, "Come on."

Without waiting to see if Markham was following, he strode along the deck toward the embarking senators. They had moved to the rail and were waving to the crowd on the dock as the band continued to play. The politicians were in their element, eagerly lapping up the attention.

Clay stepped up behind them and said in a loud voice that carried over the strains of martial music, "Senators! It's good to see you again!"

The three men turned, and Clay could read nothing on their faces but the surprise that anyone would normally show at seeing an acquaintance in an unexpected place.

Charles Emory said, "Why, it's Mr. Holt! And Lieutenant Markham, I do believe."

Morgan Ralston stuck out a hand. "It's a pleasure to see you again, Holt. You, too, Lieutenant. I didn't know you were coming on this trip."

As Clay shook hands with Ralston, Louis Haines said, "There's an old saying about a bad penny always turning up, Morgan."

"It's good to see you, too, Senator Haines," Clay said with a grin calculated to annoy the politician from New York. To Ralston he said, "The lieutenant and I both have business in New Orleans. This boat is the fastest way there. We happened to run into each other by coincidence."

"I see," said Ralston. "Well, I'm glad you decided to book passage. The two of you were certainly boon companions on that outing of poor Maxwell's."

Clay frowned. "What do you mean—poor Maxwell?" Gideon Maxwell had died during a fierce hand-to-hand battle with Clay, but as far as Clay knew, the authorities had kept his death quiet.

"He passed away suddenly," said Haines. "Bad heart. You didn't know?"

So that was the story the government was circulating. Someone should have let him know, Clay thought as he shook his head. "No, I hadn't heard."

"What about Maxwell's daughter?" Markham asked, his voice strained. "What about Diana?"

"She's gone to Europe to stay with relatives while she gets over her father's death," Ralston replied.

"That's . . . good," Markham said. He and Clay both knew that Diana was in prison, not in Europe.

The lieutenant had been more than halfway in love with Diana Maxwell—until he had discovered that she was as deeply involved in the land grab plot as her father. The revelation was made doubly painful when Diana shot him during the showdown in the Virginia woods. Clay wasn't sure what had hurt Markham more—the bullet or the betrayal. The bullet wound had healed in a matter of weeks. The other wound would take much longer.

"Well, I'm sorry to hear about Maxwell, but I reckon life goes on," Clay said.

"Indeed it does," said Emory. He gestured grandly at the magnificent steamboat. "And if we needed more proof, here it is, gentlemen. This vessel is the vanguard of the tide of civilization that is going to sweep across this entire nation. Why, once steamboats are regularly wending their way up and down the great rivers of this mighty land, there will be no limit to what can be done!"

Clay noticed a few men standing nearby, furiously scribbling on wooden slates, recording Senator Emory's words. Clay asked, "Are you going on this trip just to make speeches, Senator?"

"Of course," Emory replied without hesitation. "At every opportunity. What sort of politician would I be otherwise?"

The sort who would sell out his country, maybe, Clay thought. Or perhaps the traitor was Ralston, or Haines. At this moment he had no idea. But the villain had just been served notice that Clay Holt and John Markham intended to find out.

The gangplank was drawn in. Clay felt a growing vibration in the deck under his feet as the boat built up steam. He could almost hear the flames crackling and roaring in the firebox under the massive boiler. The band played more strenuously, and cheering spectators on the dock waved hats and hands and kerchiefs in farewell. Slowly, the giant paddlewheels on the sides of the boat began to turn, and with a faint lurch the *New Orleans* was on its way. The motion was almost imperceptible at first, but then the dock began to slide by. Clay and Markham stepped to the railing with the other passengers, drawn by the drama of the moment. History was being made here today.

It was just the beginning, Clay thought as he watched the Pittsburgh waterfront recede. Their story was waiting to unfold downriver. And how it ended was likely to be much more significant than how it began.

CHAPTER
FIVE

Audrey Stoddard's demeanor toward Proud Wolf was distinctly cool for several days after their encounter in the moonlight. She was angry with him, and he knew it. But he also knew that he had done the right thing by refusing to give in to temptation. Audrey did not love him; she was merely attracted to him because he was . . . different. And sooner or later any romantic involvement would bring trouble down on their heads. Jeremiah Stoddard might force Proud Wolf to leave the academy if he discovered that his daughter was pursuing him—and all Professor Hilliard's efforts would be for nothing. Proud Wolf could not allow that to happen.

In the meantime, the fall term at the academy was well under way, and Proud Wolf was too busy most of the time to worry about Audrey's feelings. He was thoroughly engrossed in his studies. Philosophy and natural history were not altogether different from the matters the old men discussed around the council fires of his people. His readings in literature reminded him of the tales passed down through the generations among the Sioux. Even learning Latin, though difficult, was similar to learning English and French, and he had already mastered both those tongues in addition to his native language.

Only mathematics, with its endless tide of numbers and symbols, presented a serious challenge. The concepts of counting, of many and few, of near and far, had always been sufficient to meet the needs of Proud Wolf's people. He strained to understand each day's classroom lesson, and in the evening he spent long hours working by candlelight, scratching numbers on a slate with a piece of charcoal, then wiping them out to start over again when the answers eluded him.

The time would come, he told himself, when he would return to his people and take the place of his father, old Bear Tooth, as the leader of the Teton Sioux. Of what use then would these numbers be? He was tempted to throw the slate aside and give up.

But he did not. Professor Hilliard was counting on him. He would not let him down.

On a lovely autumn afternoon when he would much rather have been outside, Proud Wolf sat in a stuffy classroom and listened to Master Bell, the mathematics instructor. Bell was a short old man with a face that reminded Proud Wolf of a fox. His voice was like the drone of insects, and Proud Wolf thought it would drive him mad.

"—the Pythagorean theorem," Bell was saying. "Mr., ah, Wolf, would you please explain the mathematical logic behind this?"

Proud Wolf suppressed his irritation. He had explained to Bell that he did not have a first name and a last name like the whites, but the instructor insisted on calling him Mr. Wolf anyway. He forced himself to concentrate on the question Bell had asked him, but his mind could not penetrate the tangle of numbers.

Impatiently, Bell repeated the question, and Proud Wolf got slowly to his feet to say, "I do not know."

"Of course he doesn't," a voice said from the rear of the room. "He's just a stupid redskin."

The insult was spoken in a loud whisper, but Proud Wolf recognized it anyway. It belonged to Frank Kirkland. He glanced over his shoulder and saw Frank and Will Brackett smirking at each other. Will had probably nudged Frank to speak up, might even have told him what to say. Frank was nothing but a puppet, like one of the crude figures Proud Wolf had seen in a bizarre performance in Boston during a visit there a week earlier with Professor Hilliard. Punch and Judy—those were the puppet figures' names, Proud Wolf remembered.

"Sit down, Mr. Wolf," Bell said with a sigh. "You really should make more of an effort to understand this material."

More hissed words from the back of the room. "All he understands is how to be a savage in the wild."

Bell either did not hear the insults or chose to ignore them. He glowered at Proud Wolf. "Perhaps you should obtain some private tutoring in mathematics. I shall speak to Master Stoddard."

Proud Wolf bit back a groan. He did not want anything else to bring him to Stoddard's attention. The more the headmaster ignored him, the better.

Bell moved on to another student, and then the class was finally over. Proud Wolf left the instruction hall and walked across the broad lawn toward the residence hall. As he did, the sixth sense that had saved his life more than once warned him that someone was coming up behind him. He resisted the impulse to turn and look.

He had a feeling he knew who it was, anyway.

"Explain the Pythagorean theorem to me again, why don't you, Frank," said Will Brackett.

"Why don't you ask our Indian friend up there?" Frank Kirkland replied. "He seems to know it so well."

Ignore them, Proud Wolf told himself. *Their words are nothing more than the chattering of crows.*

"Master Bell said our friend needs a tutor," Will

went on. "Where do you think we could find one for him?"

"A nursery, perhaps," Frank said with a laugh. "He's as ignorant as a baby."

"Or a woman. I'd like to see Audrey Stoddard try to explain that theorem. But of course she couldn't. She's good for only one thing."

"But she's very good at that one thing, isn't she, Will?"

"Very good," said Will Brackett. "Very good indeed."

Proud Wolf could stand no more. No matter how Audrey felt about him now, he would not allow anyone to insult her. He stopped in his tracks and whirled around.

"Close your filthy mouth," he snapped at Will.

The young man lifted one eyebrow. "We seem to have annoyed our red-skinned friend, Frank," he said. "It seems that the subject of Miss Stoddard is a sore point with him."

"I thought you liked Audrey," Proud Wolf said angrily.

"Her father is the headmaster of this academy," replied Will, his voice low. "It's to my advantage to cultivate her affections." His voice took on a fiercer tone. "But don't think for a second I could ever be seriously involved with a slut who chases after savages."

Proud Wolf stiffened with outrage, not only at the insult but also because he realized Will must have seen Audrey kissing him after his fight with Frank. Or someone else had seen them and reported what he had witnessed to Will. It did not really matter which.

"If we were in my homeland," Proud Wolf said tautly, "I would kill you for that, Brackett."

Will gave him a lazy smile. "Well, then, it's a good thing we're in a civilized place, where red-skinned savages can't do anything they please."

"I will meet you," Proud Wolf offered, knowing he was being rash but unable to stop himself. "I will meet you anywhere you say, and we will settle this. Just you and me this time"—he cast a scornful glance at Frank—"and none of your lackeys."

"All right," Will said without hesitation. "Boston Common, tonight at midnight. That old bastard Stoddard won't have a chance to interfere this time."

"I shall be there," Proud Wolf snapped. He turned and stalked away.

He had probably given Will exactly what he wanted, he realized. Will's goading had pierced his defenses, and tonight he would be walking into danger. But he no longer cared. Whether Audrey was angry with him or not, he had to defend her honor—and his.

For the first two days after the *Beaumont* sailed from Wilmington, Jeff was even sicker than he had expected. During the worst of it he passed beyond fearing that he would die to fearing he would not.

But on the third morning he felt an unfamiliar sensation in his stomach and realized to his amazement that it was hunger. The deck still moved under his feet when he came above, but the motion was no longer as discomfiting. Except for a mild, occasional lurch, his belly was calm.

He heaved a huge sigh of relief.

Melissa had followed him on deck. "What is it?" she asked.

"I think I'm over the worst of the seasickness," Jeff told her. "I believe I can actually eat this morning." He smiled. "You've certainly taken to sailing. This is your first sea voyage, and you look as fresh as can be."

Melissa returned the smile. "I've carried a child and given birth. Sailing on a boat is nothing compared to that."

Michael shot up out of the hatch behind them. Sailing came even more naturally to him than to his mother. During the past two days Jeff had watched his son dashing around the ship and envied him the resilience of youth.

Melissa caught hold of Michael's sleeve. "Don't

run near the railing," she admonished him. "I don't want you falling overboard."

"We wouldn't have time to turn around and come back for you if you did that," Jeff teased.

"Yes, you would," Michael said. "You can't go to Alaska without me!"

Jeff couldn't argue with that. As Michael scampered off to play, he and Melissa went to the ship's mess for breakfast.

The *Beaumont* and the *Lydia Marie* continued sailing southward, always remaining within sight of each other, and now that Jeff's seasickness had abated, he found himself almost enjoying the voyage. The ships put into port at the Spanish colony in Panama, trading some of their cargo of grain for rubber and fresh fruit for the crew. Then the two vessels looped back out into the Atlantic to circle the great outward curve of the South American continent before turning south again.

"We're bound to run into a storm or two in these southern seas," Captain Vickery told Jeff one day as they stood on the bridge. "It's the tail end of winter down here, like spring in the northern climes. Some powerful squalls can blow up."

"Nothing these ships can't handle, though, I'd wager," Jeff said hopefully.

Vickery waved a hand. "I've sailed through some rip-roarers, Mr. Holt, and so has Captain Canfield on the *Lydia Marie*. We'll be fine."

Jeff believed Vickery, but after that conversation he kept a nervous eye on the sky, watching for dark clouds that could be portents of trouble.

Days turned into weeks, and the two ships docked at Rio de Janeiro, the capital of the Portuguese empire. More grain was traded there for fruit, and the ships' crews were given a short liberty. They would not put in at any more ports of call until after the vessels had rounded Cape Horn and started up the western coast of South America.

Jeff, Melissa, Michael, Ned, and India ventured on shore to visit the huge open-air market that dominated

Rio. To the north lay Guanabara Bay, where the *Beaumont* and the *Lydia Marie* rode at anchor, overlooked by the imposing peak of Sugar Loaf Mountain. Captain Vickery had pointed out the towering landmark to Jeff and his family as the ships sailed into the bay.

Michael's eyes were wide as he took in all the sights and sounds of the busy market. All sorts of exotic merchandise was on display, from large-beaked birds to jaguar hides to finely worked gold and silver jewelry. A din of shouting voices filled the air as merchants haggled with their customers. The air was full of other things as well: the buzz of insects and the odors of cooking, overripe fruit, fish, unwashed flesh, human waste, and pigs running wild in the streets. Jeff wrinkled his nose.

The people thronging the market were equally varied and colorful. Brazil was now the hub of the Portuguese empire, so there were many Europeans in evidence, but there were also Indians from the interior of the country, clad in feathered headdresses and loincloths made of bark. Slaves were also quite common, burly black figures in ragged pants and shirts—and sometimes shackles. Jeff caught sight of a large slave market in the center of an open square and steered the others away from it. Slavery was an integral part of the economy, he knew, not only in the southern United States and here in South America but worldwide as well. But he had never been able to understand or condone it.

A man walked by carrying a large bird with brilliant green and red plumage. Michael stared at the bird in fascination. It squawked, then spoke in a language Jeff assumed was Portuguese. Michael's mouth dropped open. Then he pointed and exclaimed, "That pretty bird talked!"

"It's a parrot," India told him. "I've seen quite a few of them. Heard them, too. Many of them can speak. I don't think they know what they're saying, though. They're just repeating things they've been taught to say."

"Yes, but it *talked!"*

Jeff ruffled his son's fair hair and grinned down at him. He had wanted to expose Michael to new and wonderful sights on this trip; a talking parrot certainly fit the bill.

The five Americans wandered through the huge market for an hour, looking to India for guidance as she was the most experienced traveler among them. She had been to Rio before and knew which foods were safe to eat and which were not. Eventually Michael began to tire, and Jeff picked him up.

"I suppose we'd better head back to the ship," he said.

"I think India and I will explore a little more," said Ned. "If that's all right with you."

Jeff nodded. "Of course. We can get back to the *Beaumont* without any trouble." He nodded toward the docks. "I can see the masts from here." Carrying Michael, Jeff headed toward the ship with Melissa.

India gave her brawny companion a sidelong glance. "Exactly what did you have in mind, Ned Holt?"

He grinned. "I thought we'd get something to eat, then find a place where we could have a little privacy."

India had to smile in return. "That sounds wonderful. Lead the way."

When Jeff, Melissa, and Michael reached the wharves lining Guanabara Bay, Melissa glanced up at her husband. Michael had dozed off with his head against Jeff's shoulder, and Melissa felt a pang of mingled love, guilt, and regret. How could she have come so close to betraying this wonderful man? she asked herself. Certainly, Jeff was not without his faults: He was a Holt, which meant he was strong-willed, impulsive to the point of recklessness sometimes, and inclined to wander off at odd moments to see what was over the next hill. But he was also a loving husband and father, and anything that Melissa had felt in the arms of Philip Rattigan was only a pale shadow of what she had with Jeff.

She thanked God again that Rattigan was now thousands of miles away.

A tall, broad-shouldered man with a cleft chin and a thick shock of blond hair stepped out of the harbormaster's office and strode toward the docks of Rio de Janeiro. His trading here was done, and he was ready to set sail for England. This trip to South America had been a good idea. He had a cargo hold full of bananas and cacao beans that would fetch a good price at home. More importantly, he had gotten away from a place where he no longer wanted to be, a place full of painful reminders of something he longed for but could not have.

As he started up the gangplank of his ship, he caught sight of a woman walking with a man toward another vessel. The man was carrying a child. There was something familiar about the woman, even though her back was turned. . . .

Philip Rattigan shook his head and trotted up the gangplank to the deck, where his captain waited for orders. "Prepare for sailing," Rattigan told the man. "We're going home."

He must have been mistaken, Rattigan told himself. There was no earthly reason Melissa Holt would be in Rio de Janeiro.

Grog shops were much the same the world over, India mused. She had been in plenty of them, and they were usually squalid little places, scarcely big enough for a few tables and a bar. Sometimes there were even tinier rooms upstairs or in the back where the serving girls plied their other trade, but India had no interest in them. There had been a few awkward moments on past voyages when some of her shipmates, believing her to be an innocent young man, had tried to buy her a doxy. India smiled now as she thought about the surprise

that would have awaited those trollops had she gone
with any of them.

This waterfront tavern in Rio de Janeiro was no
different from scores of others in which India had sat,
nursing a bucket of beer or a jot of rum. The floor was
hard-packed dirt, the walls were made of mud and
straw that had not cured quite evenly, and the roof was
patched with palm fronds. Not surprisingly, the room
was cramped. She and Ned almost brushed elbows
with the occupants of the neighboring tables. Luckily it
was noisy enough that when they leaned their heads
together, they could speak in low voices and not be
overheard. The commotion was coming from a rear
room in which a cockfight was being held. The screech-
ing of savage birds and the shouts of the men betting
on one or the other filled the tavern.

"As soon as we finish these drinks, I say we get out
of here," Ned was saying. "I saw an inn just down the
road. We can get a room there."

India nodded. It had been over a month since she
and Ned had had a chance to be alone together, and
she felt the familiar warmth building inside her. She
smiled at him, and the boldness of her gaze made Ned
hurriedly gulp down the rest of his beer. India lifted
her glass and swallowed the last of her rum. "Come
on," she said as she got to her feet.

Ned followed eagerly as they made their way out
of the tavern, leaving the shouted wagers and the
squawking of mortally wounded roosters behind them.
The sun had slid down the sky until only a faint band
of red remained above the mountains to the west. India
walked quickly toward the inn Ned had mentioned.
Like nearly every other building in Rio de Janeiro, it
was set on a hillside, and it seemed to India that it was
leaning slightly. She hoped that fate would not pick the
next hour or so to collapse the building.

They climbed a set of narrow stairs and found a
man at the top sitting behind a rickety table. Ned
dropped a coin on the table and waited to see if it was
enough. The man nodded and pointed down a shad-

owy hallway lit only by a candle at the far end. If the man was surprised that two males were renting a room, he gave no sign of it. Several doors along the corridor stood open, and Ned and India went through the first one they came to. Ned found a candle and took it out into the hall to light it.

When he returned and closed the door, India was waiting for him in the bunk that was the only furniture in the room. Ned placed the burning candle on the small shelf where he had found it and turned toward the bunk. With a sultry look, India pushed back the blanket that had been covering her.

Ned grinned and went to her.

Outside, at the head of the stairs, the man who ran the inn looked up to see another stranger standing before him. This man was a sailor, too, judging by his clothes, and an American, judging by his face.

The stranger dropped a coin on the table, and the proprietor started to point toward an empty room. With a shake of his head, the stranger said in passable Portuguese, "Did two people just come in here? Two sailors?"

The proprietor nodded. "Yes."

"What room are they in?"

The proprietor hesitated. He did not like to get involved in his customers' business. Once he had their money, his dealings with them were done.

But the large knife the stranger drew from his belt quickly loosened the proprietor's tongue. He pointed shakily toward the door through which the two sailors had disappeared.

The stranger smiled and kept the knife out, but with his other hand he reached into his pocket and brought out another coin. "That's for being quiet," he said.

"I will be so quiet you will not know I am here, *senhor*. In fact, I shall not be here." The proprietor stood up and without a backward glance went down the stairs and out onto the street.

He could always clean up any mess when he returned.

The man called Donnelly walked with surprising stealth toward the room containing his quarry. In an old building such as this one it was difficult to move around without the floorboards squeaking, but Donnelly managed. Even if he did make a little noise, he doubted that those two would hear it. By now they would be too wrapped up in what they were doing to each other. Donnelly's breathing grew a little faster and harder as he thought about that. Maybe he would slit Holt's throat first, then have some fun with the little son of a bitch before he killed him.

Donnelly paused at the doorway and drew a deep breath, ready to drive his shoulder into the panel and burst it inward.

That was when he heard the soft cry from within. A voice filled with passion exclaimed, "Oh, my God! Yes, Ned! Don't stop . . . !"

Donnelly's eyes widened, but not with surprise at the heated words he had overheard. He had expected something like that.

But the voice that had spoken them was unmistakably that of a woman.

CHAPTER
SIX

From Pittsburgh, the Ohio River ran northward for some distance before turning sharply south. Wheeling was the next settlement of any size along its course, and as the *New Orleans* neared the wharf extending into the river, Clay Holt saw from his position at the forward railing that the streets along the riverfront were crowded with people who had come to welcome the steamboat. Most people had little faith that Captain Roosevelt would be successful in his attempt to take the vessel all the way to New Orleans and back, Clay knew, but in case Roosevelt did succeed, these citizens wanted to be able to say they had seen the boat steam into port on its historic voyage.

Lieutenant Markham was leaning on the rail next to Clay. He said in a low voice, "Our friends are certainly ready for the attention. It's been over twenty-four hours since any of them has had a chance to make a speech."

Clay glanced at the three senators, who stood with

Captain Roosevelt about thirty feet away. None of the politicians appeared to be paying any attention to Clay and Markham, but Clay was willing to bet one of them was all too aware of their presence. Since the *New Orleans* had left Pittsburgh, Clay had made sure that he and Markham were highly visible whenever the senators were on deck. Whoever the traitor was, Clay wanted to give him plenty of reminders that someone was on his trail.

"The captain told me we'll be stopping for the night in Wheeling," Clay said. "The town plans to put on some sort of rally for him."

"And we'll be there."

Clay shrugged. "One of us will be, at least."

"What do you mean by that?"

"You're going to attend the rally. I'm going to stay here and have a look through the senators' cabins."

Markham looked for a moment as if he were about to object, but he said instead, "That's probably a good idea. But you don't really think any of them has brought the evidence we need with them, do you?"

"Don't know," Clay said with a shake of his head. "Anybody who's so full of himself that he thinks he can steal away half a continent is liable to do just about anything. But even if I don't find anything, when the fellow we're after looks out at that crowd tonight and sees you but not me, he's likely to start worrying about where I am and what I'm up to. That's the main thing I'm trying to do."

"We're waging a war of nerves, I suppose you could say."

Clay nodded slowly. "It's a war I intend to win, too."

To the cheers of the waiting crowd, the pilot of the *New Orleans* maneuvered the steamboat next to the wharf. Crewmen jumped from the deck to the wharf and tied the vessel fast to the pilings. Captain Roosevelt had ascended to the wheelhouse, where he let loose a long, shrill blast from the whistle. The crowd shouted back in response.

Clay and Markham let the other passengers disembark first. The mayor of Wheeling was waiting at the foot of the gangplank to greet Roosevelt, his wife, and the politicians. The sooty-fingered journalists who were traveling on the *New Orleans* were busy scrawling notes, as usual. No one paid any attention to Clay and Markham as they came down the gangplank and stepped onto the dock.

"Ah, solid ground under my feet again," said Markham. "It feels good."

"I never rode in anything bigger than a canoe before this," Clay said, "but that boat didn't bother me much. I've heard Jeff talk about how sick it made him to sail on the ocean. I reckon a river's not quite the same thing."

"It was unsteady enough," Markham said. "Give me good solid ground anytime. It never jumps around under your feet."

Clay inclined his head toward a nearby tavern. "Let's get a drink."

When they were seated in a booth inside the tavern, Markham lifted a bucket of beer to his mouth and took a long, grateful swallow. He lowered the bucket, licked foam from his upper lip, and looked across the table at Clay. "Perhaps it's the spirits making me bold, but I think we need to discuss the way we're approaching this mission."

"You don't figure we're going about it the right way?"

"I wish there were some way to draw the traitor out more quickly."

"We'll force his hand soon enough," Clay assured him. "I've spent many a cold hour sitting on the hard ground waiting for a bear, or an elk, or a mountain lion. I reckon the fellow we're after is just as dangerous. We have to wait him out, that's all." He took a sip of beer. "But that's not to say we can't prod him a mite. That's what we'll be doing tonight when you go to that meeting and I don't."

Markham nodded, although he still looked skeptical.

They returned to the boat a short time later and found the passengers and crew in festive spirits. The journey had gone smoothly so far, and Nicholas Roosevelt was full of boundless optimism. The attitude was apparently contagious. Even the normally dour Senator Haines was smiling broadly when Clay and Markham joined the crowd in the salon. He lifted a glass of champagne and called out, "A toast to the most magnificent vessel ever to sail these waters!"

The other two senators echoed the toast, as did the rest of the crowd. Clay and Markham made their way to the bar, where a red-jacketed bartender pressed a glass of champagne on each of them. Clay had a feeling the liquor would be flowing freely through the night and into the morning, when the *New Orleans* was scheduled to cast off.

Charles Emory stepped up to the bar and nodded to Clay and Markham. "Gentlemen," he said pleasantly. "It seems that you're always in the middle of the excitement, doesn't it?"

Coolly, Clay replied, "I don't reckon I know what you mean."

"Well, you came with us on Gideon Maxwell's little expedition to the Virginia woods, and that was certainly an unusual outing." Emory shook his head. "Poor Maxwell."

Was the senator trying to feel them out and discover if they knew any more than they let on about Maxwell's death? Perhaps he was hoping, as well, that they would let slip something about the mission that had brought them on the riverboat.

If he was, Clay intended to disappoint him. "I reckon some folks are just in the right place at the right time," he said. "Or the wrong place at the wrong time."

Emory nodded. "That's certainly true, if not entirely germane to our conversation." He took a sip of champagne. "Are you coming to the rally this evening?"

"Of course," Markham said. "Wouldn't miss it."

"What about you, Mr. Holt?" asked Emory.

Clay rubbed his chin. "I don't rightly know. I may have something else I have to do."

"I'm sure it will be an exciting evening. The mayor of Wheeling has promised us a large crowd." The senator laughed. "Wouldn't want to waste a perfectly good speech on a small crowd, now, would we?"

"I wouldn't know," Clay said. "I've never been much of one for speechifying."

Louis Haines walked up in time to hear Clay's comment. He smirked and said, "Ah, yes, ever the laconic woodsman, aren't you, Holt?"

"I speak up . . . when I've got something to say worth listening to."

Emory laughed again. "I think our young friend here is having sport with us, Louis."

A few moments later, Morgan Ralston and Nicholas Roosevelt joined them at the bar, and the conversation turned to more general topics. When they had finished their champagne, Clay and Markham made their excuses and slipped out of the salon. As they walked back toward their small cabin next to the starboard paddlewheel, Markham said quietly, "None of them seem the least bit concerned at our presence, Clay."

"Our man's playing it pretty close to the vest, I'll give you that," Clay agreed. "But I'll bet he's starting to sweat a little."

"Then sooner or later he'll crack—and that's when we pounce on him."

"If he doesn't get lucky and pounce on us first."

That evening, from the deck of the steamboat, Clay could hear the brass band playing in Wheeling's town square. When the music stopped, a cheer went up, followed by more sporadic cheering. Someone must have started his speech, he thought. The mayor, Captain

Roosevelt, and all three senators were scheduled to address the crowd. Clay figured he had at least a couple of hours to carry out his search.

He hoped Markham wouldn't get too bored listening to all the inflated oratory.

Clay had blown out the candle in the cabin before slipping out the door so that anyone observing would not see him silhouetted against the light. He was fairly certain all the passengers had gone into town to participate in the festivities. Several crewmen were still on board, standing a skeleton watch, but by now they were likely half-drunk or in the arms of some soiled dove—or both.

As he catfooted along the deck, Clay's hand went to the butt of the pistol tucked behind his belt. He didn't expect to run into trouble tonight, but only a fool would not be prepared for it. The senators were staying in three adjoining compartments, forward on the port side. Clay kept to the shadows as he made his way toward them.

He came first to Ralston's cabin. The door was not locked. If it had been, Clay would have forced it easily enough with the blade of his hunting knife. He didn't care if he left behind any signs that he had been there. He opened the door just enough to glide into the room, then closed it softly behind him.

With tinder and flint, he quickly lit one of the small, oil-soaked wicks he had brought with him, then went through Ralston's baggage. There were only a couple of carpetbags; like the other senators, Ralston had left his wife and children behind in Washington City. All three senators claimed to have full confidence in Captain Roosevelt and his boat, but not to the extent that they wanted to risk their families' safety. Clay could not fault them for that.

It took him less than a quarter of an hour to thoroughly search Ralston's cabin. Finding nothing to incriminate the senator, he moved on to Louis Haines's cabin. The most damning thing he found there was a bottle of whiskey. Considering that half of Congress regularly showed up drunk at legislative sessions, that was hardly grounds on which to condemn a man, even such an unpleasant one as Haines. Feeling certain now that he would not find anything important in Emory's cabin, Clay nevertheless let himself in.

His hunch was correct. Searching Emory's cabin was as fruitless as his first two efforts. When he was satisfied he wasn't going to find anything, Clay pinched out the wick and stepped out onto the deck.

He told himself not to be discouraged. He hadn't really expected to find anything, but he *had* accomplished one goal. In each cabin, he had left things slightly disarrayed so that the senators would know that someone had been in their cabins. The two innocent senators would probably be outraged and think that a member of the crew had rummaged through their belongings looking for something to steal.

But the man Clay was after was different. He would know that Clay had not been at the rally, and his first thought would be to blame him for the intrusion. He was bound to be even more nervous afterward.

Clay turned toward the bow of the boat, intending to circle the long central row of cabins and go back to his own quarters on the starboard side. The port side was turned toward the wharf, and that was where a faint noise suddenly caught his attention. Clay recognized it as the scuff of a boot on the planks of the dock—

Then the roar of exploding black powder drowned out all other sounds, and a tongue of bright orange flame split the night as it spat from the barrel of a gun.

Being a lieutenant in the army, John Markham was accustomed to listening to boring, long-winded speeches from his commanding officers. But politicians were even worse, and tonight's activities had been especially tiresome.

But the crowd was caught up in the fervor of the evening, and they cheered everything the speakers had to say, especially when the senators declaimed loudly on the destiny of the nation and the spread of civilization and progress. Markham was as patriotic as the next man and might have found himself swayed by the flowery rhetoric had he not known that one of the men standing on the bunting-draped platform was a murderer and a traitor.

He stood at the forefront of the crowd so that Emory, Ralston, and Haines could see him clearly in the torchlight that illuminated the town square. His obvious presence would serve to remind them that Clay Holt was *not* here. As he peered up at the platform and studied the men's faces, Markham wished he could tell from their expressions what they were thinking. As politicians they were all too expert at keeping their emotions hidden. It wouldn't do to play poker with any of those three, Markham thought.

During a lull in the speeches, a voice spoke from beside him. "Isn't it all so thrilling?"

Markham turned his head. A young woman, blond and quite pretty, looked back at him, her face lit by the torchlight and by her own excitement.

"The speeches, you mean?" Markham asked.

"Yes, and having such important men here in Wheeling, too. And that Captain Roosevelt is so handsome and dashing!"

Markham smiled indulgently. "I hate to disappoint you, miss, but the captain is married. That's his wife up there with him on the platform."

"Oh," the young woman said, regret in her voice. Then she brightened. "Are you sure? That woman could be the wife of one of the senators."

"I'm afraid not. You see, I'm traveling on the *New Orleans*. I've met the captain and his wife, as well as the senators."

The young woman looked at him with wide eyes. "You're traveling all the way down the Mississippi River?"

Markham nodded. "Yes, I plan to."

"Oh, that . . . that's wonderful! It must be such a

grand adventure!'' She reached out impulsively and rested a gloved hand on his forearm. "You must tell me all about it. I've been stuck here in this little town all my life, and I so want to travel!"

"There's not much to tell," Markham said modestly. He was flattered by the attention this attractive young woman was paying him. "We left Pittsburgh only the day before yesterday."

The woman's hand moved up his arm, gripping it warmly. "I'd still like to hear all about it. I hope you don't think I'm being too . . . too forward, but I'm so excited to meet someone who's going all the way to New Orleans!" She gave him a brilliant smile. "Why don't we go somewhere quieter, and you can tell me everything about the trip."

Did she take him for a total innocent? Markham studied her intently for a moment, trying to determine if she was a woman of the streets, as her conversation suggested. She was a bit too well dressed, however, and she lacked the hardness around the eyes so common to the gaze of prostitutes. It could well be, he decided, that she was exactly what she appeared to be: an eager, somewhat naive young woman from a small town.

"Where did you have in mind that we go?" he asked. Her answer would give him an idea of what she was really after. If she suggested an inn or a tavern, then she likely was a soiled dove.

"There are some benches on the grounds of the Baptist Church," she said eagerly. "We often have picnics there after the services. We could sit down and talk."

Markham glanced at the platform, where Senator Haines was preparing to speak. As Haines cleared his throat and shuffled some notes in his hand, Markham leaned closer to the young woman and said, "All right. Let's go."

Clay couldn't fault him for leaving; he had put in an appearance, as he was supposed to. Besides, he would still be nearby. He could see the steeple of the

Baptist Church only a block or two away from the square.

The young woman linked her arm with his and led the way. "My name is Tamara, by the way, Tamara Dugan."

"I'm John Markham."

They skirted the edge of the crowd and then started down the street toward the church. The multitude of blazing torches in the square lighted their way. Markham saw several wrought-iron benches under the trees beside the church. It was a lovely spot, he thought.

And Tamara Dugan was lovely, too, no doubt about it. Ever since his ill-fated romance with Diana Maxwell, Markham had shied clear of women. The painful twinges he suffered from the healed-up bullet hole in his side whenever the weather got damp reminded him of what had happened the last time he gave his heart away.

But he wasn't thinking of giving his heart away now. Stealing a quick kiss, perhaps—that was as far as he would go. Besides, in the morning the *New Orleans* would resume its journey downriver, and Markham would never see the young woman again.

"Here we are," Tamara said as she led him up to a bench. A pair of trees grew closely behind it, throwing it into shadow. It was the perfect place to steal a kiss, Markham thought. Should he try? When?

He brushed some leaves off the bench and gestured for Tamara to precede him. "After you, my dear," he said.

"My, aren't you the charming one?" Arranging her skirts, she settled on the bench, then patted the seat beside her. If he did kiss her, she wouldn't be averse to it, Markham decided. He sat down.

The sudden crackle of leaves behind him was all the warning he got before a loop of rope dropped down around his neck and jerked tight.

• • •

Clay was moving even as the shot roared out. His instincts, finely honed by years of living in the wilderness, took over and sent him diving forward onto the deck. He heard an ugly thud as the pistol ball struck the wall above him. His fingers closed around the butt of his own pistol and yanked it free as he rolled to the side.

The gunman would have moved as soon as he had triggered his shot. Clay had to guess in which direction. He jerked his pistol up and fired to the right of the spot where he had seen flame geyser from the muzzle of the gun.

Another shot crashed back at him. The ball chewed splinters from the low gunwale of the deck a couple of feet from Clay's head. The ambusher had had another pistol primed and ready in case his first shot missed. Clay hoped fervently that the man didn't have yet another gun.

Dropping his empty pistol on the deck, Clay surged to his feet and leaped over the gunwale toward the wharf. As he landed lightly, he saw from the corner of his eye a flicker of movement coming toward him.

Clay allowed the momentum of his leap to carry him forward and down. He threw his right leg out behind him, and the man rushing him had no chance to avoid it. The man tripped and fell, crashing hard onto the planks of the dock.

Clay rolled over, pulled his knife from its sheath at his waist, and came up on his knees. His attacker was trying to get up, too, but the stunning impact of the fall had clearly shaken him. He was clumsy as he attempted to push himself to his feet.

In the darkness Clay could not discern anything about the man except that he was fairly large, large enough that Clay could not afford to give him any advantage. Clay came upright and launched a kick, but the man saw it coming and twisted aside so that Clay's boot landed on his right shoulder instead of his head. Nevertheless, the kick was strong enough to send the man sprawling on his back.

Clay leaped toward him, intending to get his knife against the man's throat and gain the upper hand. The man retaliated with a kick of his own, however, catching Clay in the stomach. Clay staggered back, gasping for air and cursing his overconfidence. His opponent scrambled upright. Clay saw starlight wink from polished steel as the man pulled his own knife.

"I'm gonna gut you, mister," the man growled. "Nobody kicks me like a dog."

He lunged forward, lashing out with the blade.

Clay darted back, avoiding the slashing arc. He had been in a few knife fights in his time and witnessed dozens more. He held his blade low, cutting edge up, ready to strike as he and the man warily circled each other. Although the dock was fairly wide, they had little room to maneuver. Clay knew he could not make any mistakes or he would wind up with six inches of cold steel in his belly.

The three pistol shots had drawn the attention of the skeleton crew on the *New Orleans,* and Clay could hear their footsteps as they ran toward the port side of the boat to see what was happening. Someone from Wheeling was probably on the way to investigate as well. With a growled curse Clay's opponent charged again, thrusting recklessly with his knife.

Sparks flew as Clay parried the blow with his own blade. With the fight in close quarters now, Clay jabbed his left fist into the man's face and rocked his head back. He slashed at Clay again, but this time Clay caught the wrist of his knife hand with his left. At the same instant, the man grabbed Clay's right wrist with his left hand. They stood like that for a moment, locked together, straining against each other, the only sound the harsh rasp of their breathing.

"Hey! What's going on there?"

The shout came from the deck of the *New Orleans.* Clay's assailant snapped up his head at the sound, and Clay took advantage of the moment to aim a kick at his knee. The man grunted in pain and sagged to one side as the leg collapsed under him. Clay heaved on his opponent's knife hand, and the man crashed awkwardly to the dock, pulling Clay with him.

Abruptly the man howled and stiffened, then went limp. Clay grated a curse as he pushed himself up. The man's knife hand had turned when he fell, and his own knife had been driven into his chest by Clay's weight on top of him. As Clay stood up, the man's arms fell loosely to his sides.

Lantern light spilled from the deck of the *New Orleans*. "What in blazes is going on?" exclaimed a deckhand. "Is that you, Mr. Holt?"

"It is," Clay acknowledged grimly. In frustration he shoved his own knife back in its sheath, still unbloodied.

"That fellow looks dead."

Clay glared down at the sprawled form with the handle of a knife sticking up from the chest. "That's because he is."

Now, Clay reflected bitterly, he would never have a chance to find out who had sent the man on this mission of murder.

Pure luck saved John Markham's life. As he heard the sound behind him, he started to turn his head and at the same time lifted his right hand. The loop of rope caught his hand as it was drawn tight, so that his fingers were wedged between the rough hemp and the soft flesh of his throat.

Back arched, he strained against the rope biting cruelly into his neck. Having his fingers inside the loop allowed him just enough air to keep from blacking out. Whoever was trying to choke him to death hauled hard on the rope, pulling him up off the bench. Instead of fighting against it, Markham went with the pull.

He had lost track of Tamara, but he was vaguely aware that she was not screaming for help as she would have been had she been telling him the truth. She was part of this murder scheme, he realized. She wasn't a soiled dove after his money.

She wanted his life.

Half falling over the back of the bench, Markham blindly shot out his left fist, hoping to find his assailant. The blow connected and rocked the man back. Markham toppled all the way over the bench, landing on a bed of dry, crackling leaves. The rope was still pulling on his neck, almost strangling him, and he was beginning to feel light-headed. He reached out frantically with his left hand, scrabbling along the ground until he found someone's booted foot. Markham grabbed it and heaved as hard as he could.

A man's voice cursed, low and profane. A second later there was a crash among the leaves as someone fell next to Markham. With a flash of satisfaction he knew that he had upended his attacker. He pulled hard on the rope, felt it come away from his neck. Rising to his knees, he gasped for air, filling his starved lungs.

He had barely had time to catch his breath when something smashed into the back of his head, driving him forward onto his face.

"Damn you!" hissed Tamara. "You're not going to cheat me out of my money!"

Markham groaned. At least it was nothing personal, he thought wryly. She had been paid to lure him here. He rolled over, saw her looming over him with a club of some kind held high over her head. He rolled again, desperately, as she brought the weapon down in a blow aimed at his face.

It was a broken tree branch, he saw from the corner of his eye as he narrowly avoided getting his brains dashed out. Fear and outrage made his blood race and his pulse pound in his head, and he found the speed and strength to come up on his feet and lash out at the woman. His fist cracked into her jaw, and although he felt a flash of guilt at striking a woman, it was quickly replaced by a feeling of gratification as she went sailing backward over the bench.

He had forgotten about the man. In the next instant he was forcibly reminded as arms encircled him from behind and trapped him in a crushing bear hug. Markham tried to bring his elbow back into his attacker's midsection, but he could not get the leverage he needed, so he kicked backward instead at the man's shin.

Markham threw his weight forward, against the bench. Both men toppled over it and landed on Tamara, who was lying motionless, apparently out cold. In the welter of arms and legs, Markham's opponent loosened his grip, and Markham managed to twist free. As he did, he heard shouts from the direction of the town square. Someone there must finally have noticed the fight at the church.

A crushing weight came down on Markham's belly, and a fist hammered his face. The man had managed to get on top of him. Markham arched his back, trying to throw him off, but another punch exploded against his jaw. He fell back, stunned. Through the ringing in his ears he heard the woman's voice.

"Hugh . . . Hugh?" Tamara had obviously regained consciousness when the two men landed on top of her. "Hugh! They're coming! Forget about him!"

"There's still time to take care of the son of a bitch," the man said. "Where's my knife—"

A shot rang out.

The weight was suddenly lifted from Markham's chest, and as he rolled onto his side, he heard running footsteps from two directions. People were coming from the square, and his attackers were fleeing. At the moment Markham didn't particularly care that they were getting away. All he wanted was to catch his breath and somehow ease the drumbeat of pain behind his eyes.

Strong hands took hold of his shoulders and helped him sit up, and a familiar voice said quietly, "Somebody tried for you, too, didn't they?"

Markham looked up. "Clay . . . ?"

"Make it sound as if they tried to rob you," Clay hissed in his ear.

Clay helped him to his feet. Markham brushed away the leaves and dirt clinging to his clothes as several townspeople, along with some crewmen from the steamboat, surrounded him. "What happened?" one of the townsmen asked.

"I . . . I was attacked as I walked by the church here," Markham said. "A couple of men . . . they tried to rob me."

"Good thing I happened to look over here and see it," said Clay. "I fired a shot into the air, and that scared them into running off."

"You're a lucky man, Mr. Markham," one of the men from the *New Orleans* told him. "Some of these riverfront toughs don't think anything of slitting a man's throat."

Markham gingerly rubbed his neck, which was bruised and abraded from the rope. "What they had in mind was just as bad," he rasped.

"Come on, let's get you back to the boat," Clay said. He took Markham's arm and steered him toward the square, where the rally was still in full swing despite the commotion by the church. As they walked along the rear edge of the crowd, Markham glanced toward the platform. The three senators sat listening while Captain Roosevelt spoke. None of them seemed to notice Clay and Markham.

"One of them sees us," Clay said in a low voice, as if he had read Markham's thoughts. "Count on that. The gent we're after tried to have both of us eliminated tonight."

"Someone . . . attacked you?" Markham croaked.

Clay nodded. "Yep. He wound up dead, more's the pity. I wanted to have a nice long talk with him about who paid him to ambush me. I headed for the square right away because I figured somebody might try to get to you, too. When I saw you weren't there, I started looking around and spotted the commotion by the church. That's when I came running."

"Did you really shoot to frighten them off?"

"Hell, no. I just missed in the bad light. I wanted to injure that fellow who was trying to beat you to death, so that we could question him."

"But they both got away," Markham said disgustedly. "We didn't accomplish a damned thing."

"I reckon we did," Clay said. "We know now that we've got him nervous, really nervous. It's only a matter of time before he tries again."

"And this is a *good* thing?" Markham said dryly. But he knew it was. They had taken one more step tonight—a blind one, to be sure, but a step nonetheless—toward identifying the man who wanted them dead.

CHAPTER SEVEN

S hining Moon was not sure where Matthew had
found the knife with which he had attacked Pollux, but that did not really matter. What concerned her was the damage the boy might do in the
future. Perhaps it was time to do what Clay had originally suggested following the death of Matthew's
mother: They could try to find a place for him in something called an orphanage. But the idea of turning a
child over to live with strangers went against everything Shining Moon believed in. Among her people,
children whose parents died were always taken in by
relatives or friends and raised as if they had always
belonged there. That was one reason she had opened
her heart and her home to Matthew. Her action had
been prompted as well by the Christian faith she had
embraced following the coming of the Black Robes.

Now, after all this time, she was on the verge of
abandoning her hopes that Matthew could ever understand what was expected of him. Anyone who invited

a predator to live with them was asking for trouble, be that predator wolf, bear, mountain lion . . . or human.

Castor and Pollux had wanted to lock Matthew in the harness room in the barn. There were no windows in the room, and it would have been easy to put a stout bar across the door. But Shining Moon could not countenance such harsh punishment. "He will stay in the house with me," she had decided.

"You're just letting yourself in for more heartbreak and danger, ma'am," Pollux had told her worriedly as they stood on the porch of the cabin. Matthew was sitting on a stump at the edge of the fields, out of earshot, with Castor standing guard over him. "There's nothing but hate in that boy. You're trying to reach something that's just not there."

Shining Moon feared that he was right.

"Perhaps Clay will return soon," she had said. "Then we will decide what to do."

So in the meantime she had maintained a close watch on Matthew, keeping him at her side during the day and observing him closely so that he could not get his hands on anything he could use as a weapon. She no longer asked him to do any chores, and he was not allowed to go to the barn or the fields. At night, when he slept in the loft, Shining Moon often sat at the kitchen table, keeping herself awake until exhaustion claimed her and she slumped forward with her head cradled in her arms. The strain was taking its toll. She looked and felt haggard, with dark circles under her eyes.

Life would have been much simpler were she not who she was, she reflected during those long, sleepless hours. Clay would have sent Matthew away, and Proud Wolf would have simply killed him. Her brother had offered to do just that during his visit to the Holt farm on his way east.

Or perhaps not. Proud Wolf was not a cold-blooded killer. He would not slit the throat of a child, Shining Moon decided, not even a child as empty and soulless as Matthew Garwood seemed to be. Only in battle would Proud Wolf kill an enemy.

A Sioux warrior could do no less.

"Good evening, lad! I must say, you seem to be adapting magnificently to your surroundings. Why, you look right at home here!"

Proud Wolf raised his eyes from the leather-bound volume of philosophy he was reading. The door of his room had opened a second earlier, and the visitor was speaking even as he stepped inside. Proud Wolf knew he would have to act quickly to get a word in and stem the torrent of talk that would otherwise follow.

"Good evening, Professor," he said. "I am surprised to see you."

"Why in the world would you be surprised?" asked Professor Abner Hilliard as he came into the narrow room and swept a beaver hat from his head. "After all, I am the one responsible for bringing you here. I'm hardly going to abandon you. I plan to make regular visits so that I can monitor your progress."

"Ah, yes," Proud Wolf said dryly. "I had forgotten that I am a scientific experiment."

"Not at all, not at all," Hilliard insisted. "Actually, Proud Wolf, above all else you are my friend."

"Thank you, Professor. And you are my friend." *But right now*, thought Proud Wolf, *I wish you would leave*.

Proud Wolf had an appointment this evening—an appointment to settle matters once and for all with Will Brackett.

Hilliard was wearing a long black cloak over his suit. He swept it back and sat on the bed, then folded his hands on the head of his cane. He was a middle-aged man with a florid face and a shock of white hair that stuck up nearly straight. A professor of natural science at Harvard, he had concocted the idea of taking a Sioux youth—Proud Wolf—and bringing him east to give him the same education that a young white man of means would receive.

"How is everything progressing with your studies?" Hilliard asked. "I've spoken to your instructors, and with the exception of Master Bell, they've all told me that you are a promising student."

"I am trying," Proud Wolf said, hoping that if he answered the questions to Hilliard's satisfaction, the professor would leave. "There is much to learn. And mathematics is difficult. All those numbers."

"True," murmured Hilliard. "Still, I'm confident that in time you shall master all your subjects."

Proud Wolf lifted the book he had been reading. "This philosophy is much like the stories of the elders, told around the council fires of my people."

"I was hoping you would find much to remind you of your home." Professor Hilliard leaned forward. "You know, I daresay you could teach your instructors every bit as much as they are teaching you."

Proud Wolf cocked his head. "Teach them? Me? I know so little."

"Only how to be a Sioux warrior," Hilliard said with a smile. "And that, my young friend, is something that no one else here at the academy knows. I daresay no one else in the entire sovereign state of Massachusetts knows everything that you know."

Proud Wolf had never thought of it that way. The professor was right. Other students might be more familiar with the world of books . . . but Proud Wolf knew the sound of the wind rushing over the long grass of the prairie. He knew the smell of the air when a storm loomed over the mountains and fingers of lightning clawed the black sky. He knew the beauty of a field of wildflowers, the majesty of snowcapped peaks rising into the heavens. He knew the taste of buffalo haunch, straight from the flames that had seared it.

And he knew the feel of hot blood gushing over his hand as he took the life of an enemy. . . .

The face of Will Brackett appeared before his mind's eye.

Proud Wolf's jaw tightened as he forced the image

out of his head. He could not kill Brackett. All he wanted was to pay him back for the insulting words he had spoken about Audrey Stoddard and, in the process, trounce him so badly that he would never bother Proud Wolf again.

"You're deep in thought, lad," Hilliard said. "Is there anything you'd like to share?"

Proud Wolf shook his head. "I am sorry, Professor. I allowed myself to be distracted from our conversation. You were saying . . . ?"

"That I have to go." Hilliard rose to his feet. "I'm on my way to the opera." He picked up his hat and swirled his cloak. "Perhaps you'd care to come with me."

"Thank you, but I cannot," replied Proud Wolf, concealing his relief that Hilliard was leaving. "I must study."

"Well, that's certainly a commendable attitude. I knew as soon as we met that whatever you decided to do, Proud Wolf, you would always do it to the absolute best of your ability."

Proud Wolf hoped that would prove true later, when he met Will Brackett on the field of battle—in Boston Common.

The stars glittered brightly in the sable sky above Boston as Proud Wolf made his way through the streets. It was close to midnight, and he hoped he would not get lost on his way to his appointment with Will Brackett. The city was so confusing . . . so many buildings and streets, all crowded together in such a small area. Proud Wolf found himself longing for the open spaces of the frontier, where a warrior could clearly see the world around him.

He had left the Stoddard Academy a couple of hours earlier, when all the buildings were dark and everyone was asleep. Slipping out of his second-floor room had been as simple as opening the window and stepping out onto the branch of a tree. From there he had dropped lithely to the ground, scaled the ivy-covered wall that surrounded the grounds, and walked down the hill into Cambridge.

He was wearing a long coat, and his raven-dark hair was tucked underneath a cap. No one could tell that he was a Sioux Indian from the Rocky Mountains. He strode through the streets with his usual confidence, and no one challenged him.

It had taken some time to walk all the way through Cambridge to Charlestown and the wide expanse of the Charles River, which separated the smaller communities from Boston proper. A ferry carried passengers across the river, and Proud Wolf had hoped it was still running this late at night.

It was, and again no one had asked him who he was or what he was doing out and about so late. The ferry pilot had simply taken his money and carried him across the river to Boston.

When the ferry had landed at Hudson's Point, Proud Wolf asked the ferryman for directions to the common. In a broad accent that Proud Wolf had difficulty understanding, accompanied by incomprehensible gestures, the man had told him. Proud Wolf could only nod and hope that he could make sense of the man's directions once he actually saw the landmarks he had mentioned.

Now he was afraid he was hopelessly lost. He had walked past a low eminence he took to be Copp's Hill, past a church he supposed was the Old North Church, and down a long street that led toward a pair of low hills in the distance. The larger of the two he thought must be Beacon Hill, and beyond Beacon Hill he was supposed to find the common, but instead he found himself in a welter of streets and buildings that seemed to have no logical order to them. He supposed he could stop and ask someone else for directions, but there were few people on the streets at this time of night. Those who were abroad might not be trustworthy. It seemed to Proud Wolf that most people who were still up at this hour must be on a sinister errand of some kind . . . much like himself.

Most of the buildings were dark, but a light in one of them caught his eye. A lantern burned over an alcove where a narrow flight of stairs led downward to the basement of the building. Proud Wolf paused at the top of the stairs. The door at the bottom was closed, but he could hear noise from the other side of it, laughter and talking and the scraping of a fiddle. A wooden sign suspended from a post over his head creaked as it moved slightly in the breeze. He looked up at the sign and realized the place was a tavern. There was a tavern in New Hope, the settlement near the village of his people, and he had seen taverns in St. Louis when he passed through with Professor Hilliard, but he had never been inside one.

Surely someone in there could help him find Boston Common. He took a deep breath to gather his courage and walked quickly down the stairs. He grasped the latch and swung the door open.

Hot, smoky air thick with the fumes of liquor and humanity enveloped him as he stepped inside. The room was crowded with revelers, and they paid him no heed as he closed the door and made his way toward the circular bar in the center of the room. Two men in aprons stood behind the bar, filling buckets of beer as fast as they could from great kegs.

Proud Wolf saw a place open up at the bar as a thick-bodied man lurched to his feet and stumbled toward the entrance. Several of the other patrons called jeers after him, and Proud Wolf gathered that they were making sport of the man for having to go home to his wife before the hour grew too late. The man waved at them and shambled out on unsteady legs.

Moving quickly, Proud Wolf slipped into the open spot and waited until one of the bartenders, a tall, dark-haired man, came over to him. "What can I do for you, friend?" he asked.

"I am looking for Boston Common," Proud Wolf said. "Can you tell me how to find it?"

The bartender squinted at him in the smoky light.

"You're a stranger around here, aren't you? I don't recollect ever seeing you in here before."

Proud Wolf smiled. "Yes, I am a stranger."

"Sort of red in hue as well."

The bartender had realized he was an Indian. Proud Wolf stiffened. He had no idea how the man would react; he might be helpful—or he might curse Proud Wolf for a savage and order him out of the tavern, perhaps even at gunpoint.

"I am a visitor to your city," Proud Wolf acknowledged. It would do no good to deny his heritage. All he could do was hope for the best.

The bartender shrugged, and Proud Wolf felt a surge of relief. "Go back up the stairs outside," the man said. "Turn left and go two blocks. Turn left again, and another block will bring you to the common. What's your business there?" The man closed one eye in a wink. "Going to dump some more tea in the harbor?'

For a moment Proud Wolf was baffled by the question. Then he remembered something he had read in a book. Years earlier, when the Americans in Boston had decided to rebel against their British rulers, they had dressed as Indians and raided one of the British ships anchored in the harbor, tossing the crates full of tea the ship carried as cargo into the waters of the bay. Did the bartender think that he was merely *disguised* as an Indian?

A man sitting at the bar next to Proud Wolf spoke up. "I was there, you know," he said. "It was a grand night. We showed the British what we're made of, didn't we, Sam?"

The bartender shook his head. "That was a bit before I was born, I'm afraid."

"Well, then, let me tell you all about it."

From the weary but tolerant look on the bartender's face, Proud Wolf guessed he had heard the story more than once already. Proud Wolf turned and went to the door while he had the chance, leaving the garrulous customer talking to the bartender.

The bartender's directions were accurate, and it took Proud Wolf only a few minutes to find Boston Common. He looked around for Will Brackett. The common seemed to be deserted. Was it already after midnight? Had Will decided that Proud Wolf was not coming? He walked a short distance out into the common, so that anyone who was watching and waiting could not miss seeing him in the moonlight.

"Redskin."

The voice belonged to Will. Proud Wolf turned in the direction of the voice and found himself facing a clump of deep shadows under a grove of trees that grew along the edge of the common.

"Over here, redskin," Will went on. "Let's settle things once and for all."

Proud Wolf stayed where he was and motioned for Will to come to him. "Out here we can see," he said.

"And be seen." Contempt edged Will's words. "You want the constable seeing us and throwing us both in jail for brawling? I don't. We might both get expelled from the academy."

Proud Wolf supposed Will was right, though he doubted that Jeremiah Stoddard would ever risk offending Will's wealthy and generous father by expelling his son. Proud Wolf strode toward the shadows.

He had reached the edge of the patch of darkness when a small voice in the back of his head shouted to him, *Would you trust a Blackfoot? Would you accept a Crow's invitation into the shadows?*

It was a trap. Proud Wolf suddenly knew that as well as he knew his own name.

But when he started to draw back, Will Brackett said sharply, "Get him!"

Figures poured out of the shadows, at least half a dozen of them, and though Proud Wolf hated to run, only a fool faced such odds willingly. He spun around.

It was too late. One of the young men leaped and tackled him around the waist, bringing him down. Proud Wolf landed hard on the ground, and the impact knocked the breath out of him. By the time he could gather his wits about him, strong hands had grabbed him and yanked him upright. They dragged him toward the shadows.

Will stepped up, hands in his pockets, a mocking smile on his face. "Now maybe you'll finally learn your lesson, redskin," he said. "Audrey Stoddard may be a slut, but she's a white woman. She's too good for the likes of you."

Proud Wolf struggled in the grip of the young men holding him. "Face me in battle!" he hissed at Will. "You swore that we would settle this man to man."

"The trouble with that," drawled Will, "is that you're not a man. You're just a red-skinned animal, and I'm not going to soil my hands on you." He made a careless gesture. "Go ahead, boys."

"Cowar—"

Proud Wolf had no chance to finish the furious epithet. A fist slammed into the small of his back, and pain shot up his spine. Before he could recover from that blow, someone else punched him in the belly. Then a fist crashed into his face.

"Hold him up," commanded Frank Kirkland. "When we're through with him, he's going to remember this night for a long, long time."

More blows, then more and yet more. The darkness became bright with a searing agony, and then the light slowly faded back to darkness, deeper and blacker than the shadows under the trees. Proud Wolf surrendered to the darkness and let it carry him far away, until he no longer felt the fists as they struck him.

Proud Wolf felt nothing at all.

Jeff's seasickness returned in full force when the *Beaumont* reached the angry waters off Tierra del Fuego and Cape Horn. He spent long hours at the ship's railing, shuddering from both the cold and the spasms that racked him. Captain Vickery was sympathetic, but there was little he could do to help other than press on toward calmer waters.

As Jeff straightened from his slumped posture and

wiped the back of a gloved hand across his mouth, the captain came to stand beside him and held out a small silver flask.

"I don't know if that's a good idea," Jeff said groggily.

"As poorly as you've been feeling, Mr. Holt, how can it hurt?"

Jeff thought for a moment, then took the flask. He uncapped it and lifted it to his mouth, taking a small swig of fiery rum. He swished it around in his mouth and spat it over the side. Then he took another drink and swallowed this one, and the warmth as it hit his belly did have a fortifying effect. Shaking his head a little, he twisted the cap back on and handed the flask back to Vickery. "Much obliged."

The captain put the rum away, then pointed out across the gray, storm-tossed waves to the south. "I'm told there's a whole continent made of ice down there, across the Drake Passage," he said. "Some of the fellows who hunt seals in these waters are supposed to have seen it. Don't know if it's true or not, but I wouldn't be surprised."

"Why would anyone want to go there?" Jeff asked hoarsely.

Vickery glanced at him and snorted. "Why, I'm surprised to hear you say that, Mr. Holt, considering all the things I've been told about you by Mr. March."

"What do you mean?"

"You know what it feels like to be the first one to see a place, the first one to do a thing. That's why sooner or later somebody will go down to that ice country. Because no one else has done it yet."

Jeff took a deep breath of chilly air and stared to the south. Captain Vickery was right, he realized. He should have understood. Holts had always been bitten by wanderlust, drawn to find out what was on the other side of a mountain, or a river, or an ocean. That was one reason he was going to Alaska. The fortune an enterprising man could make there certainly was not the only lure.

But the legendary continent of ice—someone else would have to explore it, Jeff decided. There were some places even a Holt wouldn't go.

Now that he was feeling a little better, he decided to return to his cabin and get warm again. He nodded to the captain and turned away from the rail.

A few moments later, Melissa looked up from the bunk as Jeff entered the cabin. She smiled affectionately. "You look as if you're feeling a bit stronger."

Jeff nodded. "For the time being, at least. God knows how long it will last." Even as he spoke, the ship lurched slightly, and so did his stomach. But then the vessel steadied, and his belly followed suit.

As Melissa stood up and came toward him, Jeff glanced around the cabin. "Where's Michael?"

"I took him to the galley," said Melissa. "He wanted to help the cook, and he promised not to get underfoot."

"For Michael, that's always a difficult promise to keep." Jeff turned toward the door of the cabin. "I'd better go see about him."

Melissa reached out and placed a hand on his arm. "He's been there only a little while," she said. "If you go and get him now, he's going to be angry."

"But I thought you didn't like for him to be out of your sight."

"I have every confidence that the cook will look after him. Besides . . ." Melissa stepped closer and rested both hands on his chest. "We have so little privacy on this ship, so few moments when we're alone."

She tilted her head back and brought her face close to his, and instinctively Jeff kissed her. Melissa's ardor took him by surprise. As her lips parted, her tongue slipped between them to tease and probe at his mouth. He opened his own lips and let his tongue meet hers. His arms went around her waist and pulled her tightly against him. Her hips molded intimately against his. He felt himself responding to the kiss and knew she was aware of his arousal.

She took her lips away from his and murmured, "It's been so long."

"Yes," Jeff agreed. "It's been a long time."

Not since the night he had come back to Wilmington from Washington City, in fact, had they shared the pleasures of the flesh. Now, with his wife in his arms and kissing him passionately, Jeff found himself wanting her badly. Everything else was forgotten: his earlier sickness, the fact that they were on a sailing ship in cold, cramped quarters, the weeks they had spent on this voyage and the weeks still to come. At this moment all Jeff wanted to do was make love to his wife.

She reached down between them and caressed him with a boldness unusual in her. With a smile she said, "I fear it's too chilly to take off *all* our clothes."

"We can take off enough of them," Jeff whispered.

That was exactly what they did, and a few moments later they were snug under the blankets on the bunk. Melissa clutched at him and cried out softly as they came together. They moved slowly at first, then were seized by an urgency that overwhelmed them. Their culmination was quickly reached, and its intensity left them breathless and softly shuddering.

Melissa whispered something that Jeff barely heard. He lifted his head and asked hoarsely, "What did you say?"

"Nothing," Melissa answered. "Just that . . . I love you."

"Oh." Jeff kissed the soft curve of her throat. "And I love you."

Even as he spoke, Jeff wondered if that was what she had really said. The words hadn't sounded like "I love you."

But under the circumstances, he asked himself, what else could they have been?

CHAPTER
EIGHT

Marietta was the next major stop after Wheeling, and as the *New Orleans* drew closer to the settlement, Clay felt himself growing impatient to see Shining Moon again. It had been months since he had held his wife in his arms and tasted her kiss. He hoped fervently that she was in good health and spirits; in the months they had been separated he had been nagged by worry about Matthew Garwood. The steamboat would be stopping overnight at Marietta, and that would give Clay plenty of time to visit the Holt farm.

Since the layover in Wheeling that had proven so dangerous, there had been no more attempts on the lives of Clay and Lieutenant Markham. When the senators had returned to the boat that evening, Clay and Markham were waiting in plain sight on the deck, and Clay had intently searched the faces of the three men, looking for something—anything—in their expressions that would give away the identity of the man he and Markham were after.

Nothing. The traitor was apparently a master at controlling his emotions.

It was late afternoon when Marietta came into view on the northwestern bank of the Ohio. As always when Clay returned to the settlement, he was surprised by how much it had grown. Marietta was a good-sized town now, no longer the tiny frontier village it had been when he was growing up nearby.

"At least we'll get a home-cooked meal out of this stop," Clay said to Markham as the two men stood at the rail and watched the shoreline approach.

"You will, perhaps," said Markham.

Clay shot a surprised glance at him. "You're not coming out to the farm with me?"

"Well, one of us should stay on the boat, don't you think? We have to keep an eye on our three suspects."

Clay scowled. Markham was right, of course. In his excitement over his coming visit with Shining Moon, he wasn't thinking straight.

"You be careful while I'm gone," he warned.

"Don't worry about me," Markham said. "Just be back here by the time the boat sails in the morning."

"I will be." Clay's frown deepened. "Damn it, maybe I shouldn't even leave the boat. Maybe we ought to both stay on board—"

"I won't hear of it. You haven't seen your wife in months. You have to go." Markham slapped him on the back and added confidently, "Nothing's going to happen tonight."

Clay could only hope the lieutenant was right.

The *New Orleans* was tied up at the dock. Word of its arrival had spread to the town, and a welcoming committee made up of the mayor, local ministers, and half the townspeople gathered to greet it. Clay stood at the railing and scanned their faces, enjoying the shocked surprise he saw on the face of old Steakley, the owner of the general store, who was no particular friend of the Holt family.

Clay clattered down the gangplank with the other disembarking passengers, and his path took him within a few yards of Steakley. He grinned at the store-keeper and said, "You never know when one of us Holts is going to turn up, do you, Mr. Steakley?"

Steakley's mouth was open. He snapped it shut and glared for a second, then turned away. He disliked the Holts, but at the same time he was afraid of them, especially Clay, who had always had a reputation for being wild and dangerous and maybe a little crazy.

The usual pompous speeches were being made as the mayor greeted Captain Roosevelt and the politicians. Clay managed to slip around the knot of people on the dock, and his long-legged stride quickly carried him away from the riverfront. He was prepared to walk all the way to the farm, but he hadn't gone far when a wagon pulled up beside him and came to a stop. "Clay Holt!" exclaimed the driver. "Is that you?"

Clay grinned up at one of his former neighbors, a man named Holmes. "Sure is, Morgan," he said.

"I didn't know you were back in town."

Clay jerked a thumb over his shoulder toward the riverfront. "Just came in on that fancy steamboat, and I'm going downriver on it tomorrow. But I had to stop and visit the farm while I'm here. My wife's staying there."

A shadow passed over the farmer's face at the mention of Shining Moon. Clay wondered what that meant, but before he could ask, Holmes said, "Climb on up here beside me, and I'll take you out there."

"That'll be out of your way, Morgan."

Holmes shook his head. "I don't mind. You walk all that way, you'll have sore feet for sure, and we don't want that."

Clay swung up onto the wagon seat and said, "Much obliged to you, then." He didn't point out that he had tramped over what seemed like half the ground between here and the Rockies without ever getting sore feet.

As the wagon rumbled into motion toward the

road that led past the Holt farm, Holmes asked, "Where have you been lately, Clay? Folks around here know that your missus is staying on the farm, along with that Garwood boy, but we weren't sure where *you* were."

"I had to go to Washington to take care of some business."

"All the way to Washington City?" Holmes shook his head. "Must've been important business."

You could say that, thought Clay. Important enough to draw the attention of Thomas Jefferson and several other highly placed people in the government. Important enough that half the country might well be at risk . . . But he couldn't explain any of that to Holmes. "How have Shining Moon and Matthew been getting along around here?" he asked.

"Folks like that wife of yours. She seems like a fine lady."

"She is." Clay noticed that Holmes hadn't said anything about Matthew, but he didn't press him. Instead he asked, "Has she made any friends hereabouts?"

"She and Cassie Doolittle were good friends for a while." Again, there was something in Holmes's manner that made Clay suspect that something wasn't quite right.

"How is Cassie?" he asked, remembering the irascible old woman.

"Dead."

Clay glanced at Holmes in surprise. "Dead? Finally passed on, did she?"

"Not naturally," the farmer replied as he flicked the reins to keep the mules moving. "She was killed in an accident. Her mule ran away with that cart she always rode around in, and she broke her neck when it turned over and wrecked."

"Damn," Clay said softly as he shook his head. "I hate to hear that."

"So did everybody else around here."

Again there was something strange in Holmes's

voice, and Clay's impatience finally got the best of him. He reached over and grabbed the reins, jerking them back and bringing the team to a halt. He knew he was being rude, but at the moment he didn't care.

"Blast it, Morgan, what's going on here? You've got something on your mind, and I reckon you ought to just spit it out." Clay remembered that Holmes had not said anything when he asked about Matthew, so he said, "This has something to do with the Garwood boy, hasn't it?"

Holmes looked a little angry himself. He pulled the reins away from Clay, who let go of them. "If you really want to know," he said, "it's got everything to do with the boy. There are some who say he had something to do with old Miz Doolittle's death."

That was the last thing Clay had expected to hear. "What? Hell, he's just a boy, not even half grown!"

"That's true enough," Holmes said. "But there have been rumors that he tried to do harm to your wife, too. You just ask the Gilworth brothers about it. They'll tell you."

Clay was silent for a moment, and then he took a deep breath. "I plan to," he said grimly. He didn't want to believe that Matthew would ever deliberately hurt Shining Moon—but the boy was a Garwood. Blood tainted with evil ran in his veins. And he was only a boy, too young to understand his heritage, much less try to overcome it.

Holmes looked at him sympathetically. "I'm sorry to be the one to tell you about all this, Clay. I reckon you should have heard it from your missus. But you asked, and I figured you had a right to know."

Clay clapped a hand on the farmer's shoulder. "No, that's all right, Morgan. Sorry I grabbed the reins like that."

"Don't worry about it." Holmes flapped the reins and called out to the mules to get them moving again. "Let's just get you home."

As quick as you can, thought Clay.

Suddenly he wanted to see Shining Moon more

than ever, to hold her in his arms again and know that she was all right.

Shining Moon heard the hoofbeats and the creak of wagon wheels outside the cabin and knew they had visitors. But she was busy at the moment, trying to roll out the crust for an apple pie the way Cassie Doolittle had once shown her, so she said to Matthew, "See who that is, please."

He was sitting cross-legged in front of the fireplace, where a small blaze was smoldering on this cool autumn day. Without looking around he said, "Don't want to."

"Do what I have asked of you," snapped Shining Moon. She was tired of the boy's sullen attitude, and she was determined not to be afraid of him. She was a Sioux woman, and she did not fear a small white boy.

Grumbling to himself, Matthew got to his feet and went to the door. Before he reached it, booted feet thudded on the planks of the porch, and the door was pushed open. Shining Moon looked around, surprised, and saw a tall, broad-shouldered man silhouetted against the fading light of late afternoon.

Her heart seemed to stop. She knew that man, even with his features cast into shadow by the light behind him. She knew him as well as she knew the rhythm of her own breathing.

"Clay," she said.

He stepped into the room, and Matthew drew back quickly, flinching almost as if he had been struck. Shining Moon could see Clay's face now, could see the mingled joy and concern. Her legs trembled as she stepped around the table. "Clay," she said again, and he held his arms out to her.

Later she would not remember crossing the room to him. All she knew was that she was in his arms once more. Happiness washed over her as his embrace tightened around her. Everything that had happened while he was gone was forgotten, at least for the moment.

She buried her face in his broad chest, breathing in

his scent, then lifted her head so that his mouth could come down on hers. All the loneliness of the past months was in that bittersweet kiss. When he finally took his lips away, she looked up at him and whispered, "We must never be apart again. I am not whole without you, Clay Holt."

She saw the pain flare in his eyes and knew that something was wrong. But instead of explaining, he brushed his lips across her forehead and hugged her tightly to him once more. Then he stepped back, keeping his left arm around her shoulders and drawing her against his side as he extended his right hand toward the boy and said, "Hello, Matthew. It's good to see you again."

Matthew looked up at him, lips curling into a sneer, and said, "Go to hell."

Shining Moon felt Clay tense, and she knew he wanted to strike the boy. In truth, Shining Moon had to restrain her own impulse to slap him. A moment went by, and then Clay surprised both her and Matthew by chuckling and saying dryly, "Well, at least you're honest about the way you feel. But I'm not going to hell. Not for you, and not for anybody else."

Matthew stared up at him, clearly uncertain what to say or do next. Shining Moon's own voice seemed to be stuck in her throat.

Clay turned and looked at the rolled-out crust and the bowl of cut-up apples on the table. "Is that apple pie you're making?"

Shining Moon managed to nod. "Yes. A . . . friend . . . taught me how."

"Cassie Doolittle," Clay said.

Shining Moon looked up at him, surprised. "You know of her?"

"Shoot, everybody around here knows Cassie. Knew her, I reckon I should say. The fellow who gave me a ride out here from town told me that she died not long ago." Clay shook his head. "That's a damned shame. Everybody liked old Cassie."

He was looking at Matthew as he spoke, and Shining Moon suddenly had the feeling that he knew more about Cassie's death than she had expected. The man who had brought Clay to the farm from Marietta must have told him about the rumor of Matthew's involvement in Cassie's death.

Matthew crossed his arms and glared sullenly at Clay for a moment, then turned his back and stared at the fireplace. Shining Moon saw a look of anger and concern pass across Clay's face. He did not know how to reach Matthew either, she realized. She had always believed that Clay Holt knew everything; in the wilderness, where one's strength and resourcefulness could mean the difference between life and death, he was easily the equal of any Sioux warrior she had ever known. But when it came to dealing with one small, twisted child, Clay was as much at a loss as she.

"If that's the way you want it . . ." Clay muttered as he stared at Matthew for a moment longer. Then he looked down at Shining Moon and embraced her again. His big, rough hand awkwardly patted her back.

Shining Moon accepted his comforting with gratitude. "I am so glad you have returned at last, my husband," she said softly. "We will go home now?"

She felt Clay stiffen, and she knew that he had more to tell her.

And his words, she feared, would not be good.

The brisk rapping on the door of his cabin made Lieutenant Markham look up. He was seated on the chair that, with the bunk, was the only furniture in the cabin. A leather-bound journal was balanced on his knee, and he was writing in it with a quill pen that he dipped from time to time into an inkwell sitting on the floor beside his chair.

Markham had been keeping a journal for several years, ever since he had joined the army. His father, Elliot Markham, had given it to him as a present. "It's an excellent habit to write down your thoughts, son," Elliot had said. "You'd be surprised at how much clearer they become in your mind."

The young officer tried to write in the journal every day, but the pressing nature of some of his assignments often made it impossible. So whenever he had the chance to catch up, such as right now, he took advantage of it. With a frown of annoyance he called out, "Who is it?"

"Senator Ralston, my boy," said a hearty voice. "Might I have a word with you?"

Quickly, Markham replaced the pen in the inkwell and set the journal aside on the bunk. He stood up and pulled the door open. "Senator," he said. "What can I do for you?"

"Aren't you going to ask me to come in?" the politician from Georgia said with a friendly smile.

"Well, the quarters are rather cramped, but . . ." Markham stepped back. "Of course. Please come in, Senator."

Ralston was well dressed, as usual. Markham couldn't recall ever seeing any of the three senators in less than impeccable attire. Ralston clasped his hands together behind his back, glanced around the tiny cabin, and said dryly, "I see what you mean about cramped quarters. My cabin is somewhat roomier."

"As well it should be, Senator."

"Rank has its privileges, eh?" Ralston grinned. "At any rate, Mr. Markham, I'm here to invite you to join me and my friends and fellow legislators in a small game of cards this evening."

Markham's eyes widened in surprise. "Me? Play with you and the other senators?"

"Captain Roosevelt will be sitting in on the game as well, along with two or three of the journalists." Ralston inclined his head toward the corridor. "I just knocked on Mr. Holt's door, intending to invite him to join us, too, but he doesn't seem to be available at the moment."

"He's gone to visit his wife," said Markham. "He won't be back until morning."

"His wife?" Ralston raised his bushy white eyebrows. "You don't say!"

"The family farm is near here, and Mrs. Holt is staying there while Mr. Holt and I travel on business."

"Well, if I was visiting my lovely wife after not seeing her for some time, I wouldn't be back until morning either!" Ralston winked knowingly. "I'm sorry Mr. Holt won't be able to join us, but you'll come, won't you? The game will commence in the salon at eight o'clock."

Markham wondered suddenly what Clay would think of this invitation. It couldn't be a trap, Markham decided, not with Captain Roosevelt and the journalists there. Not even the man they were after, daring and ruthless as he was, would try anything in front of that many witnesses.

"I'll be there," Markham promised.

Ralston gave him a friendly slap on the shoulder. "Excellent! I look forward to seeing you."

The senator left the cabin. Markham sat down and picked up his pen and journal again, wondering what, if anything, he should write about this latest development. He always tried to be honest when he jotted down his musings, even when it meant he had to admit his own mistakes. He had been harsh in his remarks about his behavior in Wheeling, where he had walked into an ambush and nearly gotten himself killed. After thinking a moment, he wrote:

> I have been invited to take part in a game of cards with our three suspects tonight. However, I wonder if some deeper game is afoot. The evening will tell the story. I may have some news for Clay by the time he returns tomorrow morning.

Just before eight o'clock Markham strolled into the salon of the *New Orleans*. The room was luxuriously appointed, with a lush carpet on the floor, papered walls with a velvety finish, and gleaming brass lamps. Tables of polished hardwood were scattered around the large room, and along one wall was a bar well stocked with rum and port and cognac. Streamers of blue-gray pipe smoke hung in the air, along with the hearty laughter of men.

Markham saw quickly that Senators Emory and Haines were present, along with a pair of journalists. Neither Senator Ralston nor Captain Roosevelt was on hand.

Charles Emory spotted Markham and raised a hand in greeting. "How are you this evening, Mr. Markham?" he asked as the young officer strolled up to the group.

"Very well, thank you," replied Markham. "I appreciate being invited to join your game."

"Holt's not with you?" Senator Haines asked, a little suspiciously, Markham thought.

Markham shook his head. "Clay had other business to attend to tonight."

Haines grunted. "A shame." He didn't sound particularly sincere, Markham noted.

"You know Mr. Burke and Mr. Gramlich, of course," Emory said, indicating the journalists.

"Gentlemen." Markham shook hands with them. He recognized them by sight, but he had not been introduced to them until tonight.

"Glad to meet you, Markham," said the one called Burke. "Say, don't I know you? From Washington, perhaps?"

"I don't believe so," Markham said. It was possible Burke had seen him in his uniform at some time, and he wanted to discourage any memory of that.

"I could have sworn . . ." Burke shook his head. "Well, perhaps not."

Haines asked, "What sort of business is Holt about this evening?"

"Personal business. He has family in this area." Markham watched the senator closely, looking for some sign that Haines's prying was more than simple curiosity.

A white-jacketed waiter appeared at Markham's elbow. "Cognac, sir?" he asked.

Markham took a crystal snifter from the proffered

tray. "Thank you." He sipped the smooth but fiery liquor and suppressed a cough.

"A bit strong for you, my boy?" The question was accompanied by a hearty slap on the back. Senator Ralston had entered the salon and come up behind him. "You should try some of the whiskey we make down in Georgia. It'll curl your toes good and proper."

Markham swallowed hard. "My, ah, toes are just fine as they are, Senator."

"Of course they are, lad." Ralston snagged a drink for himself from a passing waiter. "Are you gentlemen ready to be a little poorer?"

Emory laughed. "Not likely, my friend. I'm afraid you don't have the best face in the world for poker. Too easy to read."

"I resent that," said Ralston with a grin. "I think I have an excellent poker face. Shall we begin?"

"We're waiting on Captain Roosevelt," Haines told him. "He's not here yet."

As if he had heard them talking about him, the captain came bustling into the salon. "I'm sorry to keep you waiting, gentlemen," he said. "Some unexpected matters came up. That's the way of it on a steamboat. Nothing ever goes quite the way you expect it to."

A steward spread a cloth of green baize on one of the tables, and the men sat down to play cards. As the pasteboards were shuffled and dealt and play commenced, Markham quickly discovered that although he had sat in on many late-night poker games in the barracks, he was out of his depth here. The betting was fast and ruthless, and the three senators took particular joy in winning. Burke and Gramlich, the reporters, played well, but only seldom did either of them rake in a pot. Markham wondered if they were losing on purpose, so as to stay in the good graces of the politicians. Captain Roosevelt seemed distracted, no doubt by those unexpected problems he had mentioned. As for Markham, it was all he could do not to lose all the money he had on him.

He wondered idly if any of the senators was cheating. If so, they were very smooth about it.

The waiters kept the liquor flowing, and the haze of tobacco smoke over the table grew denser and denser. The senators chatted between hands about backroom deals they had brokered in Washington. During one such break, Ralston looked sternly at Burke and Gramlich and said, "You boys understand that none of this conversation ever took place, don't you?"

"Of course, Senator," replied Gramlich. "You won't read a word of it in the newspaper."

"I had better not," Ralston warned them. "You know that to get along in Washington, you must be discreet."

That was especially true, thought Markham, when you were trying to steal away half the country for some nefarious reason.

The evening wore on, and it became obvious to Markham that he was going to run out of money. As the bet came to him, he pushed the last of his coins into the center of the table and waited for new cards. When they came, flipped to him by Emory, who had the deal at the moment, they failed to improve his hand even a little. "I'm afraid I'm going to have to retire for the evening, gentlemen," he said as he tossed his cards into the discard. "I'm out of cash."

"We'd be happy to take your marker," Haines said.

Markham shook his head. "No, thanks. If I keep this up, one of you will own the old family home in Boston before the night is over."

Ralston extended his hand. "Well, then, we'll bid you good night. We've enjoyed your company, Mr. Markham."

As he shook hands with Ralston, Markham said, "Thank you, Senator." He shook hands with the other players. "Good night, gentlemen."

As he stepped out onto the deck, he realized that he was more than a little dizzy from the cognac and the tobacco smoke. He paused at the railing and drew several deep breaths, trying to clear his head. The hour was probably close to midnight, and the deck of the *New Orleans* was dark and deserted.

It suddenly occurred to Markham that these were the perfect circumstances for someone to clout him over the head, push him over the side, and let him drown unseen in the murky waters of the Ohio River.

That thought was struggling through his befogged brain when he heard the scuff of a soft footstep behind him. Acting on instinct, Markham spun around and threw up his left arm to block any blow that might be falling toward his head. With his right hand he groped under his coat for his pistol.

"Hold on there!" a startled voice said. "I mean you go harm, Mr. Markham."

Markham's pulse was pounding wildly in his head. He breathed deeply again to calm himself as he recognized one of the stewards. "What do you want?" he said harshly.

"Just to see that you're all right, sir," the steward answered contritely. "I didn't mean to startle you. I saw you standing at the rail, and from the way you were acting I was afraid that you might be ill."

Slowly, Markham shook his head. "No, I . . . I'm all right. Just a bit light-headed, but it will pass." He grimaced. "I'm sorry I reacted so strongly when you spoke to me."

"That's quite all right, sir."

Markham forced a chuckle. "I suppose I had too much cognac while I was playing cards in the salon."

"In the salon, sir?" Markham could hear the confusion in the man's voice. "Then that wasn't you I saw leaving your cabin a short while ago?"

"What?" Markham stiffened. "Someone was in my cabin?"

"I saw a man come out of it perhaps an hour ago. I couldn't see him well because of the darkness, of course, but I assumed it was you."

"I've been in the salon for more than three hours," Markham said sharply. "There shouldn't have been anyone in my cabin, unless it was Mr. Holt."

The steward shook his head. "No, sir. My view might not have been very good, but I'm sure the gentleman I saw wasn't large enough to be Mr. Holt."

"And he probably wasn't a gentleman, either," muttered Markham. "Come on. You must have a thief on this boat."

"Oh, no, sir!" The steward sounded shocked. "Captain Roosevelt hires only people of the highest moral character."

"Anyone can give in to temptation."

Markham hurried to his cabin, his head clearer now. Along the way, the steward took one of the small lanterns that hung from hooks along the deck and paused to light it with flint and steel. When Markham jerked open the door of his cabin, the steward was close behind him, holding the lantern high.

No one was in the cabin, but that was no surprise. Whoever had been there had already come and gone. Markham hurriedly checked his belongings.

"Is anything missing, sir?" the steward asked worriedly from the doorway.

Markham straightened from the bunk and shook his head, frowning in puzzlement. "No, everything seems to be here. I can't be sure if anything has even been disturbed."

"Oh, dear," the steward said, then hastily added, "Please don't misunderstand, sir. I'm glad nothing has been stolen, very glad indeed. But I'm concerned that I may have caused you some undue worry. As I told you, the light was bad, and I . . . I could have seen someone leaving one of the neighboring cabins and not this one."

"You're not sure?"

The steward shook his head. "No, sir. I thought I was, but . . . under the circumstances . . . perhaps I was mistaken."

"Perhaps," Markham grated. "Light the lamp in here before you go, will you?"

"Of course, sir." The steward hurried to obey.

Once Markham had closed the cabin door behind

the man, he checked through everything again, more carefully this time. Nothing was missing. Whoever had searched the cabin—if anyone had, Markham reminded himself—had been careful to leave no incriminating evidence behind.

Markham wondered if the man he and Clay were after could have paid someone on the boat to search the cabin to see if they had turned up any evidence. The three senators themselves were in the clear because they had been in the salon all evening, in front of several witnesses.

Ralston was the one who had invited him to join the poker game. Had it been his intent to lure him out of his cabin long enough that it could be searched? Perhaps. But, for all Markham knew, either Haines or Emory could have suggested that Ralston invite him.

"Damn," Markham said softly. The evening's activities had not brought him any closer to uncovering the identity of the man he and Clay were pursuing.

And on top of that, he was now considerably poorer.

"Damn!" he said again, with greater fervor this time.

CHAPTER NINE

L ike the Atlantic Ocean and the Drake Passage,
the waters along the southern tip of South America were choppy and turbulent. But as the *Beaumont* and the *Lydia Marie* sailed northward, the seas
were appreciably calmer. Everyone was relieved, especially Jeff.

The ships put in at Valparaiso, Chile's only major
seaport. The city's name meant "Valley of Paradise,"
although India would have described it somewhat less
effusively. However, it had been several weeks at sea
since they had last made port, and she was grateful for
the break. From Valparaiso the two ships would take
different routes. The *Beaumont* would continue to travel
fairly close to land on its journey north to Alaska. The
Lydia Marie would head out across the vast, trackless
expanse of the southern Pacific, bound for the Hawaiian Islands.

As night fell, India knelt by herself on the deck of
the *Lydia Marie*, coiling a line that she had just mended.

Ned was over on the *Beaumont*, going over the details of the business Jeff expected him to conduct during the next leg of the voyage. Ned was the official Holt family representative, and India had to smile at the thought of Ned being an official anything. She loved him, and she knew that he was intelligent and fast on his feet, but Ned Holt and any sort of serious responsibility had never been close shipmates.

A step sounded behind her, and she straightened to her feet and started to turn. Before she could, an arm suddenly looped around her and jerked her sharply backward, pinning her arms to her sides. She came up against a man's hard, unyielding body. At the same time, a hand was clapped over her mouth, silencing the cry that welled up her throat. The hand stank of tar and fish, and India almost gagged.

"Don't fight me," a voice hissed in her ear. "Don't fight me or I'll have my knife between your ribs before you can blink. Just listen."

Donnelly. India recognized the sailor's voice. Her eyes were wide with shock and anger, but not fear. She wasn't afraid of scum like Donnelly.

His next words made the blood freeze in her veins. "Are you and Holt going ashore tonight for some more . . ." His fingers closed roughly around her breast. Without giving her a chance to respond, he went on, "Don't scream, or I'll kill you. I swear I will." He gave a nasty chuckle. "That's right. I know you're a woman. I know what you've got hidden away under these baggy clothes. And I want some of it."

"I . . . I thought you preferred cabin boys," India gasped as the crushing grip around her chest tightened.

Donnelly chuckled. "I don't rightly care. Any port in a storm, as they say. With a slender little thing like you, it'll be almost the same, anyway."

India's head was spinning. This wasn't the first time she had been threatened with rape. There had been other occasions, back in London after she had run away from home.

"Ned's going to kill you," she hissed. "And if he doesn't, I will."

Donnelly chuckled. "Holt will never know anything about this. If you tell him, I'll spill your little secret to the whole crew. You know how fast the word'll get around. You'll never be able to ship out again without everybody knowin' you're a woman. And you know what that means."

India knew, all right. No captain would give her a berth, because no crew would tolerate having her on board. Not even Lemuel March, who knew her secret, would be able to help her. He could not force his captains to hire her because it would cause mutiny among the sailors who believed that having a woman on board, other than as a passenger, would bring the worst possible luck.

No. If Donnelly exposed her secret, it would mean the end of her life on the sea.

"Besides," Donnelly went on, "if you tell Holt, I'll just have to kill him 'fore he can kill me. Unless you give me your solemn word you won't say anything to him, I'll kill him this very night, as soon as he comes back on board. He won't be expecting a thing, and you won't be able to warn him because I'll have slit your throat already."

"What do you want?" India asked in a choked voice.

His fingers tightened painfully on her breast again. "I reckon you know what I want."

"All right," she forced herself to say, the sound of utter defeat in her voice.

Donnelly laughed in triumph, and his grip around her relaxed slightly . . . enough for India to get her hand on the hilt of the dagger tucked behind her belt.

She pulled it free and slashed the blade across Donnelly's arm. He yelped and jerked away, and India spun around. She lashed out with the dagger, aiming the stroke at his throat. Donnelly stumbled backward, clutching his injured arm. India lunged after him.

Luck was on Donnelly's side. India stepped on the

coil of line she had left on the deck, and it tangled around her feet, throwing her off balance. She caught herself before she could fall, but the momentary lapse gave Donnelly enough time to scramble farther away. "You crazy bitch!" he gasped. "Stay away from me!"

India's breath hissed between clenched teeth. "I ought to kill you."

"Stay away from me!" Donnelly said again. "I'll tell the crew about you! I will!"

The tide had turned, India sensed. Moments earlier, Donnelly had been confident and in control. Now he realized that he had unleashed something much more dangerous than he had ever dreamed.

"If you say one word about me to the crew or anyone else, *I'll* kill *you*," India promised flatly. "If you try to hurt Ned, I'll kill you. It's a long way to the Hawaiian Islands, Donnelly, and even farther to China and back. A lot of nights when you'll go to sleep wondering if you'll wake up with your throat cut. Is that what you want?"

"You're a damned lunatic. You'll be sorry you did this."

"Not as sorry as you." India gestured sharply with the knife. "Now get out of my sight. I'll let you live . . . but only as long as you're no threat to me."

Still muttering curses and cradling his slashed arm, Donnelly backed away, then turned and darted toward the fo'c'sle. India watched him go. Her breathing was ragged and her pulse was racing. She wasn't sure she had successfully blunted his threat, but she had acted instinctively. As much as she loved the sea, she was willing to risk being forced to give it up. She was damned if she was going to allow scum like Donnelly to bully her into letting him have his way with her.

He was going to realize, sooner or later, that threatening her and threatening Ned had been the worst mistake of his whole sordid life.

After leaving Valparaiso, the *Beaumont*'s next stop was a small Spanish settlement on the western coast of

North America. Autumn was well advanced, and Jeff had begun to question the wisdom of traveling so far north this late in the season. When he confided his worries to Captain Vickery, the captain was reassuring. "We'll reach Sitka before the worst of the winter sets in. There'll still be time to leave there and set sail to the south if that's what you want to do."

"But if not, we'll be there for the entire winter."

Vickery shrugged. "You understand, Mr. Holt, I've never sailed those waters. But from what I've heard, 'tis best to hunker down and lie low once the winter storms set in."

All they could do was wait and see, Jeff decided. He would evaluate the situation quickly once they got there and make the decision then whether to spend the winter in Alaska or make a run for home.

The situation with Melissa did not help ease his mind. The unexpected ardor she had begun to demonstrate on the ship had not diminished, and while he certainly had no objection to making love to his wife, Melissa also seemed distracted, even snappish at times. Something was bothering her. Jeff had wondered if she might not be with child, but when he had subtly suggested as much, she had laughed. "I'm not expecting a baby," she told him bluntly. "You don't have to worry about that."

Whatever it was, Jeff hoped her mood would return to normal soon. Between the weather and the upcoming trade negotiations with the Russians in Alaska, he had more than enough on his mind.

As for Melissa, her emotions were in turmoil. More than once, while she and Jeff were making love, she had come close to crying out Philip Rattigan's name. Why thoughts of him roused such passion in her she could not say, but it was deeply troubling. True, he had saved her life in Wilmington and had quite possibly saved Holt-Merrivale as well. She was grateful to him for what he had done. But gratitude and passion were not the same thing, and the guilt that beset Melissa every time the memory of his kiss set her on fire was eating away at her soul. Nothing she tried seemed to do any good. She could not banish the man from her thoughts.

And she knew that Jeff was aware something was wrong. More than once she had observed him standing at the railing of the ship, staring out over the waters of the Pacific, a troubled frown on his face. He was brooding over his inability to figure out what was wrong. All the Holts were that way, Melissa knew. They were men of action, and action was supposed to cure all ills. When it didn't, they were lost and confused.

The only one truly enjoying the voyage was young Michael. The sailors had become accustomed to having the boy underfoot, no matter how much his parents tried to keep him out of the way. He would have swarmed up the rigging like a monkey had Jeff and Melissa allowed it. Already he had cheerfully let loose with several bursts of profanity he had picked up from the crew. Melissa was scandalized, and Jeff had to suppress a smile. He had a feeling Michael would remember this voyage all his life.

Jeff was beginning to enjoy the trip as the *Beaumont* sailed up the western coast of North America. The ship was always in sight of the rugged shoreline and its rocky, towering cliffs and pine-covered hills. One day, as he and Michael stood at the rail, Jeff pointed at the snowcapped peaks visible far inland. "Those might be some of the same mountains your uncle Clay crossed when he was traveling with Captain Lewis and Captain Clark."

"I want to go there," said Michael. "I want to see the mountains."

Jeff put a hand on his son's shoulder. "One of these days I'm sure you will."

Michael looked up at him. "I want to see *everything.*"

"Everything there is to see?" Jeff chuckled. "That would take a long time."

"I don't care," Michael said stubbornly. "I'm going to do it."

Jeff patted his shoulder. "If you're determined enough, I reckon you might at that."

Ned leaned his weight into the line as he helped trim the mainsail. Then he climbed down out of the rigging and dropped lightly to the deck.

India was waiting for him, an anxious look on her face. "What happened up there, Ned?" she asked. "It looked as if you nearly fell."

He shrugged. "A piece of rigging snapped under my foot. Nothing to worry about. I had a good hold with my hands, and my other foot was steady enough."

"Still, you could have fallen."

Ned frowned at the harsh tone of her voice. "Accidents happen, India," he said softly.

"Not on a well-run ship," she snapped. "Not as often as they have lately."

She might have a point there, Ned reflected. He recalled the time, a week or so earlier, when a boom had come loose and swept over the deck with enough force to dash a man's brains out, or at least knock him overboard. He had been standing right in its path as it swung toward him from behind. India had yelled out a warning, and he had dropped beneath the boom and saved himself from serious injury.

Then there was the spar that had snapped and fallen from the mast, narrowly missing Ned as it crashed to the deck. Ned had thought little about these near-misses. Life at sea was dangerous; that was all there was to it. Many sailors had died in similar mishaps over the years, and more would die in the future.

But now that India mentioned it, Ned had to admit that such accidents were less common on ships of the March line. Lemuel March made sure that each vessel had a good captain and experienced crew.

"All right," Ned said slowly. "Maybe there is something odd going on here. But what could it be? Is the ship jinxed?"

India snorted. "I'm not superstitious, nor do I believe in coincidence. Someone could have cut that line partway through and weakened it so it would snap." Suddenly her eyes darted away evasively. "You be careful, Ned. Keep your eyes open. Just be careful."

"All right," he said, and India went on about her business.

But that wasn't going to be the end of it, Ned told himself. He was going to find out what was bothering her.

Neither of them was standing the night watch that evening. There was no place on board where they could count on being alone, so they never risked a kiss or any other intimacy. But they enjoyed each other's company, and they were in the habit of lingering at the rail in the gathering shadows to talk.

Tonight, though, India was nowhere to be found amidships, where they usually met. Ned went looking for her and finally spotted her up at the bow, talking to someone. He approached quietly, then froze when he heard the sound of angry words. India was keeping her voice pitched low, so Ned couldn't understand everything she was saying, but he picked up a few of the words: "warned you," "accidents," "kill you if anything," and "Ned."

She was talking about him. But who was that with her? Whom was she threatening?

The man's rumbling voice was louder. "I didn't have anything to do with what happened," he said. "You and Holt can both go to hell as far as I'm concerned, but you can't blame me for it."

Donnelly! Ned stiffened. Why would India be arguing with Donnelly and blaming him for the mishaps that had nearly taken Ned's life? Ever since their second fight, Donnelly had steered clear of Ned, had barely spoken to him, in fact. Ned had believed that the trouble with the man was over.

". . . giving you a chance," India was saying. "Next time, I'll just kill you."

Donnelly growled a curse and swung around, then stalked away from India. Ned drew back into the shadows along the fo'c'sle and let Donnelly pass. India still stood at the bow, her slender body straight and tense.

Now that he thought about it, Ned realized that something had been bothering India ever since the *Lydia Marie* had put into port at Valparaiso, before heading out across the Pacific. That something must have to do with Donnelly.

He and India had kept few secrets from each other. It was time to bring this one out into the open.

India sighed and started along the deck, but she stopped short and gasped when Ned stepped out of the shadows in front of her. "I was looking for you," he said.

"Ned! I . . . You surprised me."

"I imagine I did. What was that about?"

"What was what about?"

"Your talk with Donnelly just now," Ned said heavily. "Unless I'm greatly mistaken, I heard you threaten to kill him if there were any more accidents involving me."

"That's mad," India scoffed. "I didn't threaten to kill anyone."

"I heard you." Ned put his hands on her shoulders, felt the tension in her muscles as they quivered under his touch. "What's wrong, India? You've never lied to me. Don't start now."

India stared at him for a long moment, then drew a deep, ragged breath. "All right," she said. "Donnelly knows I'm a woman."

"What?" Ned exclaimed.

"He found out somehow, and back in Valparaiso, he . . . he accosted me."

"That son of a bitch! You won't have to kill him. *I* will!"

India caught at his arms as he started to turn away. "No, Ned! He thought he had me cowed, but I fought back. I put that gash on his arm."

Ned grunted. "Donnelly said he got it in a tavern when some *Chileno* tried to rob him."

"He lied. I did it fighting him off. And then I . . .

well, I convinced him that I was practically insane. I told him I'd kill him if he harmed you or exposed my secret." She closed her eyes and shook her head. "For a while I thought he had decided to leave us alone. Then these accidents started happening . . ."

"I heard him tell you he didn't have anything to do with them."

"You don't believe him, do you?"

Ned looked away. "I don't know what to believe. It's enough just trying to come to grips with the fact that he knows you're a woman."

She leaned against him, risking a quick embrace. "I didn't want to tell you. I knew you'd be angry."

"Damned right I'm angry. Donnelly's been a thorn in our sides since before we left Wilmington. Captain Canfield should never have hired him for this crew."

"Well, I hope I've put the fear of God in him again," India said wearily. "Perhaps he'll leave us alone now."

Ned had to grin as he thought about what she had just said. "The fear of India St. Clair is more like it. Would you really cut his throat if he hurt me?"

India's voice was suddenly cold as she said, "What do you think?"

I think I'm glad you're my lover and not my enemy, Ned mused. But he kept that thought to himself.

Jeff had never seen so many islands in his life. They thrust up from the cold gray water everywhere, some large, some small, some bare rock, others covered with pine.

"That's Alaska," Captain Vickery said as he stood at the rail beside Jeff. "And those mountains on the mainland are part of it, too."

Melissa stood on Jeff's other side, Michael in front of her. Her gloved hands rested on his shoulders. All four of them were bundled up against the cold wind in heavy coats, gloves, scarves, and hats. The sky was overcast, with thin, watery sunlight filtering through the clouds. Even in this gloom, Jeff thought the view was magnificent.

"I've been studying the charts," Captain Vickery went on, "and we should reach Sitka in another day or so. It's the only good-sized settlement of any kind up here, and I'm told the Russian-American Company is headquartered there. They're the folks you'll have to talk to about trading."

Jeff nodded. He knew from what Melissa and Lemuel March had discovered when they first hatched their plan that the Russians were doing a brisk business in furs, shipping seal and otter pelts back across the narrow straits that divided Alaska from the Russian mainland. But trade agreements such as the one Jeff would be proposing would open up a much vaster market for the Russians and would, he hoped, prove profitable for everyone involved.

"Will there be Indians here?" asked Michael, looking up at his father.

"I don't know," Jeff replied. "Captain, are there Indians in this area?"

Vickery nodded. "So I'm told. There are several different tribes, I understand. But the Russians have them fairly pacified."

Jeff wondered if the tribes had been friendly to begin with or if the Russians had had to overpower them with force in order to bring "peace" to the region. If the Alaskan Indians were anything like the Blackfoot, there would have been plenty of fire and bloodshed before it was safe for the Russians to establish a settlement here.

The *Beaumont* swung toward the coast but did not approach the islands too closely. "Might be rocks and snags out there we can't see until it's too late," Captain Vickery explained after he had given the order to change course. "I always like to be careful when I'm sailing in strange waters."

True to the captain's prediction, late the following afternoon the ship approached a large bay formed by a mountainous peninsula that jutted out into the Gulf of Alaska. A sailor, blue-faced from the cold, called down from his post in the rigging, "Smoke ho! There's a settlement in there!"

"That would be Sitka," Captain Vickery told Jeff. "Look there. You can see the smoke from the chimneys."

Jeff squinted toward the shoreline and spotted tendrils of smoke wisping up from dozens of chimneys. After such a long time at sea, the thought of bright, cheerful, warming flames burning in the fireplaces connected to those chimneys made him feel a little less chilly.

"We'll be there before dark," promised the captain. "The way through that bay looks clear."

It was, and the *Beaumont* sailed easily past the mountain thrusting up from the peninsula. The sight was awe-inspiring, and Jeff called Melissa and Michael on deck to watch the approach to Sitka with him.

The settlement was not large: several dozen sturdy log buildings scattered along the shore of the bay. A short dock extended into the water, and some large buildings nearby were probably warehouses for the furs, Jeff decided. A light dusting of snow lay over the ground beyond the settlement, and more snow had fallen on the roofs of the buildings and then melted, forming icicles that hung from the eaves. Jeff and Melissa had seen these winter phenomena before, having grown up in Ohio, but for Michael, who had lived most of his short life in Wilmington, snow and icicles were a novelty. His eyes were wide with wonder as he stood at the railing with his parents.

Several people were moving around the crude streets between the buildings, and they seemed to be converging on the dock. No doubt the approach of the *Beaumont* had been noticed. The arrival of a ship would be a noteworthy event in such an isolated place as this. As Jeff and his family watched, a group of men came out of one of the larger buildings and trooped toward the dock. Only a couple of hundred yards separated the ship from the shore now, and Jeff could make out the tall, black fur hats and the red coats the men wore. The outfits were unmistakably uniforms.

"Soldiers," Jeff muttered, half to himself.

"What did you say?" asked Melissa.

Jeff pointed to the marching men and said quietly, "We've got a welcoming committee." He looked around for Captain Vickery, intending to ask him about the soldiers, but Vickery was on the bridge, standing next to the helmsman.

When the *Beaumont* dropped anchor a short distance offshore, Vickery came to Jeff and said, "We'll take one of the small boats in. Would you like to come with us, Mr. Holt?"

"Yes, I certainly would." Jeff turned to Melissa and put a hand on her shoulder. "You and Michael stay here this time, until the captain and I have gone ashore and talked to the Russians."

Melissa looked surprised. "Coming to Alaska was my idea, Jeff. I think I should go ashore with you."

"Not this time," he said firmly. He saw anger flare in his wife's eyes but told himself that she would simply have to abide by his decision. He was not going to allow her off the *Beaumont* until he was certain it was safe for her and Michael to go ashore.

A small boat was lowered over the side, and Jeff and Vickery, along with four crewmen, rowed toward the dock. Vickery had given strict orders to his first mate that in the event of any trouble the ship was to raise anchor and get out of the bay as quickly as possible. Jeff had no reason to believe that the Russians would be hostile, but until he had established that for certain, he was not going to risk either his family or the ship.

As the boat drew closer to shore, Jeff saw that the soldiers were carrying muskets. He and the captain were armed with pistols, but those two guns were their only weapons. They were here to trade in peace, not wage war.

Jeff hoped the Russians were inclined to be as friendly.

The prow of the boat scraped against one of the piers, and the crewmen steadied the boat as Jeff and Vickery stood up and climbed onto the dock. Jeff raised one hand, palm out, as he turned toward the red-coated soldiers. "Hello!" he called. "My name is Jefferson Holt. I'm an American trader."

He wasn't sure how much the Russian soldiers could comprehend of what he was saying, but they must have understood at least some of it.

Because no sooner had he finished speaking than the Russians snapped their muskets to their shoulders and pointed the weapons straight at him.

CHAPTER TEN

P roud Wolf bit back a groan as he struggled to climb up the tree toward his room. Every muscle in his body ached with a deep, throbbing pain. His left eye was swollen almost shut, the inside of his mouth had been cut to ribbons by his teeth when his face was punched, and a ball of nausea rolled around in his belly. He had endured beatings before at the hands of his enemies, but never one quite as severe as this.

Odd that it had been inflicted by a group of young white men who would not have lasted a day in the wilderness that was Proud Wolf's home, he thought bitterly.

They would regret what they had done to him. He knew them, each and every one of them, had heard and recognized their voices as they brutalized him. Frank Kirkland had led the savage assault, but Will Brackett was ultimately to blame. He would punish all of them,

Proud Wolf vowed. But he would save the sweetest revenge for Will Brackett.

His main goal at the moment, however, was simply to get back into his room before he passed out again.

He had regained consciousness in the shadows under the trees bordering Boston Common, where Will and Frank and the others had dragged him. Someone was rapping the sole of his left foot with a club or stick, and Proud Wolf had blinked his eyes open to see a constable looming over him.

"Get out of here, ye miserable, sodden wretch," the officer had ordered. "I don't care how much ye've had to drink, when I come back by here in a bit, ye'd best be gone."

Proud Wolf had been unable to suppress a groan.

"Oh, aye, I know ye're sick. And ye know, laddie, I don't care. Now haul yer carcass out o' the Common."

With that, the constable had turned and strolled away. Proud Wolf had let him go rather than call after him for help. Let the man think he was nothing but a drunk who had passed out. If the constable discovered that he was the victim of a beating, then his identity would be discovered as well, and no doubt the authorities would get in touch with Jeremiah Stoddard. Proud Wolf could not risk that. So he had somehow hoisted himself to his feet, steadied himself by holding on to a tree until the awful dizziness passed, then began staggering back toward the Charles River.

By the time he had reached the ferry at Hudson's Point, he was still in great pain but moving more easily. Muscles that had grown stiff while he was lying on the cold ground unconscious had loosened up. He kept his cap tugged low over his face and hunched his shoulders inside his coat so that no one could get a good look at him.

Then, once the ferry deposited him in Charlestown, there was the long walk back through the riverfront village, then through Cambridge, and finally up the hill to the Stoddard Academy. His path seemed endless, as if he had decided to walk from one side of the continent to the other.

Finally he had reached the academy and made his way to the tree outside his window. It seemed so much higher now.

Moving carefully, Proud Wolf climbed the tree and edged out onto the branch that angled toward his window. The shutters were still open as he had left them. He braced himself and took a deep breath, gathering his strength and his will for the long step that remained. He half stepped, half fell into the room.

Someone gasped and said in fright, "Who's there?"

Proud Wolf broke his fall by landing on his hands and knees, and his instincts sent him rolling swiftly to the side in case whoever was waiting in the room intended to ambush him. He tried to come up on his feet, but his balance deserted him and he went over backward, landing hard on his buttocks. In the faint moonlight that filtered through the open window, he saw a figure standing over him, and when it spoke, he recognized the tremulous voice.

"Proud Wolf? Is that you?"

"Audrey," he said, trying to ignore the newly intensified pain that filled his body. "What are you doing here?"

"Are you all right?" She knelt beside him and reached out to lay a soft hand on his arm. "You're hurt. You must be."

"How do you . . . know?"

"Because I overheard Will and Frank talking earlier tonight. I heard them laughing about what they and their friends had done to you."

"You . . . heard them?" Proud Wolf did not understand. It was well after midnight. Audrey Stoddard should have been in her own bed, asleep for hours.

"I was awake and looking out the window," she explained. "I often have trouble sleeping. When I saw someone moving around, I put on my robe and went to see who it was."

"You should have . . . told your father. It could have been . . . thieves."

"I wasn't afraid," Audrey said indignantly. "I grew up here, and I know my way around, even at night. I followed the men I saw, and then I realized it was Will and Frank. They were talking about meeting you in Boston and giving you the thrashing they seemed to think you deserve."

"It was supposed to be . . . just Will and me. My honor demanded that I . . . accept his challenge."

She moved closer as she knelt beside him on the floor. "Was it your honor you were concerned about, Proud Wolf . . . or mine?"

Even in his battered state, he felt his face flushing. "Will spoke lies about you. I could not allow them to pass."

"What sort of lies?"

Proud Wolf shook his head. "I will not repeat them."

Audrey took a deep breath and said angrily, "You don't have to. I can just imagine. Will Brackett is . . . is terrible. To even hint that I would do anything . . . improper . . . with him is ridiculous!"

"I know," Proud Wolf said.

"And you defended me."

"I attempted to." Proud Wolf's mouth twisted in a wry grimace. Then he winced at the pain to his lips. He asked Audrey, "Why are you here?"

"I came to make sure you were all right. When I found that you weren't here, I decided to wait for a while and see if you came back. If you hadn't," she added grimly, "I would have had to tell my father what I heard Will and Frank say. For all I knew, you were lying dead in a gutter somewhere in Boston."

Proud Wolf shook his head. "Not dead."

Audrey put her arm around his shoulders and leaned closer to him. "You poor darling. Let me light a candle, and I'll see what I can do about cleaning your wounds."

"No! No lights." Proud Wolf did not want her to

see him looking as he must right now, nor did he want
to draw attention by burning a candle in the wee hours
of the morning.

"Are you sure? I don't mind."

"You must go back to your father's house before
anyone notices that you are gone."

Audrey laughed. "I heard my father snoring when
I left earlier. He could sleep through Gabriel's trum-
pet." She leaned still closer. "There's no need to
worry."

She was sitting on the floor next to him now, the
warm length of her thigh pressed against his. He could
feel the softness of her breast through her robe. "I'm so
sorry this happened, Proud Wolf," she went on in a
whisper. "It's all because of me."

That was not strictly true, he thought. Will Brackett's hatred for him was something instinctive. If not
Audrey, then Will would have found some other excuse for hating the young Sioux warrior.

"I'll make it up to you, I swear I will," Audrey said
as she caught hold of his hand. She pressed his palm to
her bosom, then moved it, and he felt his fingers sliding underneath her robe, guided by her touch. Suddenly his hand was filled with a warm, yielding globe
crowned by a ring of pebbled flesh. He could feel her
nipple growing harder at his touch and knew that what
he was doing was wrong, even though she was urging
him on.

But his injuries seemed not to ache quite so much
now, and as he continued to caress her, the pain re-
ceded even further. Wrong or not, what they were doing offered momentary solace, and right now he was
acutely aware of how far he was from his home and
everything he knew.

And he did not want to be alone any longer.

Shining Moon caught her breath and held it for a
long, timeless moment. She felt Clay shuddering with
the same intense culmination, and then his muscles relaxed so that his weight came down fully on her. Shin-

ing Moon did not care. She tightened her arms around him, holding him as close to her as any woman could ever hold her husband.

Then, with a sigh, he rolled to the side, pulling her with him so that they lay facing each other in the darkness, blankets tangled around them.

"I have missed you so much," Shining Moon whispered.

Clay kissed her forehead, then trailed kisses over her eyes, nose, lips, and chin. He nuzzled her throat and said, "I missed you, too. Staying in Washington so long was just about the hardest thing I've ever done."

Shining Moon stroked his head as he lowered his mouth to her breast. He closed his lips around the throbbing nipple and sucked gently on it. The fires of passion were spent for the moment, but this intimacy had a sweetness all its own.

It would have been so easy for Shining Moon to forget the look on Clay's face when she had asked him if they were going home. He had not answered, saying instead that they would talk about it after supper, after they'd had a chance to spend some time together. Fear had filled Shining Moon at that moment, ashamed though she would have been to admit it. A woman of the Teton Sioux was strong and accepted what fate brought to her.

She had accepted many things in her life, many evil things that she would have changed if she could. But she did not know if she could stand to have Clay leave her behind again.

Supper had been a mixture of happiness and worry: happiness that Clay was finally back, worry that he might not stay. And worry, as well, about Matthew, because the tension between him and Clay was almost palpable. Clay tried to draw the boy into conversation, but Matthew answered every question as curtly as possible. He was making it clear that he wanted nothing to do with Clay Holt.

"Don't reckon I've ever had better ham hocks and corn bread and greens," Clay told Shining Moon when they had finished the meal. "And that apple pie topped it off perfectly."

His praise, which would have been welcome any other time, meant little to her now. She managed to smile, but she was really wondering about the secret that lurked behind his eyes.

Castor and Pollux were more perceptive than one might have guessed from their hulking exteriors. After sharing supper with the Holts and Matthew, the Gilworths had headed for the barn—but not alone. "Matthew can stay with us tonight," Castor had said, and Pollux nodded in agreement.

"I don't want to sleep in some stinking old barn," Matthew had objected.

Pollux's huge hand closed firmly over the boy's shoulder. "You'll have a good time," he grated. He steered Matthew toward the doorway of the cabin.

"Don't worry," Castor said quietly to Shining Moon as soon as Pollux and Matthew were outside. "At least one of us will be awake all night. We'll keep an eye on the boy."

Clay seemed puzzled by Castor's assurance, and when he and Shining Moon were alone, he asked, "What did he mean by that? Are you afraid the Gilworths might let something happen to Matthew?"

Shining Moon had taken a deep breath and decided that if Clay could keep his secrets for the time being, so could she. "We will talk about it later," she said. "Right now, though you will think me bold, my husband, I want you to take me to bed."

Clay had smiled and done as she asked, and for a time both of them had set aside their concerns. But as the afterglow of lovemaking faded, Shining Moon, caressing Clay's head, said quietly, "You must tell me what you plan to do."

He chuckled. "Why, I figured I'd just reach right down here and—"

She caught his wrist and stopped his fingers before they could begin to give her pleasure. Now it was time to speak the truth.

"Tomorrow," she said. "What will you do tomorrow?"

His muscles had stiffened. Now he pulled away from her, sat up, and ran his fingers through his tangled black hair. "What do you mean?"

"You would not tell me when I asked if we were returning to my homeland. I think that means that we are not. You came to Marietta on a steamboat, you said. I know little of such vessels, but this I do know: If it can bring you, it can carry you away again."

He touched her bare shoulder with a warm hand. "Listen, Shining Moon, I wish I didn't have to tell you this—"

"But you do. You must tell me."

"All right," he said heavily. "Tomorrow morning, when the *New Orleans* pulls away from the dock at Marietta, I've got to be on board. I'm traveling down the Ohio to the Mississippi, maybe all the way to the city of New Orleans."

Shining Moon did not know whether to wail like a woman in mourning or lash out in anger. She controlled her emotions with an effort and asked, "Why?"

"Because the job that kept me in Washington for so long isn't over yet. I still have things to do."

"What things? Are they more important than your family?"

"Damn it! That's not fair. I didn't ask to get mixed up in all this . . ." He stopped for a moment, clearly trying to bring his own emotions under control. When he went on, his voice was steady. "Listen, this thing is bigger than me and you, Shining Moon. Something bad is happening, something that could hurt the whole country. It's up to me and a friend of mine to stop it."

"Why?" she asked.

"What?" The simplicity of the question obviously surprised him.

"Why is it up to you, Clay Holt? Cannot someone else save the country?"

He rasped a thumbnail along the bearded line of his jaw. "Hell, I never really thought about it that way before.'' Then he shook his head. ''But the answer's no. Maybe if somebody else had started the job, they could finish it without my help. But it's my job now, Shining Moon. The fellow I'm after may be responsible for the death of at least one man, one good man—my old captain, Meriwether Lewis. And now he's doing his damnedest to steal away half the country.'' He sighed. ''I might as well tell you the whole thing.''

She sat up, wrapping the blanket around her, and listened as he explained everything that had happened in Washington and on the first part of the voyage downriver on the *New Orleans*. Although she had trouble understanding everything he told her, she could hear the outrage in his voice as he talked about the land grab scheme hatched by the renegade senator.

''And you do not know which of these three men is to blame for this?'' she asked when he was finished.

''Nope,'' he said. ''Only that it has to be one of them. Lieutenant Markham, that army fellow I told you about, and I are trying to figure out which one.''

''So that is why you must continue to travel on the steamboat?''

He cupped her chin in his hand and gently caressed her cheek with his thumb. ''That's right. That's why I have to leave in the morning. I wish to God I could take you back to the mountains as I promised, but I can't do that until the job is finished.''

She took his hand in both of hers and kissed his palm. ''Now there are things I must tell you. You must know about Matthew and the things he has done.''

''Matthew? I was talking to the fellow who brought me out here, and he said some things that sounded plumb crazy.''

Shining Moon shook her head. ''They are not. With Matthew, many things are possible, things that in the beginning even I did not believe. . . .''

At first Clay figured he wasn't hearing her right. Shining Moon seemed to be accusing Matthew of killing old Cassie Doolittle and then trying to kill *her*.

"Morgan Holmes told me about Cassie," he said. He had gotten out of bed and lit a candle so that he could see Shining Moon's face as she told the story. "He said she was killed in an accident."

"An accident that Matthew may have caused."

Clay shook his head. "I can't figure that. Why would he do such a thing?"

"Because Cassie was my friend. That was enough to make Matthew hate her. And also because she did not trust him and warned me about him."

"And that business about you falling in the well?"

"It could have been a trap. Matthew may have lured me into the well, as a hunter lures an animal into a snare. I do not know." There was nothing but sincerity in her eyes as she looked at Clay. "But this I do know: When I was trapped there, he did not help me. He laughed and ran away and left me there to die."

Clay's jaw hardened. "The little . . . well, I started to call him a little bastard, but I reckon that's almost too good for him. He really is a bastard, but that's no excuse for what he's done."

"And I have not told you about the animals, or about what he did to Pollux."

Clay stood up, unable to contain the rage surging inside him, and paced back and forth across the room. "I never liked the boy, you know that," he said as he swung around. "I took him in and made an effort to care for him because you seemed to think it was something we ought to do. And hell, maybe I saw something in him, too, something I hoped we could get through to. Josie wasn't all bad, and Matthew's got her blood in him as well as Zach's." He rubbed his forehead. "But from what you're telling me, it sounds as if we'd all be better off if I just put a pistol ball through his head."

"No!" Shining Moon cried out. "He is a child."

"Well, under the right circumstances, a youngster can kill somebody just as dead as a full-grown man. Just ask poor old Cassie."

Shining Moon stood up, the blanket still wrapped

around her. "You speak the same kinds of words my brother did when I told him of these things."

"Proud Wolf?" Clay frowned. "Proud Wolf was here?"

"Yes. And he spoke to Matthew. Threatened him, I think. But Proud Wolf was wrong, too. Both of you are good men. You would not murder a child."

"What was Proud Wolf doing here?" asked Clay, ignoring for the moment what Shining Moon had just said.

Quickly, she told him about Professor Abner Hilliard and how he had taken Proud Wolf to a white man's school in the east. Clay shook his head in amazement. "I figured your brother was still back in the mountains with the rest of your people. I wonder how he's doing at that school."

"Proud Wolf does well at whatever he attempts."

Clay nodded. "I reckon he'll give it his best shot." His expression grew bleak. "But we still haven't figured out what to do about Matthew. I can't stay here to ride herd on him, not with this work I have to do, and I sure don't want to leave you alone with him again."

"There is an answer," said Shining Moon.

"You mean besides putting him out of his misery?"

She faced him squarely and said, "Take us with you."

Clay blinked in surprise. "On the *New Orleans*, you mean?"

"Yes. Matthew and I will travel with you on the steamboat. I am not needed here, you know that. Castor and Pollux are accustomed to taking care of the farm by themselves. And if we are with you, you can watch Matthew. Perhaps if we try one more time to teach him that he does not have to hate us . . ."

Clay's mind flashed back to the night in Wheeling, when someone had ambushed him and tried to kill him. Shining Moon might think she would be safer on the *New Orleans*, but that wasn't necessarily true.

"I don't know if that's a good idea," he said slowly. "The fellow that Markham and I are after, I reckon you could say he's after *us*, too. He's tried to have both of us killed."

Shining Moon looked intently at him. "You are in danger on this boat?"

"You could say that."

"Then that is all the more reason I should be with you. In the past, Clay Holt, we have faced danger many times together."

That was surely the truth, thought Clay. In more than one battle against their enemies, Shining Moon had held her own, striking with arrow and tomahawk and knife. Looking at her now, her long, unbound, raven's-wing hair gleaming in the candlelight, a fierce expression on her proud face as she stood straight and tall with the blanket wrapped around her, Clay felt a pang of intense emotion. It was a mixture of love and pride and worry, and he knew that she was right. They should not be parted again.

And for that matter, he told himself, having her along on the steamboat might come in handy. She would be one more pair of eyes and ears to help him and Markham in their assignment. For all he knew, she might be the one to uncover the identity of the traitor, and he couldn't think of a more appropriate conclusion to the job. The scoundrel was trying to get his hands on vast stretches of land that had once belonged solely to the Sioux and the other bands of Indians who roamed that part of the country. Who better to end his treacherous plot than someone whose homeland was threatened?

There was Matthew to consider, too. On the boat he might not have as many chances to get into mischief, Clay mused. Although "mischief" probably wasn't a strong enough word for what the boy had been doing . . .

"Do you not remember?" Shining Moon prompted him.

"I remember," Clay said quietly. "I surely do. And you're right. The two of you are coming with me. We'll try one more time with Matthew."

Shining Moon nodded solemnly. "Your decision is a good one. We will be ready to leave with you in the morning."

"That time's a ways off yet," Clay said as he reached for the blanket Shining Moon still had tucked around her. She let go of it, and it fell to the floor around her feet as she stepped forward to come into his embrace.

As his arms folded around her, Clay hoped fervently that his decision turned out to be the right one for all of them.

CHAPTER ELEVEN

Jeff fought down the impulse to yank his pistol from his belt and fire at the Russian soldiers. One shot would have little effect on the forces arrayed against him, and a volley from the soldiers' muskets would rip him and his companions to shreds. So far, none of the Russians had fired.

With his hands in the air, Jeff decided to try again. "We mean you no harm," he said slowly and distinctly. It was unlikely that the Russians spoke English, but perhaps one or two of them would understand that the visitors had come in peace and would spread the word to the other soldiers. "We are here on a mission of trade, and we would like to speak to someone in charge from the Russian-American Company."

None of the soldiers moved. Their muskets continued to point unwaveringly at Jeff and the other Americans.

"It appears that none of them understand what

you're saying, Mr. Holt," Vickery said nervously. "Either that or they simply don't care."

"Maybe we should try getting back in the boat," Jeff suggested. "If they don't want us here, they might let us sail away without trying to stop us."

As he spoke, he glanced back toward the *Beaumont*, riding steadily at anchor in the bay. Melissa had no doubt witnessed what was happening on the dock, and she was probably terrified that the Russians were going to kill him. *To tell the truth*, Jeff thought, *I can't say I'm not worried about that possibility myself.*

Before he could decide what to do, the ranks of fur-capped men suddenly parted, and a slender man of medium height stepped through the gap. Like the soldiers he sported a black fur cap and high black boots, but instead of a red uniform jacket he wore a long coat with a fur-lined collar that was turned up around his lean, angular face. As he strode confidently along the dock toward Jeff and Vickery, he spoke a curt command in Russian, and much to the relief of Jeff and the others, the soldiers lowered their muskets to their sides.

The newcomer stopped in front of Jeff and Vickery and gave them a thin smile. "Gentlemen," he said in English, "I apologize for the rude greeting my men have given you. Welcome to Sitka, the . . . jewel . . . of Russian America. I am Count Gregori Orlov, provisional head of the Russian-American Company."

Orlov extended his gloved hand, and Jeff and Vickery both shook with him. "I'm Jefferson Holt," Jeff said, "and this is Captain Niles Vickery of the ship *Beaumont*." Jeff waved a hand toward the vessel riding at anchor. With a smile, he went on, "I don't mind telling you, sir, I'm glad you got here when you did. I was about to decide we had broken a Russian law by coming ashore."

"You did," Orlov said casually. "My men would have been well within their rights to shoot you and blow your ship out of the water."

Vickery bristled. "Now, hold on a minute—"

Jeff stopped him with a gesture, then said to Orlov, "Then I appreciate your intervention that much more, Count. I assure you, we mean you and your people no harm."

"I would hardly deem one lone ship to be the vanguard of an American invasion." Orlov turned and, without looking back at Jeff and Vickery, went on, "Come with me, gentlemen. Your companions will stay here, under guard."

Vickery looked as if he was about to argue, but Jeff put a hand on his arm and nodded meaningfully. They had no choice but to follow Orlov and hope that he had nothing sinister planned for them.

Reluctantly, Vickery told the sailors to remain in the boat. Jeff turned toward the *Beaumont* and gave what he hoped was a reassuring wave, so that Melissa wouldn't worry too much while he was gone. Then he and Vickery fell in step behind Count Orlov. Four or five of the Russian soldiers remained on the dock to guard the crewmen from the *Beaumont*. The others surrounded Jeff and Vickery and marched along with them.

Orlov led the way to a sizable log building with a simple porch facing the road. Smoke rose from the stone chimney at one end of the building. Furs were piled in stacks on the porch, and broad-faced men with dark hair—Indians, Jeff judged—were tying them into bundles. Two soldiers armed with muskets stood nearby, watching them closely.

Orlov walked up the steps to the porch and pulled the latch string on a door made from a single thick slab of wood. Jeff and Vickery followed him in. Another red-coated soldier, waiting inside, closed the door behind Vickery.

Orlov spoke to the man in rapid Russian. The man nodded, clicked his bootheels together, and hurried out of the room through another door. Orlov took off his cap and tossed it on a desk, then turned toward Jeff and Vickery as he pulled off his gloves.

"Please, gentlemen, make yourselves comfortable.

I have commanded my aide, Piotr, to have more wood brought for the fire. I believe you thin-blooded Americans are more susceptible to the cold than are we Russians."

Jeff saw Vickery frown at the veiled insult. He wasn't feeling very friendly toward Orlov either, but for the sake of the venture that had brought them here he was going to be as accommodating as he could. He smiled and said, "I spent a winter on the upper Missouri River once. It was pretty cold, but I don't recall my blood getting too thin."

"You have not lived through a Siberian winter, my friend." Orlov dropped the gloves on the desk next to his cap, then took off his long coat, revealing tight black trousers like the soldiers' and a fringed buckskin jacket. He pulled back a heavy chair behind the desk and gestured toward a leather divan in front of it. "Please, sit down."

Jeff and Vickery did so, and Jeff took advantage of the opportunity to glance around the room. It was big, drafty, high-ceilinged, and chilly despite the blaze in the fireplace. The windows were hung with heavy drapes, and mounted on the walls between them were several sets of antlers from moose, elk, and antelope. Somebody was proud of the trophies he had taken, no doubt Orlov himself. This was clearly the count's office and, as such, the headquarters of the Russian-American Company.

The interior door opened, and Piotr reappeared, carrying a tray with a bottle and three glasses. He set it on the desk and poured a splash of clear liquid into each glass. An Indian servant followed him in with an armload of firewood and, kneeling in front of the fireplace, fed the flames.

Piotr handed glasses to Jeff and Vickery. Count Orlov picked up his glass and said, "To your health, gentlemen." He threw back his drink in one quick swallow.

Jeff and Vickery followed suit, and Jeff almost gagged on the fiery liquor. He could feel the blood draining from his face. Beside him, Vickery made a choking sound, and his face turned an even ruddier shade than usual.

Amusement glittered in Orlov's eyes. "Russian vodka, gentlemen. Excellent, is it not?"

Jeff managed to nod as he blinked back tears. "Excellent," he said hoarsely. He'd had whiskey just as potent, but it had been a while.

Orlov set his empty glass on the desk. "Now, then, to the matter at hand. What brings you to Alaska, Mr. Holt?"

Jeff cleared his throat, then came right to the point. "I reckon you have a pretty good idea already, Count. We've come to seek a trade agreement."

Orlov was shaking his head before the words were out of Jeff's mouth. "Impossible," he said. "The Russian-American Company has an exclusive charter from the government in St. Petersburg. Only the company is allowed to trade in Alaska or Alaskan waters." Another thin smile curved his lips. "There is a reason this land is also called Russian America, Mr. Holt."

"I'm well aware that your government claims dominion over this area," Jeff said, "but I don't see how that would prevent you from trading with an American company."

"It would compromise our sovereignty."

"How? We have no connection with the American government. We represent the Holt-Merrivale Company, and that's all."

The count leaned back in his chair and steepled his fingers. "If I may be so bold . . . you know nothing of the Russian mind or the Russian soul, Mr. Holt. This is *our* land. We will not share it, or its bounty, with anyone who is not Russian."

A feeling of despair washed over Jeff. Had he come this far, spent all those weeks at sea, only to run into a stone wall? Had he wasted not only his time but that of his family as well?

He was careful not to let his frustration show on his face as he said, "We're not trying to take anything away from you or your countrymen. All we want is to make it possible for the Russian-American Company to reap even greater profits."

"And how would you do that?"

Jeff didn't like the idea of exposing his hole card so soon in the game, but no other play was left open to him. "By establishing a three-cornered trade between Alaska, China, and the Hawaiian Islands."

Orlov's eyes narrowed in thought. After a moment he said, "That is quite an interesting idea. But we have ships as well. What would prevent the company from establishing such a trade route on its own?"

"By now," Jeff said boldly, "my personal representative has already negotiated exclusive trade agreements with both the Chinese and the islanders."

And I surely hope, he added silently to himself, *that you haven't let me down, Ned, old son.*

"It's a bloody paradise," Ned said as the *Lydia Marie* rocked gently at anchor in the harbor, a short distance off the beach of shining white sand.

India, standing beside him, looked out across the water. "Yes," she breathed, "this is a spectacular corner of the world."

Indeed it was. The waters of the bay were a clear, sparkling blue-green. To the east, as if standing guard over the bay, a steep rugged ridge curved out into the sea. The beach was bordered by tall palm trees whose fronds waved gently in the breeze. Beyond the beach, green hills rolled away inland for a short distance before the terrain rose precipitously into towering emerald mountains.

"That's Diamond Head," India said, pointing to the peninsula. "It's a volcanic crater. There's another crater to the west of the settlement—you can see it there in the distance—called Puu-o-waina. It means Hill of Sacrifice."

"I'm not sure I care for the sound of that," Ned said with a grin.

"King Kamehameha has preserved the old Hawaiian religion, but I don't think they actually make human sacrifices anymore. So you can stop worrying." India pointed at the line of mountains in the distance. "Those mountains were formed by volcanoes, too. The islanders believe that sleeping giants live there, and from time to time they wake up and become angry and shout and spit fire from their mouths."

Ned laughed. "Doesn't sound like anything I'd want to see."

"I heard stories, when I visited these islands before, of terrible eruptions that shook the earth and rained molten rock from the skies and wiped out entire villages."

Ned gave her a sidelong glance. "It doesn't do that very often, does it?"

"No . . . but when it does, there's usually little warning."

Ned shook his head. "Molten rain in the middle of paradise . . ."

"There's always a price to pay for beauty of any kind."

"I suppose you're right." Ned cast a wary glance toward the rocky slopes. "I just hope those giants stay asleep while we're here."

The voyage from South America to the Hawaiian Islands had been relatively uneventful, other than the series of accidents that had nearly taken Ned's life. But those mishaps had ended as abruptly as they began, and he was leaning toward the belief that they had been genuine accidents rather than attempts on his life. Donnelly had kept his distance and had not threatened either Ned or India, and Ned hoped that the trouble with him was over. It still made him nervous that Donnelly knew India's secret, but there was nothing he could do about it.

Captain Canfield ordered a small boat put over the side, and Ned and India saw to it that they were among the crew members selected to go ashore with the first landing party. Though Ned did his job as a common sailor, the captain was well aware of his status on this voyage as a representative of the Holt-Merrivale Company.

"The town is called Honolulu," India told Ned as the boat was rowed toward the beach. "Kamehameha has made it his capital since he unified the islands several years ago and established the Kingdom of Hawaii."

"You know a lot about this place," commented Ned.

India nodded. "I wouldn't mind living here, if the time ever comes when I've had my fill of going to sea."

There were certainly worse places to live, Ned thought. The weather here would be warm the year round, and India claimed that the natives were friendly. Ned could imagine spending his declining years here with her.

But before that time came, there were more adventures waiting and other lands to be explored. Ned was a long way from being ready to settle down, even in a paradise such as this.

Next to Boston or New York or even Ned's hometown of Pittsburgh, Honolulu was a village. Nor was it bustling with activity. People here seemed to move at their own leisurely pace, Ned saw as the boat came ashore. A fleet of fishing boats was pulled up on the beach, and men wearing only broad bands of colorful cloth wrapped around their hips sat on the overturned boats mending fishing nets. Children ran and played on the sand, watched over by women wearing the same abbreviated clothing as the men. The women's breasts were bare.

Ned leaned over to India and hissed, "You could have warned me."

"About the minimal clothing?" She grinned. "I thought it would be more entertaining to watch you gaping at the women."

"I don't gape," Ned said stiffly.

India chuckled, clearly enjoying his embarrassment.

Captain Canfield detailed several of the sailors to remain on the beach and watch over the boat while he, Ned, India, and the rest of the landing party went to the residence of King Kamehameha.

As they walked through the hard-packed dirt streets of Honolulu, Ned saw more bare-breasted women, but other natives were wearing European clothing. The group passed a market, and as Ned stared at the unfamiliar fruit piled in colorful mounds on the ground, India named them: breadfruit, papaya, mangoes, passion fruit. One grinning Hawaiian tried to hand Ned a coconut-shell bowl full of thick yellow paste. The man dipped his fingers into the stuff and pantomimed lifting it to his mouth, then made smacking sounds with his lips.

"What the devil is that?" Ned asked India. "It looks like something you'd use to patch a leaky hull."

"They call it *poi*," she replied. "It's one of their staple foods, made from the roots of the taro plant."

Ned shook his head at the Hawaiian, who was hurrying alongside him, trying to keep up with the long strides of the Americans. "Maybe I'll try it later," he said to India, "after we've talked to the king."

When they reached King Kamehameha's home a few minutes later, instead of the gaudy palace he had imagined, Ned found that the leader of this island nation lived in a relatively modest but stately house with a bamboo-roofed porch. Flowers in a profusion of colors and shapes grew wild on the grounds, on shrubs and tall bushes and vines. Ned watched in fascination as tiny, iridescent hummingbirds darted among them.

A man Ned took to be Kamehameha himself sat in an ornate bamboo chair on the porch, and he raised a hand in greeting as the Americans approached. He was a stocky, middle-aged man with close-cropped white hair and rugged features. Something about him reminded Ned of the ancient volcanoes that had formed the islands. The fires in Kamehameha might be dormant now, but Ned suspected that under the right circumstances they could erupt and wreak as much destruction as any volcano.

"Welcome," the king greeted them serenely. He did not seem surprised to see American visitors.

"King Kamehameha," Captain Canfield began, "you may not remember me, but my ships have made port here before."

"Captain Canfield," Kamehameha said with a nod. "Certainly I remember you, my old friend. Why have you come to see me today?"

Canfield held out a hand toward Ned. "To introduce you to a new friend. This is Ned Holt, a representative from the Holt-Merrivale Company in America."

Another solemn nod from the king. "Mr. Holt. How may I assist you, young man?"

Ned hesitated, unsure whether he ought to offer to shake hands with the king or not. He decided not to, since Canfield had not. "I've come to speak to you about a trade agreement, Your Majesty."

Kamehameha shrugged shoulders that were still muscular and powerful despite his age. "Many ships come to our islands to trade. We welcome them all, so long as they come in peace."

"Yes, but my company is interested in an agreement that would be more . . . exclusive in nature. We would like to work closely with your government to establish such a relationship."

"Ah." The king nodded. "I see."

Ned glanced at India and saw the warning in her eyes. He had to be careful about what he said. He hated being in this position. Negotiating was utterly foreign to him, and he had agreed to be Jeff's representative only because Jeff had asked him to. Ned couldn't refuse his cousin.

Canfield stepped in. "Perhaps I can be of assistance here, since I represent Mr. Lemuel March of the March Shipping Lines, a close associate of the Holt-Merrivale Company."

"I will listen to you also, Captain Canfield," said Kamehameha, "but only after we have dined."

Ned couldn't stop himself from grinning. "You mean I'm going to have dinner with a king? I never expected that."

Canfield glanced sharply at him, as if he had spoken too bluntly, but Ned didn't care.

Kamehameha returned Ned's broad grin. "I will have food brought, and a drink we brew that is much like your beer."

"Now you're talking, King." Ned gave in to impulse and stuck out his hand. "Put 'er there."

Canfield rolled his eyes in dismay, and even India looked aghast.

But after a moment, Kamehameha reached up to shake Ned's hand with a firm, powerful grip.

Melissa was waiting on the deck of the *Beaumont* when Jeff scrambled back up the rope ladder from the small boat and over the side. She caught hold of his arms and asked anxiously, "Are you all right? My God, I thought I would die when I saw all those soldiers point their guns at you!"

"I figured I might die, too, right about then," Jeff said dryly.

"You know what I mean," Melissa said severely. But she threw her arms around him and buried her face in his chest.

Jeff hugged her tightly. "I know, and I'm sorry. I didn't mean to make light of it. I really was worried, but more about you and Michael than about myself."

Melissa looked up at him. "What happened? I saw those men marching you and Captain Vickery away, and I thought you had been taken prisoner."

"Well, it probably came pretty close to that." With an arm around her shoulders, Jeff led her toward the stern. "The Russians don't take kindly to foreigners visiting these parts. It seems they're afraid we'll take some of their trade away from them."

"But that's not right," Melissa said. "We want to increase their trade."

"That's what I told Count Orlov."

"Count Orlov?"

"The man who's in charge of the Russian-American Company. They have an exclusive charter from the Russian government to handle all the trading in this area. The manager, Alexander Baranof, has been recalled to St. Petersburg by the czar, and Count Orlov has replaced him for the time being. You'll meet him tonight."

"Tonight?"

"We've been invited to dinner with the count and his wife."

"Dinner?" repeated Melissa, a note of dismay in her voice. "But we just got here. I'm not ready for any sort of— Did you say wife? This Count Orlov brought his wife here to the wilderness?"

"You're here, aren't you?" Jeff pointed out. "At least the count and his wife don't have any children. None that he mentioned, anyway." He glanced around. "By the way, where is Michael?"

"I sent him below while those soldiers were pointing their guns at you," Melissa replied. "I don't think he understood what was going on, but just in case, I didn't want him to see his father killed right before his eyes."

Jeff squeezed her shoulder. "That's good. Perhaps he should stay on board tonight instead of coming to dinner with us."

Melissa looked at him intently. "Do you think there might be trouble? A trap of some kind?"

"If Count Orlov wanted to kill the captain and me, he had plenty of chances," Jeff said. "But until I'm sure of what's going to happen, I want to know that Michael is somewhere safe."

"I agree, but he probably won't be so easy to convince." Melissa paused, then added, "What about this Count Orlov? Will he listen to reason?"

"I don't know. He seems fairly rigid to me. According to him, the Russians have done a little trading with Americans in the past, mostly with single ships that came up here looking for furs, and they've always ended up losing in the bargain. That's one reason the czar called Baranof back to St. Petersburg, so that he could make it clear he doesn't want anybody trading in these parts except the Russian-American Company. Orlov is a nobleman who's in the czar's favor right now, so he got the job of managing the company while Baranof is gone."

Melissa's natural business instincts were working again, now that Jeff was safely back on the ship. "Does Count Orlov have the power to make a contract?" she asked.

"I suppose so. It sounds as if the czar has put him in charge of everything."

"Then if we could get his signature on an agreement before this Baranof gets back . . ." Melissa mused.

"But Orlov's even more opposed to trading with Americans than Baranof was."

"People can change their minds, can't they?" Melissa caught hold of Jeff's hands. "I have confidence in you, darling. And I'll do everything I can to help."

"Just be your usual beautiful, charming self tonight. Maybe the count won't be able to turn you down." Jeff shrugged. "Although he doesn't seem the type of man to be swayed by a woman, no matter how lovely she is."

Melissa kissed him lightly. "Did you meet the countess?"

Jeff shook his head. "All I know is her name, because the count mentioned it: Irina."

"Irina," repeated Melissa. "What a beautiful name. I didn't expect to find another white woman here. I hope we can be friends."

"Don't see any reason why you can't be. After all, you've got something in common with her."

"What's that?"

Jeff chuckled. "Both of you have husbands who have dragged you halfway around the world."

"Not really. You've forgotten that it was my idea to come along on this journey," Melissa reminded him.

But halfway around the world was just about right, she thought. Half a world away from Philip Ratti-gan . . .

CHAPTER
TWELVE

C lay was up at dawn. He stepped out on the
cabin porch, took a deep breath of clean, crisp
air, and looked around at the familiar landscape
of his youth. The Rockies were his home now, but the
farm his parents had carved out of the wilderness
would always have a special place in his heart.

The big double doors of the barn were open, and a
lantern was burning inside. The Gilworth brothers
were already up and about, getting on with their
chores. Clay walked briskly toward the barn. As he
approached, he saw Matthew inside, carrying a bucket
overflowing with rich, foamy milk freshly coaxed from
a cow's udders.

"Morning," he said to the boy. "Sleep well?"

Matthew didn't look up at him but only grunted
and said, "What business is it of yours?"

"Just trying to be friendly," Clay said coolly.

"I never asked you to be my friend."

"No, that's true enough, I reckon. We sort of got

thrown together, didn't we? Whether we wanted it or not."

Matthew paused and glanced up at Clay. "Are you saying you didn't want me to live with you and your squaw?"

"She's my wife, not my squaw. And she's the one who wanted you, not me." The words were harsh but true, and at this point Clay saw no reason to lie to the boy. "And how did you pay her back? By killing her friend and trying to kill Shining Moon herself."

"That's a damned lie!" Matthew burst out.

"Don't cuss. You're too little to be talking like that."

"I'll talk any way I want. And I didn't kill no-body!"

"That's not the way I heard it," Clay drawled.

"She lied!" Matthew said angrily. Some of the milk slopped out of the bucket. "I didn't do anything to that old woman. And I didn't make Shining Moon fall in that well!"

"Knew just what I was talking about, didn't you?" Clay reached down for the bucket. "Give me that. You're going to spill all of it in a minute."

"Here! Take it!" Matthew slung the bucket at Clay's feet, splashing milk all over his boots.

Matthew spun around and started to dart away, but Clay was too fast for him. His hand shot out and closed over Matthew's collar, and he jerked the boy toward him. Matthew's feet came off the ground for an instant as Clay turned him around and pulled him up by the front of his shirt.

"That's the end of it, you understand?" Clay grated. "Castor! Pollux!"

The Gilworth brothers came hurrying out of a stall at the rear of the barn but stopped abruptly when they saw Matthew and Clay.

"One of you cut me a switch," Clay said.

"No!" howled Matthew. "You can't whip me!"

"Just you wait and see." Clay looked at Castor and

Pollux, who shifted uneasily under his glare. "I said for one of you to cut me a switch."

"This ain't really any of our business, Clay," Pollux said hesitantly, "but are you sure you want to do this?"

Castor added, "I know what the Good Book says about sparin' the rod and spoilin' the child, but—"

"Blast it," Clay snapped. "Are you going to cut me a switch or—"

"No," Shining Moon said from the doorway behind Clay. "They will not."

Clay looked over his shoulder at her. "You stay in the cabin—"

"No." Shining Moon came several steps into the barn. "This is my place. I am the one Matthew hates."

"I hate *all* of you!" Matthew snarled.

"Among my people, children are never beaten or whipped," Shining Moon said, ignoring Matthew's outburst. "We must make Matthew understand—"

"He'll never understand anything clearer than a switch across his rear end. That's likely the only thing that'll ever get through to him." Clay held the kicking, twisting boy easily as he spoke.

"Have you told him that we are going with you on the boat?"

Matthew abruptly ceased struggling. "A boat?" he said. "We're going on a boat?"

Still glaring, Clay set him down roughly. "That's right. The three of us are going on the steamboat that brought me to Marietta, maybe all the way to New Orleans."

Matthew's eyes widened. "I've never been on a big boat," he said excitedly. "My mama and I rode on a flatboat and in a canoe when we went to the mountains."

"That's right," Clay said slowly, surprised by Matthew's swift change in attitude. Under all the surliness he was still a little boy, he realized. "The boat I'm talking about is a lot bigger than a canoe or a flatboat. It's got wheels on the side that are turned by a steam engine, and that's what makes it go."

"I want to see it."

"You will."

Matthew looked down at the ground and dug the toe of his shoe into the dirt. "I'm sorry," he said, almost inaudibly.

"What?" Clay wasn't sure he'd heard correctly.

"I said I'm sorry. About dumping the milk on your boots. I shouldn't have done that."

Clay frowned. He had never seen Matthew contrite before, and he didn't know if he could trust the evidence of his own eyes and ears. Could the news of their upcoming journey on the *New Orleans* have had that great an effect on the boy?

Evidently it had, because Matthew went on, "I'll try to behave myself and not cause any more trouble."

Castor and Pollux looked as stunned as Clay felt. Castor asked Clay, "When are you leaving?"

"This morning. The boat will be pulling out at nine o'clock."

"We must prepare," said Shining Moon. "Matthew, will you help me pack our belongings?" She held out a hand toward the boy.

Holding his breath, Clay waited to see if Matthew would spit in her hand or knock it aside. But Matthew reached up and took it, and together they walked out of the barn and toward the cabin.

Pollux blew out his breath in a long sigh. "Well, if that don't beat all."

"Never thought I'd see that boy acting like a normal youngster," added Castor. He looked at Clay and went on, "If I was you, I'd be mighty careful while I was traveling downriver with him."

Clay could not tell them that he was already being careful, that his life and those of his family and Lieutenant Markham would continue to be in danger until the man he was after was brought to justice.

Instead he said, "I intend to be. I can promise you that. I surely intend to be careful."

• • •

More than anything else, they had to be careful. Proud Wolf had tried to impress that fact on Audrey, and he thought she understood, but deep down he was afraid that she did not. She was confident that no matter what she did, her father would forgive her.

Proud Wolf did not share her confidence. He was certain that if Jeremiah Stoddard knew his daughter and the young Sioux warrior were lovers, at the very least Proud Wolf would be banished from the academy and perhaps jailed.

Or Stoddard might just kill him.

The wisest course of action would be to tell Audrey that they could never see each other again, let alone be lovers. Proud Wolf knew that. So why was he slipping through the shadows again, on his way to yet another rendezvous with Audrey?

He had found the note from her under the door of his room earlier in the day. In her delicate script she had asked him to meet her behind the kitchen after dark. The kitchen was separate from the main building, and Proud Wolf knew that no one would be there after dinner had been served. They had met there often.

But not since their first night together, in his room, had they made love. Although they had found corners of the academy where they could be alone, none was appropriate for that kind of intimacy. But at least he could take Audrey in his arms and kiss her. He could stroke her hair and feel her warmth in his embrace and taste the hot sweetness of her mouth. For now, that had to be enough . . . though Proud Wolf suspected that neither of them was truly satisfied.

He had climbed down the tree outside his window again tonight. He had used that route so often that it was beginning to seem like one of the trails of his homeland, so familiar that he could have followed it with his eyes closed. Then he had silently crossed the grounds, keeping to the shadows.

When he reached the kitchen, he stole behind the squat, square stone building. Audrey was supposed to be here first, so he hissed her name into the darkness. Her whisper came back to him: "I'm here, my love."

Then she was in his arms, and her mouth instinctively found his. Her lips parted, and her tongue slid boldly between his. Proud Wolf tightened his embrace around her, feeling the soft cushion of her breasts as they pressed against his chest. He slid one hand down to the gently flaring curve of her hips and pressed her intimately against him. As she kissed him, Audrey made a low, moaning sound deep in her throat.

Yes, thought Proud Wolf, somehow they had to get away.

When she finally took her lips away from his, she whispered, "I've missed you so much."

"And I have missed you."

"I can't believe I wasted so much time being angry with you. Now I think about you all the time, and when I'm not with you, I ache so badly inside I can hardly bear it."

"I want you," Proud Wolf said.

"Tell me how much."

He took a deep breath. "As much as all the rivers that flow. My love for you is as tall as the mountains of my homeland and as wide as the sky. My love is as endless as the plains, as wild as the storms in the spring, as gentle as the snow that falls in the winter, as warm as the summer sun."

"Oh, Proud Wolf, you say such beautiful things," Audrey said.

"It is one of the legacies of my people. A warrior must know how to speak as well as how to fight."

She rested her head against his shoulder. "I love you, Proud Wolf."

His senses were full of her: the smell of her hair, the warmth of her skin, the sound of her soft, regular breathing . . . He thought he could even hear her heart beating.

What he did not hear until it was too late was the stealthy footsteps behind him.

Then something crashed down on his head, and a blackness darker than any night engulfed him.

Proud Wolf did not know how long he had been unconscious. All he knew was that feeling was beginning to seep back into his body. And that feeling was mostly pain.

His head throbbed savagely. In the weeks since the beating he had endured in Boston at the hands of Frank and the other students, he had been plagued with headaches, but nothing as bad as this. The agony was so intense that he felt his stomach clenching in response to it, and he wanted to retch. He forced down the impulse. His instincts told him to remain as still and quiet as possible until he figured out what was going on.

Then he heard Audrey's voice, shrill and frightened. "Stop it! Why can't you just leave us alone?"

"Because I'll be damned if I'm going to let some girl who thinks she's too good for me rut with an Indian buck instead."

It was Will Brackett, Proud Wolf realized. Audrey must not have been as successful as she had thought at keeping these rendezvous secret. Will had followed her, and now he was intent on taking his revenge yet again. It was not enough that he had masterminded the earlier beating. Now Audrey was in danger, too.

"Just let me go, and I won't tell my father about this," Audrey said shakily.

Another voice. "You're not going anywhere. Not until Will says so."

Frank Kirkland. Of course. Will never got his own hands dirty. It had probably been Frank who had slipped up behind Proud Wolf and knocked him out.

"Proud Wolf needs help," pleaded Audrey. "You . . . you might have killed him by hitting him so hard, Frank."

"He's not dead," Frank said scornfully. "Although I don't see what it would matter if he was. What's one

Indian more or less? There are millions of them out west, I hear."

"And that's where this one should have stayed," added Will.

With an obvious effort Audrey made her voice stronger. "You'd better get out of here while you still have the chance, both of you. I'm going to tell my father what you've done, and he'll expel you from the academy. He may even call the constable."

"Let him," Will said easily. "I'll just tell everyone that you let that savage have his way with you. That's against the law. Proud Wolf will hang."

"No," Audrey whispered.

"Then stop fighting us and do as I told you." Will chuckled. "It won't be so bad. You wanted it when I was courting you—you just wouldn't admit it, even to yourself. That's why you kept putting me off."

Proud Wolf heard Audrey gasp. "Oh, God, Will! Do you have to be so rough? And Frank . . . Frank's standing right there . . ."

"He might as well watch," Will said. "He's going to have you next, when I'm done with you."

Audrey sobbed.

Proud Wolf forgot the pain in his head, forgot everything but the hatred he felt for Will and Frank and the danger Audrey was in. He forced his eyes open and willed himself to get up.

Nothing. His muscles would not respond.

His lips drew back from his teeth in a grimace that had nothing to do with physical pain. Mere yards away, Audrey was about to be assaulted, and Proud Wolf's own body had betrayed him. It refused to obey him, refused to go to Audrey's aid. Were his treacherous muscles going to force him to lie helpless and witness an attack against the woman he loved?

Suddenly, over the sound of Audrey's wretched sobs and the harsh, anticipatory breathing of Will and Frank, Proud Wolf heard a low, deep humming. A moment went by before he realized that it sounded like the purring of a huge cat.

Then a snarling growl ripped through the night.

Frank Kirkland spun around and exclaimed,
"What the hell was that?"

Proud Wolf felt himself moving, but he was not
responsible for what was happening. It was as if some
other presence had filled his body and given him
strength. His night vision, already naturally sharp, became even keener, and he saw the three figures nearby:
Frank, standing in a frightened half-crouch; Will, kneeling close by with a startled look on his face; and Audrey, lying where she had been forced to the ground,
her long skirt in a tangle around her legs. Proud Wolf
saw all of that . . . and then he leaped.

For a tiny fraction of time, as he lunged at Frank,
he saw reflected in the young man's eyes what Frank
himself was seeing: Proud Wolf's slender figure surrounded by a ghostly, wraithlike form, the form of a
huge mountain lion as white as newly fallen snow. The
spirit cat . . .

Proud Wolf struck, his fist crashing into Frank's
jaw and knocking him backward. Will screamed and
tried to throw himself out of the way as Proud Wolf
lunged again. He was too slow, and a slashing blow of
preternatural strength slammed into him and sent him
tumbling over the ground. Proud Wolf pursued him,
pouncing like the great cat that was his talisman. Frantically Will kicked out, catching Proud Wolf in the
chest. Proud Wolf was thrown to the side, but he was
slowed for only an instant. Then he was attacking
again.

He landed atop Will Brackett and locked his hands
around the young man's throat. Will made faint gur-
gling noises as Proud Wolf's fingers tightened. Proud
Wolf lifted him by the neck, slammed his head down
against the ground, then again and again, all the while
choking the life out of him.

Frank came in from the side, launching himself in a
desperate, diving tackle. He crashed into Proud Wolf
and knocked him off Will. Both men lay sprawled on
the ground. Frank clubbed his hands together and

swung his arms as Proud Wolf tried to scramble up. The blow landed solidly and knocked Proud Wolf down again, but he barely felt it. As Frank loomed over him, preparing to strike again, Proud Wolf grabbed his shirt and planted a foot in his belly. A strong heave sent Frank flying over him, out of control. Frank had time to yelp once before he crashed to the ground.

Will was coughing and clutching at his bruised throat as he writhed in pain. He gasped for air and said raggedly, "Oh, God! Oh, God!"

His prayers, if that was what they were, were not answered. Proud Wolf walked over to him, leaned down, and caught hold of his shirt with his left hand. He pulled Will up easily and struck him with his right hand, again and again, jerking the young man's head back and forth. Proud Wolf had no idea how long he stood there, beating Will Brackett; his brain had retreated into a primitive state ruled by rage, and it had nothing to do with his Sioux heritage. At this moment he was no longer Indian or white or any other race but human. He was nothing more than a man, pushed too far, fighting back against his tormentors.

He did not cease until Audrey grabbed his arm, crying and begging him to stop. Her pleas finally penetrated the savage, atavistic rage that had gripped him. He paused, arm uplifted, poised for another blow. Through a red haze he saw that Will's head was lolling loosely on his neck, saw the blood, dark in the faint starlight, that covered Will's face. He let go of Will's shirt. Will fell limply to the ground and did not move.

"Y-you've killed him!"

Audrey's anguished words stabbed deep into Proud Wolf's soul. He turned to her and asked, "You are sorry?"

For a moment she stared at him in stunned silence, and Proud Wolf filled that moment with terrible thoughts of how he had been used. Audrey had never really loved him, he told himself. She had merely taken advantage of his attraction to her to make Will jealous, and that plan had backfired when Will believed she really cared for Proud Wolf.

Then she said, "Of course I didn't want you to kill him! I love you, Proud Wolf! What's going to happen to us now?"

"*I love you.*" That was what she had said. It was all Proud Wolf could hear at this moment, echoing inside his head. She really did love him. She had tried to stop him from killing Will Brackett because she was afraid it would mean their separation.

Frank Kirkland groaned as consciousness returned.

Proud Wolf's thoughts were suddenly as icy and crystal clear as the winter night. He took Audrey's arm and said, "We must leave this place."

"What? Leave? I . . . I don't understand . . ."

"We cannot stay here, not after what has happened tonight."

"But my father . . . my mother . . . I can't just—"

He put his hands on her shoulders. "They will come for me, and they will try to hang me for what I have done. I will not let them do this. I will sing my death song and fight them as long as life remains in my body, and more will die." He took a deep, ragged breath. "Unless I run. Unless I leave now, with only what I have at this moment. Audrey . . . I should not ask this of you . . . but if you truly love me . . . will you come with me?"

She looked around wildly. Will still lay motionless at her feet, but a few yards away Frank was stirring listlessly. Others were probably on their way, alerted by the commotion. Her gaze fastened on Proud Wolf, and even in the dim light he could see understanding dawning in her eyes.

"I do love you," she said. "And I'll come with you."

"Then we must go now, taking nothing with us."

She nodded, and he thought she was standing taller and straighter now. "Yes. I won't even go back for my things." She reached up and grasped his right hand with both of hers. "Let's go. Now."

With a sense that he was embarking on an even more hazardous journey than the one that had brought him east from his homeland, he turned and slipped into the shadows with Audrey beside him.

In a matter of seconds they were gone, vanished into the night. Somewhere far away, a great cat screeched. The cry echoed once and faded.

"Just lie still, son. You'll be all right. I've sent for a physician."

Will Brackett came swimming up out of the darkness. Light struck his eyes, painful as a physical blow, and he winced.

"Who did this? Who's responsible for this, damn it?"

The voice that had spoken so calmly at first was now angry and demanding. It belonged to Jeremiah Stoddard. The strong hands under his head and shoulders were probably Stoddard's, too. Will blinked rapidly as his eyes grew accustomed to the light from a lantern held by another student. The young man was one of a group of a dozen or more clustered around Will and Stoddard.

Someone groaned. Frank Kirkland was standing behind Stoddard, rubbing his forehead. A pair of dark bruises adorned his face, along with several cuts and scrapes. "It was Proud Wolf," Frank said in answer to Stoddard's question. "It was that savage."

"Damn him!" exclaimed Stoddard. "I knew it was a mistake to bring him here. I should have told Hilliard what an old fool he was even to entertain such an insane notion! You can't take a . . . a wild animal like that out of the wilderness and expect him to act like a civilized man."

"I'm . . . sorry," Will whispered through bruised, swollen lips. "I tried to . . . stop him. But he got . . . away . . . took Audrey . . . ."

Even in his condition Will was thinking furiously of how best to turn this situation to his advantage.

"What?" Stoddard asked urgently. He leaned closer to Will. "What did you say about Audrey?"

"He . . . kidnapped her," Will said. "Frank and I . . . we tried to stop him . . . didn't we, Frank?"

"Yes, that . . . that's right, Mr. Stoddard." Frank gulped audibly at Will's brazen lie.

"I'll have the law after him!" Stoddard raged. "And if he's harmed one hair on Audrey's head—if he's so much as touched her!—I'll kill him myself."

That would never happen, Will thought as he felt consciousness slipping away from him again. Stoddard would not kill Proud Wolf.

Because as soon as I'm strong enough, I'm going after them myself, Will vowed silently. *And I'll kill that redskinned bastard—and his squaw.*

CHAPTER THIRTEEN

Lieutenant Markham looked surprised as he watched Clay, Shining Moon, and Matthew coming up the gangplank from the dock. When the three of them reached the deck of the *New Orleans*, Markham said to Clay, "I, ah, was beginning to worry that you might not make it back in time."

"Told you I'd be here before the boat sailed."

"Well, actually, it doesn't really sail . . . although it could, since it has those two masts, but . . . well . . . who's this?" Markham finally asked.

Grinning, Clay turned to Shining Moon. "This is that young friend I was telling you about, John Markham. Markham, this is my wife, and the young fellow is Matthew Garwood, who's been living with us for a while."

Markham took off his beaver hat and nodded to Shining Moon. "Mrs. Holt, ma'am," he said. "I'm very glad to meet you."

"And I am glad to meet you, Mr. Markham," she said.

Markham turned to Matthew and stuck out his hand. "How do you do, Matthew."

With only a trace of his usual surliness, Matthew shook hands without meeting Markham's eyes.

"My family will be making the rest of this trip with us," Clay said firmly, letting Markham know that he would brook no argument.

"I see," Markham said slowly. "That's rather an unexpected development."

"Life's full of them, isn't it?" Clay said cheerfully. The sound of wagon wheels made him look around. "There're our things. Reckon I'd better get everything on board. How about giving me a hand, Matthew?"

"All right," Matthew replied, with little enthusiasm.

But at least he wasn't cursing and threatening any of them, Clay thought. That was progress enough.

"I'll help, too," Markham volunteered. He followed Clay and Matthew back down the gangplank to the dock, where a wagon had just came to a stop. Several carpetbags were loaded in the back.

"These are your wife's things?" asked Markham.

"Well, it's mostly clothes she's borrowed or bought since we got here," Clay explained. "We rode here from the mountains with nothing but what we could carry in a couple of possibles bags. Folks out on the frontier are used to traveling pretty light. But I reckon it's different once you've been around civilization for a while."

Clay took the smallest bag from the back of the wagon and handed it to Matthew. As the boy started up the gangplank, Clay handed another bag to Markham and then hefted the remaining two himself.

Before Clay could head for the gangplank, Markham leaned close and said in a low voice, "What do you think you're doing? How can you bring your wife and child along on a trip like this? Have you forgotten our mission?"

"I haven't forgotten a damned thing," Clay said

grimly. "It's a long story, Lieutenant. I reckon it'll do to say that they'll be better off with me than if they stayed here. And the boy's *not* my son."

"I just assumed—"

"Don't."

Markham shrugged. "You're in charge. Mr. Jefferson and my superior officers made that clear." He paused, then added, "You do realize you're putting them at risk."

"You just let me worry about that," Clay said as he started up the gangplank.

And that was exactly what he was going to do. Until this job was over and the traitor was either dead or behind bars, Clay was going to worry.

It did not take long before Shining Moon felt as if the walls of the tiny cabin were closing in on her. As she watched, they seemed to creep nearer and nearer, and although she knew it was an illusion, she felt an overpowering urge to get out. Her mind went back to the old abandoned well in which she had nearly been killed. The darkness, the close quarters pressing in all around her . . . she was grateful when Clay suggested that the three of them go back on deck.

Matthew's eyes were wide as he looked around the steamboat. He exclaimed at the height of the smokestack that rose from the boiler room belowdecks. He clung to the railing as he took in the massive paddlewheels. He stared in awe at the gold braid on the jacket of Nicholas Roosevelt, captain of the *New Orleans*, as he approached the family.

"Well, and who might this be?" asked Roosevelt, smiling at Shining Moon and Matthew.

"This is my wife and our . . . well, our adopted son, I reckon you could say," Clay replied. "His name is Matthew Garwood. They've been staying here in Marietta, but now they're going on downriver with us if that's all right with you, Captain."

Shining Moon noticed the flash of resentment in Matthew's eyes and knew that the boy did not like being described as their son, even an adopted one. But there was no other way to put it. They had taken him to raise as their own, whether it worked out well or not.

Roosevelt tugged on the brim of his cap. "Certainly. I'm mighty pleased to meet you, Mrs. Holt. Captain Nicholas Roosevelt, at your service. If you need anything while you're traveling with us, you just let me know."

"Thank you," she said politely. "I will. You have a most . . . magnificent boat."

Roosevelt grinned. "Why, thank you, ma'am. I'm quite proud of her, as you might expect." He turned to Clay. "Are you sure your accommodations will be sufficient? There are no extra cabins available, as I'm sure you know."

"We'll make do," Clay assured him.

"Will you show me around?" Matthew asked the captain.

"Certainly, young man," Roosevelt replied without hesitation. "That is, if it's all right with your folks."

Matthew glanced at Shining Moon, and she nodded.

"Well, now, what do you want to see first?" Captain Roosevelt asked.

"I want a closer look at those big wheels!"

"All right, but not too close. They're liable to start turning soon, and you wouldn't want to get caught in them."

Roosevelt led Matthew away, a companionable hand resting on the boy's shoulder. Shining Moon wondered what the captain would think if he knew the kinds of things she had suspected Matthew of doing over the past few months. He would not be quite so friendly, she was certain.

But perhaps all the unhappiness Matthew had caused was safely in the past. His attitude had changed abruptly when he found out they were leaving the Holt homestead and traveling downriver on the steamboat. Perhaps it had been a mistake to bring him back to

Marietta, Shining Moon reflected. There were too many
reminders here of his mother, and too many reminders
of the bad blood between the Holts and the Garwoods.
True, Matthew had been difficult in the mountains, but
he had grown more intractable since they had come to
Ohio. The surroundings could have had something to
do with his behavior.

Shining Moon slipped her arm through Clay's and
rested her head briefly on his shoulder. She hoped this
trip would be a new beginning for all of them.

"Where'd you find the squaw, Holt?"

Shining Moon felt Clay's muscles tense. He turned
slowly, and since her arm was linked with his, she had
no choice but to turn with him. They found themselves
facing a small man with a short beard. He wore a suit
that looked as if it must have cost a great deal of
money, yet was still uncomfortable, and clenched a
pipe with a short, curved stem between his teeth.

Clay nodded curtly. "Good morning, Senator. This
is my wife. Shining Moon, this is Senator Louis
Haines."

She knew immediately that this man was one of
the three suspects in the land grab scheme Clay had
described to her. He was not a pleasant-looking man,
but neither did he look particularly dangerous. Shining
Moon had learned, however, not to judge white men
by their appearance. Any of them could be dangerous.

She nodded politely and said, "It is a pleasure to
meet you, Senator."

Haines did not reply or even look at her. Instead he
addressed Clay with some surprise. "She speaks English."

"And French, as well as the language of her people, the Teton Sioux," said Clay. "I reckon when you
get down to it, Senator, Shining Moon is probably a
heap smarter than I am. Maybe smarter than you, too."

"No doubt." Haines turned to Shining Moon and
tipped his hat to her. "My apologies, madam. I meant
no offense."

"That is all right, Senator," she told him. "I

have grown . . . accustomed . . . to people believing things about me before they truly know me."

Haines took the subtle reprimand in stride. He turned back to Clay and said, "I've been known to rise on the floor of the Senate and recommend the removal and subjugation, if not indeed the extermination, of many of the Indian tribes in the West. But if all the women are as lovely as Mrs. Holt, perhaps I've been in error."

Shining Moon bit back the angry words that sprang to her lips. Senator Haines was an arrogant popinjay, and the fact that he was discussing the possible massacre of an entire race seemed to mean little to him. She hoped that Haines was the traitor Clay sought. If he was, sooner or later Clay would expose him and possibly even kill him. It was a keenly satisfying thought.

"Ah, here are Ralston and Emory," Haines went on. "Shall I perform the introductions?"

"I'll take care of that," Clay said shortly. He turned to the two men who were approaching. "Senators, allow me to present my wife, Mrs. Holt. She'll be traveling with us from now on."

Both middle-aged newcomers were handsomer and more distinguished-looking than Haines. One of them swept off his beaver hat to reveal a shock of white hair. He bowed gallantly, then took her hand and, to Shining Moon's surprise, kissed the back of it. "My dear Mrs. Holt," he drawled in a deep voice, "it is such a pleasure to meet you. Morgan Ralston, from the sovereign state of Georgia, at your eternal service."

Shining Moon felt herself flushing in embarrassment. She had no idea what to make of this man and his effusive charm. Awkwardly she said, "How do you do, Senator. It is good to meet you."

"I'm Charles Emory, Mrs. Holt," the third man told her. He spoke in crisp, clipped tones. "How is it that you come to be traveling with us on the rest of this voyage?"

"I have been living near here, on the farm that belongs to my husband's family. Now I will accompany him, and when we reach New Orleans, from there we will go home to the mountains."

"That's right," Clay said as he put an arm around her shoulders. "I'm looking forward to that, too. I wasn't cut out to be a flatlander."

Emory tipped his hat to Shining Moon. "Well, I hope the journey is pleasant for you, madam."

A shrill blast sounded from the steamboat's whistle. That was the signal that the *New Orleans* was about to depart. Several dozen townspeople had gathered at the dock to watch the boat resume its historic journey, and they waved and shouted farewells to the passengers on deck.

Shining Moon looked around for Matthew and felt a moment of panic when she did not see him. Then she spotted the boy in the wheelhouse with Captain Roosevelt. The captain was pointing out various instruments, and as Shining Moon watched, Matthew pulled the cord attached to the steam whistle. It gave another strident blast. Even at this distance Shining Moon could tell that Matthew was grinning broadly. She could not remember when she had seen him looking so happy.

She took a deep breath. Perhaps it was not too much to hope that the rest of this trip *would* go well, after all.

"I'm not giving up," Jeff said as he knotted a silk cravat around his neck. He didn't particularly enjoy wearing fancy clothes, but how often did a fellow get to dine with Russian aristocracy?

"But I thought you said Count Orlov was very definite about not wanting to trade with us," Melissa said from behind him.

Jeff turned to look at her, and for a moment his breath caught in his throat. His wife was breathtakingly lovely, as always. This evening she was wearing a dark blue gown with sprays of white lace around the throat and the cuffs of the long sleeves. Her dark brown curls were pulled into an elaborate arrangement on top of her head and fastened with combs and bows that matched the color of the gown. For a brief moment Jeff allowed himself to imagine taking down her hair and running his hands through it as he kissed her, and it was a very pleasurable thought.

But business came before pleasure, he reminded himself, at least tonight. As he had just told Melissa, the real purpose of this dinner was to persuade Count Orlov to change his mind about a trade agreement.

Jeff shrugged into a jacket, greatcoat, cap, and gloves, then helped his wife into a fur-lined jacket and greatcoat. Then he led her up to the deck, where Captain Vickery was waiting for them.

The captain rubbed his hands together. "Cold night, it is," he said. "Anybody with any sense would be sitting next to a stove or curled up under a pile of blankets."

"I'm sure Count Orlov's house will be comfortable," said Jeff. "Are you ready, Captain?"

"Aye. And so's the boat."

They were rowed ashore in the same small boat that had taken them in earlier that afternoon. As they skimmed over the black waters of the bay, Jeff looked up at the sky, which was lit by broad bands of eerie, undulating radiance. Beside him, Melissa had tilted her head back as well.

"It's beautiful," she breathed. "The lights shift back and forth like curtains blowing in a breeze."

"They're called the northern lights," Vickery said. "I've heard about them, but this is the first time I've ever seen them."

"What causes them?" asked Jeff.

The captain shook his head. "Now, there you've got me stumped, sir. I know about sailing, not about astral wonders."

"Well, whatever they are, they're lovely," Melissa said. She squeezed Jeff's hand.

As they drew near the dock, he saw a group of soldiers waiting for them. A couple of them held lanterns that cast circles of yellow illumination in the dark night. Jeff recognized one of them as Piotr, Count Orlov's aide. When he and Melissa and Vickery climbed onto the dock, Piotr clicked his heels together and bowed. "Good evening," he said in tolerable English. "You are to be coming with me, please."

To Jeff's surprise, Piotr had a carriage waiting for them. Instead of wheels, it was mounted on broad runners, apparently so that it could travel more easily over snow, ice, or frozen ground. Piotr held open the carriage door, and after the guests had climbed in, he pulled himself up to the high seat next to the driver. Jeff heard him say something in Russian, and the vehicle lurched into motion as the driver whipped the team of two fine black horses.

"Well, at least we're out of the wind," Vickery commented as the carriage bumped along.

Within minutes the vehicle came to a stop, and Piotr hopped down to open the door again. "You are welcome to the house of His Highness Count Gregori Orlov," he announced.

Jeff stepped down from the carriage and took a moment to look over the house. It sat on a slight rise overlooking the settlement, and unlike the other buildings, which were constructed of logs, the count's house was made of dark, heavy stone. In fact, it looked more like a castle than a house—not that Jeff had ever seen a castle other than in picture books. This castle was only one story high, but it was massive, looming in the darkness like some great beast that was crouched and ready to spring. The lanterns that flanked the thick slab of a front door only reinforced that image. To Jeff they looked like eyes, burning in the night.

Then the door between the lanterns swung open and dispelled the illusion. Count Orlov's lean figure was silhouetted against the light from inside the house. "Come in, my American friends, come in!" he called cheerfully.

Jeff wondered how much of that good cheer was an illusion, too.

He turned back to the carriage to assist Melissa. When she had alighted, he linked his arm with hers and walked toward the house, Captain Vickery following behind. Count Orlov stepped aside, his hand held out in an elegant gesture.

The door opened directly into a large, high-ceilinged room. The starkness of the stone walls was relieved by a pair of ornate tapestries woven with scenes from what Jeff took to be the Russian countryside. Heavy brocade curtains covered the windows. A huge fireplace on the left side of the room was topped by a rugged slate mantel. Flames leaped high in the fireplace, and Jeff was grateful for the warmth they gave off.

Suddenly he heard Melissa gasp. She was gazing intently at the right-hand wall, opposite the fireplace. A huge creature reared up on its hind legs, its front paws, wickedly clawed, stretched out in front of it. The thing was close to seven feet tall, Jeff estimated; he, too, had felt a surge of instinctive fear when he first glimpsed it—before he realized that the giant bear was dead and had been stuffed and preserved as a trophy.

"An impressive specimen, is it not?" asked Count Orlov as he strolled up behind them with Captain Vickery. "It is a giant bear from the interior of Russian America. I shot it last summer when I first came here."

"Shot it yourself, did you?" Jeff asked.

"Of course. I made several hunting expeditions to the interior with some of my troops and a Tlingit Indian guide. The day I killed that creature was one of the proudest of my life."

"I've run into a few of his cousins, down in the Rockies. Grizzlies, we called them. A little different breed than this one, I think, but still plenty mean. Decent eating, though . . . especially when you don't have anything else."

Orlov chuckled. "We will not be dining tonight on bear meat, I assure you." He turned to Melissa and took her hand. "You must be Mrs. Holt. When your husband told me that you had come to Alaska with him, I insisted that you join us for dinner tonight. I consider it my duty as a nobleman to see that you have at least one good meal here before you start back to your homeland."

The count was assuming an awful lot, thought Jeff. He hadn't said anything to Orlov about going back to the States yet.

"Thank you," Melissa said graciously.

"I'm sorry I didn't make the introductions as I should have," Jeff said. "Count Orlov, this is my wife, Melissa Holt. Count Gregori Orlov."

"I'm charmed," Melissa acknowledged with a smile.

"Not half so charmed as I." Gazing with open admiration, Orlov still held her hand in both of his, and Jeff began to wonder if he was ever going to let go of it.

To distract him, Jeff said, "And you met Captain Vickery this afternoon, of course."

"Of course." Orlov turned his head, gave Vickery a brief nod, and returned his attention to Melissa. Maintaining his grip on her hand, he led her toward a long table covered with a dazzling white cloth. "Come along, my dear. Dinner will be ready shortly."

Jeff's jaw tightened as he watched the way Orlov leaned close to Melissa and spoke to her in a low voice that he could not overhear. Melissa laughed at whatever the count was telling her.

From behind Jeff a woman said wryly, "I see that Gregori is up to his usual tricks."

Jeff glanced over his shoulder, then looked again, unable to contain his surprise.

The most beautiful woman he had seen in a long time—other than his wife—was standing behind him.

And as she looked past Jeff at the count and the American woman, sparks of rage practically flew from her icy blue eyes.

The sticky stuff called *poi* wasn't so bad when it was washed down with plenty of native beer, Ned discovered during the course of the dinner with King Kamehameha. Some people might have considered the Hawaiian leader an aboriginal savage, but Ned thought him a fine fellow. A little severe, perhaps, but understandably so considering the long, hard road he had traveled to unite these islands into one kingdom. There had been bloody battles along the way, some of them fought by warriors, others by diplomats. But ultimately Kamehameha had emerged triumphant, and Ned could only admire and respect him.

The visitors, along with their host and his wife and son, ate at a long, low table on a terrace behind the house. They sat on the ground with their legs crossed as servants brought bowl after bowl of food: whole fish baked between banana leaves, a roasted pig, a seemingly endless variety of fruits and vegetables. And, of course, bowls of thick yellow *poi*. Ned followed Kamehameha's example and scooped it up with his fingers.

He wasn't sure how long he was supposed to wait before bringing up business again, but just to be on the safe side, he said nothing until the meal was over and the servants had cleared the table. Then, as the king was packing tobacco into a pipe, Ned asked, "Did that tobacco come from the United States?"

Kamehameha looked up at him with hooded eyes. "As a matter of fact, it did."

"Trade is a mighty good thing," Ned said solemnly.

"I know," replied the king, equally solemn. "That is why I have always allowed the ships of the *haoles* to land here. There are many things my people need that your people can supply." He lit the pipe with a burning twig from the fire pit, sucked on it a moment, then continued, "Things made of iron. These are what we need. And guns."

Ned was a little taken aback. This was the first he had heard about the Hawaiians' need for guns.

"I will be honest with you, Mr. Holt," Kamehameha said, noting Ned's reaction. "I won my kingdom with much flame and blood. I will not lose it the same way. I control the trade among the islands—*all* the trade. No ships put in here without my approval, nor does any trading take place unless I approve. And no guns are allowed except among my supporters." He shrugged his brawny shoulders. "We are not ignorant of the ways of your people. We know they fought a war so that they could be free of the tyranny of a king. But I have brought much good to these islands, and I would not relinquish my hold on them."

"I'm not asking you to, Your Highness," Ned said. "We came here to trade, not to interfere in your personal affairs." He was feeling his way along, hoping not to make any irreparable blunders. "We can bring guns next time. This time we have some fine plows in our cargo. We'd be glad to trade them for a load of sandalwood."

"How many plows?"

"Oh, I reckon about a dozen."

Kamehameha frowned. "That will not get you much sandalwood," he said bluntly.

"How about some cannonballs to go with the plows?" suggested India, to the surprise of Ned and Captain Canfield. "We could probably spare some of those."

The king's eyes lit up at the mention of ammunition, although he kept his tone neutral as he answered, "We would be interested in cannonballs."

"All right," said Ned. He looked at Canfield. "How many can we spare?"

"I don't know," Canfield said dubiously. "I wasn't expecting to trade away any of them—"

"Two dozen," Kamehameha said. "And the plows. For that, you can have a full load of sandalwood."

"And fruit for all the crew." Ned didn't think it would hurt to haggle just a little more.

Kamehameha waved a hand magnanimously. "We are agreed."

Ned wanted to heave a sigh of relief, but he sup-

pressed the urge. The first step had been taken successfully . . . but only the first step.

"We could bring more guns on our next voyage,"
he said carefully, "but only if we had an exclusive
trade agreement with you."

The king was shaking his head before the words
were out of Ned's mouth. "Representatives from many
lands have asked the same thing of me in the past, Mr.
Holt. I have always told them what I will tell you. We
deal with all the *haoles* equally. I would not have the
British angry with me, or the Dutch, or the other Americans. But if sandalwood is what you seek, there is
plenty for all."

Ned glanced at India. She gave a tiny shrug. Canfield shook his head almost imperceptibly. Ned knew
from looking at Kamehameha's placid features that the
monarch was not going to change his mind.

Well, I tried, he thought. *Jeff will just have to understand that that was the best I could do.*

The visitors spent several more minutes chatting
pleasantly with the king. Kamehameha's wife had said
nothing throughout the meal, and neither had his son,
a broad-faced young man with curly black hair, although he had listened intently. The youngster had
neither the regal bearing nor the powerful presence of
his father, but Ned reckoned he would be king someday anyway, unless Kamehameha lost the throne before then. Looking at the old warrior, Ned thought that
unlikely.

"We have quarters for guests," Kamehameha said.
"You are welcome to stay."

"Thank you, Your Highness," Captain Canfield replied, "but I'd best be getting back to my ship. I never
feel too comfortable sleeping on dry land."

Kamehameha smiled. "You are a true sailor." He
looked at Ned and India. "What about the two of
you?"

"We'll stay," Ned said before India had a chance to
reply. He wasn't going to pass up an opportunity to be

alone with her. It had been too blasted long since
they'd had any time together.

India did not object, so Kamehameha called for a
servant to show them to a pair of small huts with roofs
made of dried palm fronds. The huts were near the
beach, and Ned could hear the hiss of waves rolling
ashore over the fine white sand.

Ned and India exchanged a look as the servant de-
parted, carrying a bamboo torch. Ned let a few minutes
pass, then slipped over to India's hut, bumping into
her in the darkness. "Oh!" she mumbled, but that was
all she had time for before his arms went around her
and his mouth came down on hers.

She softened in his embrace, melting against him.
Ned kissed her for a long time, and both of them were
breathless when their mouths finally parted. "Which
hut?" Ned whispered urgently.

"Neither," replied India. "Let's go down to the
beach."

"The beach?" Ned repeated as his eyebrows lifted
in surprise. "You mean . . . outside?"

"Why not?" India asked. He could see her impish
grin only faintly in the dim light of the stars.

Why not, indeed?

They walked hand in hand to the beach and found
a smooth, level spot beneath a palm tree. Ned sat on
the ground and watched as India took off the sailor's
tunic and trousers. Her body was slim and pale and
dappled with starlight and shadow. His need for her
was a sharp ache inside him. He held out his hands
and she came to him, and the night was filled with
softness and heat.

Twenty yards away, the man stood in the darkest
patch of shadow he could find and watched the two
figures come together beneath the palm tree. He could
barely hear the sharply indrawn breaths, the muttered
words of passion.

He snorted. It would be so easy to sneak up on
them unnoticed and use the heavy, long-bladed knife

tucked behind his belt. He fingered the hilt of the weapon and smiled.

Yes, it would be easy to kill them—but it wasn't time yet. Leave them to whatever fleeting happiness they could find, he told himself, because soon enough it would be over. He would see to that.

CHAPTER
FOURTEEN

P roud Wolf sensed that Audrey was beginning to
regret her decision to leave the academy with
him. Dawn was breaking, and they had walked
all night. She winced now with every step. But she did
not complain. She held his hand tightly and did not say
a word.

Her stoicism surprised him. He was very fond of
Audrey—at times he thought he loved her—but he
would not have guessed that she was strong enough
not to complain when she was in pain.

They were walking west on the Upper Boston Post
Road. Proud Wolf had no idea where it ultimately led,
only that it was taking them farther and farther away
from the academy—and Will Brackett's death.

Proud Wolf had killed men before, but always in
battle, to save his own life. The events of the night
before had been different. True, Will and Frank had
beaten him, but they would have left him alive. Nor
had they intended to kill Audrey. But what they had

had in mind for her was evil enough to justify Will's death, Proud Wolf told himself. He had done the right thing.

He had done what the spirit cat had driven him to do. Never before had he experienced such a feeling of power. Despite the battering he had received earlier, when he came up off the ground to attack Will and Frank, he had felt powerful enough to defeat any number of enemies. He had felt invincible.

That in itself was frightening, and he wondered about it now.

"Shouldn't we be getting off the road?" Audrey said. "It will be light soon, and they may be looking for us."

Her words shook him out of his reverie. He looked to the east and saw that she was right. The sun would be up within minutes. They should have sought shelter, a hiding place, before now.

They had left the city far behind and were now traveling through gently rolling farmland. In the gray light Proud Wolf spotted a log building on the far side of a field bordering the road. It looked like an old barn, but part of its roof had collapsed, and the walls were overgrown with vines. It was undoubtedly abandoned. That would be a safe place to hide until night fell again, he decided.

"There," he said, pointing out the barn to Audrey. "Come with me."

He held her hand as they climbed over a low stone wall and hurried toward the barn. The double doors that had once hung over the entrance sagged to either side of it, hinges pulling away from rotting wood. The opening gaped like a dark maw, and as they approached it, Proud Wolf felt Audrey's fingers tighten on his.

"Do not be afraid," he told her. "No one will bother us here."

"How do you know what we'll find in there?"

"I do not know. But we cannot stay in the open. The authorities will be searching for us."

Audrey sighed. "I know." She looked back over her shoulder.

Proud Wolf tugged her inside. A fluttering sound above their heads made Audrey flinch. "It is only owls," he told her. "They will not harm us."

Other sounds came from the dark interior, rapid, skittering sounds. "There are rats in here," Audrey said shakily.

"They are more afraid of us than we are of them. They will flee and not disturb us."

"You're sure?"

"I am sure."

Again she sighed. "I hope you're right."

They stayed well away from the area where the roof had collapsed. Enough light filtered in through the door and the hole in the roof that they could see the empty stalls where cattle or horses had once been housed. The floor was hard-packed dirt over which bits of straw were still scattered. Proud Wolf found a stall with several inches of straw piled in one corner.

"We can sleep here," he said.

"On that?" Audrey wrinkled her nose.

Proud Wolf banged on the wall and called out softly, then kicked at the pile of straw. He drew no response. "There are no rats here," he assured Audrey with a smile. "It will be dusty, but better than nothing."

"I suppose you're right. I'm so tired I think I could sleep almost anywhere." She sank down onto the straw. As she eased off her slippers, she let out a soft whimper.

Proud Wolf knelt at her feet and studied the blisters that had formed overnight on her toes. He regarded her gravely and said, "Do not worry. Your feet will grow tough and calloused. The women of my people can walk from sunrise to sunset and never feel any pain."

"I'm not an Indian woman," she snapped, then quickly added, "I'm sorry, Proud Wolf. I don't mean to complain, I really don't. I'm just not . . . accustomed to tramping all over the countryside."

He moved beside her on the straw and put his arm around her shoulders. "I know," he said quietly. "I am glad you came with me, Audrey."

"What else could I do?" She rested her head on his shoulder. He put his other arm around her and snuggled her against him. "It's my fault that Will is . . . is . . ."

"You are not to blame," he said firmly. "Now, we will speak no more of it. We will go far away from Boston, and we will make a new life for ourselves."

"Yes," she murmured, and he knew she was drifting off into exhausted sleep. "Just the two of us . . . a new life . . ."

A moment later, her deep, regular breathing told him that slumber had claimed her.

Proud Wolf was not so fortunate. As he lay on the straw in the shadowy old barn with Audrey in his arms, he thought about Abner Hilliard and how disappointed he would be when he learned that Proud Wolf had fled the academy. He thought about Will Brackett. The young man's face haunted him, and Proud Wolf could not understand why. Will had gotten only what he deserved. No man's death had never bothered Proud Wolf this much before.

The short time he had spent in the East had changed him, Proud Wolf realized. His perceptions were more like a white man's now, a civilized man's. Killing the enemy was no longer as simple as it once was. Perhaps it was a good thing he had been forced to run from the academy. If he had stayed there long enough, he might have turned into a white man altogether.

And that was something he did not want, not now, not ever. He was Proud Wolf, a warrior of the Teton Sioux. A warrior he would remain, he vowed, until the end of his days.

•   •   •

Count Orlov was a charming man, Melissa thought as he held her hand and led her to the table. What he was saying was not particularly witty or remarkable, but he said it in such a dry, elegant fashion.

"Gregori!"

The two stopped and turned around. The count finally let go of Melissa's hand. She saw a beautiful blond woman in a low-cut, emerald-green gown sweeping past Jeff. Though the woman was smiling, her eyes, fixed on Orlov, were blazing.

"Ah, my dear," the count said as he stepped forward to meet the woman. He took her arms and leaned down to kiss her lightly on the forehead.

"Gregori, you told me we were having guests for dinner, but you did not say that one of them would be a beautiful American woman."

"Forgive me, my dear," Orlov said smoothly. "Allow me to present Mr. Jefferson Holt and his lovely wife, Melissa."

Jeff had come across the room, trailing in the woman's wake.

"Mr. and Mrs. Holt," continued Orlov, "this is my wife, the countess Irina."

With a swirl of her skirts Irina Orlov turned and faced Jeff. "Nor did you tell me, Gregori, that our other guest was such a handsome man." She rested a hand on Jeff's arm.

Melissa frowned. She felt a twinge of something uncomfortably like jealousy. Irina Orlov was stunning, and the way she was smiling up at Jeff made Melissa's hackles rise.

Jeff, to his credit, looked uneasy, too. He nodded to Irina and said, "It's a pleasure to meet you, Countess."

"The pleasure is mine," she purred. Over her shoulder she shot a defiant glance at her husband, then linked arms with Jeff. "Welcome to our home. I hope you will enjoy your stay in Alaska."

"And this is Captain Niles Vickery," Orlov said, gesturing toward the captain, who stood by awkwardly. The countess gave him a brief nod as Orlov went on, "Captain Vickery and Mr. and Mrs. Holt will not be staying long in Russian America. The mission that brought them here has proven to be fruitless."

"And what was their mission?" asked Irina.

"We hoped to negotiate a trade agreement," Jeff replied. "Unfortunately, your husband tells me that such an agreement is impossible."

Irina looked at the count. "But why? You are the manager of the Russian-American Company until Alexander Baranof returns, Gregori. The czar has given you the power to make all decisions concerning the company's actions."

Orlov's face flushed. Melissa, discreetly observing the man and his wife, suspected that all was not well between the Orlovs. The count had openly flirted with her, and judging by Irina's reaction, this was not the first time he had flirted with a woman who was not his wife. Still, no harm had been done. Melissa found the Russian nobleman charming, but she was not attracted to him in the least.

"This is neither the time nor the place to discuss business, my dear," Orlov said, recovering smoothly. "We shall sit down and have our dinner. Perhaps later, over brandy, we can talk more."

Melissa saw the flare of hope in Jeff's eyes. He had not given up on the trade pact. Jeff rarely gave up when he was pursuing something he really wanted, and that was one of the things she loved about him. After all, he had searched for two long years before finding her, hadn't he? And in all that time he hadn't even known that he had a son.

Count Orlov held a chair for Melissa at the table, and Jeff did likewise for the countess. Captain Vickery was left to fend for himself. Dinner was served by Piotr and a female native servant. The main course looked and tasted like roast duck, and Melissa wondered where they had found such a delicacy in this frigid wasteland.

Her question was answered a moment later when Count Orlov remarked, "Quite good, isn't it? A native bird called the ptarmigan. I had Piotr go out and shoot one this afternoon."

"It is good," Jeff agreed. "Don't you think so, Melissa?"

She nodded. "Yes, excellent."

For a few minutes Jeff and Orlov discussed the wild game to be found in Alaska. Judging from his stories and the stuffed bear in the corner, Melissa thought, the count was an accomplished huntsman.

"Perhaps someday you can return, Mr. Holt," he said, "and we can mount a hunting expedition into the interior."

"I'd enjoy that," Jeff said. "I've been planning on coming back to Alaska all along."

Orlov smiled thinly. "Ah, there you are talking about business again. We said we would postpone that until after dinner."

"So we did," Jeff replied with a grin. "I beg your pardon, Count Orlov. It's just that the subject is very much on my mind."

"And you cannot be blamed for that, poor boy," Irina said, reaching across the table and patting Jeff's hand. "To come all this way, only to have my husband turn down your petition. The least he could do is show you some of the wonders of Alaska before you leave."

Orlov frowned and fingered his wineglass. "Irina, this is none of your concern."

"You are the one who brought me to this godforsaken wilderness, Gregori," Irina said sweetly, "so you have only yourself to blame if I involve myself in your affairs. Besides, you yourself suggested a hunting expedition."

Melissa looked at Jeff and saw the wariness in his eyes. He knew as well as she did that they were in danger of getting mired in more than pure business. There were problems between the Orlovs that had nothing to do with trade.

Captain Vickery spoke up. "Personally, I prefer getting all the business out of the way before sitting down to eat. It's much easier on the digestion."

"Perhaps you are right, Captain," said Orlov. He looked at Jeff. "I do not know how I can make things plainer, Mr. Holt. My mind is made up. I may have the authority to enter into a trade agreement with you, but to do so would be to go against everything the czar has said he wants from this land. I am not prepared to do that." He took a deep breath. "However, if you would like to see something of the interior . . ."

"I'd like that very much. Thank you, Count." Jeff set his fork down. "Your czar—he's a reasonable, practical man?"

"As much as any ruler can be. The concerns of a head of state are sometimes difficult for commoners to understand."

Jeff smiled slightly, and Melissa knew that even if he had taken offense at the veiled insult, he would not show it. "What do you believe his reaction would be if you made this company more profitable than it's ever been before?"

"If I were to go against his orders, I am not sure it would matter how much profit the company made."

"Has he specifically forbidden trade with non-Russian ships?" asked Jeff.

"Not specifically, no, but in the past, such trade has always been frowned upon."

Irina spoke up. "The czar frowns on anything that's even a little progressive, Gregori. You know that."

"Irina! You must not say such things."

"Why not? St. Petersburg is thousands of miles away!"

Her husband glowered at her. "Yes, but the czar has ears in places you would not suspect."

"All the troops in Sitka are loyal to you. You saw to that when you were posted here. Any men you could not trust you dispatched to outlying posts."

Orlov's right hand knotted into a fist and banged down on the table. "These matters are not fit for discussion at the dinner table, nor are they any business of yours!" His face was flushed when he turned to the others. "I apologize on behalf of my wife. She feels that we should not have been sent here from St. Petersburg, and she tries to sabotage my efforts on behalf of our country."

"That is a lie!" Irina exclaimed, pushing herself to her feet. "I want only what is best for Russia!"

Captain Vickery stood up as well. "It is I who should apologize, Count. I'm the one who brought the conversation back to the subject of trade."

Orlov shook his head wearily and waved off Vickery's apology. "It would have come to this sooner or later, I assure you, Captain."

"Perhaps we should go back to the ship . . ." Jeff suggested.

"No!" Irina said. She sighed and put a hand to her forehead. "I am sorry I have caused this awkward scene. Please . . ." She gazed intently at Jeff. "Do not leave." Almost as an afterthought she glanced at Melissa. "Please."

"Well . . ." Melissa said slowly, "the gentlemen did intend to have a glass of brandy . . ."

"So we did," Orlov said. "Perhaps we should proceed." He looked sidelong at Irina as he added, "I seem to have lost my appetite, anyway."

What the hell had they gotten themselves into? Jeff wondered. There was an unmistakable tension between Count Orlov and his wife, and the arrival of the strangers from America had only added to it. Jeff thought he understood part of the problem: The countess was an ambitious woman whose dreams would only be frustrated in Alaska, so far from the court of the czar in St. Petersburg. If the arrangement Jeff had proposed was implemented and proved successful, the added profits for the Russian-American Company might be substantial enough to prompt the czar to reward Count Orlov. It was Jeff's guess that Irina hoped to be rewarded with a summons back to their homeland.

The count, on the other hand, was a man who went by the book. He hadn't ordered his men to kill the

Americans and sink their ship, which he easily could have done. But although he had welcomed them into his home, he showed no signs of compromising on the issue of trade. He would follow his czar's wishes. The only concession he had made, in fact, was agreeing to meet Jeff the next morning for a short trip into the interior.

Complicating the situation now was the apparent penchant of both the count and his wife for open flirtation with other people's spouses. It was no wonder that Jeff's stomach was queasy. As they gathered around the fireplace sipping brandy, he felt assaulted by the heat and the liquor.

Orlov had insisted that the ladies remain and share the brandy with the men. Irina had agreed without hesitation, and Melissa had had no choice but to go along. Jeff noted with relief that she didn't seem to care for Orlov's attentions; she was polite to the count, but no more.

He hoped Melissa knew him well enough to realize that he hadn't taken a fancy to Irina, either, despite her beauty and provocative behavior. She was standing beside him now, regaling him with tales of the czar's court at St. Petersburg. Every so often she leaned toward him so that the soft mound of her left breast pressed against his arm.

Jeff found his eyes straying toward her breasts, which were displayed to advantage in the daringly low-cut gown. She had managed to press them together somehow—probably with a whalebone contraption of some sort under the dress—so that the valley between the globes of creamy flesh was dark and deep, mysterious and inviting. Jeff wondered fuzzily what it would feel like to bury his face in that valley.

He stiffened as that thought went through his mind. He had no right to entertain such ideas, he reminded himself. He was probably just tired from the voyage, and he had not fully recovered from his prolonged seasickness. The brandy and the heat from the fire did not help. What he really needed was a good night's sleep . . . with Irina beside him? The brazen invitation in her eyes made it clear that she would not mind at all.

Jeff gulped down the rest of the brandy in his glass. "We ought to get back to the ship," he said. He hoped his voice didn't sound as slurred to the others as it did to him.

Vickery was deep in conversation with the count, and Jeff was glad that he had distracted Orlov from Melissa. On the other hand, Melissa was now free to watch as Irina flirted with him. Her mouth was set in a hard line, and her eyebrows arched with disapproval. Surely she didn't blame *him* for what Irina was doing! Jeff had given the countess no encouragement.

But neither had he tried to discourage her, he realized. In truth, he was as human as the next man, and it was flattering to have a beautiful woman lusting after him . . . even if she was only doing it to annoy her husband.

Vickery turned to Jeff. "If you don't mind, Mr. Holt, I think we should stay a little longer. The count and I are beginning to see eye-to-eye on a few things."

Orlov nodded. "Your captain has made me see the light of reason on several important matters, Mr. Holt. Perhaps we can come to an agreement after all."

"Well, that's good news," Jeff said, a little surprised. He knew Vickery was a competent sea captain, but he would never have guessed that he was a skilled negotiator as well.

"Very good news," Irina said.

Jeff became uncomfortably aware that she was leaning on him again. He wasn't particularly steady to begin with, and he imagined himself stumbling and falling on the rug in front of the fireplace. No doubt Irina would fall right on top of him.

He closed his eyes, trying to banish the image of the two of them rolling around on the rug while the flames leaped and crackled in the fireplace.

"I need some fresh air," he muttered.

"Come with me," Irina offered. Her hand tightened on his arm.

He looked around for Melissa, hoping she would rescue him, but she had been drawn into the conversation between Count Orlov and Captain Vickery. Melissa was a shrewd businesswoman, and if any agreement was reached with the count, Jeff knew she would look out for their interests.

But, damn it, that was why *he* was here! That was why he had come all the way around South America, all those long weeks at sea, all those days of being sick. He had come to Alaska to make a fortune for Holt-Merrivale.

Instead, all he had accomplished so far was to drink too much brandy and allow himself to be snared by this blond she-devil who was tugging on his arm, leading him toward the rear of the house. He wanted to call out to Melissa to save him.

But that was exactly what she was doing, wasn't it? He had failed, and now it was up to Melissa and Vickery to salvage the mission. He couldn't disturb them.

Jeff took a deep breath and went with Irina.

But blast it, he thought, didn't Melissa even care?

Her heart was breaking, but Melissa kept her attention focused on Vickery and the count. At the start of the conversation Orlov had been rigid and hidebound, but then Vickery had started laying out some numbers—the estimated profits the Russian-American Company could expect if the Pacific trade routes were developed. Melissa had seen the light of interest flicker in Orlov's eyes, and she had stayed close, ready to buttress Vickery's arguments if it became necessary. When the count began to waver again in favor of his original instructions from the czar, Melissa had stepped in with more figures and projections.

They were going to do it, she realized: They were bringing the count around to their way of thinking. She should have been happy.

But in the meantime Jeff was getting drunk, and

the countess was doing everything but draping herself over him right there by the fireplace, in front of her husband and Jeff's wife—and she didn't seem to care who was watching.

But then neither did Jeff. Judging by the ridiculous smile on his face, he had gotten over his initial shock at Irina's shameless behavior. He was enjoying it now.

When Jeff had suggested they leave, Melissa was torn by conflicting desires. She wanted to get Jeff away from Irina, but on the other hand she and Vickery were making real progress with Count Orlov. If the discussion were to end now, he might not be nearly so reasonable when it resumed.

Captain Vickery had made the decision for her, and in a way she was grateful. But a few minutes later Irina had led Jeff out of the room, and Melissa felt her insides go cold and hollow. And then, just as quickly, she was filled with another emotion: anger. How dare Jeff behave like this? She would never forgive him. Never. She took her marriage vows seriously—

So seriously she had wound up in the arms of Philip Rattigan.

Melissa took a deep breath and forced that thought out of her head. She concentrated instead on what Orlov and Vickery were saying. What had happened between her and Rattigan had been completely different. In the end she had remained faithful to Jeff.

Sorrowfully, she wondered if he could say the same thing about her.

Jeff took a deep breath of the bracing air and immediately felt his head beginning to clear. He and Irina had stepped out a rear door of the house, and she stood close beside him now, her arm linked with his.

"You should go back inside," he told her. "You must be freezing in that . . . that gown."

"I am Russian. I do not mind the cold." She leaned against him. "Besides, if I get too chilly, you can put your arm around me."

"I'm not sure that would be a good idea."

"I think it would be a very good idea indeed." She turned toward him, and he felt the weight of both breasts against his arm. "I think it would be an even better idea if you kissed me."

Jeff felt a moment of panic. He never would have allowed this woman to maneuver him out here if he hadn't had too much to drink. Now that he was thinking straight again, he had to get back inside before anything else happened.

Damn, he thought. *Melissa probably hates me right now.*

He lifted his hands and rested them on Irina's shoulders to put a little distance between them. "Listen, Countess," he began.

"Irina," she insisted.

"Irina," he said reluctantly. "I'm flattered that you seem to be, ah, attracted to me—"

"You are the most handsome man I have seen in Sitka."

"But your husband is right inside, and so is my wife," he went on, ignoring the compliment. "We can't do this."

"What do husbands and wives matter? You are not a conventional man, Mr. Holt. If you were, you would not have come all the way to Alaska."

"I still can't—"

She muttered something in Russian—it sounded like a curse of frustration—then reached up and cupped both hands behind his head. She came up on her toes and pressed her mouth hard against his.

Instinctively, Jeff's arms went around her, and he couldn't help but compare the feel of her lush body with Melissa's more slender form. He knew he should pull away; being slightly drunk was no longer a valid excuse, because he was stone-cold sober now. But instead he returned Irina's kiss.

After a long, passionate moment, she stepped back. "There," she said with a coy smile. "Do you need more air, Mr. Holt, or are you ready to go back inside?"

Jeff didn't trust himself to speak for a few seconds.

The sweetness of her lips, the incredible heat of her mouth, had shaken him to the core. Finally he said hoarsely, "We should go back inside."

"I agree. But there will be other nights. You are not leaving Alaska yet, are you?"

"That depends on your husband. He controls the trade here, not to mention the garrison of troops."

"Gregori will not be any trouble. I will see to that," she said confidently. "But there will be many discussions before an arrangement is reached. You will come to this house, and we will see each other again. Often."

"But not like this," Jeff said stubbornly. "What we just did was wrong, Countess. You know it, and I know it."

She smiled seductively. "What I know, Jefferson Holt, is that you will be back."

CHAPTER FIFTEEN

After Marietta, the next major stop on the Ohio River for the *New Orleans* was Cincinnati, and, as in all the previous towns, word of the steamboat's arrival preceded the boat itself. Crowds of curious people lined the riverbank to get a good look at Captain Roosevelt's famous boat as it approached.

Clay stood at the railing with Shining Moon, Matthew, and Lieutenant Markham. As the riverfront buildings and streets of Cincinnati came into view, Markham looked down at the boy and asked, "How about it, Matthew? Is this the biggest town you've ever seen?"

"Of course not," Matthew said scornfully. "I've been to St. Louis. It's bigger. A lot bigger."

"Oh," said Markham. "You're a well-traveled fellow, then."

"I've been places," Matthew said simply.

Clay listened to the exchange and smiled. It was true: Matthew had journeyed all the way to the Rocky

Mountains and back, a feat about which few youngsters his age could boast.

Unfortunately, there were other unusual things about Matthew: He was the product of an unholy union between brother and sister, he had witnessed his mother being slain by a madman, and he himself was suspected of causing at least one death. Those burdens would be a heavy load for anyone to carry, let alone a child.

Matthew seemed to have left his past behind, however. In the days since the *New Orleans* had left Marietta, he had been surprisingly cooperative, even friendly. Clay was impressed, and he knew that Shining Moon was, too.

"There are so many big cities," Shining Moon said now. "Where do all the people come from?"

"All over," Clay told her. "From England, France, Spain, the Netherlands . . ."

Shining Moon shook her head. "I have never heard of these lands. Are they far away?"

"Halfway around the world. Many sleeps beyond the place where the sun rises."

"I would never have known there was anything beyond the sunrise if not for you, my husband," she murmured. Her hand stole into his and squeezed.

Clay's smile broadened into a grin. "There are many lands and countries in the world," he said, "but none I could ever love as well as our home."

"We will return there when your job is done?" Shining Moon asked quietly.

"As soon as we can," he promised.

There had been no more trouble on the boat, no attempts on Clay's or Markham's life, no one breaking into their cabins to search them. None of the senators had exhibited any suspicious behavior. He and Markham were going to have to discuss the situation in private, Clay decided. They had to do something to flush out the man they were after, or this voyage and all their work would be for nothing.

Steam whistle blowing exuberantly, the *New Or-*

leans docked in Cincinnati. Captain Roosevelt and his wife disembarked, accompanied by the senators and the journalists. Clay, Shining Moon, Matthew, and Markham stayed on board for the time being, although when Matthew overheard one of the crew members talking about the rally planned for that night, he asked Clay, "Can we go? There's going to be a brass band."

"And a bunch of speeches by politicians," said Clay. "I reckon you'd get bored quick-like."

Matthew pouted. "I still want to go."

Markham spoke up. "I'd be happy to take the lad. After spending so much time on this boat, I'm always glad for the chance to stretch my legs and walk about on dry land again."

Clay recalled what had happened the last time Markham had attended a dockside rally: He had nearly been strangled to death. Clay wasn't sure he wanted to expose Matthew to the risk of something similar in Cincinnati.

"I don't think that's a very good idea," he said slowly. Matthew's lower lip stuck out farther.

"Nothing's going to happen," Markham said, as if he knew what Clay was thinking. He lowered his voice and added, "Whoever it is has given up on getting rid of us."

"You can't be sure of that," Clay said, wishing that Markham wouldn't mention their assignment in front of Matthew. He didn't mind Shining Moon knowing about it, but the job he and Markham had taken on for Thomas Jefferson was none of Matthew's business. He was only a boy, and a youngster couldn't be trusted to keep his mouth shut about anything he happened to overhear.

"I want to go to the rally!" Matthew said, his voice rising.

"We will all go," Shining Moon said, kneeling beside him. She looked up at Clay as if daring him to disagree.

After a moment he shrugged his shoulders. What else could he do? he asked himself.

Matthew's face brightened, and for the next couple of hours, as evening fell, he was happy and cheerful again. As the hour approached for the rally, Shining Moon put on her best dress and made sure that Matthew's shirt was clean and his hair slicked down. He endured the fussing with a minimum of complaint.

A chilly autumn breeze was blowing as the four of them walked down the gangplank and toward the town square where the rally was to be held. Clay kept his eyes open for trouble as if they were in the middle of Blackfoot hunting grounds and not in a civilized city. *To tell the truth*, he thought, *I think I'd rather take on the Blackfoot.* There was something refreshing about pitting yourself against someone who was openly trying to kill you. All this sneaking around and trying to figure out what the other fellow was going to do before he could figure out what you were going to do was too devious and wearisome.

Matthew's ears perked up when strains of martial music drifted from the town square. Shining Moon was holding his hand, and he tried to pull away from her and run ahead. She kept a tight grip on him. Clay was about to advise her to let him go when she came to that conclusion herself and released his hand. He darted down the street toward the gathering crowd.

"Will he be all right?" she asked anxiously.

"I reckon he will be," said Clay. "Nobody's going to bother a little boy."

"I'll go on ahead and try to keep an eye on him," Markham volunteered. He quickened his pace and soon left Clay and Shining Moon behind.

Clay slowed down a little, glad for the opportunity to spend a few minutes alone with Shining Moon . . . although the middle of a Cincinnati street could hardly be considered private. He nodded toward the edge of the crowd, where Matthew and Markham had disappeared. "The boy seems to be coming around."

"It was good for him to leave Marietta. When we are home again, Matthew will be happy."

Clay was not sure he could agree. Marietta was full

of bad memories for Matthew, that was true, but so was New Hope. Matthew's mother, Josie, had died there. "We'll see what happens," he said noncommittally.

"Clay." The sharpness of Shining Moon's voice made him stiffen. "I cannot see Matthew."

Clay scanned the growing crowd. "I don't see Markham, either. Stay here. I'll go see if I can find them."

He left Shining Moon standing at the edge of the square and strode toward the platform where the brass band was playing.

Matthew darted through every small opening in the crowd as he made his way toward the platform. He liked the music, but he liked even more the chance to be on his own, away from the clinging hands of Clay Holt and Shining Moon. He was willing to put up with them because he was enjoying the trip down the river, away from Marietta, but when the time came—and Matthew was sure it would come soon—he was going to leave them and make his own way.

And if they tried to stop him . . . well, they would regret it, that was all.

He glanced behind him and saw the man called Markham pushing through the crowd, looking for him. Matthew didn't want anybody to watch him. He wanted to listen to the music and the speeches without someone hovering over him, making sure he didn't do anything wrong.

What Markham or Clay or Shining Moon thought was right or wrong didn't mean a thing to Matthew. He did what he wanted, and that was all that mattered.

He was almost at the front of the crowd now, and he tried to squirt through another narrow gap he spotted. But the gap closed, and he bumped hard into the leg of a man who loomed over him. The man's hand came down firmly on his shoulder.

"Well, now, what have we here?"

Matthew looked up. He had seen the man before,

on the boat. With a smile the man said, "You're Clay Holt's boy, aren't you?"

Matthew hated that. He wasn't Clay's son. His parents were dead. "I'm nobody's boy," he snapped.

"My, aren't you the feisty one?" The man reached into his pocket and brought out a piece of licorice. "Here, you can have this."

Matthew started to reach for it, then stopped himself. He frowned suspiciously. "What do you want?"

"Why, to be your friend, that's all. Do you want the candy or not?"

"I'll take it." Matthew snatched the licorice out of the man's hand.

"Just don't tell Holt or the Indian woman that I gave it to you. They might not like it."

There was something unfriendly in the man's tone as he spoke Clay's name, and it appealed to Matthew. He said, "I don't care what they like."

The man chuckled. "You have a mind of your own. That's good." He patted Matthew on the shoulder. "I think we'll be great friends, you and I."

Matthew grunted. He didn't want to be friends with anybody. But as long as the man had something he wanted, Matthew could pretend to be friendly. He could pretend just fine.

"I have to go make a speech now," the man said. "I'll talk to you later on the boat, just you and me. All right?"

Matthew hesitated, then shrugged. "Sure, mister."

The man smiled and turned away, and when he walked up the steps to the platform and joined several other men there, Matthew slipped to the front row and was still standing there a couple of minutes later when Markham came up behind him.

"There you are," said Markham. "Your folks are probably a little worried about you, the way you disappeared into the crowd like that."

"I didn't disappear," Matthew said. "I'm right here."

"Well, you and I will watch everything together, all right?"

"Sure," Matthew replied easily. He didn't care now. He had a piece of licorice in his pocket, and he had made a new friend.

A friend who evidently had as little use for Clay Holt as Matthew himself did.

With the cargo of sandalwood securely loaded in its hold, the *Lydia Marie* set sail from Hawaii, bound for China. Ned was satisfied that he had done as well as possible in his maiden effort. Kamehameha was a wily old fox. An exclusive trade agreement was probably too much to expect, given that the Pacific trade was already beginning to burgeon. But the king seemed to have taken a liking to Ned and Captain Canfield, and that boded well for the future. Their next trip to the islands would prove more profitable, Ned was certain.

He was standing night watch on a brilliantly starlit evening about a week out of Hawaii when approaching footfalls made him turn around. He thought for a second that it was India, but, unlike India, the newcomer shuffled and dragged his feet. Ned tensed as the shadowy figure drew closer.

"Good evenin' to ye, Mr. Holt."

Ned recognized the voice and relaxed. "Hello, Yancy. What are you doing out and about this evening? I thought you had the day watch."

The little sailor nodded. "Aye, that I did, sir."

"You don't have to call me sir. I'm not an officer. I'm just a seaman like you."

"Oh, not like me, Mr. Holt. We all know that you're the cousin o' Mr. March, him what owns this ship. Ye be the one who talked to that lord high mucky-muck Kamehameha, too, and got us this load o' sandalwood we're carrying. One way o' looking at it is that none of us boys'd even have a job if it wasn't for you."

Ned shook his head. "Now, I wouldn't go so far as to say that—"

"The boys an' me, we all know the truth," Yancy

went on. "And we know, too, that ye never try to lord it over us. That's why we figgered you had a right to know."

"To know what?" Ned asked with a frown.

"That that scut Donnelly's planning something. He figures he's got a score to settle with ye, and he's going to do it soon now."

Ned's frown deepened. He had thought that his troubles with Donnelly were long since over. Donnelly glared at him whenever their paths crossed, that was true, and he seldom spoke more than two words to Ned. But that was no reason to think he was planning mischief.

"How do you know this?" asked Ned.

"Because I heard 'im talking to one of his mates!" Yancy replied with some urgency. "He said ye were going to be sorry ye were ever born, and so was that little friend o' yours."

India. Donnelly must have been talking about India, Ned thought, and he felt a sudden sense of panic. Donnelly knew that India was a woman. He was the only one on the *Lydia Marie* who did. Was he prepared to reveal their secret now that they were far out at sea?

Or did he have something even worse in mind?

Ned clapped a hand on the little sailor's shoulder. "Thanks, Yancy," he said. "I don't know what Donnelly's planning to do, but I promise you, now that I've talked to you, he won't take me by surprise."

"Then I've done me job," Yancy said with some satisfaction. "Ye'll watch him close now?"

"I certainly will."

"And if he tries anything, ye'll be ready to strike back 'fore he knows what's hit him." Yancy sounded as if he was looking forward to that.

"Absolutely right. Donnelly's going to rue the day *he* was born."

"Well, sir . . . if I can be honest wi' ye?"

"Go ahead," Ned said. "Speak your mind."

"I hope ye kill the bastard. If ye don't, once he's through with you, he's liable to come after all the rest of us he's got a grudge against. I figure I may be first an' foremost on that list."

Yancy was right. Donnelly was a threat to the entire ship. "Don't worry, Yancy," Ned said. "Donnelly's not going to bother anybody again. I'm going to see to that."

"Honest, sir?"

"You have my word on it," Ned declared. He turned and, leaving Yancy on the deck, went in search of Donnelly.

It was time to put a stop to the man's trouble-making, once and for all.

India pulled herself up through the hatch and stepped onto the deck of the *Lydia Marie*, enjoying the feel of the warm breeze that rippled the waves. Near the equator the weather was eternally pleasant, except when storms blew through. But the air was always balmy, even at night.

She turned toward the stern, knowing that she would find Ned there, standing his watch. They would not dare to steal a kiss, but they could spend some time together anyway.

She had taken only a few steps when a figure loomed before her. India knew immediately that the man was not Ned; he was too short, although his shoulders were as broad. He said in a harsh voice, "I want to talk to you."

India recognized the voice immediately. "Donnelly," she said flatly. "I have nothing to say to you."

"No, but you got plenty to say *about* me."

"What are you talking about?" India asked. "I don't even think about you, let alone talk about you."

"That's not what I've heard. I know you've been spreadin' rumors about me, tellin' anybody who'll listen that I'm a poor excuse for a sailor who ought to stay on dry land where he belongs."

India was taken aback. "That's insane. I've never said any such thing about you."

"Won't do you any good to lie about it," Donnelly

persisted. "I'm here to put a stop to it. I've treated you fair, damn it. I haven't said anything about what I know about you—"

His voice was rising as he spoke, and for a second India was afraid he would blurt out her secret. But then, before Donnelly could go on, another figure suddenly appeared behind him, in time to hear his last few words. The newcomer grabbed Donnelly's shoulder and jerked him around. "Shut up!" Ned said, brandishing a balled fist. "Move on, Donnelly, or I'll—"

."You'll what, you son of a bitch?" Donnelly's right fist came up, aimed directly at Ned's head.

India had no time to call out a warning, but Ned didn't need one. He saw the blow coming and darted to one side, blocking Donnelly's punch with his left arm as he threw a punch with his right. His fist smacked solidly into Donnelly's face, rocking the stocky seaman back against India.

Fearing that she would fall with Donnelly on top of her, India pushed hard against him. He cursed and swung a backhand at her, sending her sprawling on her back across the deck.

She heard someone roar in rage. With an effort she pushed herself up on one elbow and shook her head, blinking her eyes to clear her blurred vision. As the scene on the deck before her came back into focus, she saw Ned whaling away at Donnelly, who blocked some of the punches and simply absorbed the rest. Shoulders hunched, Donnelly stepped closer and hooked two vicious blows into Ned's midsection.

India saw Ned double over and knew what Donnelly was going to do next. Donnelly's knee came up and cracked into Ned's jaw. Ned's head jerked back and he staggered, on the verge of falling. If he went down, India knew, Donnelly might well kick him to death.

She came up off the deck and threw herself at Donnelly's back, looping both arms around his neck, and hung on tightly. He stumbled forward under her weight. India thrust one leg down, between his calves, and he tripped and fell heavily, India on top of him. As he gasped for air, she took one arm from around his neck and grabbed the knife sheathed at her waist. She pressed the point into his neck just below the right ear and hissed, "Don't move, or I'll push this blade right into your brain."

Donnelly ceased struggling. "You . . . you bitch!" he grated. "Get off me!"

India pushed a little harder on the knife, and in the moonlight she saw a thin black line of blood begin to trace its way down the side of his neck.

"Not just yet," India told him. "Not until we settle a few things."

"I thought everything *was* settled," he wheezed. "I've steered clear of you and Holt."

"That's not the way I heard it," Ned said as he pushed himself to his hands and knees and shook his head groggily. "You've been planning your revenge, Donnelly. We should kill you right now and throw your body over the side."

"Then do it, damn you!" said Donnelly. "Go ahead and kill me!"

It would be easy, India thought. A little more pressure on the knife, and the blade would slide right up into Donnelly's brain.

But that would be cold-blooded murder. India had few qualms about taking a man's life in battle, or to save her own life or the life of someone she loved. But she wasn't sure she could kill Donnelly so ruthlessly.

"India?" Ned said uncertainly.

With a snarl, she pulled the knife away from Donnelly's neck and sat up. She wiped the blade on her trousers and said, "I'm not going to kill you, Donnelly. But I am tired of this. I want you off the ship when we reach Canton."

"What?" exclaimed Donnelly. "You can't do that. You're not the damned captain."

India tapped the side of his head lightly with the flat of the blade. "I've had your life in my hands often enough, Donnelly. I'm not going to let it go again."

"But you're talking about marooning me in a port full of heathen Chinee!"

"You won't be there for long," India said. "Despite the fact that you're a thoroughly unpleasant bastard, you're a competent sailor. You'll sign on with another crew, probably within a matter of days."

"Wouldn't it be easier just to kill him?" asked Ned.

Before India could answer, a voice called from amidships, "What's going on back there?"

"The second mate," Ned said. "Let him up, India."

India was already coming to her feet. She slipped the knife back in its sheath as Ned scrambled up. He bent down and grabbed Donnelly's arm.

"Mr. Donnelly tripped and fell," Ned explained as the second mate came up to them. He hauled Donnelly to his feet. "I was just giving him a hand."

The officer sniffed. "Tripped and fell, did he? Are you drunk, Donnelly?"

"No, sir," replied Donnelly in a surly voice. "I'm as sober as a church mouse, sir."

"A church mouse that's gotten into the communion wine, perhaps." The mate jerked a thumb toward the hatch. "If you're not standing watch, get below and sleep it off."

"Aye, sir," Donnelly muttered. He jerked his arm loose from Ned's grip and shambled past the second mate. His head was turned so that the officer couldn't see the line of blood that had seeped from the knife wound below his ear.

"As for you two—"

"We'll get back to work, sir," Ned said. "I'm standing watch tonight."

"See that you do." The mate turned and strode back toward the bow with the rolling gait of a veteran seaman.

When the officer was out of earshot, Ned said quietly, "You know that sooner or later one of us is going to have to kill Donnelly."

"Maybe," admitted India, "but maybe not. If he

leaves the ship in Canton, perhaps no one will have to die."

Ned snorted in disbelief. "I'll believe that when I see it. No, I've got a feeling that Donnelly isn't through causing trouble for us just yet."

India shook her head wearily. She hoped Ned was wrong—but she also knew better than to hope too much.

CHAPTER
SIXTEEN

By the time Jeff and Irina came back into the house, the discussion between Count Orlov, Captain Vickery, and Melissa had concluded, and all three were smiling. Jeff observed that Melissa's smile seemed strained.

"Feeling better, Mr. Holt?" Vickery asked.

Jeff nodded. "The fresh air cleared my head. I'm afraid I had a bit too much brandy."

"You may want to drink more, Mr. Holt," said Orlov, "when you toast the exceptional bargaining skills of Captain Vickery and your lovely wife." He put a hand possessively on Melissa's arm.

She didn't pull away this time, Jeff noticed.

He forced his thoughts back to what the count had just said. "I take it the discussion was successful?"

"Your proposal shows promise," Orlov said cautiously. "I cannot dispute that the arrangement could be very profitable for the Russian-American Company. Captain Vickery and Mrs. Holt have demonstrated that beyond argument. Although I am not yet prepared to enter into such an arrangement, I will be happy to consider it."

"When do you expect to reach a decision?" Jeff asked, hoping he was not pushing the Russian nobleman too hard.

Orlov gave an elegant shrug. "That is impossible to say. I must give the matter a great deal of thought."

Irina slipped her hand under Jeff's arm. "But now there is no reason for you to leave Alaska so soon." She looked at her husband. "Is there, Gregori?"

Orlov inclined his head. "Your ship is most welcome to remain at anchor in our harbor, Mr. Holt, while I consider the possibility of a trade agreement."

"Don't consider for too long, Count Orlov," Captain Vickery said bluntly. "Winter will be setting in before much longer, and once it does, nobody will be sailing in or out of that harbor."

"Quite true," agreed the count. "I will make my decision while it is still possible for you to leave Sitka. In the meantime, if you would care to come ashore again tomorrow, we can do a little hunting in the interior, as we discussed."

"Thank you, Count," Jeff said sincerely. "I appreciate your consideration."

He only wished that Orlov's wife wasn't squeezing his arm as he spoke those words. Of course, Jeff noted unhappily, Orlov still had a hand on the arm of *his* wife.

"I may have more questions about your proposal," Orlov said. "If so, I take it that you will answer them?"

"Anytime," Jeff promised. "I'll be happy to discuss the matter with you whenever you wish, and I'm sure Captain Vickery will, too."

"Without a doubt," said the captain. "Especially if you have more of this excellent brandy to offer while we're discussing. All that talk gives a man a dry throat, you know."

Orlov looked at Melissa. "And you, Mrs. Holt? Will you continue to take part in the negotiations?"

Melissa hesitated, then said, "I don't really think that's necessary, Count. Jeff knows so much more about trade than I do."

That wasn't strictly true, thought Jeff, but he was glad she had said it anyway. He would breathe more easily if Melissa was nowhere near Count Orlov after tonight.

"How true," Irina put in with a smile. "Jefferson spoke to me at length about the Pacific trade while we were outside."

Orlov frowned at her. "You are lucky you did not freeze in that gown. You should have put on a coat."

"I was quite warm, Gregori."

Jeff gritted his teeth. He wished Irina would stop taunting her husband. If she really wanted Jeff to be successful in his mission, she would stop trying to antagonize the count.

Melissa was not happy, either; Jeff could see the hurt and anger in her eyes. He disengaged his arm from Irina's grip and stepped to Melissa's side. "If it's all right with you, Count," he said, "we'll save that toast for when we conclude our agreement. My wife is probably tired. I know I am. We'll return to the ship now and resume our discussion at a later time. Tomorrow during our little expedition, perhaps?"

"Perhaps." Orlov looked disappointed as Jeff eased Melissa away from him. "I will have Piotr bring the carriage up and return you to the harbor."

"Thank you."

Melissa looked at Irina and said in a voice that faltered only slightly, "And thank you for a lovely evening, Countess."

Irina smiled coolly at her, then glanced at Jeff. "The pleasure was mine."

Melissa stiffened. Jeff swung her toward the door before she could say anything else.

The donning of hats and greatcoats and gloves took several minutes, and by then Piotr and a driver had brought the carriage around to the front of the house. The American visitors climbed into it, and once again the vehicle slid over the frozen ground on its broad wooden runners. The clopping of horses' hooves filled the frosty night.

There was an awkward silence inside the carriage for several minutes before Melissa said in a brittle voice, "That trollop."

Jeff glanced at Captain Vickery, who was sitting across from them. "This is hardly the time or place—"

"Did you see that gown? Ha! Of course you did. You saw it quite well, didn't you, Jeff? And at close range, too."

Vickery cleared his throat. "The countess is very, ah, attractive."

Jeff gave a little shake of his head, warning the captain to stay out of this discussion. "The countess didn't mean anything by what she said and did. She was just trying to make us feel welcome." The words rang false in his own ears even as he spoke them.

"*You* were welcome . . . welcome to anything she had." Melissa crossed her arms over her chest and leaned back against the seat, pointedly looking away from Jeff.

He sighed. Nothing he could say would persuade Melissa that she was wrong. And in fact she *wasn't* wrong, he thought wryly. Countess Irina had not been merely flirting; the unspoken invitation to share more than a kiss had been genuine.

"Perhaps it would be better if Captain Vickery conducted the negotiations with Count Orlov by himself in the future," Jeff suggested.

Vickery's eyes widened with alarm. "I don't think that would be a good idea, Mr. Holt," he said quickly. "I'm a sea captain, not a businessman. I didn't think it would do any harm to point out a few things to the count, but as for taking over the bargaining . . ." He shook his head vigorously. "I'm not prepared to do that, sir."

Vickery was right. It was a foolish idea. "Don't worry, Captain," Jeff said. "I won't ask that of you."

Vickery leaned back and sighed with relief. "Thank you."

Melissa's head was still turned away from Jeff. He said, "You know, it's entirely possible that I won't be seeing the countess again. Tonight's meeting was a social one, but I'm sure she won't be accompanying us tomorrow. From here on everything will be strictly business."

"Hmmph," Melissa said.

She would see, Jeff told himself. She would come to understand that Irina Orlov was no threat to her or their marriage.

He hoped fervently that it would indeed turn out that way.

Something was tickling his nose. Proud Wolf stirred sleepily, then reached up to brush away the pest. It retreated, only to return a moment later. Proud Wolf shifted, hearing the crackle of dry straw beneath him, then swatted again at the persistent tickling.

Someone laughed.

He opened his eyes. Audrey Stoddard was leaning over him, her face only inches from his, her lips curved in an impish smile. She was holding a piece of straw and tickling his nose with it. Proud Wolf caught her wrist and said, "Good afternoon."

"Good afternoon," Audrey said. "I trust you slept well?"

"How could I not sleep well, with you beside me all night?"

He had finally dozed off that morning, claimed by exhaustion, but he had *not* slept well. Every tiny sound had caused him to stir, and whenever he awakened, he had felt the warm length of her body pressed against his.

At this moment he was all too aware of her upper body draped over him, her soft breasts pillowed on his chest. His hand rested naturally on the sweet curve of her hip. She brought her face closer, and her lips pressed his in an urgent kiss.

Proud Wolf responded, pulling her over on top of him. His hands cupped her bottom, and she moved slowly and sensuously against him as her desire grew. His own need for her was raging now. Mouths still locked together, Proud Wolf was about to roll over so that she would be under him when he heard sounds from outside.

Voices. Shouting, angry voices.

Audrey must have heard them, too, because she stiffened and took her lips away from his. "Proud Wolf!" she whispered.

"Sshh." He slid her off him and came to his feet in one lithe motion. Standing stock-still, he listened intently, his keen ears searching for the source of the threatening voices.

After a moment, he relaxed slightly. In the quiet of late afternoon the voices had sounded as if they were coming from close by, but he realized that they were actually farther away, perhaps as far away as the road. He motioned for Audrey to stay where she was, then walked silently to the door of the barn and peered out cautiously.

Just as he had thought, the voices were coming from the road on the other side of the field. Two farmers were struggling to replace a broken wheel on a wagon hitched to a pair of mules.

Proud Wolf sighed and closed his eyes for a moment. Then he turned his head to smile at Audrey. "It is all right," he told her in a low voice. "They are not looking for us."

She scrambled to her feet. "Then who is it?"

"Farmers. A wheel has broken on their wagon. They are having trouble replacing it."

Audrey came to his side and, careful to remain in the dark shadows inside the doorway, peeked out at the two farmers. "Thank God! I thought it was someone looking for us."

"So did I." Proud Wolf squeezed her hand and pulled her back a few feet. "But we must not become overconfident or careless. Just because these men were not searching for us does not mean that others are not. Someone will come after us."

"Because of Will."

"Yes."

Audrey took a deep breath. "Damn him. I'm glad he's dead. I hope he burns in hell."

Proud Wolf looked at her, shocked by her vehemence.

"He was evil," Audrey went on defensively. "He deserved to die."

Proud Wolf shrugged. "Perhaps. But I wish I had not killed him. If we are caught, I will be hanged. I have learned enough of the white man's justice to know this."

"Oh, no!" Audrey exclaimed as she caught his arm. "They couldn't hang you. You were just defending me, and yourself."

"That is not what Frank will say if there is ever a trial. And he is the son of a wealthy man. He will be believed before you or I will."

Audrey could not argue with that. She looked down at the dirt floor and asked in a small voice, "What do we do now?"

"Wait here, just as we planned. It will be night soon. When it is dark, we will travel on."

"Is that what our life will be like from now on? Running? Hiding during the day and walking all night?"

Proud Wolf took a deep breath. "You can stay here," he said, though the offer took all his resolve. "You can walk to the nearest farm and seek help once I am gone. Tell the authorities that I forced you to come with me when I fled the academy." Bitterness edged into his voice. "Everyone will believe that a savage is capable of such behavior."

"My . . . my reputation would be ruined."

"But you would no longer be a fugitive," Proud Wolf said stiffly. "If that is what you want."

"I want *you*," she said. "I've always wanted you, from the moment I first saw you. After that, I didn't want anything more to do with Will. That . . . that's why he hated you so."

Proud Wolf's eyes searched her face in the gathering gloom. He saw nothing there but sincerity, and a little pain. "You wish to go on with me?" he asked softly.

"Of course I do." She slipped her arms around his waist and leaned her head against his shoulder. "I only want to be with you."

Proud Wolf embraced her, and his voice was hoarse with emotion as he said, "Then we will be together."

The faint creaking of wagon wheels and the clopping of hooves made him turn his head toward the barn doorway. With one arm still around Audrey he led her to the door, and they watched as the farm wagon rolled away down the road. The two men had finally succeeded in changing the broken wheel.

"The shadows are long," Proud Wolf said. "Soon it will be night, and we will go."

Many questions yet remained to be answered, he knew. They had to find food and water, more appropriate clothing, and sturdier shoes for Audrey. He hated the thought of becoming a thief, because then he would be no better than a Crow or a Blackfoot. But it might come to that if they were to go on.

He would deal with that when the time came, Proud Wolf told himself. For now, he and Audrey were still together, and she seemed determined that they stay that way.

For the moment, that was enough.

"The water's too low," Captain Nicholas Roosevelt said, shaking his head. "We'd never make it. Those limestone ledges would rip the bottom right out from under us if we tried to go on while the river's down like this."

The *New Orleans* was docked in Louisville, Kentucky, at the head of the Falls of the Ohio, a two-mile stretch of rapids. As Clay stood on the deck, listening with the other passengers to the captain's explanation of why they had stopped, he glanced downriver. Even from here he could see the water frothing and spraying around jagged upthrusts of rock a short distance away.

"It was a dry summer," Roosevelt went on, "and there hasn't been enough rain this fall to bring the water level up far enough." He scowled. "I knew this might be a problem, but what can a man do about the weather?"

His wife stood beside him, squeezing his arm to comfort him. Mrs. Roosevelt's belly had swollen over the trip, and there was talk that her baby would be born any day now. The voyage down the Ohio had been well under way before Clay had realized that Mrs. Roosevelt was expecting. He paid little attention to such matters where other men's wives were concerned.

And since it looked very much as if his own wife would never again be in the family way, Clay spent little time thinking about babies at all.

Roosevelt had gathered the passengers on the deck to announce that the rest of the trip would be indefinitely delayed. Senators Emory, Ralston, and Haines stared at the captain in consternation. The journalists began grumbling among themselves. The *New Orleans* sitting at a dock was not their idea of news.

Lieutenant Markham was with Clay; Shining Moon and Matthew had remained in the cabin. Clay caught Markham's eye and gestured toward the boat's stern. They wandered, apparently idly, in that direction while the others continued listening to Roosevelt's assessment of the problem.

Markham knew why Clay wanted to talk privately. "What's this going to do to our assignment?" he asked as soon as they were out of earshot of the others.

"I don't see that it'll have much effect on it," Clay said, "unless it makes the fellow we're after even jumpier."

"How do you figure that?"

"Maybe he has to be somewhere by a certain time," Clay said. "If he was planning to meet someone in New Orleans, for instance, this delay could cause problems for him."

"Then it's good that we're stuck here in Louisville?" Markham sounded dubious.

Clay shrugged. "I don't know, but it's a possibility. Let's just keep an eye on our three friends and see if one of them starts getting nervous after a few days."

Markham nodded slowly. "You know, I think you may be right. So we should hope that it doesn't rain and the river doesn't rise."

"Might be nice if nature was on our side," Clay said dryly.

He would have reason to remember that comment later.

One of the hotel owners in Louisville was only too glad to open his establishment to the passengers of the *New Orleans*, and many of them, including the Holt family, Markham, and the three politicians, took him up on his offer. Cramped quarters on the steamboat were exchanged for spacious hotel rooms. No one knew how long it would be before the Ohio River rose enough to allow the boat to continue safely, but in the meantime the passengers would be comfortable. And the hotel owner was assured that he would be able to attract more business in the future by advertising the fact that the passengers on the historic journey of the *New Orleans* had stayed in his hotel.

Captain Roosevelt, ever the entrepreneur, took advantage of the situation by staging several short runs back up the river to demonstrate how well the *New Orleans* could travel against the current. Many veteran rivermen had said all along that the real test of the steamboat would come on its return trip, and from what they saw of the vessel's performance, the rivermen in Louisville were forced to scratch their grizzled chins and concede that Roosevelt's outrageous claims might have something to them.

The captain had other matters on his mind as well. His wife was staying ashore now, too, because her time for confinement had come. The birth of their first child was imminent.

Matthew Garwood neither knew nor cared about any of the grown-ups' concerns. His only goal at the moment was to slip out of the hotel unnoticed.

The voyage downriver had been exciting, but sitting around a hotel room with Holt and the squaw was boring, to his mind. So he had decided to go back down to the docks to see if anything more interesting was going on there.

Clay and Markham were down in the hotel's bar, and Shining Moon had dozed off, giving Matthew the opportunity to sneak out of the second-floor room. He closed the door quietly behind him and stole down the hallway toward the rear stairway. No one else was about as Matthew moved quickly but silently. He went down the narrow stairway, being careful to stay close to the wall so that the boards wouldn't squeak. He snorted. Those redskins who lived near New Hope thought they were good at being quiet, but they weren't the only ones.

There was another hall at the bottom of the stairs, but Matthew headed toward the door that led to the alley behind the hotel. He opened it just enough to slide through, then eased it closed behind him. He smiled. No one had seen him.

A few minutes later he was walking jauntily through the streets of Louisville. Like any river port, it was a busy town, bustling with wagons and horses and people going about their business. As he walked toward the river, no one paid him any attention. That was the way Matthew liked it.

The *New Orleans* was not the only vessel docked at Louisville. Dozens of keelboats and flatboats were tied up at the piers along the river. Some of them were heading downstream to the Gulf of Mexico, and others were bound for Pittsburgh. With the river running so low, the cargo on the boats had to be unloaded and portaged around the rapids, while the boats themselves were hauled upstream by cables attached to mule teams on the shore, or carefully floated over the Falls if they were headed downstream. Flatboats had an easier time of it, by far, no matter which way they were going. Several keelboats had wrecked trying to run the rapids during the past few days.

Matthew picked up those bits of information by wandering around the docks for an hour and listening to the conversations around him. Despite his contempt for people who made an honest living, he found himself fascinated by the river lore he overheard. Maybe someday he would have a boat of his own, a boat he would take anywhere he wanted, and no one could stop him.

After a while he grew a little bored with this, too, and he was about to go back to the hotel when he spotted a familiar face. The man was standing inside a large shed at the head of one of the docks, talking to another man in the rough clothes of a riverman. Several bundles of furs, wrapped in canvas, were stored under the shed, and Matthew figured they had been taken off the flatboat tied up next to the dock. Matthew wondered why the man he had recognized was talking to such an individual. There had to be a good reason, he thought.

He decided to find out what it was.

Neither of the men had noticed Matthew. He moved closer, concealing himself behind some crates, and slipped to the wall of the shed, where he could hear the two men talking.

"Now, it's vitally important that you deliver this message, do you understand?"

Matthew recognized the voice. It belonged to the man from the boat.

"I understand, mister. Soon's I get to New Orleans, I'll go right to that hotel an' give it to the fellow."

"To the Comte de la Carde."

"Yeah. That fellow."

Matthew heard some muttering, and then the familiar voice said, "I'm putting my trust in you. If you let me down . . ."

Someone spat. "Hell, I said I'd get the word to him,

mister. You can count on me." Coins were jingled together. "Why, for this much money, I'd do about anything you want."

"Just deliver that message. It's very important."

Matthew drew back against the wall when he heard footsteps. He waited a moment, giving his quarry a small lead, then fell in behind him. Even as well dressed as the man was, he didn't particularly stand out. All sorts of people could be found along the river, from the richest to the poorest. Matthew quickened his pace, and within minutes he had almost caught up to the man he was trailing. He waited until there was no one close by before he said, "Hello, Senator."

The man stopped short and turned around quickly. His eyes widened in surprise when he saw Matthew, then narrowed in suspicion. He put a smile on his face, but Matthew knew it was about as genuine as the one he was wearing.

"Well, if it isn't my young friend," the man said. "I'm afraid I don't have another stick of licorice today—"

"That's all right," Matthew said. "I'd rather know what was in that message you sent, anyway."

CHAPTER
SEVENTEEN

I f the senator had been surprised to see Matthew
down by the docks, he was positively shocked by
the boy's question. He stared at him, his face contorted with anger and disbelief. "What did you say?"

"I said I'd rather know what's in that message you
sent to the C-Comte de la Carde." Matthew stumbled a
little over the awkward name, but other than that his
voice possessed a confidence unusual in someone so
young.

The senator attempted a hearty laugh, but it
sounded hollow somehow. "I'm afraid I don't know
what you're talking about, lad," he said. "How would I
send a message—"

"With that flatboat man you were talking to just
now. I saw you and heard you."

The politician's jaw tightened, and his face flushed.
"You're just a child," he snapped. "You don't know
what you saw or heard."

"I saw and heard more than you think I did." He

had always been mature for his age, Matthew thought proudly, but no one had ever really understood that. He ventured another twist of the verbal knife. "I think you wouldn't like it if I told Clay Holt what I heard you saying to the riverman."

"Why, you little—" The senator stopped himself and caught his breath. "Look here, Matthew, this is grown-up business, not something for children. It has nothing to do with you, and I'd appreciate it if you didn't say anything to anyone about it, not just Mr. Holt."

"Not even Mr. Markham?" Matthew thought about it, then added, "I've heard Clay call him Lieutenant. He must be in the army."

"I know Markham's in the army," snapped the senator. "He's not fooling anyone, and neither is Holt." He looked around abruptly to make certain that no one was eavesdropping on them. The doorway of an abandoned shop was close by, and the senator jerked his head toward it. "Let's go over there to talk."

"All right," Matthew said. He didn't mind being agreeable, when it suited his own purposes.

In the relative privacy of the doorway the senator looked down at Matthew and said, "I've been meaning to talk to you anyway, ever since that rally. I thought perhaps you could tell me about all the things your father has been doing."

"He's not my father," Matthew said sharply. "I told you that."

"So you did. My apologies. I don't like the man any more than you appear to. He and his brother and Markham caused me a great deal of trouble back in Washington City." He put a hand on Matthew's shoulder. "See here, young man. There's no reason you and I can't continue to be friends, even partners."

"If we're going to be partners, tell me about the Comte de la Carde."

The hand on his shoulder tightened a little. "I can't do that. Isn't there something else you'd like?"

Matthew replied without hesitation. "Money."

When he ran away from Clay and Shining Moon, he would need money to get to wherever he was going. He was old enough to know that.

The senator chuckled humorlessly. "Ah, a lad who knows what he wants. I like that. What do I get in return for my money?"

"I won't say anything to Clay about the Comte de la Carde." Matthew wondered idly what sort of name that was. "And if I hear him and Mr. Markham talking about anything I think you'd like to know, I'll come and tell you."

The senator patted Matthew's shoulder. "My little spy."

"Partner," Matthew reminded him curtly. "Now, what about the money?"

"A boy after my own heart," the senator muttered. He reached into his pocket and brought out a coin. "Will this do for a start?"

Matthew snatched the coin from the senator's outstretched hand, lifted it to his mouth, and bit on it gently, feeling his teeth sink slightly into the gold. That seemed to amuse the senator, too.

"I wouldn't cheat you, lad. This thing is too big to quibble over a few dollars."

"Tell me about it," Matthew said.

The senator shook his head. "Not now. Later, perhaps. When I've come to feel that I can thoroughly trust you. But this is a good start, isn't it? That coin should be enough to buy your silence for the time being."

"But not forever," Matthew cautioned.

"Of course not. Just be patient. You'll soon have more money than you thought there was in the whole world."

That sounded good. Matthew stuck the coin in his pocket.

"Run along back to the hotel now," the senator said. "And if you hear anything interesting, come and tell me."

"I will," Matthew promised. He still had his hand in his pocket, wrapped around the coin.

The senator might not know it now, but that payment would be only the first of many, Matthew thought. Excitement surged inside him. When the time came to run away, he would have enough money to go anywhere he wanted to.

And Clay Holt would never find him.

Matthew turned and left the senator standing in the doorway of the abandoned building. In his elation he never looked back, never saw the menace glittering in the narrowed eyes of the man he was blackmailing.

Storms at sea didn't blow up out of nowhere, but sometimes it seemed as if they did. This was one of those times, Ned thought as he stood at the railing in the bow of the *Lydia Marie* and observed the line of dark clouds that stretched across the horizon.

India was at his side. "There's no way around it, is there?"

Ned grunted. "You'd know about that better than I would. You've been sailing these seas a lot longer."

"We're in for a blow, all right. We'll just have to ride it out."

Ned and India weren't the only ones who'd noticed the approaching storm. Other sailors were scurrying around the deck, preparing for trouble.

Captain Canfield called to them from the bridge, and Ned and India went to join him. "We're going to turn south," he said. "I think there's a good chance we can skirt around the worst of that storm."

Ned nodded. "It's worth a try." But India looked dubious, and as they left the bridge and headed for their posts, he asked her, "You don't think we can avoid the worst of it?"

She shook her head. "I wasn't going to argue with Captain Canfield. He could be right. But I've seen storms like this one before, and it's almost impossible to outrun them." She nodded toward the line of clouds. "Look at how quickly it's approaching."

Ned saw that she was right. The dark clouds were looming much closer than they had been only a few minutes earlier. "Well, we'll do what we can," he said with a sigh. "I'm going to make sure that load of sandalwood is properly secured."

"I'll be in the shrouds," India said. "Once that wind hits us abeam, we'll need all the help we can get to handle those sails."

"I'll be back as quickly as I can," promised Ned, "and pitch in with the rest of you."

He lifted one of the hatches leading to the cargo hold and clattered down the ladder. The load of sandalwood was secured with stout ropes, and Ned knew that India had tied many of the knots herself. He trusted her skills, but he checked the lines anyway. While he was doing that, he felt the ship swing around to the south—and just in time, too, because a moment later the wind shifted. The floor of the hold shivered under Ned's feet as the sails filled and the *Lydia Marie* leaped forward. A few minutes later he heard a roaring sound and knew that the rain from those dark clouds had hit.

Ned bit back a curse. He had not had a chance to fetch his slicker from his cabin, so he would get soaked when he went back above. But everyone got wet during a storm like this, he told himself. His clothes could dry later.

It took him several more minutes to complete his task. When he was satisfied that the cargo would not shift around no matter how badly the ship was tossed by the waves, he scrambled back up the ladder and threw the hatch open. Huge raindrops pelted his face. He gasped at the strength of the downpour, then forced his way up through the hatch, flung it closed behind him, and dogged it shut.

In a matter of seconds his clothes were soaked. The day had gone from sunny and bright to gray-black and lightning-streaked. The sea was not too rough yet, but that was coming, Ned thought. He was sure of it.

He looked around for India and finally spotted her on the starboard side of the ship, holding tightly to one of the shroud lines. The wind was growing so strong that the sails might have been torn from their rigging had the crew not hung on to the lines. As the waves tossed the *Lydia Marie* higher with each swell, Ned made his way toward India. This was already one of the worst storms he had experienced since coming to sea, and it was only beginning. He held tightly to the rail as he worked his way along the plunging deck.

A man was stationed at one of the shrouds between Ned and India, and as he turned his head toward Ned, another flash of lightning cracked overhead and lit up the deck. Ned saw a familiar face peering at him. *Donnelly*! Was it pure bad luck that had put Donnelly on the same side of the ship as Ned and India, or had he claimed that post for a reason?

In the middle of a bad storm that was rapidly growing worse, there was no time for such questions. Ned was prepared to ignore Donnelly and move past him to reach India, but a particularly violent lurch made him grab the railing with both hands and hang on for dear life. The rain lashed at his face, almost blinding him.

But he could see a dim figure coming up behind Donnelly. He saw an upraised arm and something—a club of some sort?—clutched in the hand. . . .

Where was India? Suddenly Ned couldn't see her anymore.

"*Donnelly!*" Ned shouted without thinking. But the wind caught the cry and blew it to tatters behind him. A wave rose up and broke over the deck with crashing force. Ned clung grimly to the rail as the foaming sea tried to sweep him away in its deadly embrace. For a long, timeless moment he hung on.

Then the ship plunged forward again, out of the wave at last. Ned shook his head like a wet dog and blinked furiously, trying to see what had happened to Donnelly and India.

He spotted India still clinging to the shroud. But Donnelly was gone, vanished without a trace, so completely that he might as well never have been there.

Ned pulled himself along the rail, thinking furiously about what he had seen—or what he *thought* he had seen. Had there really been someone there with Donnelly? There was no sign of anyone else now. For an instant Ned had thought the second figure was India, and that she was about to strike Donnelly. But India was at her post. Had she had time to knock Donnelly out and then get back to the shroud she was clutching? Perhaps Donnelly had simply been washed overboard. If there *had* been a second figure, perhaps that person had been swept away by the giant wave, too. Or perhaps Ned's eyes had been playing tricks on him, and Donnelly had been alone when he disappeared.

Ned grabbed the shroud Donnelly had been holding. He held on with one hand while he cupped the other around his mouth and shouted, "Man overboard!" India jerked around to stare at him, and Ned repeated the shout.

It would do no good to sound the alarm, Ned knew. Under the circumstances the ship could not turn back to search for Donnelly, and any man unlucky enough to fall into that angry sea would have been sucked under by now. Donnelly was dead, no two ways about it. But he shouted the traditional cry of "Man overboard!" anyway. It was protocol, even in situations like this.

But had Donnelly really been washed overboard . . . or had he been murdered?

Ned had no answer for that. He didn't *want* an answer.

All he wanted at the moment was for this storm to end.

The sea lay calm, almost too calm, under a bright, flat, silver sky. Hard to believe, India thought as she slumped over the rail in sheer exhaustion, that less than an hour earlier the *Lydia Marie* had been caught in the grip of a maelstrom that had threatened to send her to the bottom.

India was soaked to the skin, and she knew that

her normally baggy clothes were plastered to the curves of her body. Anyone who studied her too closely at this moment could hardly fail to see that she was not the young man she pretended to be. And yet she was too tired to go below and change into dry clothing, too tired even to worry about being found out.

Instead, she was worrying about something else that had happened during the storm. She was brooding about the one crew member the ship had lost.

Donnelly.

He had been positioned at the shroud just aft of hers, and she believed that his presence there had been sheer happenstance. When a storm struck as suddenly as this one had, people went where they were needed and seldom gave a thought to whom they would be working alongside. She had been surprised to see Donnelly, and when their eyes had met for a second just before the squall broke over them, he had looked surprised, too. Then both of them had had their hands full staying alive and keeping the wind from ripping the sails to ribbons.

Donnelly hadn't stayed alive. The sea in its rage had claimed him.

Hadn't it?

A low groan made India look to her right. Ned was leaning over the railing as she was. All over the ship, exhausted men were trying to catch their breath. The passing of the storm had left the sea tranquil, and the crew was taking advantage of the respite.

"Lord, that was . . . a blow," Ned said. His head hung down, and he was breathing deeply. He sounded as if he had just run ten miles.

"Aye," India said. "I've seen worse . . . but not often."

"I don't want to see worse." Ned shook his wet hair. "I don't care if I never see another storm cloud again."

"If you remain a sailor, you'll see worse, bucko," India told him. "It's part of life out here."

Ned grunted. "And death."

India shot him a look. "What do you mean by that?"

"Nothing. I was just thinking about Donnelly."

India's reply was blunt. "I won't miss him." Then her voice softened. "But I wouldn't wish an end like that on my worst enemy, which Donnelly very nearly was."

"I saw the wave hit," Ned said, "but there was nothing I could do."

"Nothing any of us could do."

But had it been entirely the fault of the wave? she asked herself. For a split second before the wall of water had crashed across the deck, she had thought she saw someone else with Donnelly, someone about to strike him from behind. If that had happened, it would explain why Donnelly had been washed overboard. He could have been knocked out.

That was insane, she told herself. The force of the wave had been strong enough by itself to carry Donnelly off. She shouldn't complicate matters by giving in to her imagination. Who could have clouted Donnelly over the head like that?

Ned was back there. The thought prodded insistently at the back of her mind. Ned had been close by, and it had been he who raised the shout "Man overboard!"

Donnelly had been a thorn in the sides of both of them for months now. Ned had every reason to want him dead. But then so did she, India reminded herself. She probably had even better reason than Ned. And she knew that *she* hadn't done anything to him.

Ned wouldn't kill a man just to settle a grudge. India was sure of that. But if he thought he was getting rid of a threat to her, the woman he loved . . .

She put her head in her hands and moaned.

"Sick?" asked Ned.

"No, just . . . tired," India lied. It was only half a lie. She *was* tired, utterly drained, in fact. But she was sick, too, sick with worry.

Because she could not be sure that the man she loved was not a murderer.

Count Gregori Orlov was a very stubborn man. Jeff hoped that Ned and India had had better luck with the Hawaiians than he was having with the Russian.

The two men were being rowed by Russian soldiers across the strait separating the island on which Sitka stood from the Alaskan mainland. "Your proposals are most intriguing, Mr. Holt," he said, "and I am convinced that they would prove profitable for both the Russian-American Company and your own enterprise. However, I am still not certain that would be enough to satisfy the czar that I have done my duty here in Alaska."

Jeff suppressed a groan and said, "I can understand why you feel that way. You want to protect your country's rights."

"Exactly."

"But no one is disputing those rights," Jeff went on. "This has nothing to do with politics or sovereignty. This is simply a business arrangement."

A faint smile curved Orlov's lips. "Do you really believe that any business arrangement between representatives of two different countries does not involve politics, my friend? They are so tightly intertwined that they cannot be separated."

"I don't see it that way. I don't represent the United States. I represent the Holt-Merrivale Company."

"So you say," Orlov countered with a dismissive wave.

Jeff allowed his anger to flare momentarily. "Do you think I'm some sort of secret agent for my government?"

"Anything is possible."

Anything but getting you to accept a reasonable offer, Jeff thought.

Since he had arrived in Sitka that morning for their expedition into the interior, Jeff had attempted again and again to explain how lucrative the proposed venture could be for everyone involved. But the count was unyielding. For every advantage that Jeff pointed out, Orlov countered with yet another dubious objection. Jeff blew out a loud sigh. Maybe he should concentrate on the hunting trip for now, he thought. After all those weeks on board the *Beaumont*, it would be good to get back into the wilderness again.

And Alaska was certainly a wilderness, he thought as he studied the mainland. Foothills covered with dense pine forests came all the way to the water's edge, and rising behind them were majestic, snowcapped peaks. Jeff felt a sense of homecoming. Those mountains were linked to the Rockies in which he and Clay had roamed, part of the long chain that stretched all the way down the spine of the continent.

As the hull of the boat grated on the narrow gravel beach, the first one to hop out was the Tlingit guide Count Orlov had brought along. Orlov called him Vassily. "His real name is quite unpronounceable," he had told Jeff when they picked up the guide at the Tlingit village just outside Sitka.

The village had been something of a revelation for Jeff. Unlike the hide-covered lodges of the Sioux with which Jeff was most familiar, the Tlingit lived in houses made of wood. Tall wooden poles were installed in front of many of the houses, and as Jeff got closer, he saw that they were carved and painted with grotesque faces the likes of which he had never seen.

"Those are the gods of the savages," Orlov had explained scornfully. "They call those things totems."

"The natives here are very different from the Indians I've known," Jeff had observed.

"They are all savages. Almost a decade ago they attacked our settlement of St. Michael and massacred all the men. The women were carried off into slavery. Since then we have treated them with an iron hand. It is the only way," he added with grim satisfaction.

Perhaps, but Jeff had not failed to notice the veiled resentment on the faces of the Tlingit as they regarded their Russian masters. Someday, no matter how firm a grip the Russians kept on them, that resentment was liable to boil over into bloody rage once more.

For the moment, however, as their Tlingit guide led the party ashore, everything seemed peaceful. Vassily's demeanor was calm and unthreatening.

The group entered the pine forest. Jeff had brought a flintlock rifle from the ship, and it felt good to be tramping along with a weapon in his hand, a shot pouch and powder horn bumping against his hip. If he'd had his old buckskins on instead of a greatcoat and fur hat, he would have felt right at home.

Orlov's plan was to walk into the interior until midday, then return to Sitka in late afternoon. He had told Jeff he hoped they would encounter a bear. He seemed anxious to demonstrate his prowess as a hunter, no doubt because of the way his wife had behaved the previous evening.

"So, what do you think of Alaska, Mr. Holt?" he asked as they walked.

"It's fine country. Reminds me of places my brother and I used to trap beaver, down in the Rocky Mountains."

"I would wager it does not get as cold there as it does here."

Jeff thought about the first winter he and Clay had spent in the Rockies, holed up in a stockade fort with the fur-trapping party sent up the Missouri River by Manuel Lisa. He shook his head. "I don't know. I've seen it plenty cold."

"But not as cold as here."

Orlov was determined to establish that Alaska was the coldest place on earth, Jeff thought wryly. He shrugged and let it go.

Ahead of them, Vassily stopped, pointed to the ground, and addressed Orlov in Russian. Jeff saw the droppings. Bear sign. Orlov smiled thinly and said, "I knew we would find one of the beasts."

The watery sunlight barely penetrated the dense growth of the forest. Led by the Tlingit guide, the hunters moved through gloom and shadow. Jeff studied one of the tracks Vassily had indicated. It was fairly recent, probably made within the previous couple of days.

Around midmorning, Jeff caught the tang of wood-smoke in the air. He mentioned it to Orlov, who questioned Vassily in Russian. The Tlingit replied, and Orlov turned to Jeff and translated. "There is an Indian village nearby. Vassily asks if we wish to visit it."

"I'd like to," Jeff answered without hesitation. He had enjoyed his time in the Rockies with Bear Tooth, Shining Moon's father, and his band of Sioux, and he welcomed the opportunity to see the Tlingit in their own environment.

A short time later they reached the village, which sat on the banks of a foaming, fast-flowing creek. The wooden huts here were similiar to, but slightly smaller than, the houses in the Tlingit village outside of Sitka. Totem poles were prominently displayed in front of many. Like the coast Indians, these people were fishermen, although their methods were different, Jeff noted. Instead of fishing from boats, they scooped fish out of the stream with nets fastened to the ends of long poles. The men handled that chore, while the women and children were given the task of cleaning the fish.

Several men from the village came striding forward to greet the visitors. Vassily spoke to them in the Tlingit language, and they seemed to welcome him warmly. Orlov explained quietly to Jeff, "I believe he came originally from this village. Those savages are probably relatives."

Vassily turned and spoke in Russian to Orlov, who translated for Jeff. "We are welcome here. They have seen a bear prowling in the area recently. He is a great bear, very tall and powerful." His eyes burned with anticipation. "He will make a fine trophy for my wall. There is nothing quite like taking the head of something you have conquered."

The party rested briefly in the Tlingit village. Jeff was handed a pole by a fisherman, who instructed him

in its use by means of gestures. Grinning, Jeff dipped
the net at the end of the pole into the fast-moving water
and almost immediately felt a slight jerk as a fish swam
into it. He twisted the pole as the Tlingit had shown
him, closing the net and trapping the fish. When he
lifted the net from the water, he saw a fine trout thrashing around in it, sunlight gleaming off its silvery scales.
A small child standing nearby laughed and pointed delightedly.

Jeff was enjoying himself so much he almost hated
to leave. But Orlov was determined to find the bear, so
the hunters once again entered the woods. Jeff smiled
and waved to the Indians as he left with the Russians.
No one returned the wave except the children. The
adults merely watched with their habitual stony, un-
readable expressions.

"That bear is here somewhere. I know he is," Orlov
said. "I think we should split up until we find him.
That will allow us to search more ground."

Jeff frowned, unsure how to reply. With a huge,
dangerous bear lurking around, splitting up might not
be the wisest course. It might take all the guns in the
party to bring the beast down if they found him. But
Jeff knew even from his limited experience with Orlov
how stubborn he could be once he'd made up his mind
about something.

At the base of a slope where Vassily found some
droppings no more than an hour old, Orlov signaled to
his soldiers to spread out. "We will form a line and
move up the hill," he said. "That way we are certain to
flush out the bear."

Jeff nodded agreement. An unsettling thought suddenly occurred to him: If Orlov wanted to get rid of
him, a "stray" shot would be a good way to do it. All
Orlov had to do was get Jeff alone with him so there
would be no witnesses.

But it quickly became apparent that Orlov had no
such intention in mind. "We will form into groups of
two and spread out across the hillside, Mr. Holt. You
will go with Vassily," the count suggested. "He is the

most experienced among us at these things. Piotr will accompany me." He raised his voice and gave the order to the others in Russian.

Jeff found himself at one end of the line with Vassily. A couple of Russian soldiers were some fifty yards to their left. Fifty yards beyond them were Count Orlov and Piotr, and past them more pairs of soldiers. At Orlov's shouted command, the line of men began to move up the thickly wooded hillside.

Within a matter of moments Jeff could no longer see the others, although he could hear them moving through the undergrowth. Other than that, he and Vassily might have been alone in the wilderness. Jeff gripped his rifle tightly.

Quickly he lost track of how long it had been since he and Vassily had separated from the others. In this shadowy world beneath the pines, time seemed to move more slowly. All Jeff knew was that he and Vassily had been climbing up the hillside for some time when a loud roar suddenly sounded directly ahead of them. In a cluster of trees not ten yards away, the branches were thrashing back and forth.

Before Jeff could comprehend what was happening, out of the trees burst the bear they were tracking. Instantly its small eyes spotted the two men. With another ferocious roar and a flash of its hideous fangs the huge grizzly charged straight at them.

CHAPTER EIGHTEEN

This wasn't the first time Jeff had been charged by a bear. He had faced grizzlies before. But this creature was larger and more daunting than any bear Jeff had ever seen.

It was also lumbering toward them faster than anything that enormous had a right to.

Instinctively Jeff brought his rifle to his shoulder. Beside him, Vassily was lifting his flintlock. Surely the other men on the hillside had heard the bear's roars by now and would be on their way to help, Jeff thought fleetingly. The plan had been for everyone to converge when the bear was spotted before anyone closed in on it. The bear, however, had other ideas.

And if Jeff and Vassily didn't bring it down with their first shots, they might well be mauled to death before help arrived.

The familiar, steely calm Jeff always felt in the face of danger settled over him. But his confidence took a serious blow when the hammer of Vassily's rifle fell and nothing happened save for a tiny spurt of smoke in the pan. The rifle had misfired.

The single lead ball in Jeff's rifle was their only hope now.

A jolt of fear shot through Jeff. A bear's skull was notoriously hard. If a rifle ball struck it at an angle, the ball would likely only glance off, annoying the bear more than anything. The only way to kill the creature quickly and surely was to send the shot through one of its eyes into its brain—but a bear's eye was a small target indeed, especially when it was charging. Clay might be able to manage such a shot, but Jeff . . .

He thought of Melissa, and Michael. His aim steadied, and he squeezed the trigger. The rifle bucked hard against his shoulder. Smoke and flame geysered from the muzzle of the gun, and for a second Jeff couldn't see through the smoke. He heard the bear howl, but he couldn't tell if it was from rage or pain.

As he lowered the rifle, the great beast stumbled, its onrushing stride broken. It fell, crashing to the earth so hard and so close that Jeff could feel the impact through the soles of his boots. It came to rest barely ten feet away.

The bear's right eye was a gory mess where Jeff's ball had penetrated. The animal was dead, although its massive paws were still twitching.

Breathing heavily, Jeff looked at Vassily and saw admiration shining in his eyes. The Tlingit had not budged after his rifle misfired, even though he could have turned and run. But he had not fled, and Jeff felt a surge of gratitude for the faith the Indian had placed in him.

Then, as he was struck by full realization of what he had just done, Jeff's knees begin to shake. He rested the butt of the long rifle on the ground and leaned against it to steady himself.

Orlov and the other Russians hurried up a moment later.

"No!" Orlov exclaimed when he saw the body of the bear. For several seconds he stood staring at it, his face flushed and angry. Jeff knew why. He had slain the trophy that Orlov had wanted to take himself. And there was Irina to consider, too—Orlov would have to return to Sitka and tell his wife that the American, not he, had made this stupendous kill.

With a visible effort Orlov summoned up a facade of enthusiasm. "A magnificent shot!" he said. "I assume it was you who made it, Mr. Holt?"

"Seemed the proper thing to do," Jeff said dryly. "It was either that or let that big fellow tear us to pieces."

Orlov glowered at Vassily. "The savage was no help? I heard only one shot."

"His rifle misfired," Jeff said with a shrug. "It couldn't be helped."

"Still, he will be punished when we return," said Orlov, a tiny muscle jumping in his tightly clenched jaw.

Jeff started to protest, then decided to remain silent. It might make matters worse for the Tlingit if he rushed to his defense. Orlov was in a sour mood as it was.

The count gestured toward the fallen bear. "There will be bear steaks tonight!" he said with false heartiness. "You will take some back to your ship, Mr. Holt?"

"I'd be glad to, if you're sure your people don't need them."

"It was your kill," Orlov said. "To the victor belong the spoils."

"I don't know that I'd call myself the victor. All I did was shoot a bear."

"Ah, but you are," said Orlov. "You have won your life this day, Mr. Holt."

There was no denying that, Jeff thought. If he hadn't made the shot, he would be dead now, and so would Vassily. He wondered if his luck would hold when negotiations began anew for the elusive trade agreement.

• • •

Proud Wolf found a small stream not far from the abandoned barn, and he and Audrey drank their fill. That helped ease the gnawing in their bellies, as did the berries and nuts he found. They would need more food than that to survive, he knew.

They had left the Upper Boston Post Road and taken a smaller lane that led to the south. Proud Wolf had no plan in mind, no ultimate destination, but he knew they would be safer off the main road.

"We must find shoes and stockings for you," he said. "Otherwise, your feet will be too sore for you to go on."

"I'm all right," she said bravely. "Don't worry about me."

He stopped and bent to pick up her right foot. In the moonlight he saw a dark stain on the soft fabric of the slipper where a blister had burst and bled. He put her foot down and straightened, sliding one arm behind her knees and the other around her waist. Audrey gasped as he picked her up.

"I will carry you," he said.

"Proud Wolf! You can't. I'm too heavy."

"You are as . . . light as the leaves on the trees," he said through gritted teeth.

"Put me down." Her voice was stern. "You don't have to be ashamed of the fact that you can't carry me. I'm a good-sized girl."

That was true. They were almost the same height, and Proud Wolf had always been slender and wiry. Reluctantly, he lowered Audrey to the ground.

"That's better," she said, though he knew it really wasn't. "Let's keep walking."

They had no choice but to do exactly that. The nighttime hours were fleeting, and soon it would be morning, time to hide again.

A short time later they came to a small village, a cluster of houses around the intersection of the lane they were following and another, smaller one. One of the houses had a sign hung over the door, and Proud Wolf read the words painted on it: DAVIS GENERAL STORE.

That was exactly what they needed. Ever since he had reluctantly reached the conclusion that he would have to become a thief, he had been looking for just such an opportunity.

The night was quiet. Proud Wolf drew Audrey into the shadows beneath a tree and whispered, "Stay here."

"What are you going to do?" she whispered back.

"Get clothes for us, shoes for you, food."

"You're going to steal from that trading post, aren't you?"

Proud Wolf's mouth tightened into a grim line. He could have pointed out that he had already killed a man. Stealing a few things from a store did not sound so terrible compared to murder. "Stay here," he repeated.

Audrey hesitated, then nodded. "All right."

Proud Wolf left her in the shadows and, with all the stealth he could muster, circled the trading post. The building was dark and silent. If anyone was inside, they were asleep. Proud Wolf intended for them to remain that way.

He stepped up onto the narrow porch that ran along the front of the building. Carefully he grasped the handle of the latch and lifted it. If the door was barred on the inside, then he was out of luck.

Good fortune was with him. The latch clicked open, and the door swung inward on leather hinges that barely creaked.

Proud Wolf slipped inside and paused to let his eyes adjust to the deeper darkness. Scarcely breathing, he listened intently. Somewhere, probably in a back room, someone was snoring. From the sound of it, the man was sleeping quite soundly.

The big main room of the trading post had several windows covered with oilcloth, and the shutters were not closed. Proud Wolf was thankful that the autumn weather had been so mild. In the faint light that filtered in through the oilcloth he saw a long counter at the rear of the room, and along the walls were shelves filled with merchandise. Barrels were lined up in front of the counter, and Proud Wolf knew they were probably full of molasses, salt, pickles, and crackers. He avoided them for the moment and glided toward the shelves. Working by touch, he rapidly located several pairs of shoes.

He chose a pair he hoped would fit Audrey's feet, then groped along the shelf near the shoes and found some stockings, wool by the feel of them. He took a couple of pairs and stuffed them into the shoes. Then he went in search of a heavier dress to replace the thin gown Audrey was wearing.

Painfully aware that the minutes were flying by, Proud Wolf found an empty burlap sack and began filling it with food. He could still hear the snoring in the back room, but he could not be sure the man would continue sleeping. He took down a ham that was hanging from the ceiling and put it in the bag, along with several loaves of bread and some small, hard apples.

Had he been in the mountains and valleys of his homeland, he could easily have survived for weeks. But here, in a land that was supposedly civilized, he had discovered an entirely different kind of wilderness, and he wondered if he had the skills to hide himself and Audrey from the pursuit that would inevitably be mounted. He would have preferred being chased by a band of marauding Blackfoot.

That thought was going through his head as he turned too suddenly away from the counter. The bag in his hand swung out and brushed a glass jar full of something he couldn't make out in the dark. The jar toppled over, and although Proud Wolf lunged desperately to grab it, he missed.

The jar fell to the floor and shattered.

Instantly, the snoring in the back room ceased. A man's voice snorted and muttered, then called out, "What in—? Who's out there?" Heavy footsteps thudded on the floor.

Proud Wolf was already running toward the front

door, the bag of food in one hand, the shoes and stockings and dress tucked under the other arm.

"Hey! You there! Stop! Stop, I say!" shouted the man as he came scurrying out of the back room. "Stop or I'll shoot!"

That threat only prompted Proud Wolf to run faster. Behind him, gunpowder exploded with a deafening roar that filled the store. A flash of orange fire geysered from the muzzle of an old-fashioned blunderbuss and lit up the dark interior of the trading post for an instant.

Proud Wolf plunged through the door as a heavy lead ball slammed into the jamb only inches from his head. Flying splinters stung his cheek.

Ignoring the steps, he leaped off the porch. He flew through the air and landed running, heading for the tree under which he had left Audrey.

Suddenly he realized that he was leading his pursuer directly to her. He veered to the side, hurdling a low rock wall and tearing out across an open field. He hoped Audrey understood what he was trying to do.

The blunderbuss roared again, but as far as Proud Wolf could tell, the ball did not come anywhere near him. He glanced over his shoulder. The man was standing beside the rock wall, reloading his weapon, but by the time he had finished that, Proud Wolf would be out of range of the gun. There was a line of trees on the far side of the field, and when he reached them, he would circle back toward the spot where he had left Audrey.

Another blast came from the blunderbuss just before he got to the trees, and Proud Wolf felt something slam hard against his right hip. He found himself falling, knocked off balance, and as he pitched forward, he was astounded by the storekeeper's blind luck—to actually hit his target with a shot aimed clear across a field by moonlight. The things he had stolen spilled from his arms as he landed, rolled over, and tried to come back to his feet. His right leg was numb, and he fell again.

Proud Wolf grimaced as he got his hands under the leg and heaved himself upright. This time he was prepared for the numbness and compensated for it well enough to stay on his feet. He looked toward the wall. The man from the trading post had climbed over it and was now running across the field toward him, yelling, "Hold it right there, you damned thief!"

Proud Wolf bent, retrieved as many of the things he had dropped as he could, then turned and hobbled into the woods.

The numbness was already wearing off, but he began to wish that it was not. Pain took its place. He reached down to his hip and felt the torn, wet place on his trousers where the ball had creased him. He winced as his fingers probed the shallow gash in his flesh. The wound itself was not serious; no bones were broken, and although it was bleeding, the flow was not heavy. The injury simply slowed him down and made it difficult to move without pain shooting all up and down his right side.

He stumbled through the welcoming darkness among the trees. The storekeeper was still shouting somewhere behind him. If the man caught up to him, Proud Wolf thought, he might have to knock him out. His intention in breaking into the trading post had been to steal a few things he and Audrey needed, not to hurt anyone, but he would never let himself be captured. He would try not to hurt the man too badly.

The storekeeper was closing in on him. Proud Wolf stopped and stood motionless, trying to slow his breathing. Perhaps the man would move past him in the darkness without seeing him.

Then, from in front of Proud Wolf, the sound of someone else pushing through the undergrowth came to his ears. Whoever it was seemed to be trying to move quietly, but without much success. Even as Proud Wolf heard the brush crackling, so did the man from the trading post. As he plunged past the spot where Proud Wolf waited, he yelled, "Hah! Got you now, you damned robber!"

A gasp sounded from up ahead, a distinctly feminine gasp. *Audrey!*

While Proud Wolf's brain was still reeling from the implications of what he had just heard, the blunderbuss exploded again, and Audrey screamed.

It never did rain in Louisville while the *New Orleans* was delayed there, but after a few days, the Ohio River began to rise steadily. Clay, Shining Moon, and Matthew were in the dining room of the hotel one evening, eating supper with the other passengers, when Captain Roosevelt came hurrying in, red-faced and out of breath. To the room at large he announced, "I have good news!"

The three senators were dining together, and Ralston looked up with a smile to say, "By all means, tell us about it, Captain."

"I have a son!"

Instantly the politicians and journalists were on their feet and crowded around the captain, pounding him on the back and offering hearty congratulations. Clay joined the group and pumped Roosevelt's hand.

"Oh, and one other thing," Roosevelt said. "It appears that we'll be able to negotiate the falls in another day or two, if the river continues to rise at its current pace."

"That's good news indeed, but what about your wife and child, Captain?" asked Emory. "Surely you don't plan for them to accompany you the rest of the way to New Orleans."

Roosevelt rubbed his chin worriedly. "I've already spoken to Lydia about that, and she insists that she and the baby are coming along. Nothing I could say could persuade her to change her mind. I even suggested that she and the child travel around the falls by land and rejoin us below, but she would have none of it. She insists that her place is by my side."

Clay glanced at Shining Moon. He had a hunch she would feel the same way if she had been in the same position. And he knew from past experience how stubborn she could be.

But Shining Moon wasn't in the same position, and it wasn't likely that she would ever be. More and more it appeared that she and Clay would not have children of their own. The only child they would raise was Matthew Garwood.

Senator Haines said, "I think all this good news calls for a drink." He glanced at Clay and added reluctantly, "Care to join us, Holt?"

"Don't mind if I do, Senator," replied Clay.

He waited with the others while Haines signaled to a waiter to bring brandy for the group. When everyone had their drinks, Haines lifted his snifter. "To Captain Roosevelt's new son and heir."

"Hear, hear!" Ralston said, and the other men joined in, lifting their glasses and drinking.

"And, if I may be so bold," Roosevelt cried, "to the *New Orleans*, the best boat on the river!"

"To the *New Orleans!*" Clay said along with the others.

When they had finished their brandy, the men returned to their tables. Shining Moon smiled at Clay. "That is good news for the captain," she said. "He must be proud. A son is a good thing."

Clay nodded slowly. "And so is the fact that we'll be getting under way again soon."

He and Markham had been trying to keep a close eye on the senators, and so far they had seen no sign that any of them was cracking under the pressure of the delay. Of course it was impossible to watch them all the time, especially since there were three politicians and only two of them. Shining Moon would probably have been willing to help, but Clay had no desire to involve her in the assignment. He was taking a chance as it was with her life and Matthew's by bringing them along on this journey.

Matthew asked, "Did the captain say we'd be heading downriver soon?"

"That's right," Clay answered. "The river is rising

again. I reckon he'll get the boat ready to travel, then leave as soon as the water is high enough."

"I hope it's not much longer," Matthew said. "I don't like staying here."

"Neither do I, son." As soon as the words left his mouth, Clay glanced at Matthew and saw the slight tightening of the boy's face. Then, to Clay's surprise, Matthew seemed to relax. Maybe he was finally getting over his sensitivity about his parentage. For the boy's sake he hoped so.

When they all went upstairs a little later, Clay stopped and rapped softly on the door of Markham's room. He told the young officer Captain Roosevelt's good news—all of it.

Markham listened, then glanced up and down the hallway. It was empty at the moment, Shining Moon and Matthew having gone on to their room. In a low voice he asked, "What are we going to do if we get all the way to New Orleans and still don't know who the traitor is?"

"That's a problem, all right," Clay agreed. "I never saw a fellow as good at covering his tracks as this one. I was sure he would have done something by now to give himself away."

"We can't just arrest all three of them."

"No, we've got to pin down the right man. I'll think some more on it."

"So will I," Markham said bleakly, "but I'm afraid we're running out of time and ideas."

Clay sighed heavily. He had a feeling that Markham might be right.

By the next day the river had stopped rising. The senators accompanied Captain Roosevelt to the docks when he checked on the water level, and Clay and Markham made sure that they were along, too. Roosevelt looked out at the broad surface of the Ohio and shook his head. Just downstream, the water still foamed and boiled around the rocks that formed the rapids.

"I wish it had come up some more," Roosevelt said. "We'll have to wait another day or two and see what happens."

No one complained aloud about being forced to wait, but a distinct impatience had begun to grip the entire party of travelers. Two more days went by, but the river did not rise. A grim-faced Nicholas Roosevelt called a meeting of his passengers in the steamboat's salon.

"I'm going to try to take the falls just as they are," he announced. "I've had a dozen or more soundings taken, and I'm confident that the river is deep enough for our hull to clear the bottom. All we have to do is avoid the rocks. But it will be a risky venture, and I wanted you all to know. You can stay in the boat or travel overland and meet us downstream."

Senator Ralston spoke up immediately. "Now, how would it look to the folks back home who voted for me, Captain, if I took the easy way out? I'll stay right here on board the *New Orleans*, if that's agreeable to you. I have every confidence in her—and in you."

"I appreciate your confidence, Senator," Roosevelt said sincerely. "But I can offer no guarantees that we will make it through the falls safely."

"Nothing in life is guaranteed," said Haines. "I'll stay, too, Captain."

"As will I," Emory chimed in.

The journalists had no choice but to stay on the boat with the senators, although some of them looked dubious about the idea.

Roosevelt looked at Clay. "What about you, Mr. Holt?"

Clay glanced at Shining Moon and Matthew. He couldn't risk their lives any further. He knew that Shining Moon would agree to whatever he decided, but Matthew's face was flushed with excitement. He wanted to take the rapids on the steamboat.

Well, Matthew would just have to be disappointed, Clay thought. He said, "I reckon the best thing for us to do would be to—"

"What about your wife, Captain?" Shining Moon suddenly asked, interrupting Clay. He stared at her, unable to recall the last time that had happened.

Roosevelt smiled resignedly. "I'm afraid Mrs. Roosevelt is determined to make every single foot of this voyage with me. She and the babe came back on board earlier this evening and are even now settling into our cabin."

"Then we shall stay as well, because I know my husband wishes to remain on the boat," Shining Moon said.

Clay looked at her, thunderstruck. After a moment he said, "Now, wait just a minute—"

"Was I mistaken, my husband?"

"Well, no," admitted Clay. "I didn't much want to travel overland, but that doesn't mean—"

"Then it is settled."

Evidently it was. Clay knew how hard it was to budge Shining Moon once she had made up her mind about something. And Matthew's eagerness to run the rapids would only make it harder to convince her that she was making a mistake.

With a sigh, Clay looked at Roosevelt and nodded. "I reckon we'll stay on board."

"And so will I," Markham added.

"All right, I suppose it's unanimous," said Roosevelt. "First thing tomorrow, then. That will give the river the rest of tonight, in case it wants to rise some more." He looked around the salon. "Good night, gentlemen—and madam. Sleep well tonight."

But Clay didn't. Not with tomorrow's adventure weighing on his mind.

The river had not risen any higher by sunrise. The passengers had all moved out of the hotel the evening before and spent the night on the steamboat, and they were lining the rail along the bow as the crew made ready to cast off the lines tying the *New Orleans* to the dock. The boilers were at full pressure, even a bit beyond. Clay felt the faint shiver of the deck vibrating under his feet as he stood at the railing with Shining Moon, Matthew, and Lieutenant Markham.

Captain Roosevelt leaned out the open window that ran all the way around the wheelhouse and bellowed the order to cast off. He blew a long, shrill blast on the steam whistle as the paddlewheels slowly began to turn. The slapping of blades against water grew louder as the great wheels revolved faster and faster. The *New Orleans* knifed out into the current of the Ohio, leaving the dock behind. Along the shore, spectators waved and shouted.

As the boat approached the Falls of the Ohio, Clay unconsciously tightened his grip on the rail. He glanced at Shining Moon. Her face was placid and unworried, and as her gaze met his, she smiled. Her serenity, he realized, sprang from the simple fact that they were together. Whatever dangers might await them, that was all that mattered to her.

Matthew was leaning over the railing, eagerly scanning the river ahead. Markham, standing nearby, seemed not to share the boy's excitement.

The three senators stood nearby, with the usual entourage of reporters. If they were nervous, they did a good job of concealing it. But, Clay reflected, politicians were accustomed to hiding their true feelings, which was one of the reasons he and Markham were finding it so difficult to ferret out the traitor. The man they were after could smile and laugh and put a knife in his best friend's back, all at the same time.

As the boat drew closer, the roaring of the rapids could be heard even above the rumble of the engine. The *New Orleans* picked up speed, outpacing the current. The paddlewheels became twin blurs, so fast were they churning. Captain Roosevelt could not allow the boat to drift wherever the current would carry it; it had to move independently of the current to avoid the rocks. The roar of the water was deafening. Clay pried a hand off the rail and put it on Matthew's shoulder, then muttered, "Hang on tight, boy."

The boat plunged between the first of the rocks and

lurched forward as the river began to drop through the rapids.

It was a thrilling ride, Clay had to admit. Again and again the boat seemed to be headed straight for a jagged rock and certain doom when, at the last instant, Roosevelt's pilot spun the wheel and sent it careening past. No sooner had one rock been avoided by a hairsbreadth, however, than another loomed straight ahead. The passengers lined up at the rail shouted in horror, then relief, then horror again. Clay kept a tight hold on Matthew's arm as the bucking and pitching threatened to throw them off their feet. Everyone should have been belowdecks in their cabins, he thought, but no one had wanted to miss the experience of running the rapids.

He and Shining Moon had made similar journeys in the past, riding down fast-moving mountain streams in the Rockies. They had been in small, lightweight canoes then, not a ponderously heavy steamboat. Under the expert hand of Roosevelt's pilot, however, the *New Orleans* seemed somehow to grow lighter and swifter as it slipped past the rocks, sometimes with only inches to spare.

The trip through the two-mile stretch of rapids took only a few minutes, but it seemed much longer to Clay. Finally the *New Orleans* neared the end of the falls. A flat, open stretch of water beckoned ahead. Like an arrow, the boat shot past the last of the rocks and into the calmer water. It was moving so rapidly that Clay thought it might rise and skim over the top of the water like a stone skipped on a pond. Up in the wheelhouse, Roosevelt shouted orders into the speaking tube that connected with the boiler room, telling his engineers to shut everything down and blow off the pressure. He helped by hauling down on the whistle cord and blowing a long, sustained blast.

Gradually the *New Orleans* slowed, and along with everyone else Clay finally allowed himself a sigh of relief. It would have been ironic, he mused, to make it safely through the rapids and then have the boilers explode in calm waters and destroy the boat and everyone on it. Roosevelt took the wheel and turned the vessel toward the south bank of the river. It glided to an easy stop.

Clay turned and watched as the captain descended from the wheelhouse. He was shaky, and despite the cool autumn day his shirt was soaked with sweat under his jacket. He drew a deep breath and announced, "That's as far as we're going today, folks. We'll tie up here and move on in the morning."

No one complained about the loss of the rest of the day. Indeed, everyone seemed relieved for the opportunity to relax for a while before resuming the voyage.

"Well, that's something I'll never forget," Markham said as he leaned against the rail. "Several times there I thought we were dead for certain."

"I liked it!" said Matthew. His face was wreathed in a broad grin, and his eyes shone. "I didn't care if we died or not. I never rode a boat that went so fast."

"You may never ride one that goes that fast again," Clay told him.

Matthew looked up at him. "Yes, I will. I'll see everything and do everything I want to."

"Maybe you will," Clay said. "Keep thinking that way, and maybe it'll come true."

Clay himself had no great desire to repeat the experience. The only excitement he needed now was that of capturing his prey and completing the assignment he and Markham had been given by Thomas Jefferson—and then heading home to the Shining Mountains with his wife.

Those were the thoughts going through his mind when he was distracted by a rumbling sound, similar to the thrumming of the boat's engine and the roaring of the rapids. He listened intently. This sound was deeper, more intense, and so powerful that it seemed to shake him inside.

Then, amid the screaming and yelling that suddenly erupted around him, Clay realized that he *was* shaking—and so was everything else. The branches of the trees on shore were swaying eerily back and forth, huge waves were rolling over the surface of the river that only moments earlier had been calm, and the boat was bucking and heaving. Some tremendous force was sweeping through the landscape.

With a frightened cry, Shining Moon grabbed Clay's arm. "What . . . what is it?"

Clay could not tell her. It was almost as if the world were coming to an end.

CHAPTER NINETEEN

In the week since the hunting trip, Jeff and Count Orlov had been meeting daily, trying to hammer out the details of an agreement. Jeff had conceded almost every point the Russian had demanded, willing to forsake some of his own profits now for the promise of more in the future. But now Orlov was on the verge of backing out again.

Jeff scraped his chair back and stood up. "I don't know what else I can say to you, Count Orlov. I've given you every argument I can think of. Perhaps I should wait until Alexander Baranof returns and negotiate with him."

Orlov's face stiffened. "You will have even less success with Baranof, I can assure you. Not to mention the fact that I have no idea when he will return. It will be next spring at the earliest."

"I could come back then," Jeff suggested. "My ship will have to sail soon anyway, before winter makes sailing impossible."

Orlov slapped a palm on the desk. Jeff knew he was taking a calculated risk by goading him, but he had to do *something* to break this stalemate. Orlov might feel confident that Jeff would not be able to strike a bargain with Alexander Baranof, but he couldn't be completely certain. And if Baranof consummated a trade agreement that made the czar even richer, how would Orlov look, having passed up the same opportunity?

"Do not leave," Orlov said grudgingly. "I must consider your proposal at greater length." He paused, then added, "Perhaps it would be wise if you and your lovely wife would come to dinner at my house again. I would appreciate her opinion on some of these matters. She struck me as an astute businesswoman."

There was more truth to that statement than Orlov knew, thought Jeff. It had been Melissa who had kept Holt-Merrivale operating while he was stuck in a jail cell charged with her father's murder, and then later while he was in Washington City with Clay. But he didn't want Melissa subjected to Orlov's advances again. The count had done quite enough touching and flirting during that first meeting.

Of course, Orlov hadn't kissed Melissa, and Jeff couldn't say the same about himself and Irina. . . .

"All right," he said, seeing no way to decline the invitation. He would simply have to be careful not to leave Melissa alone with Orlov—or allow himself to be trapped alone with Irina again.

Orlov stood up. "I will send the carriage to meet you later. I still have great hopes that we can come to an agreement, Mr. Holt."

"As do I," Jeff said.

He left the count's office after putting on his greatcoat and hat. The howling wind was bitingly cold, even through his heavy clothes, as he walked back to the dock where the boat from the *Beaumont* was tied up. The sailors who had brought him ashore were waiting nearby in a tavern, and they hurried out when they saw him coming.

Jeff was glad to get back to the ship and his own cabin. As he walked in, Melissa looked up from where she was sitting on the bunk. After he kissed her forehead she asked, "How did the meeting with Count Orlov go? Did he sign an agreement?"

Jeff shook his head. "I wish I could say he did." Melissa seemed worried about something. "What's wrong?"

"Michael doesn't feel well. He has a cough, and I think he may have a slight fever." She glanced at the bunk where the boy was lying asleep under a heavy blanket, then looked imploringly at her husband. "I wish we could leave here."

Jeff refrained from pointing out that it had been her idea to come along on the trip, and to bring Michael as well. "Will Michael be all right?" he asked.

"I think so."

Jeff took a deep breath. He had a perfect excuse now not to mention the dinner invitation from Count Orlov. "The count wants to talk to me again later this evening. Will you be all right here?"

"Of course. I'll look after Michael."

"With any luck, we'll soon be on our way home," he said with confidence—a confidence he was no longer sure he truly felt.

Piotr, Count Orlov's aide, looked confused when Jeff stepped out of the small boat alone at Sitka's dock. In halting English he said, "Please to be explaining. The count sends me to bring your wife and you, Mr. Holt."

"Our son is feeling ill," Jeff said, "so my wife remained on the *Beaumont* to care for him. She won't be joining us for dinner tonight."

Piotr looked out at the ship, then back at Clay. "But the count is sending me to bring both of you—"

"Not tonight," Jeff said sharply. "I'm sorry, but there's nothing I can do about it."

As far as Melissa knew, he was simply returning to

Sitka for another meeting with Count Orlov. He had said nothing to her about dining at the count's house.

Piotr gave a sullen nod. "Get in carriage."

Jeff clambered in, then spread the plush lap robe over his knees. The night was crystal clear, stars sparkled in the sable sky overhead, and the air was already so cold that it felt like a knife in Jeff's lungs whenever he took a deep breath.

Jeff expected Piotr to climb up beside the driver, but instead he swung up into the saddle of a horse that was tethered nearby. He jerked the reins loose and rode quickly toward Orlov's house, well ahead of the slower-moving carriage. Jeff wondered if he was warning the count that Melissa had not come ashore as expected.

A surprise awaited him when he got to Orlov's house. The door was open, and a smiling Countess Irina stood alone in the doorway. Jeff saw no sign of Orlov.

Jeff climbed out of the carriage and stepped up onto the porch. "Good evening, Countess," he said as he tugged off his fur cap. A glance told him that Piotr's horse was here. The aide had indeed carried word of Melissa's absence—but to Irina, not the count.

"Mr. Holt," she murmured. "Please, come in. I am sorry to hear that your child is ill."

"Michael will be all right." Jeff hesitated. "I was supposed to have dinner with your husband—"

"Gregori will be here later. There have been problems to which he must attend."

"Problems?"

She waved one elegant, bejeweled hand. "Nothing that need concern you. Word has reached Sitka that the Indians may be considering another revolt. They burned the entire settlement to the ground several years ago, or so I have been told. That was before Alexander Baranof crushed their opposition." She stepped back, and Jeff had no choice but to follow her into the house. She closed the door behind him and went on, "Gregori is meeting with his military advisers, trying to determine a course of action should these rumors prove to be true.''

The thought of an Indian uprising sent a chill through Jeff. The Tlingit Indians far outnumbered the Russians, and only the vastly superior weaponry of the invaders had allowed them to subdue Alaska's native inhabitants. If the Tlingit decided to rise once more, they might crush the Russians through sheer force of numbers, though the casualties on both sides would be devastating.

Irina did not seem particularly concerned. She was smiling serenely as she turned toward Jeff. ''I will . . . entertain you myself until Gregori arrives.''

Warning bells sounded in the back of Jeff's brain. He didn't like the tone of Irina's voice, nor the predatory gleam in her eyes. She was wearing another low-cut gown, and as she came toward him, he found his gaze drawn irresistibly to the valley of creamy flesh between her breasts.

''I'm not sure I ought to wait for the count,'' Jeff heard himself saying. Even to his own ears the words sounded hollow. ''If there's trouble with the Indians, there's no telling how long he'll be occupied.''

''That is true,'' Irina murmured. ''Gregori may be gone for . . . hours.''

This was outrageous, Jeff thought. She was taking advantage of the fact that her husband and his wife were absent and flirting with him even more brazenly than at their first meeting. Well, she wasn't going to get away with it, he promised himself. He couldn't just turn around and leave, not without risking giving offense to Count Orlov, but he could certainly resist any temptation Irina chose to dangle in front of him.

Besides, Piotr was here somewhere, and there were probably some Indian servants in the house, too. Nothing improper could happen.

''We must have a drink,'' Irina went on. ''And not brandy this time, but good Russian vodka.''

Jeff eyed her warily. ''All right. I don't suppose I've ever wrapped my tongue around that, but it can't be

any stronger than the corn squeezings folks brew up
back where I come from."

Irina went to a sideboard and poured a clear liquid
from a crystal decanter into two glasses, then brought
one to Jeff and kept one for herself. "And where is it
you come from, Mr. Holt?"

"I grew up mostly in a state called Ohio, a long
way back east. But since then I've been out to the
Rocky Mountains and back, and up and down the east
coast of the United States and over the Cumberland
Gap to Tennessee. The past few years I've been living
in North Carolina."

Irina smiled and shook her head. "I am afraid I
know little of your country. Perhaps someday you can
show me the places on a map."

"I'd be glad to."

She lifted her glass and spoke in Russian. Jeff
guessed that she had made some sort of toast, so he
smiled and raised his own glass. They clinked together.
He sipped the vodka.

The stuff had a real bite to it, he had to admit that.
In fact, it chewed on his insides all the way down to his
stomach. Irina downed a healthy swallow and seemed
not to be affected in the least. Jeff wasn't accustomed to
seeing women drink hard liquor so easily. He took another swallow.

This one went down a little more smoothly, and
the next one more smoothly still. Irina fetched the decanter, and he allowed her to splash more vodka into
his glass. As he sipped the second drink, he recalled
that he hadn't had anything to eat in several hours.
Drinking like this was probably not a good idea, especially given the delicate nature of his stomach since the
sea voyage. But it was difficult to refuse Irina when she
smiled so coquettishly and offered more.

"Should we go ahead and have dinner," Jeff suggested, "since we don't know when the count will return?"

"I am not really hungry."

He thought about it for a moment, then said, "You know, come to think of it, neither am I."

"I hope you do not mind. I sent the servants away when Piotr brought word that your wife did not accompany you from the ship. Without her, and without Gregori, it seemed too much trouble to have a, how do you say it, fancy dinner."

Jeff blinked as he struggled to understand the implications of what she had just said. "So . . . there are no servants here?"

"No. And Piotr has gone back to the company headquarters to be with Gregori."

"Then . . . he'll tell the count that I'm here."

"Piotr will say what I want him to say," Irina said confidently. "He may be Gregori's aide, but he is loyal to me as well."

And just how had Irina secured and maintained Piotr's loyalty? Jeff wondered. Looking at her now, she seemed to be capable of almost . . . anything.

Irina turned toward a lushly upholstered divan, then glanced back at Jeff almost shyly. "Will you sit with me?"

"I suppose it wouldn't hurt." He had to be polite, after all. Carrying his drink, he went to join Irina on the divan.

It was Jeff's intention to keep plenty of distance between them, but somehow, when they were both seated, Irina wound up right beside him, so close that he could feel the warm pressure of her hip against his. Once again she clinked her glass with his and repeated what she had said earlier in Russian. Then she downed what was left of her vodka, and Jeff followed suit. As he lowered the glass and licked his lips, he said, "Tell me, Irina, what is that you keep saying?"

She leaned closer and let her glass slip from her fingers. Jeff heard it thud on the carpet. "I am saying, Jefferson Holt, that soon you will be mine."

Jeff dropped his glass, too.

He wanted to get up. He knew he ought to get up and get the hell out of here while he still had the chance. But maybe he didn't have a chance, not any-more. He was dizzy, and the divan was so soft it seemed to reach up and suck him down. Suddenly Irina was no longer beside him; she was in his arms. Her mouth pressed hotly against his. She caught his wrist, lifted it, and brought his hand to her breast. As warm, soft flesh filled his palm, he discovered that the low-cut gown was no longer in the way. The breast that he cupped in his hand was bare, and the erect nipple that crowned it prodded maddeningly against his palm. Instinctively he caressed her, sliding his finger-tips over the ring of pebbled flesh around the nipple, then pulling gently on the hard bud itself. Irina moaned and thrust her tongue between his lips.

Jeff had closed his eyes when she kissed him, and now he was afraid to open them again, afraid the room would be spinning crazily around him. Besides, the darkness seemed to sharpen his other senses, and at the moment he was reveling in the taste and smell and feel of the woman. He brought his other hand up and cupped her other breast. The gown had somehow got-ten pushed down around her hips, and she was nude to the waist.

Irina urged him back, and Jeff found himself reclin-ing on the divan. Her fingers flew to the buttons of his trousers and flipped open the first one with practiced ease. Jeff was full of vodka and desire, and he knew he could not stop Irina from doing whatever she wanted to. He didn't *want* to stop her. . . .

Melissa. Michael. Their images sprang into his mind as Irina unfastened his trousers, pausing between each button for a brazen caress. Jeff groaned, but not from passion. As he thought about his wife and son, guilt flooded through him, sickening him. He knew he had to act now, or he might weaken and give in to what Irina wanted—to what *he* wanted. Keeping Me-lissa and Michael foremost in his mind, he suddenly grasped Irina's shoulders and pushed her away. She fell back against the cushions as he bolted up.

"What . . . what are you doing?" she gasped.

"Getting out of here," Jeff said shakily. "I'm sorry, Countess, but I . . . I just can't do this."

"Yes, yes, you can!" she cried. "I saw and felt the evidence myself!"

"I *won't* do this," Jeff grated. He stumbled toward the doorway, trying to button his trousers, but like Lot's wife, he made the mistake of looking back. Irina was sprawled on the divan, raised on one elbow, her glorious breasts bare. Jeff had never seen a more wanton, desirable woman. He was frozen to the spot, his fingers still on the buttons of his trousers, and he heard only vaguely the sound of the door opening.

But he heard Irina loud and clear when, her face contorted, she shrieked, "So, you . . . you American dog! You think you can seduce me and have your way with me and then just walk out?"

"*Irina!*"

Jeff's head whipped around. Count Gregori Orlov stood in the open doorway.

"Oh, hell," Jeff whispered, watching in horror as the count raised a steady, unwavering hand, pointed a pistol at him, and fired.

Proud Wolf lunged forward with the sound of the shot and Audrey's scream echoing hideously in his ears. "Audrey!" he shouted. A figure loomed in front of him. The man from the trading post, the man who had just shot Audrey! Proud Wolf clasped his hands together and brought them down like a club on the back of the man's neck.

The storekeeper groaned and pitched forward. Something thudded to the ground next to him. Proud Wolf realized it was the blunderbuss. He bent and snatched it up, oblivious now to his own injury. The weapon had just been discharged, so it was empty, but Proud Wolf did not care. It would still serve as a club. As the storekeeper struggled to rise, Proud Wolf slammed the stock of the blunderbuss against the side of his head. The man went down again. Proud Wolf lifted the gun, intending to use the barrel this time to smash out the man's brains.

"Proud Wolf! No!"

He froze for an instant, then dropped the gun. Audrey was stumbling toward him, and he leaped forward to meet her and pull her close. His hands flew over her body, checking for wounds.

"Proud Wolf, I'm all right," Audrey said as she returned the embrace. Her hand fell on his hip. She jerked it away when she felt the blood-soaked trousers. "You're hurt!"

"I am fine. You are alive, and I am fine!"

"I don't even have a scratch, but you—"

Proud Wolf stepped back and gripped her shoulders. "What are you doing here?" he demanded. "I told you to stay under that tree by the road."

"I heard the shots and the shouting, and I saw you running across the field," she explained. "I . . . I had to come to you, to make sure you were all right. So I circled around and into these woods—"

"And nearly got yourself killed," he finished. "That man from the trading post shot at you thinking that you were me."

"I'm sorry," Audrey said. "I didn't mean to cause trouble."

Proud Wolf pulled her close again. "You are not hurt. That is all that matters."

A groan from behind warned him that the storekeeper was regaining consciousness. Proud Wolf turned. He still felt like cracking the man's skull with the blunderbuss, but now that his anger had passed, he knew that would be cold-blooded murder. A killer he might be, but only when he had no other choice.

He clutched Audrey's hand. "We must leave while we still can. Come. Help me gather the things I took from the trading post."

He had dropped the bag and clothes and shoes when he struck the storekeeper. Now he picked them up, wincing at the pain in his side as he bent over. Audrey helped, and soon they were making their way deeper into the woods, leaving the half-conscious storekeeper far behind.

Proud Wolf's wound was still bleeding, and he was beginning to feel dizzy. He was worried that he might lose consciousness if he did not get a chance to rest soon.

Another concern was that when the man from the trading post finally regained his senses, he would seek help and come after them. A skilled tracker would be able to follow their trail through the forest. If Proud Wolf had been alone and uninjured, he could have traveled so stealthily as to leave no sign of his passing, but he could not expect that of Audrey, and he himself was too exhausted and had lost too much blood.

Still, they had to try to throw off any pursuit. Proud Wolf forced himself to think clearly. "Look for a stream," he said to Audrey, "or a patch of stony ground. We must . . . stop leaving . . . tracks."

"All right." She slipped an arm around his waist as he staggered. "Here. Let me help you."

"I am . . . fine," he said stubbornly.

"No, you're not. You've been shot, and you need to rest while I try to do what I can for you." Her voice trembled a little.

He accepted her help gratefully, and they stumbled on for several minutes before Proud Wolf abruptly stopped. "Wait," he whispered. "Listen."

After a moment Audrey whispered back, "I don't hear anything."

"I hear . . . running water. A stream." He lifted his arm and pointed. "That way."

"All right." Audrey led the way, pushing aside the thick undergrowth. A few minutes later, she stumbled and would have fallen had Proud Wolf's hand not shot out and grabbed her wrist to steady her. "It's a creek," she said, looking down from the high bank off which she had almost tumbled. "I think we can get down to the water over there."

Moonlight flooded the opening in the trees above

the creek, illuminating the path Audrey indicated. Proud Wolf nodded. "Yes. This is . . . what we need."

Carefully they made their way down the steep bank and stepped out into the water. The creek was deeper than Proud Wolf had expected; the water rose almost to their waists when they reached the middle. The bottom was rocky and fairly solid. As near as he could judge, the creek ran north and south, so he turned south.

The water was cold, so cold that it numbed the pain in his wounded hip, and as they walked, he began to feel stronger and more clear-headed. He peered up at the narrow band of stars visible above them and calculated by their position that they were indeed moving in a southerly direction. An odd sound caught his attention, and he glanced at Audrey. She was shaking violently. The sound he had heard was the chattering of her teeth.

"H-how long . . . do we have to stay . . . in the water?" she asked.

"As long as we can, so that anyone who comes after us will not be able to find our tracks when we leave the creek."

"A-all right," she replied gamely.

The minutes dragged by as they stumbled along the creek bed. Audrey could not keep her teeth from chattering, and the blessed numbness Proud Wolf had felt in his wounded hip was spreading. They would have to get out of the water soon.

He spotted a dark circle ahead on the bank that rose above their heads. Hope sprang up in his breast. If that was the mouth of a cave . . .

It was. The opening was about four feet above their heads. He pointed to it and said weakly, "Up there."

"I . . . I don't know if I can climb," said Audrey.

"You can," Proud Wolf assured her. "I know you can."

He reached up and caught hold of a root that protruded from the bank. Relying primarily on the strength of his arms, he hauled himself up the steep slope. He had no way of knowing what was in the cave or how big it was, but there was only one way to find out. He pulled himself through the dark mouth.

Luck was with him. The cave was perhaps ten feet deep, and the ceiling rose almost high enough to allow Proud Wolf to stand at his full height. It seemed to be empty, too, and he was grateful no skunk or badger had recently taken shelter there.

Proud Wolf turned back to the opening and stuck his head out. He extended his arm down to Audrey, who was leaning against the bank in exhaustion. She was holding the things he had taken from the trading post, careful to keep them above the level of the water.

"Audrey!" Proud Wolf called softly. "Give me the bag and the clothes. Then I will help you up."

Audrey lifted her hands wearily and gave him the food, the dress, and the shoes. Proud Wolf put them in the cave and then leaned out farther and grasped her wrists. As he pulled upward, she climbed out of the water, her feet slipping in the mud at the edge of the stream. Proud Wolf hung on grimly and called on all his reserves as she clambered into the cave.

She sat on the cave floor hugging herself, teeth still chattering, while he felt around and found some twigs and dead leaves. With cold fingers he fumbled for the little packet of flint and steel he always carried in his shirt pocket. In a few moments he had a tiny fire going. The little flames licked hungrily at the meager fuel, but the light they cast helped Proud Wolf find more dry leaves that had blown into the cave.

He also saw charred circles on the rock floor, the remains of other fires. Children probably played in this cave during the summer, he thought. The young men of his people were fond of caves.

While the fire was still burning, he said to Audrey, "Take off that wet gown." As she pulled off the sodden dress, he emptied the stolen food and clothing from the bag and handed it to her. "Dry yourself with this, and then put on that dress."

Audrey did as he told her. Proud Wolf stripped off

his trousers and examined the wound on his hip. Immersion in the cold water of the creek had stopped the bleeding, for which he was thankful. He took the sack when Audrey had finished drying herself with it and tore some strips from one corner. He was trying to bind them around his hip when Audrey said, "Let me do that," and took over. She had already slipped into the stolen dress.

By the fading light of the fire she patched him up as best she could. Proud Wolf had no dry clothing, so he settled for wrapping the bag around his legs. It was damp, but not nearly as wet as his trousers. They took off their shoes and held their half-frozen toes close to the flickering flames.

The fire wouldn't last much longer, but it had already taken some of the chill out of the air. Audrey looked at the flames and said, "I'll go look for more firewood."

"No," Proud Wolf said without hesitation. "I should go—"

"No, you should not," she said. "You're exhausted. Sit there and rest. I feel better now, and I'll look just outside the cave."

Normally Proud Wolf would have argued, but a lethargy was stealing over him that took away his will. "Be careful," he muttered as he leaned back against the rock wall and closed his eyes. "Do not fall into the creek. We have no more dry clothing."

"I'll be careful, don't worry." Audrey stood up and, stooping slightly, stepped to the mouth of the cave and disappeared.

Proud Wolf waited, breathing deeply and trying not to fall asleep. A few minutes later he heard Audrey returning and opened his eyes.

"There's a fallen tree on the bank just above the mouth of the cave," she said, kneeling to feed the branches she had gathered into the softly glowing fire. "I reached it without much trouble."

"Thank you," Proud Wolf murmured as he watched the branch catch fire and fresh flames lick upward, brightening the cave. The blessed warmth spread over his limbs.

"You just rest," Audrey told him. "I'll feed the fire and keep an eye on things."

That was his responsibility, he thought dully, but in the condition he was in, doing anything more strenuous than breathing seemed an insurmountable task. Now that Audrey had returned, it was hard not to surrender to sleep.

She sat down beside him, arranging the wood close at hand. Proud Wolf closed his eyes again as she leaned against him, her body warm and soft on his side. The darkness of exhausted slumber swept over him like a river.

Gratefully he allowed the ebony current to carry him away.

CHAPTER
TWENTY

With one arm around Shining Moon, Clay reached out to grab Matthew's shoulder and steady the boy. Matthew might have enjoyed the perilous ride through the rapids, but even he was frightened by this sudden, violent shaking of the earth.

Markham grabbed the rail and hung on for dear life. "It's an earthquake!" he shouted.

Clay had never experienced an earthquake. He spread his legs wide and planted his feet firmly on the deck to brace himself and his family as the *New Orleans* rocked back and forth like a ship on a stormy sea.

Some of the trees swaying crazily on the shore toppled over, and huge chunks of the bank sheared off and were heaved into the river, throwing muddy water high into the air. For what seemed like an hour but was probably only a few moments, everything in sight shuddered and jumped and shook. The noise was deafening.

And then, after a short burst of tremors, it was

over. Clay stood unmoving, still holding Shining Moon and Matthew and drawing deep breaths into his lungs. A few feet away, Markham seemed reluctant to let go of the railing, as if he thought the shaking might start again with no warning. Elsewhere on the boat, people were shouting questions. Some of the passengers had been thrown off their feet, and now they were carefully picking themselves up and checking for bumps and bruises. No one seemed to be badly injured, Clay thought as he looked around.

But everyone was clearly frightened out of their wits. Even the three senators, accustomed as they might be to camouflaging their emotions, looked badly shaken.

"Good Lord!" exclaimed Ralston. "What was that?"

Captain Roosevelt mopped his dripping face with a handkerchief and said, "That was an earthquake, Senator. I've heard of them happening along the river before, but I've never been in one myself. Nor do I ever want to be again." His eyes widened. "I've got to check on Lydia and the baby!" He dashed off toward his cabin.

Charles Emory tried to summon up a smile. "Well, we'll certainly have some exciting tales to tell when we get back to the Senate, won't we, Louis?"

"I'd just as soon not have any more excitement, thank you," Haines replied, shaking his head. "In fact, the sooner we get to New Orleans, the better!"

A quick survey by the crew determined that no one had been hurt beyond a few scrapes and bruises. Mrs. Roosevelt and the baby had come through just fine, the captain reported when he returned to the main deck several minutes later.

"My wife was rather frightened, of course," added Roosevelt, "but who wasn't?" He paused, then went on, "I've changed my mind about staying here the rest of the day. We're going to cast off and head on downriver. I'd like to put some distance between us and this spot."

Clay couldn't fault him for that decision, but he also wondered just how much good it would do.

Markham echoed the thought. "The captain may want to leave the earthquake behind, but that may not be possible. There's no telling how far up and down the river it reached."

"Only one way to find out," Clay commented.

Markham shrugged. "True. And I wouldn't think it would hurt to push on."

Matthew looked up at Clay. "Do you think the ground will shake any more?"

Clay shook his head. "I don't know . . . but I hope not."

Over the next few days, as the *New Orleans* continued down the Ohio toward its junction with the Mississippi, more quakes shook the landscape. Most were not as severe as the first shocks, but a few were worse. Roosevelt kept the steamboat as close to the center of the river as he could, for the water acted as a buffer of sorts, absorbing some of the effects of the turbulence. Still, some passengers were laid low by an illness very much like seasickness.

Matthew wasn't particularly bothered by the tremors, but he was awed by the devastation visible on both banks of the river. Fallen and uprooted trees, flooded fields, houses that had collapsed into piles of kindling, the bloated bodies of dead animals . . . all blended together into a gigantic, continually unfolding picture of destruction.

Clay and Shining Moon seldom let him out of their sight, but whenever he could, he stood at the railing and watched the ravaged landscape slide past. That was where he was when the *New Orleans* reached the confluence of the Ohio and Mississippi Rivers. He had slipped out of the cabin while Shining Moon was resting.

The bluffs that rose along the banks of the Ohio fell away where the two great rivers merged. Matthew stared to starboard and saw the huge, flat expanse of the Mississippi. He had thought the Ohio was a big river, but now that he could see what the Indians called the Father of Waters, he understood what big really was. The Mississippi was so wide that it looked more like a lake than a river.

Someone stepped beside Matthew and rested his hands on the railing. "Quite a sight, isn't it, young man?"

Matthew glanced up. "Oh, good afternoon, Senator. I like looking at the river."

"Yes, it's magnificent." The politician lowered his voice. "Have you been keeping your ears open, Matthew? Has Clay Holt or Lieutenant Markham said anything about me recently?"

"No . . . but they're worried that they're not going to find the man they're looking for before the boat gets to New Orleans." Matthew squinted shrewdly at the senator. "I reckon you're that man."

The senator chuckled. "And what if I am?"

"I could tell Clay."

"Don't be ridiculous. You and I have already established a partnership. Remember the coin I gave you?"

"I remember," said Matthew. "But I could use another one."

The senator didn't chuckle this time. "Don't overstep your bounds, my young friend," he said sharply. "I'll give you another coin, but you'll have to earn it, and with more than your silence, too."

"What do you want me to do?" asked Matthew.

"I want you to speak to Clay Holt, and this is what I want you to tell him. . . ."

Clay and Markham had had another fruitless discussion about how to smoke out their quarry, and Clay was in a somber mood when he returned to the cabin. Matthew was gone, and a worried Shining Moon was about to go looking for him.

"I'll find the boy," Clay said as he turned back toward the cabin door. "The river's calm now, but you never know when it'll start jumping around again."

He stepped out onto the deck and looked in one direction, then the other. He spotted Matthew standing alone at the starboard railing, up toward the bow. Clay strode toward him. His hand came down on Matthew's shoulder, causing the boy to jerk a little and look around. "You snuck off again," Clay said. "Shining Moon's worried about you."

"I didn't mean to worry her," Matthew said off-handedly. He pointed. "I just wanted to see the Mississippi River."

Clay glanced outward. Indeed, they had reached the junction of the Ohio and the Mississippi. Clay had seen the mighty river before, in St. Louis, and so had Matthew, he realized, on the journey to New Hope with his mother, Josie. But he had to admit that there was something awe-inspiring about the way the Mississippi swallowed the sizable but still smaller Ohio.

Matthew looked up at Clay. "I saw something funny a while ago," he said.

"Oh? What was that?"

"Senator Haines. He was talking to one of the crewmen, and he gave him some money and then pointed toward our cabin."

Clay stiffened and looked down at the boy. "What did you say?"

"I saw Senator Haines giving some money to one of the crewmen. And then he pointed toward our cabin."

What in blazes did *that* mean? Clay asked himself. Was there going to be another attempt on his life? Had Haines accidentally revealed himself as the traitor?

It was too soon to be jumping to conclusions, Clay warned himself, and the evidence, such as it was, was flimsy: the word of one little boy, a boy who was none too reliable himself.

But Clay was on the alert now, and he would continue to be. If anything suspicious happened in the next day or two—anything at all—he was going to have a long talk with Senator Louis Haines.

• • •

Jeff threw himself aside even as Count Orlov was pressing the trigger of the pistol. The ball whipped harmlessly past his head and thudded into the thick log wall near the fireplace. On the divan, Irina screamed and cringed, holding a cushion in front of her to shield her nudity.

"Bastard!" grated Orlov as he tossed the empty pistol aside and grabbed for the short, curved saber sheathed at his hip. "American bastard! I will gut you for this!"

"Damn it, hold on a minute!" Jeff said. "You've got this all wrong, Orlov."

Firelight glinted on the blade of Orlov's saber as he slashed the air. "Wrong?" he repeated, his voice shaking. "What is wrong is for a man to come into his home and find his wife with another man!"

Jeff felt sick, not only from the vodka but also from the realization of how the scene must have appeared to Orlov: There was Irina, lying on the divan, nude to the waist, while stumbling away from her was the visitor from America, fastening the buttons of his trousers. Irina's strident accusation hadn't helped. She had clearly acted out of spite; Jeff had refused her advances. How many men could have walked away as he had?

The knowledge was no consolation. Orlov was going to believe his wife, and even now Irina was crying, "Kill him, Gregori, kill him! He has dishonored me!"

Finally Orlov took his blazing eyes off Jeff and looked at her. "Shut your mouth, slut," he growled.

"Gregori!" she gasped in horror.

"Do you think I do not know what kind of woman you are?" Orlov spat. "I know you went behind my back with my friends in St. Petersburg. I know you hated it when I brought you to this place."

"Gregori, none of that is true!" Irina protested.

"Do not waste your breath lying to me." His voice was as cold as the frigid wind outside. "By now you have probably been with every man in my command, all of them laughing at me as they rutted with my wife." He lifted the saber. "Now you will pay. First you, then this American!"

With that, he rushed toward the divan. Irina shrieked in terror. The count evidently did not consider Jeff a threat.

That was Orlov's mistake. Jeff's mistake had been coming alone in the first place. It was too late to rectify that error, but he would not stand by and watch Orlov butcher Irina with his saber.

He flung himself toward the count, tackling him around the waist. Orlov grunted under the impact as both men crashed to the floor. Jeff chopped at the wrist of the hand holding the saber, and the weapon slipped from Orlov's fingers onto the floor.

Orlov twisted around and struck at Jeff, who took the blow on his shoulder. Loath to make the situation any worse than it already was, Jeff grabbed Orlov's wrist as he drew back his arm for another punch. "Stop it!" Jeff said. "Damn it, listen to reason, Count! I didn't do anything to the countess!"

"Don't listen to him, Gregori!" Irina screamed from the divan. "He attacked me!"

Orlov suddenly stiffened and stopped struggling under Jeff, who had managed to get on top of him and pin him down. He stared up at Jeff for a moment, his breath hissing between his teeth, and finally said in a hoarse whisper, "Get off me."

"Not if you're going to try to carve people up with that saber," Jeff told him.

"Damn you, American—" Orlov caught himself and drew a deep, shaky breath. "It is all right, Mr. Holt," he said, and although his voice was hollow, it seemed to be under control again. "There will be no more violence here tonight."

Jeff warily let go of Orlov's wrists and straightened, then came to his feet and stepped back. He glanced toward the divan. Irina still lay there, the cushion held in front of her. She was looking at him with an odd mixture of anger, sorrow, and pleading.

Count Orlov climbed shakily to his feet. Jeff noticed that the top two buttons of his trousers were still undone and turned discreetly to fasten them. When he turned back, Orlov was standing in the middle of the room, running a shaky hand over his hawklike features.

"Mr. Holt," he said, "please accept my apologies. I realize that in my rage I almost did you harm, and I regret that."

That statement could be taken more than one way, Jeff thought wryly. Orlov might be sorry that his pistol shot hadn't splattered Jeff's brains all over the rug. But for now he was willing to give the Russian the benefit of the doubt.

"I'm sorry, too, Count," he said. "My actions here tonight were . . . unforgivable."

A small, humorless smile plucked at Orlov's thin lips. "You were a victim, my friend, a victim of a game my lovely wife has played quite often."

"Damn you, Gregori!" Irina burst out. "You know I . . . I have always been faithful to you."

Without looking at her, Orlov said, "My dear, that is such a laughable statement that I shall not honor it— or you—with a response."

Irina sagged back, aghast.

Orlov strode over to his fallen saber and bent to pick it up. He slid it back into its scabbard, then turned to Jeff. "I regret that I was delayed this evening," he said calmly. "I had hoped that over dinner we could come to a final agreement regarding the trade pact you wish me to sign."

Jeff tightened his jaw so that his mouth wouldn't drop open. Orlov had come very close to shooting him and then had gone after his wife with a saber. Now he was talking as if nothing unusual had happened this evening except that he had been late for dinner.

"You had . . . other things to worry about," Jeff forced himself to say.

Orlov nodded. "Yes, the rumors of an Indian uprising." He waved a hand. "Nothing will come of them. I am sure of it. The Tlingit are totally under our domination."

Jeff wished he could share Orlov's confidence. For a man responsible for the lives of everyone in the settlement, Orlov was taking the threat too lightly, in his opinion. But a Tlingit uprising wasn't the most pressing problem right now. Jeff couldn't forget that the man's half-naked wife was lying only a few feet from them.

But Orlov hadn't forgotten about Irina, either; his eyes frequently narrowed and shot in her direction.

Jeff said, "I think I'd better head back to the ship."

"Under the circumstances, that would be wise," Orlov said with a stiff nod. "I'll go out and speak to Piotr. He will have the carriage brought round."

Jeff considered warning Orlov about the influence Irina evidently had over Piotr but decided not to. If the count was unaware of it, it was not Jeff's business to tell him.

Orlov stalked out of the room, and Jeff went to get his coat and hat, ignoring Irina. He heard the rustle of cloth behind him. As he shrugged into his coat, her arms snaked around him and she pressed her head against his back.

"I am sorry," she said piteously. "I . . . I was so frightened of Gregori, I didn't know what else to do. I had to blame you, Jefferson. Surely you can understand that."

"I understand that I don't like being caught between two people who ought to solve their own problems," Jeff snapped. He jerked out of Irina's embrace and turned to look at her. He was glad to see that she had pulled her gown back up so that her breasts were covered again. "I should have left when I realized what you were trying to do," he went on. "I love my wife, Countess."

Irina's contrition vanished in an instant, replaced by contempt. "Your wife!" she spat. "That simpering little fool! I saw the way Gregori drooled over her. So did you."

"Your husband didn't get her drunk and try to seduce her." Jeff settled his fur cap on his head and wound a scarf around his throat. "Well, I'm not drunk anymore. Nearly getting my head blown off by a jealous husband has that effect on me."

"Damn you." A note of regret crept into her voice. "We could have had . . . a wonderful time together."

"Not likely, Countess. I would have had to sober up sometime."

With that, Jeff turned on his heel and strode out of the room, leaving Irina behind. He could feel her eyes on him, stabbing like daggers into his back.

He met Count Orlov on the porch. The count nodded curtly and said, "The carriage will be here in a few moments. Perhaps you will come back tomorrow, so that we can resume our discussion of the trade agreement?"

Again Jeff fought to control his surprise. "You . . . still want to consider signing the agreement?" he finally asked.

"Of course. What sort of businessman would I be if I made a decision based on the actions of a foolish woman?"

"Well, that's mighty . . . generous of you. I suppose I could come back . . ."

"Good," Orlov said heartily. "We will forget that this night ever happened."

That was easier said than done, Jeff thought, at least for him. He would not forget the sight of the pistol exploding almost in his face. But if Orlov was willing to make the effort, then so was he.

Business, after all, was business.

Several minutes passed in awkward silence, and Orlov said impatiently, "Where is Piotr and that blasted carriage?" He was about to stomp off the porch and check when hoofbeats sounded and the carriage came around the corner of the house. The driver, a wizened man with a drooping gray mustache, brought his team to a halt in front of the porch. There was no sign of Piotr.

Jeff wondered for a moment where the aide was, then discarded the thought. All he wanted was to get back to the *Beaumont*, where he would try to make sense of this bizarre evening.

He stepped up into the carriage, and the old man whipped the horses into motion. As the carriage slid toward the harbor on its runners, Jeff heaved a grateful sigh.

Behind him, on the porch, Count Orlov stared with narrowed eyes at the dwindling shape of the carriage. Holt had believed him when he said that he bore him no ill will.

Stupid American fool. Orlov knew exactly who was to blame for what had happened, or almost happened, tonight. Irina had played these games before. Whether or not Holt had actually made love to her mattered little. What was important was that he had witnessed Orlov's humiliation—and that was a sin the count not forgive.

Jefferson Holt would regret coming to the land called Alaska. He would pay dearly for his folly.

With that thought, Count Orlov turned and went into the house to deal with Irina. She had finally pushed him too far, and she would have to be punished . . .

Everything looked normal on the *Beaumont* as the small boat carrying Jeff neared it. He hoped that was true; normal was what he needed right now. He wondered how Michael was doing. He never should have left the boy tonight. Blinded by the prospect of concluding the trade agreement with Orlov, Jeff had brushed aside his son's illness. In fact, he had used Michael's fever as a convenient excuse to leave Melissa on the ship. Shame burned his face—or maybe it was just the cold wind.

Things were going to be different now, Jeff told himself. He had come close to betraying his marriage vows tonight. That would never happen again. He was not going to let business blind him to the needs of his family.

Captain Vickery was waiting for him when he came up the ladder onto the deck. "Evening, Mr. Holt," the captain greeted him. "How did the dinner go? Did that rapscallion finally see the light and sign an agreement?"

"There was no dinner," Jeff said flatly, "and no agreement. The count was dealing with talk of an Indian uprising."

"Good Lord," muttered Vickery. "The savages aren't about to attack the settlement, are they?"

Jeff shook his head. "The count says the threat is exaggerated. I don't know. But if I were you, Captain, I'd keep the ship ready to sail fairly quickly."

"You can count on that, Mr. Holt," Vickery said with an emphatic nod. "If those Indians make any trouble, we'll catch the first breeze out of here."

Jeff started to turn away, saying, "Well, good night, Captain."

Vickery stopped him. "I'm glad to see you back safely tonight, sir. When the count's aide showed up with a message that he insisted on giving to Mrs. Holt herself, I was afraid something was wrong."

Jeff stared at the captain, his eyes widening in surprise. "Piotr was here?"

"Aye, just a few minutes ago. He rowed out in one of the Russian boats. I'm surprised you didn't see him on his way back to shore when you came out."

"I must have missed him in the darkness. You say he had a message for my wife?"

"That's right. It was sealed, and he wanted to put it in her hand himself, but I insisted that I would do it. That's what I did."

Jeff could think of no reason for Piotr to bring a private message to Melissa, but the sudden sick feeling in the pit of his stomach told him that something was very wrong. Piotr carried out the orders of only two people: Count Orlov . . .

And Irina.

Jeff left the captain gaping after him as he raced toward the companionway that led down to the passenger cabins. His bootheels thudded heavily on the stairs as he descended, echoing the thudding of his heart.

He went straight to the door of the cabin he shared with Melissa and Michael, jerked it open, and stepped inside. The first thing he saw was Michael, asleep in one of the bunks. The lamp on the tiny table next to the bunk was turned down low, and the small circle of flickering yellow light it cast was the only illumination in the room. Jeff stepped over to the bunk and reached down to rest the back of his hand against his son's forehead. It was blessedly cool. The fever had broken.

"Whip," Jeff whispered, and all the love he felt for his son was expressed in that simple nickname.

"You should have thought of your son before you left tonight." Melissa's voice from behind him cut like a scourge. Jeff jerked around and saw her stepping out of the shadows, holding a piece of paper that had been folded and sealed with wax. The seal was broken now and the paper unfolded. Her face was pale and drawn as she looked at Jeff and went on, "But no, you were too eager to see *her* again to consider your wife and son."

Jeff swallowed hard. "Melissa, you don't understand—"

"Oh, I understand!" Melissa hissed. Her hand clenched, crumpling the message. "I understand that you spent the evening in the arms of another woman. Another man's wife!" She flung the paper aside. "And I'll never forgive you for it, Jeff. Never!"

CHAPTER
TWENTY-ONE

T he first things Proud Wolf became aware of were
a warm weight against his left side and a gentle,
regular movement. After a moment he realized
that the warmth was Audrey's body and the movement
was her breathing. She was sound asleep, curled
against him as they both leaned back against the wall
of the cave.

The light of the rising sun slanted through the
opening. Proud Wolf squinted against the glare. He
must have slept through the day and the following
night. The fire had long since burned out. He wondered how long Audrey had been asleep.

He could hear the bubbling of the creek outside the
cave, and the sound made him aware that his mouth
was parched and he was very thirsty. In fact, he felt as
if all the moisture in his body had been leached out of
him. Carefully, so as not to disturb Audrey, he slid to
the side. He gently eased her down until she was lying
on the floor, still asleep.

Proud Wolf's right hip throbbed as he moved. He grimaced at the pain and moved the canvas bag aside so that he could look at the wound. The flesh around the gash was red and swollen. He bit back a groan of dismay. The wound was beginning to fester. A chill shook him. It was cold in the cave, but what he felt had little to do with the temperature. He had a fever. The dry mouth, the dizziness, the chills—all were sure signs.

There were plants that could help heal his injury and ease the fever, if only he could find them. He needed to open the wound and pack it with moss. Bracing one hand against the cave wall, he climbed slowly and carefully to his feet and took a step toward the opening.

Suddenly the world was spinning madly, and he felt himself falling. Though he tried not to cry out, he grunted in pain when he landed hard on the dirt floor.

"Oh!" Audrey exclaimed. She sat up sharply, startled out of sleep. "Proud Wolf!" she cried when she saw him. "What are you doing?" She scrambled to her knees and crawled over beside him, then rolled him on his back and hugged him. "Are you all right? You shouldn't have gotten up."

"I . . . I need . . ."

"Whatever you need, I'll get it." She laid a hand against his cheek. "You're burning up." Lithely she sprang to her feet. "I'll get some water."

Proud Wolf was too weak to stop her or to say anything else as she hurried out of the cave. It was broad daylight outside, which meant that it was dangerous for her to be out where she could be seen. If anyone was still hunting for them and noticed her . . .

The man from the trading post had never gotten a good look at her, Proud Wolf recalled. If he had roused his friends and neighbors to look for the thief who had raided the store, they would have no reason to suspect a young woman. For that matter, the storekeeper had seen him only fleetingly, and in the dark. Proud Wolf doubted that either of them could be identified.

But pursuit from Cambridge was a different story. Anyone searching for him in connection with Will Brackett's death would probably know both him and Audrey on sight. Silently, Proud Wolf urged her to hurry.

After what seemed like a long time, he saw her shadow as she entered the cave. She dropped to her knees beside him and began to wash his face with a strip of cloth torn from her old gown. She had soaked it in the creek water, and the cool touch on his brow felt wonderful beyond description. He closed his eyes and let her bathe his face. Then she folded the cloth, laid it across his forehead, and slipped a hand under his head to lift it slightly. Water trickled into his mouth as she squeezed another wet strip of cloth. He swallowed greedily.

"I have to find someone to help you," she said, as much to herself as to him.

Proud Wolf opened his eyes and looked up at her. Her red hair hung in matted tangles around her face, which was smeared with mud. She was still the most beautiful woman he had ever seen.

"No," he said. "We cannot . . . risk it. I will be all right. We need moss to pack the wound . . ."

Audrey shook her head, and her eyes shone with tears. "I don't think I can do it," she said miserably.

"You can," Proud Wolf told her. "Together . . . we can. We must." He gripped her arm. "Help me . . . stand up."

She got to her feet, holding his arm and supporting him as he rose. He was trembling and weak, and his head was swimming.

"Perhaps we should . . . wait until night," he suggested. "That way no one can . . . see us."

Audrey shook her head. "I won't let you just lie here with that fever all day, not if there's anything I can do about it. Come. We're in the middle of nowhere. No one will see us."

With their arms around each other, they hobbled to the mouth of the cave. Proud Wolf paused there, leaning against the wall for support, while Audrey went out first. She turned to face the creek bank and braced herself. "Come along," she urged Proud Wolf. "I won't let you fall."

She was stronger and braver than he would have guessed, he thought as he eased himself out of the cave mouth. At the academy he had seen only her flighty, flirtatious side; after all, she was very young and very pretty. Now he was seeing another, more mature side of her, and he could only marvel at it.

He slipped a little, but she was there to steady him, her hands strong but gentle. They slid down the bank to the water, but with Audrey's help Proud Wolf managed to stay upright.

She bent, cupped a hand in the stream, and brought it to his mouth. He sucked greedily at the cold water. She scooped up more until he shook his head to tell her he had had enough. He hadn't, not really, but he knew he would make himself sicker by drinking too much on an empty stomach.

"Now we must . . . find some moss . . . to pack the wound." He looked around.

He saw nothing he could use, but he did get a good look at the area. The creek was perhaps a dozen feet wide, and steep banks rose on both sides. The banks were covered with trees, and although many of them had lost their leaves with the onset of autumn, the branches were interlaced so tightly that they cast a deep shade.

Proud Wolf turned slowly, taking in his surroundings, and stopped abruptly when he was facing south. In that direction, the direction in which he and Audrey had been traveling before they found the cave, the creek gradually widened. A quarter of a mile away it was three times as wide, and judging by the way it foamed around the rocks, it was correspondingly shallow. The banks were still about ten feet high, and steep on both sides.

Proud Wolf noted all these details peripherally. His

concentration was riveted on something else: a stone bridge spanning the creek.

"A road!" he exclaimed as he stared at the bridge. "I thought you said we were in the middle of nowhere!"

Audrey was staring, too. "I . . . I never noticed that bridge! I was just so worried about you—"

Somewhere, not far away, the creaking of wagon wheels sounded.

"Someone is coming!" Proud Wolf said. "We must get back in the cave—"

As he spoke, he took a hurried step, and his feet went out from under him. Audrey clutched his arm but could not keep him from falling. With a great splash, Proud Wolf toppled backward into the creek.

"Proud Wolf!" Audrey cried.

In his feverish state the icy water seemed to pierce through to his very core. He thrashed weakly, trying to fight both the cold and the current. But he began to lose feeling in his limbs, and then even his soul felt numb. He was barely aware of Audrey screaming his name and pulling at him, trying to haul him out of the water.

Suddenly the chill was gone, replaced by an unexpected warmth. Proud Wolf welcomed it, relaxed his flailing arms, and allowed the warmth to flow into him, calm now in its grip. Yes . . . perhaps he could even sleep again.

His head broke the water. Gasping for air, he realized that the deceptive warmth had been that of unconsciousness. He had blacked out for a moment and would have drowned had Audrey not pulled his head out of the water. But she was not strong enough to lift him bodily from the creek, and he heard her calling loudly, "Help me! Oh, please, help me!"

"N-no!" he exclaimed, pawing feebly at her. "We must . . . hide."

It was too late for that. He heard a man's voice shouting to a team to stop, and then more voices were calling out questions.

"They're coming," Audrey panted in Proud Wolf's

ear as she held up his head and shoulders. "They'll help us."

He was too weak to protest. He could see little more than a mad dance of blurry shapes. A large, dark figure loomed over him, and then a man's deep voice boomed, "Good Lord, what have we here? A poor fellow like unto a drowned rat, cast up on shores of woe?"

The odd, stilted words seemed to come from far away. The warm darkness engulfed Proud Wolf once more, and this time he could not fight it off. All he could do was surrender.

Donnelly was the only sailor who had been lost in the storm. With him gone, life should have been easier on board the *Lydia Marie* for Ned and India as they sailed on toward China. Instead, the man was still between them even in death, his memory as much of an irritant as his presence in life had been.

The more Ned thought about it, the more he realized that India could have knocked Donnelly senseless just before the crashing wave washed him overboard. Then she could have slipped back to her position in the shrouds with no one being the wiser.

No one, that is, except Ned, who was the only man who had been close enough to witness what had happened.

But the whole idea was preposterous, Ned chided himself. If India had wanted to kill Donnelly, she could have done so on several other occasions when her own life would not have been at such great risk.

Everyone else on board regarded Donnelly's death as nothing but an unfortunate accident, the kind that happened all too often at sea when a ship encountered such a violent storm. Perhaps that was what India wanted. Ned was the only one who was suspicious of her . . . and he hated himself for the disloyalty and doubt that struck him sometimes when he looked at her.

And then there were the times he caught her looking at him, too, as if they shared a secret. Did she know that he suspected her?

One evening, when by Ned's estimate they were less than a week out of Canton, India came to him while he was standing watch on the bridge. The second mate was on duty, too, but he had gone belowdecks for a moment to consult with Captain Canfield concerning a minor course change. The vicious storm a couple of weeks earlier had blown the *Lydia Marie* a ways off her course, and since then such corrections had occasionally been necessary.

"Hello, Ned," India said as she came up to him.

"You ought to be below getting some rest," he said gruffly.

"What kind of greeting is that?" she demanded.

In a low voice Ned replied, "Well, I can't very well give you a proper one, not out here where anyone could see us."

India turned and surveyed the ship. "No one else is on deck right now. A quick kiss wouldn't hurt anything." She laughed quietly. "I never used to have to cajole you into stealing a kiss, Ned Holt."

"Maybe I'm just being more careful these days." And maybe it was just his suspicion that she had killed Donnelly in cold blood, he thought.

But if she had, did it really make a difference? he asked himself. India's actions had been motivated by a desire to remove a threat from their lives, so that they could be happy. Ned had blood on his own hands; he had killed men before. But only in defense of himself or those dear to him, he reminded himself. Perhaps India regarded Donnelly's death the same way.

He ran a hand through his hair. These emotional waters were too murky for a simple soul like Ned Holt to navigate. He needed more time to think.

India sighed. "All right. If that's the way you feel, that's fine. We'll be careful." She stepped closer, and her voice became a sensuous purr. "But when we get to China, we'll find a chance to be alone, and then . . ."

There was a world of meaning in the way her voice trailed off.

"Maybe," Ned said.

India's sigh was louder and more exasperated this time. "Good night, then," she snapped.

"Good night."

Ned watched her go, wondering if anything would ever be the same between them again.

India paused at the entrance to the companionway leading to the fo'c'sle. She looked up at Ned's figure, silhouetted against the starlight. She had hoped to get close to him again, to draw him out and get a sense of whether or not her suspicions had any basis in fact. He had been so cold, so distant, since Donnelly's death.

Was it because he had killed the man and felt guilty about it? India wondered if she would ever know. She sighed, then stepped down the ladder into the companionway.

Unknown to either of them, another pair of eyes had watched their brief meeting. The man was concealed in deep shadows, where he stayed whenever possible. From what he had observed he guessed that Ned and India had no idea what had really happened to Donnelly. That was the way it should be. They would have no warning when the proper time came and they met their own deaths.

The *New Orleans* had been slowed greatly by the delay in Louisville and by the terrible earthquake that followed. The course of the mighty river itself had been vastly altered in places, and many of the landmarks were now unrecognizable. Captain Roosevelt and his pilot spent most of their time in the wheelhouse, trying to chart a safe course. The river channel had shifted so much that the best they could do was keep the steamboat where the current ran the fastest, on the assumption that that was where the channel had moved. So far that assumption had steered them safely.

The terrible earthquake had not completely subsided. Nearly every day the ground shook again, and the same fearful rumbling could be heard. Some of the tremors were mild, others more violent. The passengers on the steamboat, nerves frayed as they waited for the next bout, began to wonder if the monstrous heaving would ever end. The river was full of obstacles that had not been there before. Huge trees floated by, flung in when the banks on which they had grown collapsed. The river was choked with dead animals as well—and more than one human body had been pulled out of the muddy water by the crew as the *New Orleans* made its way downstream. Once, Clay saw an entire barn, largely intact, come floating near the boat. It had taken all the pilot's skill to steer around it.

Clay had thought the devastation he and the others were witnessing from the deck could not possibly get any worse. When the steamboat reached the settlement of New Madrid, he saw how wrong he was.

The settlement on the west bank of the river was the only one of any size between Louisville and Natchez, Mississippi—or at least it had been once. Buildings were flattened, trees were downed, and a raw scar along the bank showed where a huge section had been sheared away. Clay saw the ruins of a church perched precariously on the edge of the river. Whatever had once been behind the church—a graveyard, most likely—was gone, swept away in the cataclysm.

Clay stood at the rail on the starboard side of the *New Orleans* with Shining Moon, Matthew, and Markham. They stared solemnly at what was left of the settlement.

"Dear God," muttered Markham. "The poor people who lived here—what will happen to them now?"

"I expect those who survived the quake will rebuild," Clay said. "If the earthquake ever stops, that is."

Matthew looked up at the adults. "Maybe it won't ever stop," he said. "Maybe the earth will just keep on shaking and shaking until it shakes itself apart."

Clay frowned. He wondered if the boy was right—maybe this really *was* the end of the world. He considered it a moment longer, then shrugged. There was nothing he could do about the forces of nature. But earthquake or no earthquake, he was going to finish the assignment he had been given.

The three senators, with their ever-present entourage of journalists, were standing nearby, watching silently as the scenes of destruction and tragedy along the riverbank slid past. As the steamboat left New Madrid behind, Clay walked over to join them. He waved his hand toward the shore.

"Never saw anything like it before," he commented.

"Nor have I," Emory said somberly. "And I hope I never do again."

"The power of nature is much greater than anything we puny human beings can ever build or invent," Ralston observed.

"Bah!" grunted Haines. "If I could legislate against things like this, I would." He glowered at Clay. "You know, this is just one more example why President Jefferson never should have been so foolish as to buy all that land from the French. Suppose things like this happen out here all the time? You never hear anything about earthquakes in New York!"

"They may have felt this one that far away," said Ralston. "I'm sure they did in Georgia."

"Well, I still think it was a mistake," Haines sniffed.

Clay watched the man surreptitiously. Ever since Matthew had told him about Haines, he had been keeping a close eye on the senator from New York. Unfortunately, other than his unpleasant manner, Haines had done nothing else to warrant suspicion.

Clay ambled back to join Shining Moon, Matthew, and Markham. "It looks as if we won't be stopping at a settlement until we get to Natchez. Maybe by then all this shaking will be over." He tried to sound hopeful.

The rest of the day passed without incident. Clay

allowed himself to think that perhaps the earth had finally settled again. Given the current condition of the river, it was too dangerous to travel at night, so the *New Orleans* was tied to a stand of trees on an island in the middle of the river. Captain Roosevelt avoided the banks as much as possible, for fear they would collapse.

The earthquake had effectively dissipated the festive atmosphere that had prevailed during the earlier stages of the journey. No one felt like celebrating, and even the historic nature of the trip had been largely forgotten. Survival was uppermost on the minds of the travelers now.

John Markham and the Holts dined in the salon with the other passengers, then returned to their cabins. Shining Moon and Matthew would be turning in early, but Clay and Markham quietly made arrangements to meet later.

After seeing Shining Moon and Matthew settled in for the night, Clay left the cabin and found Markham at the railing, near the great paddlewheel on the starboard side of the boat.

"If nothing else happens to slow us down, we may reach New Orleans in a little more than a week," Markham said worriedly. "We've got to do something, Clay. We're running out of time."

"I agree. I reckon we're going to have to confront the three of them and see if we can tell which one is lying."

Markham regarded him dubiously. "They're politicians, remember? How in the world would we ever tell?"

"A fellow generally tells the truth when he's staring down the barrel of a gun," Clay said impatiently.

Markham stared. "You're going to try to force the truth out of our man at gunpoint? What's next? Torture?"

"I picked up a few things from the Blackfoot," Clay said, remembering a terrible night when he and Shining Moon had been held prisoner with some of their friends by Blackfoot warriors. It had taken Shining Moon a long time to recover from the ordeal, if in fact she ever really had, and he knew that he could never sink that low. But at the moment it was tempting to think about it.

"Well," said Markham, "I certainly hope it never comes to that. I don't know how we'd explain to President Jefferson—"

The rush of feet interrupted him. A dark figure loomed behind him, and something swooshed through the darkness. Clay heard a thud, immediately followed by a grunt from Markham. The young officer slumped against him.

Even as Clay caught Markham with one hand, his other hand was flashing under his coat toward the pistol tucked behind his belt. The shadowy attacker gave him no time to reach it. A bludgeon slapped the side of Clay's head. The blow was a glancing one, but the impact was strong enough to send Clay staggering against the rail. Markham's limp body slid to the floor. The club swung again, this time smacking against Clay's upper right arm. The blow deadened his arm all the way to the fingertips.

The attack had been a long time coming, but Clay knew it for what it was: Their quarry was finally striking back at them before the boat reached New Orleans. Though Clay could barely see the man swinging the club, he was definitely too large and burly to be any of the senators. A crewman, more than likely, paid by the senator to eliminate his pursuers. The crewman Matthew had seen taking money from Louis Haines? Had to be, Clay thought grimly as he ducked beneath another sweeping blow of the club.

With his right arm still numb, Clay stepped over Markham, lunged toward the attacker, and hooked his left fist into the man's belly. The man grunted and stumbled back but managed to bring the club down on Clay's back. Clay grunted under the impact and kept crowding the man, lowering his head and butting him in the face. It was a deadly dance, Clay knew. If the man succeeded in knocking him out, he could easily dump both Clay and Markham over the side to drown in the murky waters of the Mississippi.

Clay wrapped his good arm around the man's waist and forced him backward against the wall separating the cabins from the deck. Maybe someone would hear them and come to investigate, Clay thought.

The man grabbed Clay's throat with one hand, his fingers digging cruelly into the flesh. The move caught Clay between breaths, and in a matter of seconds he felt as if his lungs might explode. He fought back by bringing his knee up into the man's groin. The man howled, let go of Clay's neck, and doubled over, clutching at himself. Clay stumbled back, gulping down air, but did not let up on the attack. He swung his left fist in a backhand that caught the man in the jaw.

The attacker staggered to one knee, and Clay sensed that the tide of battle was turning now. He jabbed with his left, rocking the man's head back. Clay was about to finish him off with a kick to the face when the man lunged forward, tackling Clay around the waist. Both men sprawled on the deck.

Why the devil hadn't Markham come to and started helping him? Clay wondered fleetingly. Had the blow that had knocked him out been fatal?

His attention was jarred back to his own predicament. The man was fumbling at Clay's throat again, trying to get a choke hold. Clay put his left hand in the man's face and shoved hard, knocking him aside. Clay rolled away and bumped hard against the railing. The dark waters of the Mississippi flowed ponderously past only a few feet below him.

The attacker reached his feet first and came after him again. Clay kicked out, but the man grabbed his foot and twisted, trying to shove him under the bottom rail and into the river. Clay yelped in pain but caught hold of the rail with his good hand. Feeling was seeping back into his right hand now, and he tried once more to reach the pistol behind his belt. His fingers found the smooth wood of the butt but slid off on his first attempt to draw the weapon. He tried again and this time pulled the pistol and lifted it, his thumb looping over the hammer of the flintlock to pull it back.

A gun boomed, but not the one in Clay's hand. The shot had come from farther along the deck, toward the bow. Clay's assailant grunted and stiffened, and his hands fell away from Clay's foot. He took a couple of stumbling steps to the side, then pitched forward on his face and lay motionless. As Clay scrambled away from the railing and came up on his knees, he saw a dark stain spreading across the back of the man's shirt.

People were running to the deck now, shouting questions or screaming in panic. Closer at hand, Markham let out a groan. Clay put his gun away, then knelt beside his attacker and checked for a pulse. Finding none, he turned his attention to Markham, who lay sprawled a few feet away.

He rolled the young officer on his back. "It's all right," he assured him. "You just got a clout on the head, but I reckon it'll take more than that to dent that hard skull of yours."

Markham moaned again as Clay helped him sit up. He lifted a hand and gingerly touched his head. "My skull's not . . . that hard," he said, his voice a little fuzzy. "What the hell—"

"Down there!" an authoritative voice said loudly. "Bring that light."

Several men came striding down the deck. One of them was holding a lantern. Clay saw Captain Roosevelt, Senator Morgan Ralston, and several members of the crew.

Senator Ralston had a pistol in his hand, smoke still curling from the barrel.

Clay and Markham got to their feet. Both men were shaky, Markham more so than Clay.

Roosevelt pointed to the dead man and demanded, "What happened here? Mr. Holt, Mr. Markham, are you all right?"

"I reckon so," Clay replied. "As for what happened, this fellow here"—he nudged the corpse with the toe of his boot—"tried to knock us over the head and throw us overboard." He looked at Ralston. "I reckon we owe you our thanks for helping us. You're the one who shot him, aren't you?"

Ralston stared down at the small pistol in his hand as if he had forgotten it was there. Then he looked up at Clay and nodded. "Yes. I shot him. I came out on deck and saw some kind of altercation down here. I couldn't really tell what was happening, but it looked as if someone was about to shove someone else overboard. I . . . I took out my pistol and fired a shot, thinking that I might frighten the man away. I never meant to . . . Good Lord, I never shot a man before . . . I didn't mean to kill him."

"Don't worry, Senator," Clay said. "He was doing his damnedest to kill Markham and me. I was about to shoot him myself." He prodded the corpse again. "Of course, I figured on just wounding him so that he could tell us who hired him to get rid of us." Clay figured he already knew the answer to that question, but it would have been much more helpful to hear it from the thug's own lips.

Captain Roosevelt grunted. "Let's take a look at him."

As the dead man was rolled over by a couple of crewmen, more people came out to the deck, drawn by the gunshot and the agitated voices. Among them were Emory and Haines, several journalists . . . and Shining Moon and Matthew. Seeing Clay, Shining Moon hurried forward and caught his arm. "You are hurt?" She touched his face, and her fingers came away dark with blood.

"I'm fine," Clay assured her. "That must belong to the other fellow. I butted him in the face, and I reckon some blood from his nose must've got on my head."

The crewman holding the lantern brought it closer as the dead man was turned over. The light fell over a rugged face that was now and forever contorted with the agony of violent death.

"He was a member of the crew, all right," Roosevelt said. "Name was Richards. I hired him in Pittsburgh. This was his first trip with me."

"And his last one," Markham said, still rubbing his head where he had been clubbed.

"Wait a minute," a childish voice piped up. "I know him. I know that man."

Clay felt his heart leap when he heard Matthew's words. Carefully he put his hand back on the butt of his pistol. "What do you mean, son?"

"He's the one I told you about, Clay," Matthew said. "The one who was being given some money by that man." He turned and pointed.

Straight at Senator Louis Haines.

Haines gaped at the boy and for once seemed to be at a loss for words. His mouth opened and closed a couple of times before he sputtered, "What . . . how dare you . . . I never—"

Clay lifted his hand, and the pistol was in it. He pointed it at Haines. "Looks like you've got some talking to do, Senator. I've got a pretty good idea why you wanted Markham and me dead, but why don't you explain it to all these other folks?"

CHAPTER
TWENTY-TWO

J eff felt as if his insides had dropped to his feet. He
heard a strange ringing in his ears, and his stomach
was churning. He gestured at the piece of paper
Melissa had crumpled and thrown aside and asked in a
hollow voice, "Is that a note from the count?"

"What?" Melissa sounded surprised. "Count
Orlov knows about this, too?" She sniffed in contempt.
"Then I'm surprised you're not dead. I would think
that the count would kill a man who dishonored his
wife."

"I didn't dishonor anyone," Jeff snapped. "Nothing happened, Melissa."

She folded her arms across her chest and glared at
him. "That's not what the countess says in her note.
She's boasting—boasting!—that she made you happier
than I ever could. That . . . that bitch!"

"It's not true, Melissa," Jeff said stubbornly. He
had to get through to her somehow, had to break
through the wall of anger she had erected. Damn Irina!

Jeff knew now why Piotr had disappeared after summoning the carriage: He had been summoned by his mistress and given that lying message to bring to the ship.

Melissa was still glaring at him. "It's not true that you spent the evening with her . . . alone?"

"Well, that does happen to be the way it worked out—"

"I thought so." Melissa started to turn away.

Jeff stepped across the room, caught her shoulder, and tried to pull her toward him. But she resisted stiffly and refused to look at him.

"Listen to me," Jeff said urgently. "I was supposed to have dinner with Count Orlov and discuss the trade agreement, but when I got to his house, he wasn't there. There was some sort of trouble—rumors that the Indians were going to revolt—and he had to deal with that. But the countess was there, and she insisted that I come in anyway, and . . . and—"

"And you made love to her." Melissa's voice was as cold and flinty as the stone of the hills that rose around Sitka.

"No!"

"Keep your voice down," Melissa hissed as she jerked away. "I don't want Michael to wake up and hear any of this. It's disgusting."

Jeff scrubbed a hand over his face and fought down the urge to grab her again, to try to shake some sense into her. That wouldn't do any good and would likely only make things worse. After a moment he said bluntly, "The countess tried to seduce me."

Melissa gave him a contemptuous glance, her mouth twisted in a sneer. "If you only knew how ridiculous and vain that sounds."

"It's true, damn it. She got me to drink some of that Russian vodka, and then we . . . she was on this divan . . . I don't really know how it happened—"

Blast it! thought Jeff. This was sounding worse and worse, and he knew that no matter how he explained things, he couldn't make them sound good. But he had to try.

He was searching for the words when Melissa said icily, "Don't bother. I don't need all the details. I'm a married woman, remember?" She laughed hollowly. "I know what happens between a man and a woman."

"Nothing happened."

She seemed not to have heard him. "That Russian trollop threw herself at you, and you responded. You're a man, and you couldn't help yourself. Isn't that it?"

"No, damn it!"

Melissa lifted her chin. "Well, I'll have you know that *I* could have been unfaithful to *you* more than once. I've had plenty of chances, you've been gone so much the past year, but when another man kissed me, *I* didn't just—" She caught her breath, her eyes widening in horror, then tried awkwardly to press on. "—didn't just give in, I . . . I remembered my family and I . . . I . . ."

Jeff was staring at her. "Another man . . . kissed you?" he said. "Who?"

"That doesn't matter," Melissa said quickly. "I told you, I didn't—"

"The hell it doesn't matter!" Jeff's voice was rising, but he couldn't help it. "Who kissed you?"

"A man named Philip Rattigan!" Melissa burst out. "But he just kissed me. That's all that happened!"

"Rattigan," repeated Jeff, and now his voice was soft with shock. "I've heard of him. An Englishman, isn't he? Has a small shipping line?"

"That's right. He . . . he helped me during that trouble with the sabotage in Wilmington—"

"And I reckon he expected to be thanked for his help," Jeff said.

"It wasn't like that! Don't make more of it than it really was."

"As you're doing with me and the countess?"

"Did you kiss her?" Melissa demanded.

"Yes." Jeff wasn't going to lie about it, especially not after what he had just learned.

"Was she . . . clothed?"

Jeff remembered the soft, creamy breasts and the way they had filled his hand. "Not fully, no."

"Then even if nothing else happened, you still went much farther than I did. I was fully clothed, and—"

"What about Rattigan?" Jeff broke in.

He saw Melissa's eyes widen again, and he wondered if she was going to lie. He would know it if she did, he told himself.

Instead she said, "He had taken his shirt off, but it's not the same thing and you know it. We had just come through a very dangerous experience together, when that warehouse nearly blew up—"

"So naturally you wound up in the arms of the first fellow who took his shirt off," Jeff said dryly.

"Damn you! This isn't about me."

"No, but it's about us," Jeff said. "You don't trust me, and I reckon from what I've heard tonight, I've got reason not to trust you."

"Nothing happened!"

"Yep. That's what I said, too." He looked at her with narrowed eyes. "But you found out about the countess here and now, right after it happened. I didn't find out about you and Rattigan for months. You've been carrying it around like your own little secret."

"I just didn't see any point in . . . in worrying you."

"So you lied to me, and like a fool I believed you."

Melissa shook her head. "I never lied to you, Jeff."

He didn't know what to believe anymore. The encounter with Irina had left him shaken, but the revelation about Melissa was much more difficult to accept.

"Maybe I should have taken her up on her offer," he said softly. "I might just do that if the opportunity ever arises again."

Melissa caught her breath. "You don't mean that."

"I don't know. Maybe I do."

"I want to go home," she said miserably.

"So you can look up Rattigan again?"

Her arm came up and her hand flashed toward his face, but Jeff was quicker. He caught her wrist before she could slap him. She struck at him with her other hand, but he grabbed that wrist, too, and then, holding her powerless, jerked her against him and brought his mouth down on hers. There was no love in the kiss, only anger and lust. Melissa tried to pull away, but Jeff held her too tightly. Her lips were cold and hard under his.

Jeff let go and stepped back. Her eyes were blazing. "I'm leaving," she said.

"Fine."

"And I'm taking Michael with me."

He nodded. "All right. It's high time this ship headed home anyway, before the weather gets any worse."

"You can move to another cabin," she said, crossing her arms sternly.

Jeff shook his head. "I'm not going anywhere. I haven't done what I came here to do."

"What do you mean?" Melissa exclaimed. "You . . . you're staying here . . . in Alaska?"

"Send a ship for me in the spring. By then the agreement with Orlov will be signed, and we'll be ready to start building up the trade here."

Melissa stared at him for a long moment, then said quietly, "You're staying here . . . to be with her."

Jeff shook his head, though he doubted it would do any good to deny what Melissa's anger and resentment had implanted so firmly in her brain. "I'm going to stay as far away from the countess as I can—but I'm not going to abandon the plans we made. That wouldn't be fair to the company, or to Lemuel."

"So you're leaving me," Melissa whispered, "again."

"You're the one who's leaving," he countered. "And I'm hoping that by the time I'm home again, you'll have come to your senses. Either that"—he shrugged—"or you'll have left me for Rattigan."

"Is . . . is that what you want?"

Jeff took a deep breath but didn't answer Melissa's question.

Because right now, after everything that had happened tonight, he didn't have the slightest idea what he wanted.

Once again, Proud Wolf climbed out of the black, seemingly bottomless pit of unconsciousness, and every step of the grueling climb was shot with pain.

Pain was good. Pain told a man that he was still alive, still capable of fighting his enemies.

Proud Wolf opened his eyes.

A face the same size and shape as a full moon peered down at him, and a voice as deep as the pit Proud Wolf had just escaped said, "Well, well, well. The sleeper awakens at last. 'To sleep: perchance to dream.' Did you dream, lad?"

It seemed to Proud Wolf that he might still be dreaming. In fact, the figure looming over him was like something out of a nightmare.

The man's eyes were large and protruding, and his prominent nose had been broken more than once. His eyebrows were thick and bushy and grew so close together that they seemed to be one dark line across his face. His eyes were dark and deep-set in pits of gristle. A network of scars from ancient battles marked his features, and what little hair he had left was gray and bristly, standing straight up from his scalp.

When Proud Wolf did not reply to his question, the man said impatiently, "Well, speak up, my boy." He frowned, which only made him uglier. "Or perhaps you don't speak English. I can tell from the cast of your features that you are not a white man. But you don't dress like one of the woodland savages, either. What about it? Do you understand me?"

"I . . . understand," Proud Wolf rasped. His throat was painfully dry. "Where . . . where am I?"

"In my wagon, of course. Where else would we have put you?"

"Wh-who are you?"

The man stepped back, and Proud Wolf noticed that he was holding a hat with a broad, floppy brim and a long feather in the band. He swept out his arm and bowed. "Ulysses Xavier Dowd, at your service, good aboriginal sir."

Dowd was wearing an old-fashioned suit with a waistcoat that barely buttoned around his ample belly. His torso looked like a full barrel with bulging sides, and his legs were disproportionately short and slender. It all made for a rather comical figure, but as Dowd clapped the silly-looking hat back on his head, he held himself with genuine dignity.

Proud Wolf looked around in wonder. He was lying in a wide bunk—considering Dowd's size, it would have to be wide—built solidly against the wall. The bunk was, indeed, in a wagon, but a wagon that was completely enclosed, like a small cabin on wheels. A table and chair were the only other furniture. Curtains of a cheerful print adorned two small windows. There were built-in wooden shelves lined with leather-bound books, more books than Proud Wolf had ever seen in one place outside of the library at the Stoddard Academy.

Proud Wolf shifted his body slightly and felt bandages wrapped tightly around his hip. This bizarre man Dowd, whoever he was, had taken good care of him.

"We've cleaned and doctored your wound," Dowd said, "and given you a tonic to counteract that nasty fever. You should be feeling much better by now."

"How . . . how long?"

"It's been three days since we responded to the calls for assistance from your lovely young companion. You've been awake here and there since then, but I doubt that you remember any of those occasions. You were rather out of your head, as mad as good Mercutio seemed to be."

Proud Wolf had no idea who Mercutio was, but at Dowd's mention of Audrey he tried to sit up. "Audrey," he croaked. "Where is she?"

Dowd came closer and put a big hand on Proud Wolf's shoulder to hold him down. "There, there," he murmured. "You must rest, lad, and not perturb yourself so. The young lady is fine, except for the fact that she has worried herself to distraction over you. I'll have her fetched here immediately."

Proud Wolf sank back, dropping his head on the pillow. The news that Audrey was all right was a great relief; now he could concentrate on the other thing that was bothering him.

"Th-thirsty," he said.

"I shouldn't be a bit surprised, considering that fever you endured. I'll have some broth brought to you as well. Body, mind, and soul all require sustenance, and we aim to provide for all three." Dowd let himself out the door at the rear of the wagon.

Proud Wolf closed his eyes for a moment. They flew open again when he suddenly remembered how he had come to be here. Dowd and his companions, whoever they were, had taken pity on Proud Wolf and Audrey and helped them, but their generosity would surely be withdrawn if they found out he was a fugitive who had killed a man.

But why did they have to find out? Proud Wolf asked himself. In the eyes of the law he was already a murderer and a thief; surely he could become a liar, too.

The door opened, and Audrey ran into the little chamber. She dropped to her knees beside the bunk and threw her arms around Proud Wolf. "You're awake," she said, her voice catching in a sob. "Have you really come back to me this time?"

"Here now, give the lad room to breathe." A woman stepped up into the back of the wagon behind Audrey. She was carrying a large, steaming mug. "And let me get some of this broth down him. He needs his strength."

The woman was attractive, with long, fair hair and deep brown eyes. Her face was sweet and kindly,

Proud Wolf thought. She pulled the chair next to the bunk and told Audrey, "Help him sit up."

Proud Wolf caught a whiff of something savory, and his stomach suddenly cramped with hunger. With Audrey's assistance he sat up and bent forward to reach for the cup.

"You're not that strong yet," the woman said gently. "Here, we'll help you."

As the woman held the mug to his lips, Proud Wolf began to sip the broth. The first taste of it threatened to make him sick, but then the roiling in his belly settled. He gulped greedily at the delicious brew.

The woman sat back. "There, that ought to make you feel better," she said with a smile. "In a few days you'll be back on your feet . . . almost as good as new."

"Thank you, Vanessa," Audrey said as she gently lowered Proud Wolf back into a reclining position. "I don't know what we would have done if you and Mr. Dowd hadn't been passing by."

"You would have found some other way to help your young man," said the woman called Vanessa. "I could tell right away that you weren't going to let him die, not without a struggle." She patted Audrey's shoulder. "But it was probably a good thing we came along when we did."

Proud Wolf's voice was stronger as he asked, "Who are you?"

Audrey answered the question. "They're actors," she said, a hint of excitement in her voice.

"Actors?" Proud Wolf repeated, not sure what the word meant.

"Players," said Vanessa. "Performers, if you will. We enact scenes from the great plays of the ages, from the ancient Greeks to the immortal Bard of Avon."

Proud Wolf had no idea what she was referring to, but when she spoke like that, she reminded him of Dowd. "You are the daughter . . . of the man called Dowd?"

"Daughter?" Vanessa let out a peal of laughter. "Ulysses will enjoy that. I'm his wife."

Proud Wolf tried not to stare. True, Vanessa looked somewhat older than he, but she did not seem old enough to be married to Ulysses Xavier Dowd. And it was hard to believe that a woman so attractive would be matched with a man so undeniably homely. But that was none of his business, he told himself.

Proud Wolf had already determined that the wagon was not moving, so he asked, "Have you made camp for the night?"

"That's right," Vanessa said with a nod. "The wagons are drawn up beside a nice little stream."

"Wagons?"

"There are four of them," Audrey supplied. "It's a whole acting troupe."

Proud Wolf had never heard the phrase and was still vague about what exactly actors did. But they had saved his life, apparently out of the kindness of their hearts, and he was grateful. "Thank you," he murmured.

"For the broth?" Vanessa said. "You're welcome. It was no trouble."

"Where is this camp? Are we still in Massachusetts?" The woman might wonder why he asked, but he could not rest until he had an idea of how close their pursuers might be.

"Massachusetts?" Vanessa shook her head. "Oh, no, we're in Connecticut, bound for Maryland and then Virginia."

Proud Wolf closed his eyes in relief. They were heading in the right direction—away from Cambridge and Will Brackett's death.

"You'd best let him sleep now," Vanessa quietly advised Audrey. "He seems to be out of danger now that the fever has broken, but he's going to need lots of rest."

Audrey slipped her hand into Proud Wolf's. He felt her smooth, cool fingers and closed his own around them.

"I'll just stay for a few minutes, until he dozes off."

"Well . . . all right."

Proud Wolf heard Vanessa leave the wagon, then felt Audrey's warm breath on his face as she brushed her lips against his cheek. "I'm right here," she said, still holding his hand. "Right here."

With Audrey as his anchor, Proud Wolf let himself drift back off to sleep.

On the deck of the *New Orleans*, Senator Ralston stepped closer to Haines. Clay hoped he wouldn't get in the line of fire. Haines might be desperate enough to do almost anything, including using a fellow senator as a shield.

"See here," Ralston barked at Clay. "What are you doing, Holt? Have you gone mad, pointing a gun at a United States senator?"

"No, I'm not crazy," Clay said. "Fact is, I'm finally seeing things straight. Tell them, Matthew."

Clay glanced at the boy. Matthew was figeting, apparently uncomfortable with all the attention he was getting from the grown-ups. Shining Moon put her hands on his shoulders and said, "If you have something to tell us, Matthew, do so."

Matthew nodded. "All right." He pointed again at Haines. "A few nights ago, I saw the senator talking to that man there, the one who was shot."

"You mean Richards?" The question came from Captain Roosevelt.

"Yes, sir," Matthew said. "Senator Haines was pointing to the cabin where my . . . my folks and I are staying. He talked to that fellow for a while, then gave him some money."

"You saw all this clearly?" asked Roosevelt.

"Plain as day, Captain," Matthew replied without hesitation.

"The boy's lying!" Haines burst out. "I never saw this man Richards before, unless it was simply as a member of the crew. And I certainly never gave him any money." He glowered at Clay. "I know what you're implying. You think I paid this man to attack you and Markham. But why in the hell would I do that?"

"To get rid of us before the boat reaches New Orleans," said Clay. "You've covered your tracks well until now, but you didn't want to take a chance on our finding out what you're really up to. Are you meeting somebody there—say, another partner in that scheme of yours?"

"Scheme?" Haines blustered. "What scheme?"

Markham laid a hand on Clay's arm and nodded toward the journalists. "Perhaps a bit of discretion would, ah, be in order here, Clay," he said quietly.

Clay realized how avidly the reporters were following the conversation, and he knew Markham was right. Thomas Jefferson had made it clear that their mission was to be kept as secret as possible. Still, under the circumstances, they were going to have to take at least Nicholas Roosevelt into their confidence. Clay said, "Captain, Markham and you and I need to go somewhere quiet so that we can talk with the senator."

Haines said angrily, "I'm not going anywhere at gunpoint!"

Roosevelt took off his cap and rubbed his jaw. "Perhaps it would be a good idea to straighten this all out in private," he said. "We can go up to the wheelhouse. The pilot's already turned in for the night, so there's no one up there."

Clay nodded. "That's all right with me." He lowered his gun but held it ready to use at an instant's notice. "What about you, Senator?"

Emory said to Haines, "I don't know if you should go with them, Louis. Holt seems to have lost his mind."

Haines quickly regained some of his composure now that the gun was no longer pointing at him. "No, I want to clear this up," he snapped. "But I warn you, Holt—when we reach New Orleans, I'm going to press legal charges against you!"

"Reckon I'll worry about that when we get there,"

Clay said dryly. He didn't think Haines would be able to do anything to him from behind the bars of a jail cell.

Roosevelt and Haines started toward the steep, narrow stairs that led to the wheelhouse. Markham trailed them. Clay hesitated long enough to pat Matthew on the shoulder. "Thanks, son," he said, with more genuine fondness than he had ever felt toward the boy. "You've been a big help." He looked at Shining Moon. "Better take him back to the cabin now."

She nodded and gave him a smile. Clay knew she was relieved that he had finally discovered the traitor's identity, because once the boat reached New Orleans, the three of them could return to the mountains. Clay smiled back at her. Then he turned and followed the others toward the wheelhouse.

Damned fool. Matthew tried not to smile too broadly as he watched Clay walk away. Everything had worked just the way the senator had said it would. Clay had believed every lie he had spouted.

Matthew had done a lot of thinking about the things the senator had asked him to do. He was sure he had it figured out. The senator was a criminal of some kind, and Clay and Markham were after him. The lie Matthew had told about seeing Haines giving money to the dead crewman was designed to make Clay think that Haines was the real culprit. Pretty clever, thought Matthew. No matter what had happened tonight, the senator had had every possible outcome covered.

Except that he still thought Matthew was just another stupid youngster.

Matthew let Shining Moon take him back to the cabin, and he pretended to go to sleep while he waited for her to doze off. He hoped she did before Clay got back. When he was satisfied that she was sleeping soundly, he slipped out of his bunk and went to the door. He opened it quietly and stepped out onto the deck.

It was time to pay a visit to his partner.

• • •

"Senator, I need to talk to you."

He had been about to go into his cabin for a good night's sleep, well satisfied with the way events had unfolded. Holt and Markham and the captain were still up in the wheelhouse with poor Louis. Poor, stupid Louis. Well, thought the senator, by the time Haines convinced them that he was innocent, it would be too late. The boat would have reached New Orleans, and the man Clay Holt was really after would be long gone, on his way to a rendezvous with the Comte de la Carde and his new home.

But then that blasted boy showed up, lurking in the shadows. As the senator turned toward him, Matthew stepped out into the moonlight.

"You startled me, lad," the senator said, injecting the habitual note of bluff heartiness into his voice. "Bit late for you to be out and about, isn't it? Shouldn't you be in your cabin with your mother?"

"She's not my mother," Matthew hissed. "My mother's dead, and so is my father. Holt and the Indian woman don't mean anything to me."

The senator shook his head. It always amazed him how a child so young could sound so mature—and so cold-blooded. Young Matthew Garwood was a bit of an aberration. Perhaps more than a bit.

"What do you want?" he asked curtly.

"More money," Matthew answered. "And I want you to tell me what you've got planned with that fellow, the Comte de la Carde."

The senator waved a hand brusquely. "You'd never understand. You're too young."

"I wasn't too young to lie about Senator Haines, the way you told me to."

"And you did a fine job. But it's *over* now. I appreciate your help, but I don't need you anymore."

Matthew smiled. "Yes, you do. You need me to keep my mouth shut. You'll have to pay for that, Senator."

The older man sighed in frustration and fought down the impulse to pitch the boy into the river and be done with it. But that wasn't the way he did things. It would be . . . well, crude.

"All right. I'll give you the money—within reason, mind you—and when we get to New Orleans, I'll introduce you to the Comte de la Carde. How would that be?" The senator slid a cigar from his vest pocket and clamped it between his teeth. "Perhaps we could use a partner like you, Matthew."

"Nobody pays any attention to a child," Matthew said. "I could come in handy."

"You could be right at that."

Matthew held out his hand. "I reckon another double eagle would be all right for now."

The senator took a coin from his pocket and slapped it into Matthew's palm. "There you are, my young friend."

"Partner," Matthew reminded him.

"Partner."

Matthew held up his hand with the gold piece clenched inside it. "Much obliged, Senator Ralston." Then he turned and sauntered back to the cabin he shared with Clay Holt and Shining Moon.

Morgan Ralston, senior senator from the state of Georgia, watched him go with narrowed eyes. It had been easy to promise to introduce Matthew to the count when the boat reached New Orleans. Young Master Garwood was not going to live that long.

No, indeed; the child who was too precocious for his own good was going to meet with an unfortunate accident. . . .

CHAPTER
TWENTY-THREE

In the wheelhouse of the *New Orleans*, Senator Haines flushed bright red and stared aghast at Clay. "How . . . how dare you accuse me of treason?" he sputtered.

"Only one man on this boat has any reason to want to have Markham and me killed," Clay said. "That's the man who was working with Gideon Maxwell to steal half the country."

Captain Roosevelt shook his head, obviously struggling to believe the story he had just heard. "This strains my credulity, I'm afraid," he said. "Are you quite sure of your facts, Mr. Holt?"

"Sure enough," Clay replied grimly. "I heard one of the three senators talking to Maxwell one night on Maxwell's estate in Virginia. Whoever it was admitted to having my old captain, Meriwether Lewis, killed when Lewis stumbled across the land grab scheme."

"It wasn't me you heard," Haines insisted angrily.

"If, in fact, you heard anyone saying anything of the sort. Frankly, Holt, I think you're insane."

Roosevelt looked at Markham. "What's your part in this, young man?"

"I'm on detached duty from the army," Markham explained. "At the request of President Thomas Jefferson, I've been assisting Clay in this matter."

"Jefferson is no longer president," Roosevelt said.

"No, sir, he isn't," agreed Clay, "but he initiated the investigation into the land grab. Everyone figured it was too delicate a matter for President Madison to get involved in."

Roosevelt sighed and shook his head again. He looked at Haines. "These two young men sound rather convincing, Senator."

Haines was still fuming. "I don't care how convincing they sound," he snapped. "Everything they're saying is a pack of lies. It's true I was acquainted with Gideon Maxwell—hell, practically everyone in Washington City knew the man—and I knew that his background was rather shady. But he made substantial contributions to the party, and I've never been one to"—he cleared his throat uncomfortably—"hold a man's past against him." He crossed his arms, stood stiffly erect, and glared at Clay defiantly.

Captain Roosevelt looked at Clay. "I suppose I'm to keep all this to myself?"

"We'd appreciate it, sir. President Jefferson would prefer that the journalists in particular don't get wind of it."

"That's understandable," mused Roosevelt. "News like that could throw the country into a panic. It would be devastating."

"What I want to know," said Markham, "is what the senator and his cronies were planning to do with all that land?"

"I don't have any cronies, damn it!" Haines exploded. "And I have never plotted to steal any land from the government!"

"That's one thing we still have to find out," Clay said, as if he had not heard Haines's outburst.

"What can I do to help you?" asked Roosevelt.

"Well . . . we're going to need to keep the senator in some sort of confinement."

Haines's face flushed with renewed outrage. "You mean you intend to lock me up like a common criminal?"

"There's nothing common about what you tried to do, Senator," Clay said.

Roosevelt frowned worriedly. "You realize, Mr. Holt, that you're basing your theory on the word of a small boy?"

"Not entirely, Captain. Senator Haines is on record as opposing the Louisiana Purchase, but now that the western half of the continent belongs to us, he thinks it ought to be exploited. He hates Indians and thinks they should be wiped out. I reckon he figures that if anyone is going to make a fortune out of the West, it ought to be him and his partners."

"Flimsy reasoning," sniffed Haines.

Clay shrugged. "I didn't have to prompt Matthew into identifying him. The boy came to me with the information."

"I'm not saying that your boy is lying, Mr. Holt," Roosevelt said. "But he could have been mistaken."

"Matthew couldn't have taken Senator Haines for either of the other two senators," Markham pointed out. "They all look quite different from one another."

Roosevelt looked out at the river and sighed. "I'm at a loss, gentlemen. Mr. Holt and Mr. Markham make a convincing case against you, Senator. On the other hand, I can't place too much stock in the word of a mere child, not when a United States senator is involved." He rubbed his jaw and thought for a moment, then said, "Senator, would you be willing to give me your word that you'll remain confined to your cabin until we reach New Orleans?"

"That's not good enough," said Clay, before Haines had a chance to reply. "If Markham and I are correct about him, he's a killer, and he can't be trusted."

"And if you're wrong, I'm an innocent man," Haines snapped. "An innocent man with a great deal of power . . . and a very long memory."

Markham flushed and glanced sidelong at Clay, clearly nervous about the implied threat. Clay understood his dilemma. When this was all over, Clay intended to go back to the Rockies, where any power wielded by some fancy-pants politician meant little. But Markham's situation was different. If they were wrong about Haines, the senator could ruin Markham's military career.

And they *were* placing an awful lot of weight on the word of a boy who had a checkered past himself, despite his years.

"All right, Senator," Clay said abruptly. "You claim you're an honorable man. If you'll give me your word that you'll stay in your cabin until we get to New Orleans, I reckon that'll do."

Haines glowered at him. "I won't be locked up."

"We aren't talking about locking you up, Senator," said Markham. "This is simply a . . . gentlemen's agreement, I suppose you could say."

"And what is my alternative?" asked Haines.

"We could tie you up and toss you down in the cargo hold, I reckon," Clay said.

Haines's lip curled and his hands clenched into fists, but he finally nodded. "I'll remain in my cabin." He glared at Roosevelt. "But I'll expect excellent service from your stewards, and an apology when this is over."

"I can pledge the service," Roosevelt said, "and the apology as well, if it turns out to be warranted."

"It will, I can assure you that." Haines turned to Clay and Markham. "But I'm afraid an apology won't do from you two. As I said before, I'll be pressing charges. And you, young man—"

Markham gulped.

"You can say farewell to any hopes you might have

had of advancing in the ranks," Haines continued. "In fact, I'm going to do everything I can to see that you're removed from the army in disgrace."

Markham swallowed hard again. "You do what you feel you have to, Senator," he said, "and so will I."

Clay was proud of Markham at that moment. The young man was learning.

"Will I be allowed to have visitors?" asked Haines.

"Not the journalists," Clay said quickly. "We don't want this story getting out."

"I suppose Senator Emory and Senator Ralston can see you," Roosevelt said.

"Very well. But not tonight." Haines looked at Clay and Markham with narrowed eyes. "Tonight I'm going to be busy . . . figuring out how I'm going to settle the score with these two buffoons."

Roosevelt opened the door of the wheelhouse. "I'll escort you down to your cabin, Senator."

Haines and the captain left, the senator still glowering ferociously. Clay and Markham stayed in the wheelhouse for a moment, and Markham asked quietly, "Do you think he'll keep his word and remain in his cabin?"

"Don't reckon it matters," Clay said.

"But if he gets away—"

"He won't." Clay's voice was grim. "The captain said he wouldn't be locked up. But nobody said anything about having a guard outside the door. We'll take turns, and I can promise you one thing: Senator Haines won't be going anywhere until we get to New Orleans."

Jeff stood on the dock and watched the crewmen from the *Beaumont* unload the last of his bags from the boat they had rowed in to shore. He glanced toward the ship with mixed expectations. Part of him hoped that Melissa would come up on deck to look at him one last time before the ship sailed away. On the other hand, seeing her again wouldn't make this separation any easier.

What the hell had happened? How could two people have gone so quickly from so much love and passion to the cold, stiffly polite resentment that existed between them now? Jeff sighed heavily as he gazed across the water at the graceful sailing ship. He had no answers, only regret and a painful sense of loss.

The sun shone weakly through a sparse layer of gray clouds. Here and there the overcast was thin enough to allow shafts of pale yellow light to slant through. At one time Jeff might have regarded the sight as a good omen—but no more.

His parting with Michael earlier this morning had been especially sorrowful. He had tried to keep the boy from seeing how upset he was. But that was not easy when Michael wrapped his arms around Jeff's neck and said plaintively, "I don't want to go without you."

"I'll be back before you know it," Jeff had said, forcing a lighthearted note into his voice.

"Why can't you come with Mama and me?" Michael had demanded.

"I have work here in Alaska that I have to do." That explanation was difficult for a child to understand or accept, Jeff knew . . . but it was better than telling him the truth. *Your mother doesn't want me anymore—and I don't know if I want her.*

Perhaps time and distance would cure some of their problems. Jeff fervently hoped so.

"What are you going to do?" he had asked Melissa when they were alone.

"Go home," she said. "See to the business."

"What about Rattigan?"

"What about him?" she had snapped. "I haven't seen him in months, and I don't expect to see him. I think he's gone back to England." She had paused, then added, "The same can't be said of the countess, however."

"I told you, I intend to stay as far away from her as I can." Jeff had chuckled humorlessly. "I don't reckon the count's going to be inviting me to any more dinners."

Melissa hadn't seemed to find that amusing, and neither had Jeff. He went on, "Take good care of yourself . . . and Michael."

"You don't have to worry about Michael," she had assured him. "He'll be fine."

"He'll miss his papa. It's a long time until spring."

"Yes," Melissa had echoed. "A long time . . ."

Soon after that, Jeff had left the cabin. His bags were already loaded on the small boat, and after one last tearful hug with Michael, he had gone ashore. That was where he stood now, gloved hands jammed into the deep pockets of his greatcoat, the cold wind in his face. There was no sign of Michael on the deck of the *Beaumont*; Melissa must have taken him back down to the cabin.

"That's the last of it, Mr. Holt."

Jeff looked over at the sailor who had spoken. "What?"

The man inclined his head toward the small stack of carpetbags on the dock. "The last of your gear. Want us to take it to where you're staying?"

That was a good question. Jeff had no answer to it, because at this moment he had no idea where he would stay. He shook his head. "No, that's all right. You men head on back to the ship. I know Captain Vickery is ready to cast off."

"Aye, sir." The sailor touched a finger to the brim of his cap. "See you next spring, Mr. Holt."

Jeff nodded as the man and his companions climbed back into the small boat and began rowing out to the *Beaumont*. He stood watching as preparations continued for the ship's sailing, and he was still there a short time later when the anchor was hauled up, the sails were unfurled, and the *Beaumont* turned slowly and gracefully toward the mouth of the harbor.

Hoofbeats sounded behind Jeff, and a moment later an agitated voice asked, "What . . . what you are doing here?"

Jeff turned and saw the startled face of Piotr, Count Orlov's aide . . . and Irina's lapdog. Jeff smiled faintly. "I've come to stay. For the next few months, Sitka is my home."

Melissa fought against the impulse, and until the last minute she thought she had conquered it. Then she knew she could stand it no longer, and she started up to the deck to look back at the shore and perhaps catch one last glimpse of her husband.

Michael followed on her heels, asking excitedly, "Are we going back to get Papa?"

Melissa stopped halfway up the companionway stairs. She looked down at Michael's eager face, and her heart broke a little. She shook her head. "No, Papa wants to stay here. But perhaps you can wave good-bye to him."

"Papa's sad."

Papa is a thoughtless bastard who doesn't care who gets hurt as long as he gets his own way. Melissa took a deep breath and swallowed that thought before it could form into words on her lips. Hearing it wouldn't do Michael any good. Besides, it wasn't true . . . at least not all the time.

She reached down and took Michael's hand. "Come along."

They hurried up on deck and went to the railing astern. The sails were filled with wind, and the *Beaumont* had come around so that Sitka was behind it. Michael came up on his toes and hopped up and down as he tried to see over the gunwale. Melissa swept him up in her arms and pointed to a tall figure on the distant dock. "There," she said. "See him? There's your father."

Michael said, "I see him!" and began to wave.

No answering wave came from the distant figure, and Melissa realized with a sinking heart that Jeff had already turned away. He was talking to a man in a red coat, one of the Russian soldiers.

The last chance for a farewell was gone.

Melissa stood there anyway, with Michael in her

arms, as Sitka—and Jeff—fell farther and farther behind.

The time he had spent in an eastern academy had not softened Proud Wolf. His lean, muscular body was still resilient. By the morning after he had regained consciousness in Ulysses Dowd's wagon, he felt much stronger, and his appetite was no longer satisfied by broth. Audrey brought him a plate of biscuits and thick slices of ham, and Proud Wolf ate eagerly, washing down the food with a cup of strong tea.

Fortified by the meal, he began to feel restless. "I would like to get up and see the camp," he told Audrey.

She smiled and caressed his cheek. "You only woke up last night from a terrible fever. You need to rest."

"In my land there is little time for resting. A man must recover quickly from his injuries if he is to fight again."

"Well, I hope you won't have to fight anymore. I'm tired of fighting." Audrey sighed. "And I'm tired of running away."

Proud Wolf felt a pang of guilt. Audrey had certainly gotten more than she had ever bargained for when she'd fallen in love with him. She had been involved, if only peripherally, in several brutal fights, a killing, a robbery, being shot at, running through woods, tramping along an ice-cold stream . . . and she had come through with strength and poise and only a few moments of despair. But she had a point: He could not continue to ask her to risk her life for his sake.

"Do you like these people?" he asked.

Audrey seemed surprised by the question. "You mean Mr. and Mrs. Dowd and their friends? Why, yes, I . . . I like them very much."

"Do you believe them to be trustworthy?"

"Oh, yes. They helped us without asking any questions at all, and I know they must have been curious."

Curious about finding a beautiful but bedraggled

young white woman traveling with a gun-shot Teton Sioux in the middle of Massachusetts? Yes, Proud Wolf thought dryly, he could see how that might prompt anyone's curiosity. But he said, "Then you should stay with them, and I should leave. We have spoken of this before. If you go back to Cambridge and tell everyone that I forced you to go with me, they will believe you."

Even before he had finished speaking, Audrey was shaking her head stubbornly. "I've told you before, I won't do that. We were meant to be together, Proud Wolf."

"Meant by whom? Fate? The Creator, Wakan Tanka? The one you call God?"

"That's right," Audrey said with an emphatic nod.

From the doorway of the wagon, Ulysses Xavier Dowd said in his booming voice, "And whom God hath joined together let no man put asunder."

Proud Wolf caught his breath. For such a large man, Dowd could move silently when he wanted to.

Dowd stepped up into the wagon. "It sounds to me as if you young people have some serious problems." He looked solemnly at Audrey. "You ran away from home, didn't you, young lady?"

Audrey swallowed, then nodded.

"Because your young man here is a savage? Your parents did not approve of him?"

"Proud Wolf is *not* a savage," Audrey said sharply.

Dowd waved a large hand. "I was speaking purely in racial terms. From what little I've seen of it, the young man's demeanor seems quite civilized."

"I take no offense, Mr. Dowd," said Proud Wolf.

"There, you see? Quite civilized." Dowd clasped his hands together behind his back, straining the buttons on his waistcoat. "And I was correct about the other matter, too, I'll wager. 'A pair of star-cross'd lovers,' if ever I've seen one."

Vanessa came into the wagon behind him. "What are you blathering on about, Ulysses?"

Dowd turned to her with an affectionate smile. "Ah, my dear, I was just speaking with young Lady

Capulet and Lord Montague here. It seems—and I must admit here that I was eavesdropping—that Romeo wants his Juliet to leave him and return from whence they came."

Vanessa looked at Proud Wolf and Audrey. "Is that true?"

Proud Wolf could only guess at the meaning of what Dowd had said. He thought of Professor Hilliard and wondered fleetingly why it was his fate to encounter white men who spoke so much and so strangely. But there was one thing of which Proud Wolf was certain.

"It would be better if Audrey returned to her home," he said.

"No!" she exclaimed. "I won't go back, and I won't leave Proud Wolf!"

"No one is asking you to, dear," Vanessa said gently. "What you've done is none of our business."

Her husband looked askance at her. "It's not?" he asked. "Are we not placing ourselves at risk by assisting them? What if they be brigands or cutthroats?"

That question hit too close to the mark, but as Proud Wolf and Audrey involuntarily stiffened, Vanessa said, "Look at them, Ulysses. Do they look like thieves or killers?"

Dowd regarded them solemnly for a moment, then said, "Well . . . now that you mention it, no. They seem like charming young people who have encountered ill fortune."

"We need to move on," said Vanessa, "but you're welcome to travel with us, at least until Proud Wolf has regained his strength."

"Thank you," Audrey said. "We can't tell you how much we appreciate—"

"We have no money with which to pay you," Proud Wolf cut in.

Dowd waved off that objection. "No matter. As soon as you're back on your feet, you'll earn your keep, right enough. We'll put you to work, we will."

"Doing what?" asked Audrey.

Vanessa smiled. "Have the two of you ever considered becoming actors?"

By the time the troupe reached Hartford, Connecticut, a week later, Proud Wolf's hip was still stiff and sore, causing him to limp when he walked, but the bullet wound was healing nicely.

During that week, Proud Wolf and Audrey had become acquainted with the other members of the group. There were eight of them: Kenneth and Philippa Thurston, a middle-aged married couple; Theodore and Frederick Zachary, twins in their twenties; Walter Berryhill, an elderly man with a shock of white hair; Elaine Yardley and her adolescent daughter, Portia; and Oliver Johnson, who was thirty years old and barely three feet tall.

All of them were friendly to the newcomers, although young Portia Yardley could not stop staring at Proud Wolf. Walter Berryhill was rather forgetful and asked several times why an Indian was traveling with them. "Proud Wolf is not simply an Indian," Dowd explained to the old man. "Why, he is a prince among his race, a man of noble blood who will one day rule over all the red people of the West."

That was stretching the truth a little, Proud Wolf thought. He was the son of a chief and might one day lead his father's band of Teton Sioux, but he was no royal prince.

But Berryhill nodded solemnly, satisfied with Dowd's answer.

Life with the acting troupe was pleasant, Proud Wolf discovered. The wagons moved at an easy pace. After a couple of days, Proud Wolf left the Dowds' wagon so that they could reclaim it. At night he rolled his blankets under the wagon belonging to the Zachary brothers, and Audrey stayed with Elaine and Portia Yardley in their wagon. By day, at Dowd's insistence, Proud Wolf rode on the wagon seat beside him, listening to the rotund actor's seemingly endless supply of stories interspersed with long speeches from plays

Proud Wolf had never heard of. By the end of the week he was becoming increasingly familiar with the works of a man called William Shakespeare and a host of Greeks with names Proud Wolf could not pronounce, let alone remember.

Always in the back of his mind was the knowledge that the authorities were somewhere behind him, seeking him for the murder—that was what they would call it, no matter what the circumstances—of William Brackett.

As the wagons neared Hartford, Dowd pointed out a cluster of tents that had been set up in an open field on the edge of the town. Wagons lined the periphery. "A traveling fair," he explained to Proud Wolf. "We shall stop there and enact several scenes from the tragedy *Julius Caesar*. I believe you will make an excellent Roman centurion, my young friend."

"A what?" asked Proud Wolf.

"A centurion. A soldier. Fear not, I shall provide all the costuming and the necessary equipage." Dowd boomed out a laugh. "I daresay, given your heritage, this will not be the first time you've carried a spear, will it, lad?"

"I have killed buffalo with a lance," said Proud Wolf.

"Well, there are no buffalo here . . . though if the audience becomes restive, perhaps you could skewer one of them and liven things up."

Proud Wolf stared at Dowd, not completely convinced the actor was speaking in jest.

"And Miss Stoddard can participate as well, though when the Bard wrote his plays, women were never allowed to take part in them. All the feminine roles were played by young men."

"Men . . . who dressed as women?"

"Yes, indeed."

Proud Wolf nodded gravely. "There are some among my people who do this."

Dowd made a rasping, gravelly noise, and Proud Wolf could not tell if he was clearing his throat or laughing. "Ah . . . yes," Dowd finally said. "At any rate, Miss Stoddard can play one of the young women of Rome, with Elaine and dear little Portia and Philippa. It will be an excellent performance, I'm quite sure."

Dowd led the wagons into the field where the fair was being set up. Dozens of people were gathered there already, and over the next few hours Proud Wolf was treated to sights the likes of which he had never seen before. Many of the men and women strolling the fair were swarthy of face and dressed in flamboyant clothing. Dowd explained that they were called Gypsies. "Some say they be the descendants of the ancient Egyptians, and that's how they came by the name. As for myself, I don't know, but they're uncommonly good performers, and they travel with these fairs all over the land."

Proud Wolf watched in awe as one Gypsy practiced sliding the long, thin blade of a knife down his throat—and back out again. Another man juggled brightly painted wooden balls, moving them faster and faster until they were a blur of color. Fiddles scraped, pipes piped, voices were raised in song, and dancing feet flew until they blurred, too. Booths selling different kinds of food were set up, and a whole pig was roasted in a pit. As evening approached, torches were driven into the ground. Their flames cast a garish glow over the entire field.

The wagons of Dowd's acting troupe were pulled into a circle in the middle of the field around a broad, empty space. "This will be our stage, our Globe Theater," Dowd told Proud Wolf. "Come along, lad. We must make ready."

Trunks were lifted out of the wagons and opened, and the clothing that was lifted out of them was novel and strange to Proud Wolf: leggings tighter than any of buckskin he had ever worn, silk shirts with billowing sleeves, feathered hats like the one Dowd wore.

Proud Wolf looked skeptically at the hat Dowd handed him. "I am to wear this?"

"Certainly."

He prodded the feather with a finger. "It reminds me of the headdress favored by the Cree and the Arikara."

"Well, in this case you're a Roman. Remember that. But don't worry. All you have to do is stand there and hold a spear and look fierce. You can do that, can't you?"

Proud Wolf nodded. "I will be a Roman."

As the performance was about to begin, Audrey came up to Proud Wolf. She was wearing a long white gown not altogether different from the dresses she had worn at the academy. "Good luck, Proud Wolf," she said. She brushed a kiss against his cheek. "Isn't this exciting?"

He grinned. "I am a spear carrier," he said, holding up the weapon. It was much shorter than the lance his people used, and the head was so dull it would have bounced off a buffalo's side, no matter how hard he threw it.

"You'll do a wonderful job," Audrey assured him.

A commotion near the tents caught Proud Wolf's attention. One of the Zachary brothers was coming toward them. Unsure whether the man was Theodore or Frederick, Proud Wolf did not address him by name. He nodded toward the knot of people and asked, "What is that?"

Zachary paused and looked over his shoulder at the crowd. Several people seemed to be arguing. "I'm not sure," he said. "But I know the constable from Hartford is here, and I believe I heard someone say that he's come looking for a murderer."

CHAPTER TWENTY-FOUR

B ut . . . but this is impossible!" Piotr exclaimed. "You cannot remain here. You are not Russian."

Without looking back, Jeff inclined his head toward the harbor. "The *Beaumont* has already sailed. I don't have much choice."

"We will send up a signal rocket and call the ship back," Piotr suggested frantically.

Jeff shook his head. "I don't think so."

"But Count Orlov—" Piotr stopped short and stared at him. Jeff had no doubt he knew what had transpired between Jeff and Irina, and he had to know as well that the count had taken a shot at him. And now the insane American was saying that he was going to impose on the hospitality of the Russians for the entire winter!

Jeff could read all those emotions on the aide's face. Piotr was probably right, too, at least about the insane part. Jeff had told Melissa that he was staying in Sitka in order to conclude the trade agreement, but that wasn't the real reason. He was staying because of the argument they'd had, because his own stupid Holt pride wouldn't let him back down.

"Take me to see the count," he said quietly.

Piotr shook his head emphatically. "I cannot do that. The count would . . . would . . ."

"What? Shoot me? He's already tried that." Jeff stalked past him, jerking a thumb at his bags. "Have a wagon come for those and bring them to the headquarters of the Russian-American Company. That's where I'll be."

Piotr sputtered a little and then spewed a stream of Russian words that sounded like curses. Jeff ignored him and kept walking. After a moment Piotr mounted up and rode past him, trotting the horse toward Orlov's office.

The thin layer of snow on the ground crunched under Jeff's boots as he walked. He saw Piotr give orders to one of the soldiers near headquarters, and the man hurried off, probably to fetch a wagon. Piotr dismounted and scurried into the building. Jeff arrived a few minutes later.

The aide was waiting inside, next to the closed door of Orlov's office. He said stiffly, "The count will be seeing you now," and leaned over to open the door. Jeff nodded his thanks and strode inside.

Orlov sat behind his desk, leaning back in his chair and calmly regarding his visitor. Jeff took off his hat and gloves and stomped some of the snow from his boots, then bowed slightly. "Count Orlov."

"Mr. Holt. Your presence here surprises me. And I am even more surprised by what Piotr has told me."

"That I intend to stay in Sitka for the winter?"

"Exactly." Orlov reached out and toyed with a paperweight on his desk. It was a chunk of stone, hewn out of a larger rock. "This stone is from the Ural Mountains, in Siberia. A cold and unpleasant land. A land where I might find myself posted permanently if I were to offend the czar."

"The czar won't be offended by your putting extra money in his pockets."

Orlov slammed the piece of rock down on the desk, gouging out a splinter of wood. "Again you mention money!" He snorted. "I think it is the god you Americans truly worship. Do you know *nothing* of honor, Mr. Holt? Do you think that sufficient profits cure all ills, right all wrongs, and redeem all lost souls?"

Jeff took a deep breath and tried to control his own anger. "I know better than that, Count," he said. "And I don't blame you for being angry that I'm still here. I reckon if our positions were reversed, I wouldn't be very happy about the situation either. But I can assure you that I do not mean to cause further trouble. All I want is to reach an agreement with you on a trade pact, and then I'll stay out of your way until next spring."

"And where will you stay?"

"You've got an empty cabin or two around here. I've seen them."

Slowly, the count nodded. "True. And I suppose, if what Piotr tells me is true, that there is nothing I can do other than make you welcome. Your ship has sailed."

"That's right."

Orlov leaned forward. "Then I have no choice," he said harshly. "You are welcome here in Sitka until the spring. But I warn you—"

"You don't have to warn me about anything, Count," Jeff cut in. "I've no intention of causing problems for you—or anyone else."

Orlov looked balefully at him. "Very well," he said with a curt nod. "I will instruct Piotr to see to it that your belongings are taken to one of the vacant cabins. As soon as you are settled in, we will meet again."

"And iron out all the details of the trade agreement."

Orlov's mouth twisted as if he had just bitten into something that tasted bad, but he nodded. "Yes. Business is business, as you Americans say."

"You won't regret this, Count Orlov."

The Russian merely grunted. Jeff waited a moment,

then turned to go. Orlov called Piotr in from the outer office, and Jeff heard them speaking in rapid Russian. Then Piotr emerged behind Jeff and said, "If you will be coming with me . . . ?"

"All right," said Jeff. The two men left the building. A wagon with Jeff's bags in the back was waiting, with the same elderly soldier with the drooping gray mustache on the seat, holding the reins.

"Alexander Ilyavitch will take you to your cabin," said Piotr.

"Much obliged." As Jeff stepped up onto the wagon box, he looked back at Piotr and couldn't resist adding, "I suppose you'll go tell *her* now that I'm back."

Piotr made no reply, only stared straight ahead as if he had not heard Jeff's gibe. But then his eyes flicked toward Jeff for an instant, gleaming with hostility.

Jeff Holt had more than one enemy in Sitka. He was going to have to watch his back all winter.

Murder! The word shrieked in Proud Wolf's brain as Zachary bustled on to whatever errand needed his attention. Proud Wolf looked around for Audrey, trying not to appear frantic. He spotted her near one of the other wagons, talking to Elaine and Portia Yardley, both of whom wore white gowns like hers. Proud Wolf hurried over to them, and although he was trying to suppress his panic, the women broke off their conversation and Audrey asked, "What's wrong, Proud Wolf?"

"I must speak with you," he said quietly, taking her arm.

"But the performance will be starting in a few minutes—"

"Please, Audrey. It is important."

"All right." She gave Elaine and Portia a weak smile, then allowed Proud Wolf to lead her around the corner of the wagon. In a whisper she asked, "What in the world is the matter?"

"The local constable is here. He is looking for a murderer."

Audrey's hands flew to her mouth. "Oh, dear."

"That is all you can say?" demanded Proud Wolf.

She flushed. "What do you want me to say? That we should run?" She looked pointedly at her costume, then at his. "Dressed like this?"

She was right, of course. In these costumes they would be all too conspicuous if they attempted to flee.

"We have to brazen it out," Audrey went on. "No one in Hartford knows we joined the troupe only recently."

"The Dowds and all the others know it."

"They won't betray us." Audrey's voice was hollow. "I'm sure they won't."

She was no more certain of that than he was, thought Proud Wolf. But they had no choice except to hope that the other actors would keep their secret.

Ulysses Dowd bustled up to them. "Everyone to your places, as we rehearsed."

Audrey gave Proud Wolf a quick kiss on the cheek and said, "Good luck."

"No, no, my dear," Dowd exclaimed. "Never wish anyone in the theater good luck. That's a sure way of bringing down misfortune. Say 'Break a leg' instead."

"Are you sure? That sounds . . . I don't know . . . risky."

"Trust me, my dear," said Dowd.

"All right, then." Audrey summoned up a smile as she turned back to Proud Wolf. "Break a leg."

"And you, too," he replied solemnly.

A pair of whitewashed columns made of lightweight wood had been set up about ten feet apart in the center of the open space. These were meant to represent the Roman Forum, and the scenes the troupe would enact would take place between them. As the actors moved into position, Dowd stepped out of the rough circle formed by the parked wagons and bellowed, "Ladies and gentlemen! For your edification and entertainment, the world-famous Dowd Players will now present a series of dramatic scenes from *Julius Caesar*, written by the immortal William Shakespeare! Come one, come all, and thrill to this exciting presentation!''

Dowd continued his exuberant pitch as Proud Wolf, Audrey, and the other members of the troupe stood ready to begin. Spectators trickled through the openings between the wagons and gathered around the performers. Dowd had explained to Proud Wolf during the trip to Hartford that the troupe rarely charged an admission fee for their performances but relied on passing the hat afterward. Tonight was no exception.

Proud Wolf's grip on the spear tightened when he caught a glimpse of the man who had been at the center of the arguing crowd earlier. He was a tall, powerfully built individual in a sober dark jacket and trousers, and Proud Wolf took him to be the constable. He had a firm grip on the collar of a smaller man and was prodding him along. The second man had his hands tied behind his back.

Proud Wolf let out an audible sigh. He knew he might be jumping to conclusions, but it looked as if the constable had come to the fair in search of someone else. Proud Wolf kept his eye on the two men until he could no longer see them.

A sizable crowd had gathered, and Dowd walked imperiously through them to the center of the performing area. He swept his hat from his head and bent low in a bow. "Welcome, ladies and gentlemen! And now . . . let the performance begin! Our scene is Rome, and several important members of the Roman Senate are meeting in private to conspire a dark and bloody fate for their emperor, Julius Caesar.''

The performance proceeded, with Walter Berryhill portraying Julius Caesar, Kenneth Thurston playing Marc Antony, the Zachary brothers and Oliver Johnson performing as senators, and Audrey, Elaine, and Portia as female citizens of Rome. The crowd laughed at the idea of someone as small as Oliver playing a Roman politician, and when he made faces at them, they laughed even harder. Dowd provided narration between the scenes.

As for Proud Wolf, he stood stiffly between the columns, holding the spear and looking solemn. He was reminded a little of the rituals of his people, but there was nothing real about this. It was all make-believe.

When the play was over, Oliver and Portia each took a hat and moved through the crowd, collecting coins. As the spectators trickled away, Audrey came to Proud Wolf and took his hand. "You see, I told you everything was going to be all right. I . . . I think we may have found a home with these people, Proud Wolf."

He could not imagine spending the rest of his life with the acting troupe, but for now he supposed that Audrey was right. He squeezed her hand. "We will stay with them, and we will be safe."

He hoped he had spoken the truth. He and Audrey had suffered enough pain and hardship.

A hundred miles north of Hartford, two men strode into the main room of a tavern and looked around. One of them moved stiffly, as if he were in pain. Long days spent in a saddle before he was ready to travel accounted for his halting gait.

But Will Brackett had waited as long as he was going to for his revenge. With an ugly smile pulling at his lips, he said to Frank Kirkland, "There are some rough-looking men here. We ought to be able to find some who are willing to do what we want."

"Kill that damned redskin, you mean?" Frank asked with an equally vicious grin.

"Exactly," said Will.

Clay spent the night lounging on the deck of the *New Orleans* not far from the door of Senator Haines's cabin. Toward dawn, with only a faint rumbling sound as a warning, the earth began to shake once more. Even with the waters of the Mississippi acting as a buffer, Clay could feel the mighty vibrations rolling across the landscape. In the grayish light, he saw the trees waving back and forth on shore.

Suddenly a huge sucking sound welled up and filled the air. The steamboat lurched violently. Clay had to grab the rail to keep from being pitched off his feet. Then another jolt shook the *New Orleans*, and before Clay's disbelieving eyes, the island in the middle of the river where the boat had been tied . . . *sank*.

Clay shook his head and blinked, unable to comprehend what he had just seen. A couple of heavy ropes had run from the boat to some trees on the island, and now those ropes led down into the river at a sharp angle. They were still tied to the trees, Clay realized, but the trees were now below the surface of the water.

All up and down the deck, cabin doors banged open. Sleeping passengers had been thrown from their bunks. Shouting in fear and confusion, they poured out onto the deck, Senator Haines among them. Clay ignored him for the moment. He had something more important to worry about.

The *New Orleans* was beginning to list to one side. Clay lurched away from the rail to keep from sliding into the water.

The sunken island was pulling them down! Even as that realization hit him, Clay yanked his knife from the sheath at his waist and broke into a staggering run toward the closest of the ropes. He heard Captain Roosevelt yelling for the crew to get up some steam and start the giant paddlewheels turning. That might stabilize the boat to a certain extent, but the only way to save the *New Orleans* was to cut the ropes.

The rope nearest to Clay was wrapped securely around a large metal stanchion at the bow of the boat. He grabbed the stanchion with his free hand and slashed at the rope with his knife. The rope was thick and tough—it had to be to keep the boat moored safely under normal circumstances—and Clay knew it was going to take a while to cut through it. Still, he had to try.

A moment later, one of the crewmen appeared at his side carrying an ax. "Get out of the way!" the man bellowed, and Clay moved gladly. The crewman swung the ax, and with the damage Clay had already done to the rope, only a pair of strokes was required before it parted with a loud twang. Clay grabbed the rail again as the bow swung sharply around. Now the *New Orleans* was facing north, instead of south as when it was tied up.

What the devil was going on?

As the sky grew lighter, Clay saw that the waters of the Mississippi were rushing along much more swiftly than their usual ponderous pace. But, far more ominously, the river was also flowing *backward*.

The rope at the stern parted under the ax of another crewman, and the boat surged into motion, carried to the north by the surging current. Clay could not comprehend what he was seeing. Somehow this freak occurence of nature had to be connected to the earthquake. The shore was still shaking wildly. This tremor was the lengthiest and perhaps the strongest yet.

Clay stumbled away from the rail and toward his cabin on the other side of the boat. He had to make sure that Shining Moon and Matthew were all right. As he passed the wheelhouse, he heard Roosevelt shouting, demanding more power from the engine. The paddlewheels had started to revolve, but so far they were making no headway. The *New Orleans* was being swept along by the runaway river.

The door of the cabin was open when Clay got there, and he saw to his dismay that Shining Moon and Matthew were not inside. Where in blazes could they have gone? He looked around wildly. Maybe they were looking for him to make sure he was all right. They knew he had been standing guard at Haines's cabin when the quake hit. That was where they would have gone.

As Clay turned in that direction, Markham stumbled up to him and caught his arm. "What the hell is going on?" he yelled. "The river's gone crazy!"

Clay had no answers for him. Urgently he asked, "Have you seen Shining Moon or Matthew?"

Markham shook his head. "They're not in your cabin?"

"They must have gone looking for me!" Clay replied grimly. "Come on!"

With Markham at his side, he started again around the long row of cabins toward the one Senator Haines occupied, as the *New Orleans* struggled to right itself against the turbulent, backward-flowing river.

Matthew had loved the excitement of traveling over the rapids at the Falls of the Ohio, but this ride back up the Mississippi while the world was shaking crazily was too frightening even for him. He clutched at Shining Moon's dress as they made their way along the tilting deck toward Senator Haines's cabin.

"Do not worry," Shining Moon said over the rumbling of the earthquake and the roar of the steamboat's engine. "We will find Clay, and everything will be all right."

Matthew wasn't so certain. What he had said to Clay about the world shaking and shaking until it shook itself apart had been intended merely to annoy him. But now he was beginning to worry that he might have been right.

He didn't want the world to end. He didn't want to die. Until this moment Matthew had never known he could be so scared. Even in the most threatening situations in the past he had always known that he could fool people and get what he wanted. But he couldn't make the world stop shaking. He couldn't make the river flow the right way again. All he could do was stumble along the deck, holding on to Shining Moon's dress as she gripped his shoulder, and hope that they would live through the next few minutes. . . .

Senator Morgan Ralston pressed his back against the wall, bracing himself in a small alcove midway along the deck where he had come stumbling out of his

cabin. He wished there was something more solid to
hang on to.

But there didn't seem to be anything solid about
the world anymore. Everything was shifting and shaking, and he, who had always prided himself on being
in control, could not do a damned thing to stop it.

He couldn't die now, not when he was on the
verge of having everything he wanted! So close, so
close . . .

Then, as it always did, fortune smiled on Morgan
Ralston, and he saw the solution to one of his problems
staggering toward him.

The Garwood boy—that damned little black-
mailer—was coming along the deck with the squaw
who was Clay Holt's woman.

Ralston's lips pulled back from his teeth in an evil
smile. A few feet away, the giant paddlewheel was
spinning faster and faster as Captain Roosevelt called
on his crew for more power to fight the unnatural pull
of the river. Matthew and Shining Moon hadn't noticed
Ralston yet; they were concentrating on keeping their
balance on the tilting, vibrating deck. All he had to do
was step out to meet them, and one quick shove for
each would send them toppling into the paddlewheel.

The churning wheel itself might not kill them, but
it would injure them and surely knock them unconscious. Once they were in the river, they would die,
and their bodies would probably never be recovered.
Everyone would blame their disappearance on the
earthquake, and if their bodies were ever found, their
deaths would be regarded as tragic accidents. All Ralston had to worry about now was the possibility that
someone might see him push them.

He could take that chance. He looked up and down
the deck and saw that no one was paying attention to
anything but their own safety. He stepped out of the
alcove just before Matthew and Shining Moon drew
even with him.

Finally they saw him. Shining Moon looked at him

with desperation in her eyes. "Senator Ralston! Please help us. Have you seen Clay—"

That was when Matthew—damn the boy!—read the truth in the senator's eyes. He shouted, "Watch out! He's going to—"

Too late. Ralston's right hand slammed into Shining Moon's chest and drove her backward, toward the railing. The paddlewheel spun madly a scant yard away. At the same time, Ralston's left hand grabbed Matthew's arm and slung him after Shining Moon. Her back cracked against the rail, and the momentum of Ralston's shove carried her up and over. She plunged straight toward the revolving wooden blades of the giant paddlewheel.

CHAPTER
TWENTY-FIVE

The *Lydia Marie* docked at Whampoa, China, at the mouth of the Pearl River a dozen miles downstream from the city of Canton. This was the only Chinese port where trade with the West was allowed, and the Americans were required to remain in compounds known as *hongs* that had been set up by the Chinese for the express purpose of doing business with outsiders.

The cargo of sandalwood from the Hawaiian Islands was unloaded after several Chinese merchants—all of whom spoke a bizarre but understandable dialect called pidgin English—had come on board and struck a suitable bargain with Captain Canfield. Ned and India had sat in on the discussion.

The sandalwood was being traded for silks, spices, tea, and camphor. Ned had never considered himself a businessman, but as he watched the crates being brought aboard and stored in the hold, he kept a running estimate in his head of what the Chinese goods ought to bring when the Holt-Merrivale Company sold them in the United States. He stopped when his calculations reached thirty thousand dollars. Sums larger than that were beyond his comprehension.

"Jeff and Melissa will be pleased," India commented quietly as she stood beside him at the railing.

"Aye," Ned said with a nod. "I've lost count of how much money the company stands to make off this journey. But it'll be well worth our while."

"You're glad you came, then?"

Something in her tone made Ned look at her. "Of course I'm glad," he said. "Why wouldn't I be?"

She shrugged her slender shoulders. "I don't know. You've been a bit . . . distant lately."

"Oh." Ned looked away. "Well, I've got quite a bit on my mind." *Like worrying whether or not you killed Donnelly during that storm.*

The thought was still plaguing Ned. Donnelly had been a brutal bastard whom no one else on board had particularly liked. In fact, many had despised him. Good riddance—that was what he ought to be thinking about Donnelly, Ned told himself.

But for some unknown reason he had not been able to come around to that way of thinking, even though he knew it would be better if he could. He had sown his wild oats as a young man. More than once he had known the satisfying feeling of a man's nose pulping under the hard knuckles of his fists during a tavern brawl, and on even more occasions he had plunged out the bedroom windows of married women, narrowly avoiding the wrath of their husbands. But deep down, instilled in him by his God-fearing parents, was the knowledge of right and wrong, and blast it, he simply couldn't bring himself to believe in cold-blooded murder, not even of scum like Donnelly.

Unfortunately, he couldn't explain all that to India. At times all the questions, all the concerns, had threatened to come bubbling out of him, but at the last minute he had been unable to speak. He might be able to live with the suspicion . . . but he was not sure he could live with confirmation.

While those dark thoughts were going through his head, someone came up beside him and clapped a hand on his shoulder. Ned looked down and saw Yancy, the wizened little British sailor.

"Hello there, lad. Watchin' the heathen Chinee at work, are you?"

Ned grinned. "That's better than working myself."

"Aye, that it is." Yancy nodded toward the dock and the crates still waiting to be loaded. "Going to be a lucrative trip, from the looks o' things. Yer cousin will be pleased."

"Which one?" asked Ned. "Jeff Holt or Lemuel March?"

"Both, I'd wager," Yancy said with a cackling laugh. Then he grew more serious and added, "Seems to me you ought to be in for more of a share yourself, laddie. You're a Holt, after all."

Without hesitation, Ned shook his head. "I signed on to work as a member of the crew and to keep an eye on things for Jeff and Lemuel. They're the ones who have taken all the financial risks, not me. I don't want to be in charge of anything."

"But ye could be the captain of your own ship someday, or run the business back in the States—"

"I'm a sailor, plain and simple," Ned cut in. "That's all I want to be."

"Ye've no ambition to be something more?"

Ned grinned. "You're starting to sound like my father, Yancy." He shook his head again. "No, too often ambition doesn't gain a man anything but gray hair, a pain in his belly, and a weight around his neck. I'm content to be a sailor."

Yancy looked at India. "What about you?"

In a husky voice she said, "Too many men let the business own them, instead of the other way round. I'm for the freedom of the sea."

"Well, I can't say as I blame either one of ye. An

old salt like me just sometimes gets to thinking o' what he's going to do when he's too old to go to sea."

"That'll be a long time yet, Yancy," Ned assured him.

"Maybe so, maybe so," Yancy muttered as he moved off along the deck.

India watched him go and said quietly to Ned, "That was certainly a strange conversation."

"Oh, Yancy's just feeling sorry for himself. Once he's had a chance to go ashore and cut loose a little, he'll feel better."

India's lips curved softly in a smile. "And how would that make you feel, Mr. Holt?"

He took a deep breath and tried once more to put all his worries behind him. "I think that may be exactly what I need."

At the other end of the ship, three sailors, all burly and hard-faced, waited for Yancy to join them. When the little Englishman hobbled up to them, one of the men asked, "What about it? Any chance of bringing Holt over to our side?"

Yancy shook his head. His weathered face had a sinister cast to it now. "He'll never come round; he's just a lackey for those damned cousins of his, without a lick of ambition of his own."

"And St. Clair?"

"He does whatever Holt does, ye know that."

One of the other men said quietly, "Then when the time comes, both of them will have to die, just like Donnelly."

Yancy chuckled humorlessly. "Well, not *just* like Donnelly. I don't think we'll be lucky enough to have another storm come along so one of us can push them overboard, the way I did with Donnelly."

"I thought sure Donnelly would join us," said the third man. "A bastard like him."

"A man can be a bastard and still be honest," said Yancy. "That was Donnelly's mistake, right enough." He looked toward the bow, where Ned and India still stood, paying no attention to him. "It was a fatal mistake for Donnelly . . . and it will be for those two, as well."

After rounding the great eastern bulge of South America, the *Beaumont* swung up through the Caribbean, then across the Gulf of Mexico, and put in to port at New Orleans. There it would take on a cargo of furs and cotton to carry back to North Carolina.

Melissa was thinking about that as she stood at the railing of the ship and watched the teeming hordes on the docks of the Crescent City. She and Captain Vickery had hatched the idea of stopping at New Orleans during the weeks-long voyage around the Cape. Since the *Beaumont* would not be returning with Alaskan furs in its hold, as everyone involved in the enterprise had hoped, at least they would have something to show for the trip.

Something, Melissa thought bitterly, besides a ruined marriage.

Though she fought against them, images of Jeff in the arms of the countess had haunted her ever since the ship had sailed from Sitka. Jeff had sworn that he was going to stay far away from Irina while he was in Alaska, but Melissa doubted that would be possible. That woman went after what she wanted, and it had been clear that she wanted Jeff.

But how was the count going to react? Was Jeff in danger?

Why should she care? Melissa had asked herself every time that question occurred to her. Jeff had made his own decisions; now he would abide by them and take the consequences. But it was easier to think that than to feel it. After all, Jeff was still her husband, the man she had thought to be the love of her life, the father of her child—

"Mama? Mama?"

Melissa became aware that Michael was standing beside her, tugging on her dress. She looked down at

him, frowning in annoyance, as she did all too often
these days.

"What is it, Michael?"

He pointed into the throng on the dock. "Isn't that
Uncle Terence?"

Melissa looked in the direction Michael indicated,
and her eyes widened in surprise. She saw a tall, muscular man with broad, powerful shoulders, a shock of
black hair, and a rawboned face moving easily through
the press of dockworkers, sailors, and merchants. She
recognized him immediately, as Michael had. Terence
O'Shay was the kind of man who always stood out in a
crowd.

Melissa could not imagine what O'Shay was doing
in New Orleans. The last time she had seen him, they
had both been in Wilmington, where O'Shay had become a staunch friend of the Holt family. Though a
smuggler by trade—some even said a criminal—
O'Shay had always been an honorable man where his
friends were concerned. He had helped Jeff and Melissa on more than one occasion.

Melissa waved an arm over her head and called,
"Terence! Terence O'Shay!"

At first she thought he hadn't heard her over the
hubbub, but then he paused and looked back over his
shoulder. She waved again. O'Shay spotted her, and
his craggy face split in a grin. He turned and began
pushing his way back along the dock toward the *Beaumont*.

Melissa and Michael moved toward the gangplank
to meet him. He bounded up the plank with long-
legged strides and reached out with both hands to
grasp the hand Melissa extended to him. "Mrs. Holt!"
he said. "Didn't expect to run into you here!" He let go
of Melissa's hand and swooped the boy up in his powerful arms. "And little Whip! Danged if you haven't
grown a foot since I saw you last, lad!" Still grinning,
he looked back at Melissa. "Where's Jeff?"

"He . . . he's not with us." Melissa tried to keep

the regret and anger out of her voice, but she knew she failed miserably.

O'Shay frowned. "Back in Carolina, is he?"

"No. Jeff's in Alaska."

"He's talking to the Russians," Michael put in.

"Russians," repeated O'Shay. He looked at Melissa with raised eyebrows.

"It's a long story, Terence," Melissa said. "What are *you* doing here in New Orleans?"

"That's a bit of a yarn, too," O'Shay said dryly. "The climate back in Carolina got rather . . . warm. The legal climate, if you know what I mean."

Melissa knew exactly what he meant. The authorities in North Carolina must have cracked down on his smuggling activities. He might even have been in danger of being arrested again.

O'Shay confirmed her suspicion. "I needed to take a wee holiday as soon as I could, and the first boat sailing from Wilmington was headed to New Orleans. I got here a couple of weeks ago, and I've been casting around since, trying to decide what to do with myself." He paused for a second, then went on, "I had a thought about that the other day, and oddly enough, it had to do with the Holts."

"If there's anything we can do to help you, Terence, you know we would," Melissa said without hesitation.

"Well, actually, I was thinking about that brother of Jeff's."

"Clay?" O'Shay had never met Clay Holt, as far as Melissa knew.

"Aye. Jeff told me about that settlement up in the mountains that Clay started, what's it called . . . ?"

"New Hope?"

"That's it," said O'Shay. "So I was thinking, and it came to me that that's just what I need: a new hope. A new start, if you will. So I thought I'd go out to the Rockies and find the place and make a life for myself as a fur trader."

Melissa stared at him for a moment, thoughts whirling madly in her head. O'Shay must have thought something was wrong, because after a minute he said, "What is it? Did I say something wrong?"

"Not at all," Melissa assured him. O'Shay's words about a new start had struck a chord. That was exactly what *she* needed, too, she told herself. He marriage to Jeff might be over—she wouldn't know until next spring, at the earliest—but her life wasn't, and she had never been the type to sit idly by. She wanted to *do* something, and O'Shay had just pointed her in the right direction.

"Then what is it, lass?" he asked. "I can tell something's going on in that head of yours."

"I'm going with you," Melissa announced simply. She knew it was a hasty decision, but sometimes first impulses proved to be good ones, and every instinct told her that this was a good one. She wasn't ready to return to the house in Wilmington, as full of memories as it was.

"What?" exclaimed O'Shay, staring at her.

Michael pushed himself down, out of O'Shay's arms, and tugged on Melissa's skirt. "Where are we going, Mama?"

"To the mountains," she told him. "We're going to start a fur-trading business with Mr. O'Shay. That is, if he agrees." She looked at O'Shay. "I know that I may be . . . imposing, but what do you think, Terence? I'm a good businesswoman, you know that."

"Aye, I saw how you kept Holt-Merrivale afloat while Jeff was in jail." O'Shay rasped a thumbnail along his beard-stubbled jaw. "But still, a woman going all the way out there to the Rockies . . ."

"Not just any woman," said Melissa. "I'm a Holt."

"There is that," O'Shay agreed.

Melissa held out her hand. "Partners?"

O'Shay hesitated for only a moment, then abruptly grasped her hand and pumped it hard. "Partners," he said.

Michael let out a whoop and jumped up and down. "The mountains!" he said. "I'm going to the mountains!"

"Aye, lad," O'Shay told him with a broad grin. "Before you know it, we'll be calling you Whip Holt, mountain man."

For the first few days of Jeff's stay in Sitka, Count Orlov refused to see him again. The count was always busy with other, more pressing matters whenever Jeff came to the headquarters of the Russian-American Company, or so Piotr informed him. Jeff suspected the aide of lying, but even so, there was nothing he could do about it except wait.

This was going to be a long winter, Jeff thought dismally. Darkness lasted almost around the clock during the winter months, he had been told. The time he spent here would be one long, endless night . . . a night without Melissa.

The pain of their separation was more wrenching than he had expected. Sitting in the nearly empty cabin, which was lit only by the weak, flickering glow of a candle made from whale tallow, Jeff had nothing to do but think about everything that had gone wrong in his life. His thoughts were a mad whirl: Melissa, Irina, Orlov, Rattigan . . . He did not know Philip Rattigan, but he hated the man anyway, just as he hated Orlov and Irina because of what they had done to drive the wedge between him and Melissa.

But in his more objective moments he knew he wasn't being fair. True, Orlov had been stubborn about accepting the trade pact and had kept the Americans in Alaska longer than Jeff had anticipated. And Irina *had* tried to seduce him. But she had not forced him to drink the vodka. Nor had she held a pistol to his head as he kissed her and fondled her bare breasts.

No, Jeff decided, ultimately the blame was his. And these long, cold months alone would be his punishment.

After several days, however, the solitude of his own company was more than he could stand. Not far from the cabin he occupied was a long, low-ceilinged log building used by the Russian soldiers as a tavern.

Jeff shrugged into his greatcoat, settled the fur hat down around his ears, wrapped a thick scarf around his neck, and set out into the chilly night.

The *Beaumont* had sailed from Sitka just in time. True winter was settling in. The ice on the harbor grew thicker every day. The wind had picked up, and it was so cold it cut through a man like shards of ice. The earlier snow flurries had turned into a near-constant curtain of falling snow. A fog of white, whirling clouds surrounded him.

He could tell he was on the right path by the feel of the ground beneath his boots. The snow on the roads was packed down hard, and whenever he found himself angling off into the softer drifts to the side, he moved back onto firmer footing.

Finally a light appeared ahead of him, seeming to float in the darkness. That would be the lantern on the front porch of the tavern, he thought. With the light as a beacon, he headed straight for the building, eager for company again, though he wasn't sure how the Russian soldiers would welcome him.

He was still some twenty yards from the tavern when someone came out of the blowing snow behind him.

The howling wind drowned out the sound of footsteps. The first warning he had that he was being followed came when something was suddenly flung over his head, cutting off his view of the lantern light. Rough canvas rasped against his face, and the stench of old fish filled his nostrils. He stumbled, thrown off balance. Gagging from the smell, he fumbled at the canvas shroud and tried to pull it off his head.

Someone struck him a powerful blow in the middle of the back, sending him staggering forward. He felt himself falling, but even as he pitched headlong into the snow, he finally succeeded in ripping away the stifling canvas. He rolled over and kicked out with his right leg.

His heel slammed into something soft and yielding, and even over the noise of the wind Jeff heard an explosive grunt of pain. He rolled again and came up on his hands and knees, then surged to his feet. A dark shape loomed in front of him. He threw a punch at it.

That blow connected, too, and Jeff was rewarded with a satisfying shiver of impact up his arm. Before he had time to enjoy it, though, someone grabbed his left shoulder and hauled him around. Instinct made him jerk his head to the side. Something scraped along his left ear and then thudded against his shoulder. Jeff gasped in pain and stumbled a couple of steps to the right, trying to avoid another blow from the unseen club. He hated fighting blind like this.

"Damn you!" he shouted. "Come out where I can see you!"

Too late, he realized that was a mistake. His opponents were doubtless having as much trouble seeing in the snowstorm as he was, and his shout had only given them something to aim for.

He was struck in the back again, and even as he bellowed involuntarily, another blow fell on his right shoulder. Both arms were almost paralyzed now. Someone grabbed him in a powerful embrace and bore him down to the ground. Once again a canvas bag was yanked over his head, blinding and nearly suffocating him. Jeff writhed futilely, unwilling to give up the struggle.

Then a final blow crashed down on his head. His muscles went limp, and even though he was still half conscious, he couldn't put up a fight anymore.

Lying on the frigid ground, breathing in the putrid reek of rotten fish, he heard a voice speaking a language he could not identify. Then, suddenly, the voice was next to his ear, speaking through the canvas.

"You are being a fool, Holt," it hissed, "and now it will kill you."

Piotr. Jeff knew the canvas would muffle his words, but he shouted anyway, "You son of a bitch! I knew I couldn't trust you. When Count Orlov finds out what you've done—"

Piotr's harsh laugh cut into Jeff's tirade. "Who do

you think gave me my orders, stupid American? In return for my life, I now do the count's bidding, and the count's alone.''

So Orlov was behind this attack, Jeff thought. The count's words had been a lie. He had allowed Jeff to remain in Sitka only so that he could take his revenge on him.

And like a fool—Piotr was right about that—Jeff had accommodated him.

With a groan he tried to wriggle out of the grip of the strong hands that held him. It was too late for that. Not only had he lost the strength, but cords were already being whipped around his wrists and ankles, binding him tightly. More rope was wrapped around his legs and his torso. They had him trussed up like a sheep going to market.

That was a pretty apt description, Jeff thought bleakly. The same fate probably awaited him as it did the sheep.

Piotr spoke to him again in a gloating voice. "These Tlingit will take you away from Sitka and dispose of your body in a place where it will never be found. You should not have come to Alaska, American.''

Jeff knew that now. His desire to build up the company had led him into a series of unwise decisions—but the worst of them had had nothing to do with business. He had failed to cut and run as soon as Irina Orlov brought out that damned vodka.

Piotr spoke in Russian, or maybe it was the Tlingit tongue, or a mixture of both. Jeff felt himself being picked up, then carried away. Piotr's mocking laugh followed him for a short time, but then the wind swallowed the sound, leaving Jeff alone in a black, reeking silence.

Considering all the mistakes he had made, he was exactly where he deserved to be, he told himself grimly.

CHAPTER
TWENTY-SIX

C lay had just rounded the corner of the row of
passenger cabins when he heard, even over the
rumbling of the earthquake and the rushing of
the runaway river, a terrified scream. Despite the cha-
otic circumstances, his keen eyes instantly found the
source of the cry. Midway up the boat, next to the giant
paddlewheel, a woman hung over the railing, clinging
for dear life. Clay's heartbeat slammed into a gallop as
he realized who the woman was.

Shining Moon!

And beside her, only a few feet away, a smaller
figure was struggling desperately with a man who was
trying to force him over the rail. Clay recognized the
boy, and as he broke into a frantic run, he shouted,
"Matthew!"

The man struggling with Matthew suddenly struck
the boy with a vicious, backhanded blow, knocking
him against the railing. He started to slip under it, but
he grabbed the rail at the last instant and hung on.

"Clay!" he screamed when he saw the frontiersman racing toward them.

Clay recognized the larger figure now. The usually dapper attire was disheveled, and the shock of white hair was askew, but the man was unmistakably Senator Morgan Ralston. The senator's normally jovial face was twisted in murderous hatred, and Clay knew in that instant that he had been wrong about Louis Haines. Clay was looking at the traitor now. He was sure of it.

Ralston yanked a pistol from under his coat, probably the same one he had used to kill the crewman the night before, Clay thought fleetingly. He threw himself to one side as the pistol in Ralston's hand cracked wickedly. The lead ball whipped past Clay's head, close enough for him to sense the stirring of the air.

With a shouted curse, Ralston turned back toward the rail and struck at Shining Moon's hands with the empty gun. Her fragile hold was all that kept her from falling into the maelstrom below, and in a matter of seconds, Clay knew, Ralston would knock her fingers loose. It would happen before he had time to reach her.

Then Matthew, still holding tightly to the railing himself, twisted and brought up his leg in a kick aimed at Ralston's groin. Ralston screeched, doubled over, and staggered back from the railing. Matthew whirled around, reached over the rail, and grabbed Shining Moon's arm. He was not strong enough to lift her, so the two of them clung there, the railing between them, as the boat pitched wildly back and forth.

Ralston caught himself against the wall and stayed there for a second, hunched over in pain. Then he looked up, a snarl on his patrician face, and readied himself to launch another attack.

Clay slid to a halt several yards away and raised his own pistol, aiming quickly and pulling the trigger. Ralston shifted just as Clay fired, and the ball thudded into the wall a foot to his left. The shot was enough of a distraction to make Ralston abandon his plan to force Shining Moon and Matthew over the side. Instead he turned and sprinted toward the bow, away from Clay.

As soon as he had fired, Clay was running again toward his wife and the boy. He thrust the empty pistol behind his belt as he slid to a halt and lunged halfway over the railing to grab Shining Moon under the arms. Matthew stepped back to give him room. The muscles in Clay's arms and shoulders bunched as he lifted Shining Moon up and over the rail. He took a couple of unsteady steps back as she fell into his arms. They came to a stop against the wall of the cabins.

Shining Moon was still gasping, but she was dry-eyed. Sioux women did not cry in the face of danger. Clay lifted his voice above the chaos around them and asked, "Are you all right?"

Her head jerked in a nod. Then her eyes widened and she exclaimed, "Matthew!"

"I'm here," the boy said as he grasped her skirt and hung on tightly. She turned to him and caught him up, hugging him to her chest.

Matthew squirmed around until he could look at Clay. "It was him!" he said. "Senator Ralston! He's the bad man you're looking for, Clay!"

Clay had already come to that conclusion himself; no one but the man he and Markham had been trailing for so long would have had any reason for trying to kill his family. But how did Matthew know this?

"He gave me money and told me to lie about Senator Haines!" Matthew babbled on. "He said he was just playing a joke, but I figured out later it was more than that. He's a bad man!"

"Damn right he is." Clay looked around. What in blazes had happened to Markham? The lieutenant had been right behind him only a few minutes earlier. Once he had seen Shining Moon and Matthew in danger, however, Clay had forgotten everything else.

Now, as Matthew's words reminded him of the mission that had brought him here in the first place, Clay cast a glance around and spotted Markham hurrying toward them from the bow of the boat. The young officer was panting, and he had the fingers of his right hand clamped over his left arm, just above the elbow.

In the early morning light, Clay saw blood welling between Markham's fingers.

"He got away!" Markham said miserably. "I tried to stop him, but he had a knife. He slashed my arm, then went over the side."

"What?" exclaimed Clay. "He jumped in the river?"

"I couldn't believe it either," Markham said, his face drawn and haggard, "but the boat was fairly close to shore when he jumped, and I guess he thought he could make it. He may have been right. The last I saw of him, he was still afloat and swimming toward the bank."

"Damn!" Clay burst out.

"Ralston's our man, isn't he?"

Clay nodded. "And he's not going to get away. Not when we've come so far, not when we're this close."

As he turned, intending to look for the captain, he saw Roosevelt hurrying along the deck toward them. "Is everyone all right?" the captain asked anxiously.

Clay glanced at the shore and saw that the trees had stopped moving and the ground was no longer jumping around. For whatever ungodly reason, the Mississippi was still flowing backward, but the worst of the tremor seemed to have passed.

"We're all right," Clay told Roosevelt. "Can you put in to shore?"

"What?" Roosevelt looked askance at him.

Clay grabbed the captain's arm. "Half the country may be at stake! I've got to get ashore and find Ralston!"

"Senator Ralston?" Roosevelt was still baffled. "I don't understand—Good Lord, Markham, your arm's bleeding! You're hurt!"

Markham nodded. "Ralston did this, Captain. He's the man Clay and I have been seeking, not Senator Haines."

Roosevelt gaped, clearly incredulous. "You're certain?"

Shining Moon pushed a tangle of raven hair away from her face. "Senator Ralston just tried to kill me and Matthew," she said.

"And he took a shot at me," added Clay. "I need you to put me ashore, Captain."

Roosevelt hesitated only a moment, then nodded. "All right. I'll have the pilot put in to shore as soon as possible." He hurried away toward the stairs leading up to the wheelhouse.

A few moments later, the *New Orleans* angled toward the western bank of the Mississippi, where Ralston had disappeared. Roosevelt had given up on trying to fight the unnatural current, so the steamboat proceeded quickly to shore.

Clay reloaded his pistol, then fetched his flintlock rifle from his cabin. He waited impatiently at the bow as the boat drew nearer to the shore, Shining Moon and Matthew at his side. Markham had been taken to the salon by one of the stewards, who would clean and bind up the knife wound on his arm.

Clay looked intently at his wife. "You're sure you're all right?" he asked.

Shining Moon nodded. "Ralston did not hurt me. I was afraid I would fall into the river, but Matthew helped me, and then you came."

Clay put a hand on Matthew's shoulder and squeezed it. "You did a good job, son. If not for you, Ralston might've killed you both and gotten away with the bad things he's been doing."

"He lied to me," Matthew said. "I didn't know I was going to get Senator Haines in so much trouble."

"It's all right," Clay assured him. "We'll get it all straightened out."

The boat's engines slowed, and crewmen jumped from the bow into the shallow water along the shore to fasten mooring ropes to the trees. Clay turned to Shining Moon and gave her a quick, hard kiss, then followed the men into the shallows, holding his rifle and powder horn high so they wouldn't get wet. He waded ashore and paused, turning back for one last look at

Shining Moon and the boy, then plunged into the dense undergrowth and disappeared.

This hadn't worked out very well, thought Matthew as he watched Clay vanish into the woods. His partnership with Senator Ralston had come to an abrupt end. But it would never have amounted to anything anyway, Matthew told himself. Ralston had never intended to honor their agreement, or else he wouldn't have tried to kill them.

Matthew decided that he had come out of the affair about as well as could be expected. He was alive, after all, and Clay thought he was some sort of hero for helping Shining Moon and telling the truth—partially—about Ralston.

For a moment Matthew allowed himself to enjoy the sensation. He tried to tell himself that Clay Holt's approval meant nothing to him, but he could not deny the warm feeling Clay's gratitude had given him. It would have been easy, at that moment, for Matthew to let himself care. . . .

But then I'd be as big a fool as Holt and the squaw, he told himself firmly. The warmth faded, and as Matthew stared out at the woods into which Clay had plunged, he hoped that Clay and Ralston would have the decency to kill each other and dispose of two problems at the same time for him.

If Ralston had made it ashore safely, the spot would have been about a mile upstream from where the *New Orleans* had stopped, Clay estimated. He wished he had a horse—he could have covered that ground quickly and picked up Ralston's trail sooner. Instead he loped along a game trail that took him south along the river.

He hoped that Ralston *had* survived the dangerous swim. After everything he had done, he deserved to die, right enough, but not until he had a chance to tell everything he knew about the land grab. Other conspirators could still be operating, and until Clay knew exactly what Ralston and Gideon Maxwell had been planning to do with those vast tracts of virgin territory, the assignment he had been given by Thomas Jefferson would not truly be completed.

Clay ran on. He had feared that the time he had spent in Washington and on the steamboat had softened him, but as he stretched his legs in a swift stride, he felt his muscles responding. It felt good to be on the trail again, to be hunting.

After a few minutes he spotted some landmarks that looked familiar: a lightning-ravaged tree leaning far out over the bank, a large round rock poised on a small hillock, a finger of land jutting out into the river. If Ralston had come ashore, it would have been somewhere in this area. Clay made his way down to the bank and began searching for signs of the renegade senator's trail.

Clay's instincts had served him well again. It took him only a few minutes to locate the spot where Ralston had slogged out of the water and onto the bank. From the way the dead grass was pressed flat, Clay guessed that the senator had thrown himself down to rest and catch his breath for a few minutes before forcing himself to his feet and stumbling toward the southwest.

As if he were tracking a wounded animal, Clay read the sign Ralston had left behind and followed the trail. Clay knew he was closing on his quarry. Ralston was not accustomed to traveling quickly or efficiently through the wilderness; Clay Holt was.

In less than half an hour Clay had closed the gap, and he could hear Ralston pushing through the brush up ahead. He pushed on, eager now to get the business over with. It had been hanging over his head for too long.

As he hurried along, though, he suddenly realized that he could no longer hear the crackling of the brush ahead. Clay stopped short at the edge of a short dropoff and listened intently.

He heard harsh breathing behind him and started

to turn, but he was only halfway around when something crashed into him. "You bastard!" Ralston screamed as he tackled Clay. Both men went off the brink of the little bluff, toppling some ten feet onto a stretch of rocky ground.

The fall knocked the breath out of Clay when he landed, especially with Ralston on top of him. The senator grappled wildly with him, trying to wrest the rifle out of Clay's hands. Clay gasped for air, unable for a few seconds to fight back. Then he drove a short punch into Ralston's side and heaved himself up, throwing Ralston off.

Ralston rolled one way, Clay the other. Clay still had his rifle, but as he came up on his feet, he saw Ralston had managed to pluck the pistol from behind Clay's belt. The senator was earing back the hammer on the lock of the North & Cheney as he lifted it.

Clay brought the rifle up, cocking it as he did, and brought the barrel to bear on Ralston's chest. The two men stood watching each other, breath heaving, guns leveled, tense with impending violence and ready to deal death.

After a moment, Ralston broke the strained silence. "You had to keep prodding," he said harshly. "You couldn't just let things go."

"Half a continent? Damn right I couldn't let it go," snapped Clay.

"I gave you Haines!" Ralston shouted, red-faced. His clothes were still sodden from his swim in the river, and his white hair was plastered to his skull.

"Framed him, you mean. And used my boy to help you do it." Clay snorted. "You're the one who paid that crewman to try to kill Markham and me, and when you saw he wasn't going to be able to do it, you stepped in and shot him, and not by accident, either. Hell, you didn't want him talking about who really paid him. Then Matthew spoke up and pointed the finger at Haines. I reckon by then he knew it wasn't really a joke, but he didn't know what else to do. He was probably a mite scared of you, too."

Ralston gave a hollow laugh. "That boy of yours . . . there's a lot you don't know about him, Holt."

Clay ached to press the trigger, but he held off. "What do you mean by that?" he demanded.

Instead of answering, Ralston laughed and went on, "There's a lot you don't know about everything! You and Markham and that damned Jefferson! You think you're all so smart! Well, you won't feel that way in a few years when you're all speaking French!"

French? What in blazes . . .

Clay didn't have to prod Ralston for answers. In his fury, the senator was only too glad to provide them. "None of you have ever had any idea what's really going on," he said, his lips curling in contempt. "You think of our efforts as a mere land grab, a simple quest for riches. The fate of nations is at stake here, you idiot! One new nation in particular—"

"The nation you're supposed to be serving," Clay cut in.

Ralston shook his head. "Not at all. The United States will be nothing but a short-lived dream once La Carde establishes his empire."

"La Carde?" Clay repeated. "Who the hell is La Carde?"

"The Comte Jacques de la Carde, late of Napolean's court, soon to be the emperor of New France." Ralston wagged the barrel of the pistol. "Not everyone in France supported Bonaparte's plan to sell the Louisiana Territory to Jefferson, you know. But only La Carde was bold enough to do something about it!"

Clay was getting glimmerings of the truth now. He felt a chill travel down his spine. "You mean this French fellow is the one who's grabbing all the land in the West, so he can start his own empire there?"

"Exactly! Once I've rendezvoused with him, I'll be his first minister—and a richer man than I ever dreamed of being back in Georgia! And in a few years, when he's established, his armies will pour out of the west and take the rest of this country. He'll expand the new empire."

Clay took a deep breath. "That's just about the craziest thing I've ever heard."

Ralston laughed. "You can say that now, but you'll see that I'm right."

"Damn it, Ralston, you have a wife, children! It's bad enough you've turned traitor to your country. You're betraying your family, too."

"Well, now, you're right about that, and I'm truly sorry about them," Ralston said ruefully. "But La Carde offered me too much money and power to turn him down."

"You'll never see the money or the power, Ralston. You're going back to Washington to stand trial for your crimes."

Ralston shook his head. "I don't think so. Perhaps I'm not a frontiersman and a crack shot like you, Holt, but I'm too close to miss."

"I'll kill you, too," warned Clay.

"Yes, but you'll be just as dead, and you won't be able to do a thing to stop La Carde's plan, will you?"

Ralston was right, and Clay realized he was going to have to take the desperate step of giving the traitor the first shot. He had to avoid the ball from the pistol Ralston was holding, then wound the senator and take him prisoner. Clay's muscles tensed in readiness to throw himself to the side and draw Ralston's fire.

Before either man could move, the earth suddenly leaped upward under their feet.

Ralston screamed in frustration as the ground lurched and his finger involuntarily jerked the trigger. The pistol roared, but the weapon had already been thrown wildly out of line with Clay. The ball soared off harmlessly into the sky. Clay snapped the rifle to his shoulder, trying to aim as he fought to keep his balance, but before he could fire, the ripple of the aftershock jolted him again. The ground seemed to drop from under his feet. He pitched forward, headlong onto the shaking earth.

From where he lay, he saw Ralston stagger backwards, then suddenly disappear. Clay scrambled to his feet and lunged toward the spot. He heard Ralston scream.

Clay jerked to a halt at the edge of a jagged gash in the earth that might have been put there by a giant knife. The crevice was some twenty feet deep, and at the bottom of it, twisted and broken, lay Morgan Ralston, still alive. He lifted his head and looked up at Clay.

"Help me!" he shrieked. "Oh, God, help me, Holt!"

Clay wasn't sure how he could reach the senator, let alone get him out of the crevice, but before he could do anything, another loud rumble sounded and the earth shook violently. Ralston screamed, and Clay staggered back from the crevice. Before his horrified eyes it closed as suddenly as it had opened, with a grinding, deafening sound.

Clay stared at the spot where the crevice had been a few seconds earlier, imagining millions of tons of sundered earth and what they would have done to Ralston as they came together. As the tremors died away, leaving an eerie silence over the landscape, Clay muttered to himself, "Looks like the land grabbed *him*, instead of the other way around!"

Then he turned shakily and started back toward the river. He had to get to the steamboat, and he hoped it would be able to move down the Mississippi as soon as possible. He needed to get word to Thomas Jefferson and explain who was really behind the scheme. Jefferson and his allies in the government had to be warned that although the earth itself had disposed of one of the players, the greater conspiracy had not yet been eliminated.

Out there somewhere in the West was a whole new snake that needed stomping, Clay thought grimly.

A snake named Jacques de la Carde.

• • •

Jeff lost consciousness somewhere along the way, and when he came to, he had no idea how much time had passed. All he knew was that his head hurt tremendously.

That, and he was moving.

Gradually he realized that he was still tied up. He was lying on his back on something that shifted and bounced beneath him. He realized he was still outside, too; he could feel a cold wind blowing. He could see nothing because of the canvas bag over his head.

Men's voices sounded somewhere nearby, speaking what sounded like the same language Jeff had heard earlier. He heard dogs barking as well. It dawned on him that he was on a sled of some sort, probably being pulled by a dog team. The sled suddenly jolted to a stop, and the bag was yanked off Jeff's head.

The light was blinding. He winced and closed his eyes. Someone laughed. Jeff opened his eyes again slowly, letting them grow accustomed to the dazzling sunlight that reflected off a vast expanse of snow. Pine-covered mountains rose in the distance.

A figure loomed over Jeff. A man with a round, swarthy face, wearing a heavy coat with a fur collar that stood up around his ears, looked down at him and grinned. Jeff recognized Vassily, the Tlingit guide whose life he had saved during the hunting trip.

"Russian man say we kill you," the Indian said in English. "But we not kill you. Man who kills bear will come with us, live with our people."

Jeff nodded weakly. He had no other choice. Better to live as a prisoner of the Tlingit than to be killed and thrown into an icy ravine. Sooner or later he would find an opportunity to escape, he told himself. And when that day came, he would make his way back to Sitka. He had a score to settle with Piotr—and with Count Gregori Orlov.

The Tlingit leaned over him. "I cut you loose, you not run away?" he asked.

Jeff had to swallow a couple of times before he

could force words out of his dry mouth. "I won't run away," he said. *Not yet, anyway.*

"Good." Vassily produced a knife from under his big coat and cut the ropes holding Jeff. Jeff winced again as blood began to flow painfully back into arms and legs that had grown numb from the tight bonds.

He sat up and looked around. Half a dozen grim-faced Tlingit men stood around the sled. The dogs were resting, lying on the snow with their tongues lolling, their breath puffing in front of their noses.

Vassily extended a hand, and Jeff accepted the assistance as he stood up. It felt good to be on his feet again, although he was a little shaky.

"I speak English good," the Tlingit said proudly.

Jeff nodded. "You speak English good. Who taught you?"

"Men who come on ships and hunt whales. Before Russians come to Alaska." Vassily spat, then laughed. "Count think I not speak English. Many things he not know about Tlingit, like how much we hate him and all Russians."

Englishmen had taught Vassily the language, more than likely, Jeff thought. He had heard that they had done some whaling in the waters off the coast of Alaska in previous decades.

Vassily changed the subject by pointing to another canvas sack lying on the sled, close to where Jeff's head had been. "That is yours?"

Jeff frowned. "I don't know. What's in it?"

"Russian man give it to us, tell us put with your body after we kill you. Maybe you want it."

Jeff shook his head. "I don't even know what it is."

Vassily grinned. "I show you." He snatched up the bag, loosened the drawstring, and upended it.

Jeff recoiled in horror when he saw what fell out onto the snow.

It was the severed head of Irina Orlov.

AUTHOR'S NOTE

Captain Nicholas Roosevelt was real, as was his steamboat, the *New Orleans*. Roosevelt's historic trip down the Mississippi River occurred in the autumn of 1811, as described in this novel, although of course the events relating to Clay Holt and his allies and enemies are the invention of the author. The series of massive earthquakes is also historical fact, and the Mississippi River did flow backward for a time. These quakes, the strongest in recorded history in North America, have become collectively known as the New Madrid Earthquake.

From Dana Fuller Ross

WAGONS WEST

THE FIRST HOLTS. The incredible beginning
of America's favorite pioneer saga

*Dana Fuller Ross tells the early story of the Holts, men
and women living through the most rugged era of
American exploration, following the wide Missouri,
crossing the high Rockies, and fighting for the future
they claimed as theirs.*

WESTWARD!
_____ 29402-4 $6.50/$8.99 in Canada

In the fertile Ohio Valley, the brothers Clay and Jefferson strike out for a new territory of fierce violence and
breathtaking wonders. The Holts will need all their
fighting prowess to stay alive . . . and to found the pioneer family that will become an American legend.

OUTPOST!
_____ 29400-8 $6.50/$8.99 in Canada

Clay heads to Canada to bring a longtime enemy to
justice, while in far-off North Carolina, Jeff is stalked by
a ruthless killer determined to destroy his family. As
war cries fill the air, the Holts must fight once more for
their home and the dynasty that will live forever in the
pages of history.

Ask for these books at your local bookstore or use this page to order.

Please send me the books I have checked above. I am enclosing $_____ (add $2.50 to
cover postage and handling). Send check or money order, no cash or C.O.D.'s, please.

Name _____

Address _____

City/State/Zip _____

Send order to: Bantam Books, Dept. DO 34, 2451 S. Wolf Rd., Des Plaines, IL 60018
Allow four to six weeks for delivery.
Prices and availability subject to change without notice.   DO 34 6/98